Praise for Can Xue's *Barefoot Doctor* (2022)

"During the Cultural Revolution, minimally trained 'barefoot doctors' were sent to the Chinese countryside. . . . The author of this novel was one of them, and she draws on her experiences in the story of Mrs. Yi, a village herbalist who gathers her remedies on a nearby mountain . . . [but] events become increasingly surreal. As the mountain changes shape and ghosts visit the living, mysterious connections between the body and nature emerge."
—*New Yorker*, "Best Books of 2022"

"A complex and illuminating portrait of a group of healers in China . . . [that] offers profound insights about what it means to pursue and live a fulfilling life."
—*Publishers Weekly*

"Over the course of the novel, *Barefoot Doctor*'s odd, fable-like logic becomes more insistent, and more persuasive. . . . The genres of historical commentary and autofiction aren't big or wild enough to encapsulate this ambitious, mystical novel."
—*Full Stop*

"Out of all of Can Xue's books in English translation, this novel is especially intimate, as she was a barefoot doctor herself once upon a time. I have no choice but to call this novel my favorite of hers yet—a feeling I have with every single book."
—Porochista Khakpour, author of *Brown Album*

Praise for *I Live in the Slums* (2020)

LONGLISTED FOR THE 2021 INTERNATIONAL BOOKER PRIZE

"There's something inescapably cosmic about [Can Xue's] writing: the grandness of her vision, the abstraction of her thought, the way the details of lived reality seem to shrink and assume an equal significance, as though one were orbiting a distant star and peering down."
—Bailey Trela, *Los Angeles Review of Books*

"[An] eerie, unpredictable, cracked and crazy world. . . . Sheer reading pleasure for sophisticated readers and a worthy starting point for initiates."
—*Library Journal*

"[An] exquisite collection. . . . Can Xue is a master at twisting philosophical ideas into realities that seem simple but are incredibly thoughtful and intricate. These sixteen poetic stories have astonishing depth that will transfix readers."
—Emily Park, *Booklist*

Praise for *Love in the New Millennium* (2018)

LONGLISTED FOR THE 2019 INTERNATIONAL BOOKER PRIZE

"Translator Annelise Finegan Wasmoen conveys a remarkable linguistic simplicity while maintaining the weirdness of [Can] Xue's descriptive passages and dialogues, which are rather like non-sequiturs. . . . This is a challenging but worthy path into [her] body of work."
—Aaron Robertson, *Literary Hub*, "The 10 Best Translated Novels of the Decade"

"Tackling age-old themes of love's many iterations, Can Xue continues to upend comfortable notions of structure, narrative, plot, and character while crafting stories that linger in the mind long after the last page has been turned."
—*World Literature Today*

"*Love in the New Millennium* is, as always with Can Xue's work, a marvel. She is one of the most innovative and important contemporary writers in China and, in my opinion, in world literature."
—Bradford Morrow, author of *The Prague Sonata*

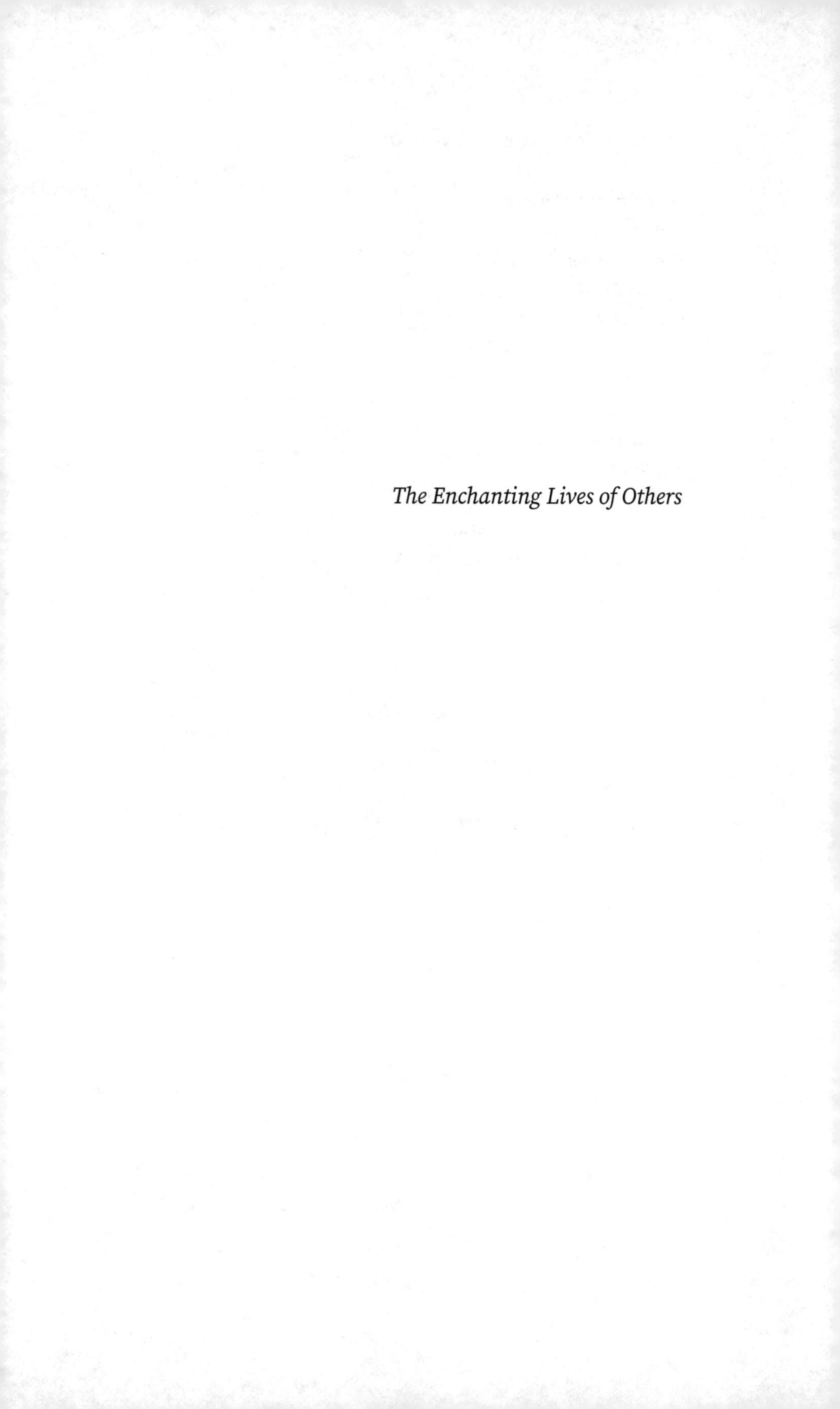

The Enchanting Lives of Others

BOOKS BY CAN XUE IN ENGLISH TRANSLATION

The Enchanting Lives of Others
Mother River
Barefoot Doctor
Mystery Train
I Live in the Slums
Love in the New Millennium
Frontier
The Last Lover
Vertical Motion: Stories
Five Spice Street
Blue Light in the Sky and Other Stories
The Embroidered Shoes: Stories
Old Floating Cloud: Two Novellas
Dialogues in Paradise

CAN XUE

The Enchanting Lives of Others

A NOVEL

Translated from the Chinese by
Annelise Finegan

A MARGELLOS
WORLD REPUBLIC OF LETTERS BOOK

Yale UNIVERSITY PRESS | NEW HAVEN & LONDON

The Margellos World Republic of Letters is dedicated to making literary works from around the globe available in English through translation. It brings to the English-speaking world the work of leading poets, novelists, essayists, philosophers, and playwrights from Europe, Latin America, Africa, Asia, and the Middle East to stimulate international discourse and creative exchange.

English translation copyright © 2026 by Annelise Finegan.
Originally published in China as 激情世界 [A World of Passion] by People's Literature Publishing House, 2022. Copyright © 2022 by Can Xue. First part originally published in China as 迷人的异类生活 [The Enchanting Lives of Others] by *Flower City* magazine in 2022.

All rights reserved.
This book may not be reproduced, in whole or in part, including illustrations, in any form (beyond that copying permitted by Sections 107 and 108 of the U.S. Copyright Law and except by reviewers for the public press), without written permission from the publishers.

Yale University Press books may be purchased in quantity for educational, business, or promotional use. For information, please e-mail sales.press@yale.edu (U.S. office) or sales@yaleup.co.uk (U.K. office).

Set in Source Serif type by Motto Publishing Services.
Printed in the United States of America.

Library of Congress Control Number: 2025941807
ISBN 978-0-300-28165-1 (hardcover)

A catalogue record for this book is available from the British Library.

Authorized Representative in the EU: Easy Access System Europe, Mustamäe tee 50, 10621 Tallinn, Estonia, gpsr.requests@easproject.com.

10 9 8 7 6 5 4 3 2 1

Contents

The Enchanting Lives of Others

Part One

XIAO SANG AND HER FRIENDS AND PARENTS

Xiao Sang sat at her desk writing in her diary. She let her thoughts wander at random for a while, chin propped on hand, and then said to herself: "When I go back to that time, I'll have all kinds of other choices." "What choices will they be?" a voice inside her asked. "I don't know, but they will flow forth and show themselves at that time." She spoke out loud. She blinked. Just now she'd seen some of the scenery from *that time*: for example, a jade shoehorn, a full weeping willow. "I sat there talking with my loved ones who are dead. At the far end of my vision was a place where a stream curved, where a kingfisher flew toward me, but vanished in an instant." Her voice reverberated through the room. Then Xiao Sang lowered her head and wrote down the words "jade shoehorn." Was this her choice? She hadn't yet returned to *that time*, so she didn't know. She merely knew about a few of these striking tableaux. Reading is good labor. She could read certain books a hundred times without boredom.

When Xiao Sang finished writing in her diary, she stood and paced the room. She felt that she read fiction in order to return to *that time*. Maybe, in some obscure and fateful way, she had made choices many times before. How could she not have, when everything became so intense? Then a smile appeared on her face—she had been so young back then. Was she that much older now? Maybe, maybe not. She raised her eyes to look at a book with a grayish-white cover on her bookshelf. This book had been her partner over the past few years. The book's contents were plain to her, as if—as if she were living them herself. The book told about a sanitation worker, in whose time it seemed the city had not had street cleaning trucks. Every day before dawn she used a long bamboo broom to sweep the asphalt, with her head wrapped in a patterned scarf, her face unseen. The broom made a *sha sha sha* sound. Every time Xiao Sang read up to here she imagined herself as this woman. The asphalt road cooling again in the long night after being scorched by the sun; the mild contact of the broom with the ground . . . Xiao Sang sighed: "How lifelike!" She took that beloved book down and casually turned to a page in the middle. This page depicted a fanatical driver. "The sedan leaped into the air, then violently fell into the thick weeds and slid for a distance . . . The driver went limp, collapsing onto the steering wheel." It seemed as though the driver had fallen asleep in the wilderness. Xiao Sang liked these types of plots best—a wasteland under the starlit sky, and someone serenely entering another world, with no one knowing . . . Ah! She was slightly excited each time, each time so invested, even though the plot was already familiar. She didn't know whether other readers felt this way, but for her this is how it was.

Outside her window there was a little girl jumping rope. The swaying of her rope made what was portrayed in the book even more vivid. Xiao Sang sensed how the atmosphere around her captivated her. Sometimes she even liked to read on the street, especially when she was waiting for a ride. Xiao Sang held the stubborn belief that if an author were unable to weave the book's contents into her everyday life, then it wasn't a book she needed to read. She loved reading novels on the train the best, while the train moved slowly, stopping and starting as people from all classes chatted in loud voices, in the sleeper cars or gathered playing cards, so that there was noise everywhere. Xiao Sang usually read half-lying on the berth. With one ear she listened to the voices outside the novel, while her other ear listened to the voices inside the novel. At such times her body would feel very content. She could immerse herself for a whole day in this half-attentive reading, aside from the two meals on the train ride. "How lovely!" she would say to herself, once in a while. Unfortunately Xiao Sang had few opportunities for taking the (old-fashioned) train, so most of the time she read at home. Reading fiction at home was good, too, but not as enjoyable as in the sleeper car. Thinking of her most recent business trip on the train, she smiled again. Xiao Sang turned the pages of the book in her hand to the end.

The ending of this book was its best part, still exciting, but gradually returning to a steady state: like a whetstone tracing an arc through the air and then dropping into a secluded lake. Oh, that feeling of happiness passed too soon. Read it again then. A book that can give you a feeling of happiness—a remarkable author! She read it another time, looking through the window to where the little girl was still jumping rope, the jump rope swaying and swaying. She remembered again that scene of taking the train on a rainy day: holding a good book in her hands. Things couldn't be more sentimental or nostalgic. On the sleeper berth with tears in her eyes—tears, though, of happiness. That book! In the course of reading year after year had passed, while her reading partners had changed—fewer in number now, the four or five books to which she was faithful from start to end.

"Xiao Sang, Xiao Sang!" her friend Xiao Ma rushed in. "I came to tell you, because you've been guiding us all. I've just read the most brilliant novel. The title is *XXXX-XX*. I read it all night, and my mind's still spinning. How can there be such beautiful novels in the world?"

"I read that book, too, fifteen years ago." A smile floated across Xiao Sang's face as she fell into recollection. "It was a very good book, written with such tenderness, such quality . . . I can remember reading it by the sports field at school. There were people playing soccer in the distance, and once in a while I'd raise my eyes so the blurry shapes of the players flashed past me. I was so young then. Now you've experienced this book, too. Wonderful."

"Haha, I'd worried that my insights weren't real. Since you have the same feeling, it shows my good judgment. Have other people in the reading group recommended this novel to you?" She eagerly watched Xiao Sang.

"No, you're the only one."

Xiao Ma clapped her hands with excitement and shouted: "I want to be elevated! Elevated!"

She rushed out shouting, probably impatient to get back to enjoying the novel.

Xiao Ma was five or six years younger than her. Xiao Sang murmured: "Ah, youth." She vividly sensed herself growing older, although this transformation inspired her rather than making her sad. She no longer read the kind of book Xiao Ma was reading. Had she become an elevated reader then? She must have, otherwise Xiao Ma wouldn't come to her so anxiously seeking confirmation. Next Xiao Sang imagined Xiao Ma's reading environment—had she read in the study for the whole night, or lying down in the bedroom? Or else under the streetlight by her building? Xiao Sang felt that the streetlight was the most suitable place to read that book: stillness on all sides, a black cat with shining fur slinking around the courtyard, the apricots on the large tree at the entrance glowing in the lamplight. Reading a beautiful book, then urgently running over to tell a friend. What a strong impulse this must be. Xiao Sang was more experienced than her friend, so her passion wasn't as fervent, and instead was like the whetstone arcing into water. She understood this eagerness, though. Such a memorable scene.

That night for a long time Xiao Sang roamed the city inside the book that she loved. There was a shadow—but it also wasn't a shadow, because it had an expression—that led her along the way. She and the shadow passed through many outdoor stalls along the side of the road before finally reaching a suburb where there was a deep well.

"Where have I read up to now?" her voice abruptly thundered in the air, startling her.

The shadow suddenly jumped down from the edge into the well, with an extremely natural gesture. Xiao Sang slowly approached the well's edge and looked down into it, into the pitch-black below. A voice inside her said: "You've read up to here."

Then she joyfully entered a dreamscape.

"Xiao Sang, Xiao Sang!" Xiao Ma shouted as she ran after her.

She had come over from across the street and now she walked with Xiao Sang together to work. The two women were cashiers at the same large department store.

"I've been thinking that the novel will bring me good luck," Xiao Ma said foolishly.

"Yes," Xiao Sang nodded in admiration. "Books melt into life. This in itself is good luck."

"I'm becoming more intelligent."

"Yes." Xiao Sang started to laugh, glad in a heartfelt way for her friend.

"Let's go to the coffee shop after work."

"Sure."

Xiao Sang sensed that Xiao Ma still had many things that she wanted to say to her. Could she be in love?

The coffee shop was a tony lounge with velvet curtains blocking the light from the main room, giving them a sense of it being late at night. Sitting there felt more than just pleasantly cool, and even a bit chilly. Xiao Ma loved this kind of atmosphere.

Their coffee arrived, hot. The women slowly drank, distractedly watching the candle.

"Look, the flame is straight. There's no draft here. I had hoped . . . ," Xiao Ma said.

Xiao Sang sensed her friend entering the plot of a story. What did she hope for? She was still young and could hope for anything. She read fiction, naturally, because she was full of hope. Something inside of Xiao Sang softened.

"Xiao Ma, you actually—" Xiao Sang was about to say that Xiao Ma already had everything her heart desired, but what she came out with was: "We are fortunate, you and I."

"Oh!" Xiao Ma gasped with excitement. She made a vague gesture with her hand. "Do you still remember the first time we met? It was at XXX."

"No, it wasn't there. It was chapter 3 of the novel *Cloudy Sea*. I can see it before my eyes. You were looking at the book, and I was looking at you. I thought to myself that you were my youth."

They told the server that they didn't need cake, but to bring another cup of coffee. When the server left, a leopard silently appeared. It placed its front paws on the table and lowered its head. The leopards here were so gentle.

"Kiss me," Xiao Ma said to it softly.

Without touching her cheek, it kissed her symbolically.

"This place can return me to those scenes, but it's also very different here," Xiao Ma worriedly said.

Xiao Sang sensed her friend's anxiety. She turned her face away, smiling. Let youth worry. This was the power of that book. Who had she fallen in love with now?

Xiao Ma seemed to have heard Xiao Sang's inner voice. Pointing at the leopard, she said:

"Who else could it be? That's it."

"Oh, Xiao Ma, Xiao Ma . . ."

"Shh, quiet. I will be elevated, right now. Listen, can you hear?"

Then the leopard disappeared, disappeared suddenly, vanishing into thin air.

Why couldn't she hear the voice inside of Xiao Ma? Xiao Sang felt a little regret. She wondered if maybe Xiao Ma were the better reader. Even though she was young, even though she made such a fuss over things, even though she had read fewer novels than Xiao Sang . . . Oh, oh.

It was already the middle of the night when they left the coffee shop. The lights were out in the buildings of the residential area, but there were many people in the bars along the road. When a warm breeze blew against Xiao Ma's face, she grew unexpectedly sorrowful. She held tight to Xiao Sang's arm.

At that moment they both saw the leopard. It perched on an enclosing wall in the distance, beyond it the glimmering sky. How could the sky be so bright at night? It seemed unimaginable to them both. Then all at once Xiao Sang understood: this was the sky in that book.

"Goodbye, Xiao Ma."

"See you tomorrow, Xiao Sang."

Another weekend came. The book Xiao Sang had ordered still hadn't arrived, so she'd borrowed a copy from the library. In her time outside of work she'd already browsed a few paragraphs, and she planned to make a night of it Saturday. She worked with extra drive once she thought of the enjoyment soon to come. Reading novels was solving mysteries, ones that were without exception the mysteries of life. Was there anything that could fascinate her more? No.

Xiao Sang began to read earlier than she'd planned. The book placed on the table sent invisible waves in her direction. She couldn't stand it, in fact, so it ruined her plan to study a foreign language.

She soon knew this wasn't a novel that could be read easily to the end. She could even tell it was a profound novel. Its characters were filled with longing, continually meditating on similar things. Their conversations were implicitly understood. The dialogue had a kind of excessive passion flowing through it. Xiao Sang thought while she read that maybe ordinary readers wouldn't like this book, but in her it produced a sense of familiarity right away. She adored how the style was given free rein. She sat beside the window holding the book in both hands and saw the ground in the courtyard covered with flowers from the scholartree, and a pair of lovers she didn't recognize who sat on the stone bench talking, their voices, *weng weng weng weng,* reaching her ears. She brought her eyes back to the book and continued to read slowly, wave upon wave rising in her mind. She finished reading the most beautiful passage. Though it was still a little obscure, though she didn't fully grasp it, she confirmed to herself: beautiful. Its artistic conception would go well with fragrant Longjing tea, so Xiao Sang went into the kitchen to heat up some water.

When the tea was brewed and placed on the table, another kind of thirst took her by surprise. She quickly returned to the book. What was this? The view of someone's figure from behind was a bit familiar, this shoulder—in which book did she seem to have met her? No, she hadn't met her, not even once. Xiao Sang slowly finished reading the passage, which seemed to leave no impression. Then she went back to the beginning and read it again. Now she began to drink the tea. It was truly good tea, and her thoughts immediately became livelier—she recognized that person. It wasn't from which book, it was the setting of *that time*. The woman seen from behind was mature, maybe a little older, only she couldn't be sure. Xiao Sang felt for no particular reason that a woman like this must appear everywhere. Yet she'd encountered her for the first time in a book. And the woman had never turned around. After recognizing her figure, Xiao Sang felt more sure about this book. She tried again, as hard as she could, to return to the artistic conception of *that time*: it was autumn in the outskirts, a slightly dry, cool wind gusting through the sky. The backs of figures appeared beside a marble gravestone. One, two, three of them . . . Xiao Sang thought she was just about to call that woman's name. Then she finally, suddenly remembered that her name was difficult to pronounce, that she simply couldn't say it out loud. The sky was so blue.

"Xiao Sang, you're sitting under the streetlight reading a book. Isn't it tiring?" Uncle Yi quietly asked her.

"No, Uncle Yi. I'm enjoying it."

"I know, I know. You're such a good girl."

Uncle Yi walked on past, his brisk steps pleasant to hear. The black cat hadn't come yet, the apricot tree had been picked clean, but these things didn't affect the atmosphere under the streetlight at all. Under the streetlight—reading a novel: this was a significant pairing, just like many years ago with the pairing of a well and a village girl. Xiao Sang raised her eyes and saw a light shining in the room on the third floor. Uncle Yi was also reading a book. Then her line of sight rested on the book page, and she swiftly entered its plot. The character in this chapter kept pursuing something, his feet flying through the air, but his goal was always changing form . . . Xiao Sang accompanied him somewhat tensely, wanting to see what was ahead.

Suddenly Uncle Yi spoke from above her.

"Xiao Sang, I'm worried you'll catch a chill."

He tossed down a wool scarf. Deep blue, it might have been one he used himself. Dear old man.

Xiao Sang wrapped herself in the scarf and advanced to victory with the book. While she read she reflected on how Uncle Yi was also reading a novel, a different book. People who read fiction are imprinted on each other's hearts . . . Later she grew a little tired and closed her eyes to rest for a few minutes.

She remembered a few days ago when she had been in Uncle Yi's study discussing fiction with him. It wasn't a large study, but books were piled all the way up to the ceiling. "There are only five or six genuinely useful books," Uncle Yi had said. Xiao Sang understood what he meant. When he said "useful," it indicated those few novels that one could frequently review and consult. Xiao Sang knew that the books Uncle Yi cherished included three classic novels and two modern novels. He'd bought several editions of each of these books, which were tidily placed on a corner of his generous desk. Xiao Sang finished resting, and her thoughts returned to her book.

Xiao Sang didn't know how long she'd been sitting when she heard the building's night shift workers returning. At first their conversations came through the enclosing wall, then they entered the courtyard. The workers lowered their voices as they came through the entrance, probably because they'd seen that she was reading. They walked past her and went into the building. Just now Xiao Sang had read exactly up to the chapter about the main crisis of the book. A life crisis and an emotional crisis. She noticed that her knees were trembling slightly. When the workers came in, did they sense the crisis in her book? They were so careful! There'd been several crises in Xiao Sang's life, the same as with the characters in this book. She'd suffered then, but the suffering had held a dreamlike quality. She often felt that she couldn't endure it, but later facts proved: any kind of suffering could be endured. She liked this type of novel, because, without exception, on reading these books up to the endings a feeling of happiness would rise from the depths of her soul.

After Xiao Sang finished reading the chapter about the crisis, she stopped. She raised her eyes and saw that the light in Uncle Yi's study was off, so that it looked as if the window had disappeared. She reflected that after all Uncle Yi couldn't be as full of energy as she was. She remembered that many years ago he could sit up all day and night, not moving, reading continuously. That was when he'd become her guide. Afterward he slowly taught her, leading her into an entrancing world. Her progress with reading would have been much slower if it weren't for Uncle Yi. People on the same path are so important, especially for this undertaking of reading. The main character undergoing the crisis kept reading no matter how much mental suffering there was—wasn't this the tactic of fighting poison with poison? Uncle Yi had said that it's difficult for people to truly despair. She hadn't yet been able to genuinely understand what he meant. Back then she hadn't read enough books.

The black cat came closer, its fur like satin. Xiao Sang stroked the cat and thought of the dialogue in the book.

"Dad, where are you going?"

"Not far from here. I'll be back soon."

"Come back soon. I'm scared."

The black cat stayed for a while then serenely left. It would patrol, safeguarding the atmosphere of this place. Xiao Sang was full of thankfulness toward it. Would the fear of the child in the book ever be dispelled? Xiao Sang remembered that this kind of fear was incurable. He must wait, wait until he became a different person. It was already after midnight. The sound of elderly people snoring emerged from a few windows, gently vibrating the air, as if they were saying: "I'm really comfortable, so comfortable . . ." Xiao Sang turned to the last few pages of the book, hurriedly swept her eyes across them a few times, then suddenly changed her mind. She was certain this book wouldn't disappoint her. Now she wanted to recall it in her dreams before dawn, even go herself to “meet” those several companions.

As she carried her chair upstairs, she was startled to see someone standing on the staircase.

“It’s me, Xiao Sang. I woke up and saw that you were still struggling bravely. I was worried, so I was coming down to warn you not to catch cold.”

It turned out to be Uncle Yi.

They said good night to each other. He lived on the third floor, and she on the fourth.

Xiao Sang didn’t meet the characters from the book in her dreams. Yet the night of reading left her contented. She comfortably turned over a few times and sank into deep, deep sleep.

The next day when she woke up she couldn’t recall what had happened during the night. She asked herself: “Who said that I was ‘struggling bravely’?”

She saw the novel on the table. She had taken up a part of the book’s battle; some obscure places had become clearer. Besides, she still had an afternoon. There would definitely be results.

She carefully made breakfast to warm her body.

After she finished breakfast, she also ate two pretty mangoes. Then she sat in the rocking chair squinting and lightly laughing. She thought of last night’s guardian, the black cat. It must know the contents of the book, because it took part in reading. You shouldn’t look down on this type of animal, especially black cats and spotted leopards.

“Everyone should learn from Xiao Sang: study her accomplishments and her enthusiasm,” the store’s manager announced at a short meeting before the shift started.

Xiao Ma took the lead with the applause. Xiao Sang’s heart warmed. The store manager praised her for not having made mistakes for many years. But this work was so simple, of course she didn’t make mistakes. How was this an accomplishment?

Xiao Sang sat calmly working at the cash register. She was ready to serve the customers. First, because she’d enjoyed the weekend and was in a good mood, and second, because these customers would come to trust her store and come back here to buy things, resulting in an increase in her bonus, so that she could buy even more good books. During the short break she thought about this and unexpectedly started to laugh out loud. Her gaze swept toward Xiao Ma opposite and saw that she was busily taking money and giving change to the customers. Xiao Ma sometimes made mistakes, not of course because she wasn't highly accomplished, but because her habits were just that way—inattentive. There wasn't anything wrong with this.

The morning passed quickly, and it was time to eat again.

"Xiao Sang, could you tell me what you read last weekend?" Han Ma asked Xiao Sang.

"*XXXX*," Xiao Sang kept eating while she spoke. The younger woman imitated Xiao Sang's every move, and whatever books Xiao Sang bought, she also bought. Xiao Sang appreciated Han Ma. She felt that her coworker had a manly quality, like the pillar of a family. Xiao Sang had never seen her depressed.

"Reading this book is hard. I still can't get into it."

"Oh? If it's hard for you, then I'll be far behind. But I want to try."

"Of course, Han Ma, you should definitely try," Xiao Sang earnestly said.

There were many young women who worked at the department store, and also a few young men, who enjoyed reading books. A few years ago they'd naturally formed a reading group. Every Wednesday they gathered in the conference room. They'd elected Xiao Sang to be their leader.

On that evening, in the flickering candlelight, a young man had excitedly stood and said:

"I nominate Xiao Sang. By reading books we want to better ourselves, and we can't go wrong following Xiao Sang."

"Aye!!!" twenty-some young people said together.

Xiao Sang's face had been feverish. She felt a reaction similar to when she was entering into a novel.

Xiao Sang rode the bus after getting off work. She was still thinking about Han Ma's reading. How would Han Ma enter into this somewhat obscure novel? She thought that this young woman had potential and might enter it through an unexpected passageway. An incident like that had happened two years ago. Han Ma hadn't been at the department store for long when, with a red face, she spoke to Xiao Sang about a novel that they both had read. Her insights surprised Xiao Sang, because Han Ma's history of reading novels was so brief. A sophisticated charm that no one would have expected emerged from her apparently disordered speech. From then on Xiao Sang had paid attention to Han Ma. Later Xiao Sang found out that she'd only been to middle school and then switched between quite a few jobs before coming to their store. She was a salesperson, which was a job she especially liked. "It's a good store, I like the atmosphere." When she told Xiao Sang this, the expression on her face was relaxed, and her body looked entirely at ease.

Before long Xiao Sang started encouraging Han Ma to study writing.

"No, I can't do it." She shook her head emphatically, as if scared.

Xiao Sang hadn't insisted on her suggestion, but she predicted that someday this girl might pick up the pen. Why not? Weren't even elderly people pursuing their passion and happiness?

Xiao Sang reached home thinking over these past events.

She lived in an older style of six-story building without an elevator. In the courtyard out in front of the building there were a number of large weeping willows and also a few scholartrees. The shapes of these trees were pleasing. Every time Xiao Sang entered the courtyard, she searched with her eyes for that black cat. Sometimes it was there, sometimes it wasn't. It belonged to everyone in the courtyard. Xiao Sang always felt that this courtyard was a natural reading place. You could tell that a reader like Uncle Yi lived here.

On work days Xiao Sang ate at the department store's cafeteria. After she got home she would just drink tea, without having a snack. Now she heated water and brewed a cup of Longjing tea, then her gaze fell again onto that book on the shelf. There was an unfinished battle inside of it. But on workdays Xiao Sang didn't want to tire herself out too much. When she'd finished drinking the tea, she thought of Uncle Yi.

Once she'd taken a seat in Uncle Yi's tiny study, her restless mood disappeared.

"All of the words and sentences sneak past my eyes like ghosts. The structure behind them hasn't appeared yet."

While Xiao Sang complained with her mouth, with her mind she thought about how suitable it was to talk with Uncle Yi about this mystical novel.

"When you sense that there is a structure behind them, you will be halfway to success."

Uncle Yi's voice was pleasant to listen to. Every time he spoke, Xiao Sang felt able to enter into the artistic conceit of an otherwise dim or unclear novel. Yet as soon as she left his study that atmosphere dispersed. Today Xiao Sang hoped Uncle Yi would talk about something different. The best thing would be to talk about his personal life.

"Are you asking about my old life at the North Sea? It was a small, bleak fishing village. There was a white sand beach by the sea called Silver Beach. Every day when I wasn't working I would just read books, because there was nothing else to do. In the first year I was restless, because I was young. Later I gradually came to like the North Sea. Yes, I liked its bleakness. The people there were so plain." Uncle Yi thought he had said enough by way of introduction.

These few simple words made Xiao Sang's thoughts leap. She felt that his narrative was similar to the tone of her novel. She stood to go, saying that she had to get back to reading right away.

"All right, good! You will have some results." Uncle Yi nodded profoundly.

Once Xiao Sang returned to her home she immediately opened the book. She read almost ten lines at a time, up to the thing that she was seeking. She nodded as she read, sighing: "It's really magical, magical . . ." It seemed as though when she realized what she wanted, she would be able to read about it. This situation had occurred many times before.

After she finished reading the passage, and read it again, she closed the book. She planned to digest it slowly. Tomorrow, too, she had to wake up early for work.

Xiao Sang lay in bed thinking carefully about the plot, discovering a few passageways, some interesting connections. The more she thought the more excited she was. Then she controlled herself and went to sleep wrapped in happiness.

"Sometimes, entering a different world is accidental," Xiao Sang thought as she waited for the bus. "For example, last night, in Uncle Yi's memories about his past life, an emotion was communicated through his slow speech. This emotion entered my world, and all at once burst open my inner (outer) door. Behind the door were many twittering sounds, rising and falling in the darkness."

The bus arrived, and Xiao Sang followed everyone on board. There were no seats today, so she grabbed on to the metal loop on the back of a seat and stood there. Opposite her was a middle-aged man with a distinctive profile, who smiled toward Xiao Sang, and she smiled at him.

"I entered the world of the novel with Uncle Yi's unintentional guidance. What does this prove? It shows that there are some people in this world who are always thinking of the same thing, doing the same thing, who are moved by the same artistry. Looking at it this way, entering a different world isn't completely accidental . . . For example, there's Han Ma . . . ," Xiao Sang thought.

The bus reached her stop. She walked a short stretch of road, then suddenly realized that the man she had run into on the bus looked like a classmate from when she was in college. "It *was* him! Damn it," she slapped her forehead. Then she busied herself after she'd entered the department store.

When Xiao Sang sat down at the cash register, that distinctively shaped face appeared in front of her again.

"Heishi! Where have you been all these years?" she nervously asked him.

"I've been here in the city the whole time," he answered calmly, handing Xiao Sang a ticket.

A certain book club was holding a group discussion. Heishi invited her to take part. Xiao Sang nodded and agreed. Then he turned around and went to browse the products on the shelves.

Xiao Sang's work began to get busier because there were a lot of customers in the store.

She was so busy the entire day that she nearly forgot about Heishi. Only when she reached her hand into her leather bag and felt the ticket did she remember. At school Heishi had always been the most inconspicuous boy, and he still was now. Even so, Xiao Sang had noticed his broad shoulders back then. She ate, showered, and changed into casual clothes. Just a few steps from the store's door, she heard Heishi calling to her.

"Shall we take a taxi?" Xiao Sang asked him.

"No, let's walk. It's not far," he said.

So it wasn't far! How had she never heard of this book club?

While the two of them made their leisurely way back and forth through small alleys, the sky grew dark and the streetlights came on.

"These alleyways are so interesting. We're not at the Pigeon Book Club yet?" Xiao Sang asked Heishi.

"Soon. What do you think of this area?"

"It's like a street in another province where I went to a used bookstore. It's really nice here. Look, there're still a lot of customers in the bookstore over there," Xiao Sang said.

Then Heishi told her that the book club was just behind the largest of the used bookstores.

There was a narrow passageway through the shelves of thread-bound books. They walked out of the passageway and saw a spacious tearoom. There were only four people seated in the tearoom. A small lamp hung from the ceiling.

"They're here, they're here," an enthusiastic voice said.

Xiao Sang noticed that the speaker was a young woman, probably not even twenty-five. Sitting beside her were three men who might have been in their thirties. The woman was brewing tea for everyone.

"Which book are we discussing today?" Xiao Sang inquired.

"We're having a casual chat. My name is Qiaozi," she answered on everyone's behalf. "We've heard that you're reading *XXXX*?"

"Yes, but I haven't finished it." Xiao Sang was startled. "How did you all know?"

"We're well-informed in the world of reading," a square-faced man said. "We're all reading that novel and have been for a long time. We want to hear your impressions."

At Xiao Sang's side Heishi encouraged her in a low voice to "boldly elaborate." He said that this was a rare opportunity.

Xiao Sang thought deeply for a while, then said:

"I think of this as a lofty book. All of the plots it depicts are indefinite, are not what they seem, precisely because there is a powerful intention behind the words. For the past few years I've enjoyed literary works of this type. In them, language expands into another kind of function . . . It isn't some mysteriousness that can't be understood, no, it isn't that. I think that it's an unusual power."

At this last part Xiao Sang gradually became excited and raised her voice slightly, because even she hadn't expected that she would say all of this. It seemed like there was an automatic speaking device installed inside her.

"See, Xiao Sang just began to read this book and has already entered into it. She really is experienced. As for me, I only entered the world of the book slowly, after half a year. Before that I kept revisiting its plots in my mind, like going over a lover's figure." It was the thin man named Fei speaking.

Next Xiao Sang heard everyone whispering among themselves. She turned her face toward Heishi and saw his eyes flickering with light. Was this an effect produced by the book?

"Xiao Sang, have you been to the rock garden in the middle of the lake?"

Heishi was speaking in the shadows, but his voice seemed to be floating from a distance.

Xiao Sang said that of course she had. She'd been about to bring this up and never thought that Heishi would first. But what did the novel have to do with that rock garden in the center of the lake? Now she was slightly agitated because she felt that she'd slipped into the atmosphere of the book. She couldn't interpret this atmosphere—maybe she had to wait until later to do so. In a chaos of emotion, she saw Qiaozi's pretty face approaching her, then moving far away again . . . What was Qiaozi saying? Xiao Sang apparently hadn't heard, yet she was filled with gratitude toward her—such intriguing communication, which was characteristic of this type of book.

"I've met you before, Xiao Sang," Qiaozi stated at last.

"And I can confirm that. It was at the library," Xiao Sang immediately remembered.

The two women took hold of each other's hands excitedly, holding tight for as long as half a minute. They had brushed by each other in the hallways of the library. Their acquaintance now was half a year later.

"I respect you, Xiao Sang."

"I . . . should have joined the reading group earlier," Xiao Sang said regretfully.

"Now is good. Water finds its channel. I benefited from your speech! Each person has a unique perspective, which together will bring that book into our midst. Before I came here today I was at home, and there were lots of random creaking sounds in the walls. I felt terrified. But then, once I sat down at the book club and met these friends of books, some vague patterns appeared in my mind."

Qiaozi was very excited about Xiao Sang's arrival and had especially liked her speech. She said that she imagined herself sharing her own ideas in this way, but obviously she hadn't practiced enough yet.

"I forced myself to say a few random words. I can tell that this book club really stimulates the imagination," Xiao Sang said.

Only at this moment did she truly understand what she had said. She felt saturated with happiness.

While they were talking Heishi's diamondlike eyes glistened in the dark. Xiao Sang heard him sigh ambiguously from time to time. Could he be in love with Qiaozi? Xiao Sang remembered Heishi's invitation, which she thought could be rich with implications. She'd been living in the same city as her college classmate without seeing him for many years, and now, the first time she saw him, there was a book club that much to her surprise met her standards. Did Heishi know her way of life? If so, through what channels had he obtained this information? Also, she worked in the city of Meng, so how hadn't she known before about there being an alley of used bookstores nearby, or about this hidden book club? Just as Xiao Sang became distracted, her classmate Heishi, who was sitting beside her, spoke up.

"Xiao Sang, what do you think of the book club?" he quietly asked her.

"It's wonderful! For me it's just like coming home. There's a new force at work here . . . ," Xiao Sang said.

"I won't hide from you that I've become crazy about reading over the years. I first met Fei and Li Hai a long time ago. My life was stuck in a rut, then Fei led me into the world of novels . . . We founded this book club. It's an exceptional life, don't you think? Everyday life becomes more meaningful in relation to it," Heishi said.

"Of course I think so, Heishi. Thank you, we'll all be able to form long-term connections."

"Xiao Sang," Qiaozi said, tugging on her hand, "you should focus on looking after me."

"In fact, you're the one who is looking after me—you inspire me," Xiao Sang responded.

The man with the rugged face, who'd seldom spoken throughout, stood up and said:

"Welcome into the book club, Xiao Sang! I'm Li Hai. I'm still at the beginner level, because I'm not diligent enough."

Qiaozi stifled a laugh at what he'd said and, lowering her voice, added to Xiao Sang:

"Li Hai reads books like a detective. He's a unique reader."

Xiao Sang felt a tiny flame leaping up from the bottom of her heart. She realized that this was the atmosphere of her way into this book *XXXX*. Her thoughts extended out very far all at once, and she thought of it being thirty years later, at this same place, sitting here with these few companions. Would she still burn then as she did at this moment? "I'm so lucky," she said to herself. Then she thought of Uncle Yi, with numerous emotions. Originally these friends had all been inside the book, so that her meeting with Heishi on the bus was the logical next chapter. Her mood grew incredibly bright, the fog that had been obscuring her reading dispersed, and some passageways appeared to her through the book's words and in between its lines. Naturally, she still needed to do battle with her reading.

When it was time to leave the book club, only Heishi went in the same direction as Xiao Sang. The others disappeared all at once and went another way. Xiao Sang wondered, a bit confused, why Qiaozi hadn't left with Heishi. The human heart is unfathomable. However, Xiao Sang went along with him cheerfully. The used bookstores on both sides of the small alleyway were still lit up bright and shining, so that they could see the customers clustered inside moving around. Heishi told her that several of the bookstores remained open all night.

She asked him who would spend the night in used bookstores. Heishi answered that they were sailors.

"They want to enjoy the embrace of their loved ones after many days of drifting on the water."

"You're speaking abstractly now, but I love to listen to it," Xiao Sang said, slightly mocking him. "Now tell me, how did you find me the other day?"

"I've never been far from you, but there are blind spots in your vision. You never stopped by this street with the used bookstores."

"You're right, I'm no good."

"I'm the one who felt inferior. Until one day when I resolved to read like you . . . Thank you."

"I'm the one who should thank you for letting me spend an evening like this. It was a priceless gift."

The two of them parted at the bus stop, each seeing the same thing in the other's face. Xiao Sang's mind began to churn as she rode the bus. She thought that the events of the evening had been slightly fantastic. That unfamiliar street of used bookstores, her companions in that book club at the back of a bookstore—what were these after all? Unexpectedly, she had made so many friends among people she hadn't met before—when it wasn't her style at all to form a wide group of friends. Though she realized that these people were not ordinary friends. An atmosphere that was hard to describe wound around them. My classmate Heishi, you have become so mystical!

When Xiao Sang lay down to sleep, she happened to start imagining those sailors. She sensed that the atmosphere of the small bookstores suited them. She recalled seeing someone who'd squatted on the floor reading an old thread-bound book when she entered the bookstore and later, when she left the store, seeing that person still sitting in the same place. She wondered at how much concentration that must take. Xiao Sang's single life had been a little disturbed by her classmate Heishi. She wasn't in love with him—she loved the indescribable atmosphere that surrounded him . . . Why hadn't he fallen in love with Qiaozi? They were such a good match! At this thought Xiao Sang started to smile, conscious that she was troubling herself over nothing. No matter what, this had been an uncommon evening in her life, for which she thanked Heishi. It was remarkable that, after so many years had passed, he still thought of his former classmate.

Xiao Sang felt that recently her personal life centered on the novel *XXXX*. Was this normal or not? As soon as she raised this question she felt it was meaningless. Wasn't reading a novel that tugged at her soul and entangled her dreams with longing exactly what she had been seeking for so long? It was the kind of book that wouldn't let go of any reader who was interested in it. With each week Xiao Sang would find her experience of reading renewed. It was a marvelous book. She hoped that Heishi would invite her to the book club again, but there was no sign of him for well over a month. The reading group at her department store was great, too, but the standards were a little lower than at the book club. Xiao Sang wondered if maybe her own standards had disappointed Heishi. Maybe those words the book friends had used to praise her had been spoken out of politeness. They'd already researched this book for a long time and were sure to have many different opinions than hers. They must have had reservations and were probably worrying that she wouldn't be able to adapt to the way people in their circle expressed themselves. These thoughts extinguished Xiao Sang's newly inflamed passion. Puzzled, she continued to read the novel and had numerous new inspirations. Naturally, her confusion didn't disappear. Sometimes while reading she would have the sensation that the book was also reading her. It would ask her outright: "To the left, or to the right?" Xiao Sang answered: To the left. Then, before her eyes, the kind of landscape that she yearned for would unfold. Just as if she were writing this book. Even though her new friends weren't there to encourage her passion, a certain degree of emptiness and disappointment deepened her comprehension of the novel's text. That's what Xiao Sang thought. She thanked those friends for this.

At dusk Xiao Sang and Uncle Yi stood talking under a large scholartree.

"What does it mean if a book makes you read it again and again endlessly?" Xiao Sang asked.

"It means you're maturing quickly," Uncle Yi answered, smiling.

"But I want to be sure that something's ultimately there."

"You're already there," he affirmed.

"Thank you, Uncle Yi. I'm so happy."

"That's good. Have you been back to the Pigeon Book Club?"

"Oh, did you know about this book club, too? It's remarkable! I haven't been back—they haven't asked me. Maybe they've forgotten about me."

"A young friend of mine goes there. You don't need to wait for them to ask you. Can't you go on your own?"

"Yes, yes! I see that, now that you've pointed it out." Xiao Sang jumped up in excitement. "Who is your young friend?"

"His name is Heishi."

"Oh? How come I've never heard you mention him before?"

"Because you never asked me. He's my ex-girlfriend's son . . ." Uncle Yi added with deep feeling, "Children in single-parent households sometimes have problems, so his mother had him come visit me."

"I see. Who wouldn't love you? Even someone like me who has both parents. Uncle Yi, no one can resist your charm. If it weren't for you, I wouldn't know even the basics about the world of reading yet."

"Xiao Sang, you're speaking in the voice of a character. Which book is this from?"

"Living downstairs from you, it's the same as my living in a novel—every day."

They joked with each other as they went upstairs, then each returned to their home.

Xiao Sang brewed a cup of tea to calm her sense of surprise. The shock Uncle Yi had given her was too much, her mind was almost in chaos.

So there *were* such fortuitous events in life! Could it be that the novels she had read were slowly transforming the environment around her? Many years ago Uncle Yi had led her into this special world of fiction; now, without her knowing how or when it had started, he'd also let his former lover's son burst into her life. Oh, Uncle Yi, Uncle Yi! Xiao Sang didn't know what to think about her mentor, when her experience of him was so complex. There was still a doubt in her mind: Uncle Yi and Heishi ought to see each other often, so why had she never come across him before this? Could it be that the two men met secretly someplace in the city? As she thought about these questions, Heishi's features blurred. He no longer seemed to be the classmate she had known before, but instead changed into someone odd and unfathomable. Xiao Sang had experienced this before: a familiar friend suddenly become strange, their behavior unpredictable. Now, encountering it again, Xiao Sang wondered how to approach things, especially with Uncle Yi involved. Uncle Yi had urged her to take the initiative to go back to the book club, which must be because he cared for her deeply . . . but what could the even deeper meaning be? No matter what, Xiao Sang was willing to go there. She would clarify what all this meant. She decided that the next time she met Heishi she would be sure to observe him carefully and discover from his perspective another, unfamiliar Uncle Yi. While Xiao Sang was thinking of these unusual and fascinating events in her life, the plot of the book she'd just been reading kept flashing through her mind. These plots didn't correspond to reality, but there always seemed to be some connection.

On a day off, Xiao Sang thought of Heishi as soon as her eyes opened. She planned to go on her own to the Pigeon Book Club toward evening. After she got out of bed she ate breakfast and then began to clean the apartment. After cleaning the apartment she showered and washed her hair. She'd resolved to appear at the book club with a brand-new face. She would boldly declare her opinions and speak as much as possible, even if she had no grasp of what she was saying.

To prepare for the evening, she sat back down to read *XXXX*. The sky outside sparked with lightning and thunder rolled while she read. She took a look outside the window, then at the book in her hand. She enjoyed this kind of reading atmosphere so much that her heart filled with inspiration.

The rain, heavy rain, kept falling almost until evening. Xiao Sang's thoughts kept leaping at the sound of the rain. She saw cities, passageways, enormous caves among throngs of people. Lastly, she took an elevator up to the forty-fifth-floor balcony. Looking at the dome of the sky above, she shouted over and over in her mind: "So high, so high!"

The rain stopped when she'd eaten dinner, and the passion in her heart quieted down. After debating for a few minutes, she decided she would go to the Pigeon Book Club to make a speech.

"Xiao Sang, are you heading into battle?" Uncle Yi asked her as he came in through the courtyard entrance.

"Yes!" Xiao Sang laughed.

There were obstacles on her way to the book club. She couldn't find the original street. Why not? Could it be that her classmate Heishi had played some trick to make her lose her sense of direction? Xiao Sang started to feel worried, because the sky would soon be dark and finding the way would be even more difficult then. She asked quite a few people the way, but they all shook their heads and said there was no street of used bookstores nearby. An old woman even remarked, "That kind of bookstore ought to be in the neighborhood of chiseled stone streets by the river." She didn't know why she believed this. "Anyway, there are no bookstores like that near here. I've lived here for forty years and haven't seen any," she said.

Xiao Sang's despair was indescribable. Still, she kept searching and asking around. Some of the small alleyways she walked through were familiar and some were strange, but none were the one she and Heishi had taken the previous time. Probably she hadn't paid enough attention when she'd passed through with him. The sky was dark now, but fortunately there were streetlights along every alley. Her friends at the book club wouldn't wait for her. It was likely none of them had expected her to come barging in, and now she was late!

"Ma'am, who are you looking for?" a seven- or eight-year-old girl asked her.

"Oh, little friend, I'm looking for the Pigeon Book Club. Do you know where it is?"

"This is my uncle's book club. You're going the wrong way. Keep walking along this street, turn left, and you'll be there."

Xiao Sang walked a long ways while the girl stood there and shouted after her:

"Turn left, turn left . . . Look for the archway!"

Xiao Sang thought: "This girl is so conscientious!"

She walked to the end of the alleyway and then turned left with the road. Here this street was narrower, only wide enough for two people side-by-side. The squat houses along both sides pressed closely in, with a wooden post placed every so often on which were hung old-fashioned streetlamps. Xiao Sang said to herself: "This isn't the street of used bookstores. Why did she trick me? Was it an archway or the gates of hell? . . ." She walked for ten minutes without seeing a single person. She hadn't thought there were any places like this left in the city.

When Xiao Sang was about to return to the main alley, a wooden door creaked open and a young woman's flat face looked out.

"Are you here for the meeting? Come in."

Xiao Sang, happy as a flower in bloom, walked quickly toward the open door.

Entering the room she saw the same pattern again: a small lamp placed on a table arranged with a teapot and teacups. The five friends swept expectant looks toward Xiao Sang.

"We've been waiting for you," their individual voices said together.

"So you knew I would come! But the location has changed." Xiao Sang tried to temper her excitement.

"Xiao Sang, you still found it," said Qiaozi, pouring tea for her. She added: "Just a moment ago I said to them: a reader of the book *XXXX* will definitely be able to find us."

The four men laughed knowingly.

"Qiaozi's right!" Xiao Sang started to feel moved. "That book encouraged me to find this place. Friends, no one understands my ideas better than you. Today it rained heavily . . . No better weather for reading, then I just knew we'd be able to meet again. This is written about in the book . . . No, I wasn't so sure, not until a moment ago when Qiaozi brought it up, then I was sure all at once . . ."

Continuing, Xiao Sang spoke about some things inside the book and some outside the book. Her five friends quietly listened to her, urging her on with their eyes. She sensed that Heishi and Qiaozi had shifted to be beside her. Their movement made her more self-confident.

"Who was that darling little girl?" Xiao Sang paused and asked.

"She's the daughter of this book club's owner," the four men answered.

"So, could you understand my random words just now? I don't seem to be talking about my impressions of the book—I seem to be very far off-topic. I'm so sorry . . ." Xiao Sang was a little bewildered.

"Xiao Sang, you've spoken very well," Qiaozi said enthusiastically and took hold of her hand.

"Yes, your speech was brilliant!" Fei echoed Qiaozi.

The small lamp suddenly went out, but quickly was lit again. Xiao Sang felt Qiaozi's grip urging her on.

"Friends, what was I just saying?" she asked everyone absently.

"You were talking about a nameless animal that appeared in the courtyard of your home," Li Hai, who was sitting opposite, prompted her.

He'd risen slightly as he was speaking, as if he were approaching Xiao Sang to shake hands with her. She was touched.

"I've heard that you study this unusual book with the tenacity of a detective. I admire you! . . ."

Xiao Sang kept speaking for a long while. She felt her thoughts set loose and said almost everything she wanted to.

Everyone's eyes were watching her seriously, especially Heishi's eyes, diamondlike . . . How had she studied alongside him for so many years and never noticed that his eyes were different from other people's? Maybe because her interactions with him had all taken place in the daytime. Xiao Sang finished her speech with infinite emotion.

The room was silent. She looked all around her, discovering that Qiaozi was gone. The men were watching her kindly, as if each wanted to speak but held back.

"I would very much like to hear Li Hai's views on this magnificent novel," Xiao Sang said directly.

Li Hai immediately grew bashful. Even though he sat in the shadows, Xiao Sang could sense his face reddening.

"It's like this, I, I place my book in the sunlight, and I stare at those, those sentences, hope, hoping that the character behind the curtain will emerge on its own . . . Xiao Sang, I can't say it well. I like listening to you speak."

"No, Li Hai, you've spoken very well. Who is that character? What is that character like? I think this is what we all want to know. Li Hai, you've said what we all wanted to say.

"Fei, how do you read this book?" Xiao Sang added.

"I've already said that for some time now this book has been my lover—naturally, his (her) sex isn't clear, sometimes it's male, sometimes it's female. In real life I have no actual lover. Now, though, I have a secret lover. Once I think of him (her) I just smile. We're never apart, ever since I formed this attachment to him (her). I'm a household electrician, and sometimes I have rush jobs. I feel agitated when I go home after these jobs are finished. But I take the book out and place it on the table, and then my mood gradually calms down. What is this book about? I don't think of this question at all—I think about other things. For example, what if someday I came across the sort of scene described in the book? That would be so joyful! This is the book's magic for me."

"It really is a book with magic power . . ." The square-faced young man sighed as if he were dreaming.

Xiao Sang felt Heishi shifting his chair a little closer to her. What did he want to say to her?

He said nothing.

"Heishi, I understand a bit more now. You came looking for me because of this book, didn't you?" Xiao Sang asked.

"You could also say that you were always in the book, so I was destined to find you at some point," Heishi softly said.

"You flatter me too much. It will go to my head," Xiao Sang answered him in a whisper.

"Why? Are we inferior to the characters in the book?"

"No, that's not what I meant. You and Uncle Yi are both better than me. Of course, I'm not so bad myself."

The two of them looked at each other for several seconds, then laughed out loud together. The rest of the group also had smiles on their faces.

Xiao Sang felt that this evening's wonderful encounter had reached the peak of happiness. She became a little incoherent. She repeated the sentence: "If it weren't for this book *XXXX* . . ." She heard everyone chiming in with her, saying: "Yes, yes . . ."

On the way home the scene played out just like before, with the three men abruptly disappearing and leaving only Xiao Sang and Heishi standing at the entrance. Xiao Sang asked, "Qiaozi? Qiaozi?" Heishi told her that Qiaozi's mother had paralysis and needed her care, so she had gone home early. Xiao Sang was startled to hear this.

Going out the door, Xiao Sang discovered that the narrow alley from before had changed back into the street of used bookstores. They had walked for a while when she suddenly saw a silhouette that looked like Fei in one of the bookstores. She hurriedly pulled Heishi inside.

It did turn out to be Fei. He was standing in front of a shelf paging through a book.

"It's so late. You're not going home yet?" Xiao Sang asked him.

"Haha, there's never time to finish," he said.

"This is a holiday for Fei. We shouldn't disturb him," Heishi said to Xiao Sang.

Xiao Sang looked back as they went outside, discovering that there were many customers in the bookstore holding books, looking like colorful tropical fish slowly swimming—were they all wearing brightly colored clothes by coincidence?

After they left the street of used bookstores, they unexpectedly came to an alley without any streetlights, only faint lamplight from the windows of the houses on both sides.

"Xiao Sang, you're nearsighted. Hold on to my hand," Heishi said.

"All right, all right," Xiao Sang replied with pleasure. "Were all the customers in that bookstore just now sailors?"

"Most of them. It's such a lively atmosphere there. I've always wanted to be a sailor out on the ocean, but my mother doesn't approve."

"Do you live with your mother?" Xiao Sang couldn't help asking.

"No, I live in my company's housing. My mom's a very independent woman."

Xiao Sang said to herself: "Independent woman? Why won't she let her son go to sea?"

They walked a long stretch of road together in the dark, discussing the book again. Heishi's views surprised Xiao Sang. She felt that her former classmate was much more profound than her. She was filled with gratitude toward him. Besides this gratitude, though, Xiao Sang also wondered why he hadn't been in touch with her for such a long time.

"I felt like I kidnapped you the last time we went to the Pigeon Book Club," Heishi said calmly.

Xiao Sang wanted to tell him that it was exactly the opposite. It wasn't kidnapping, it was helping her open up a new universe of life. Because of meeting these friends, she had enough energy now to do anything! For example . . . but she didn't say these words. She watched in silence as the road before her eyes gradually widened—they had reached the bus stop, and Heishi was waving goodbye. "He's that rare man who's considerate of other people," she finally said aloud, "and people like that are suited to reading this kind of novel."

Once Xiao Sang got home she picked up the book, turned to the passages that she liked the most, and rapidly skimmed them one by one again. She wasn't using her own eyes to read these passages, but instead at one moment used Heishi's eyes, and the next moment Fei's. Besides these two sets of eyes there was also a third—Uncle Yi's. So, why had her classmate Heishi come looking for her? What did it have to do with Uncle Yi?

Xiao Sang went to sleep, without completely falling asleep. She walked far, very far, along a path in the countryside, without feeling tired. Everything around her was shimmering with light; there were no shadows. Was this place somewhere outside the city where she lived? It seemed to be. She remembered that at first she knew where she was going, then she was no longer interested in her destination, only in keeping on walking. Now she unexpectedly thought of what her book friend Fei had said about his lover. Had she also become the lover of this miraculous book? Her overwrought emotions really were like being in love. Xiao Sang had experienced love many times, until the past few years when she had quieted down and turned her passion toward reading fiction. Her ambition was to reach Uncle Yi's level, then to continue her efforts and spend the coming years in the enjoyment of books. She hadn't anticipated how great a novel's magic power could be, even changing the rhythms of her everyday life. She took a strong breath of fresh air and said to herself: "My friends from the Pigeon Book Club are like sailors!" She imagined a picture of them going to sea and returning, as if she could smell the sea salt on their clothing—especially Qiaozi's clothing. Qiaozi was such a remarkable young woman. She had to care for her paralyzed mother . . . Xiao Sang thought again that Heishi ought to be with Qiaozi, but it seemed as though they weren't together. On the ridges in the fields before her a silhouette appeared, a person who was a little like the young woman Han Ma from the store. Oh, it really was her! "Han Ma, Han Ma!" Xiao Sang shouted, but no sound came out. Then she dropped into darkness—in darkness was happiness.

The woman had a mature beauty. Uncle Yi stood talking with her under the persimmon tree. When Xiao Sang passed them he nodded to her. Back at home, her heart pounded. This woman didn't seem to have been here before. Could it be Heishi's mom, Uncle Yi's former girlfriend? She and Uncle Yi looked like such a good match. Xiao Sang couldn't help going to the window, where she saw that they were no longer there. Had the woman read this book, too? Could she be discussing the book with dear Uncle Yi? Xiao Sang felt a bit jealous, but even more curious. Thinking over this incident, she picked up the book again and turned to the chapter that she had most recently read over and over, skimming through it, now with the eyes (imagined) of that beautiful woman. Strangely, she seemed to reach some new comprehension. It was as though her realizations were always connected to Uncle Yi. The Uncle Yi whom she knew so well suddenly became unfamiliar, unfathomable.

Xiao Sang hadn't seen Heishi for another long time. She didn't dare to crash the Pigeon Book Club again. Without knowing why, she thought that if she went looking for the street of used bookstores, like last time, she would surely lose the way and the trip would be for nothing. Why hadn't Heishi arranged another meeting with her when they'd said goodbye? Naturally he had his reasons, but so far she hadn't been able to figure out what his reasons were.

"Uncle Yi, was that your girlfriend?" Xiao Sang asked.

"No, my ex-girlfriend. She's Heishi's mom," Uncle Yi answered calmly.

"She's beautiful."

"Did you get a good look at her?"

"Yes. She must have been even more beautiful when she was young."

"Yes."

As they went upstairs together Xiao Sang chattered: "Such a pity."

"What's a pity? You're imagining things, Xiao Sang."

Back at the apartment, Xiao Sang sighed at the ways of the world.

She mused: was Heishi's personality like his mother's? The beautiful woman had a gentle appearance. Xiao Sang read the book and thought: would Uncle Yi be able to get to sleep tonight? At ten-thirty she couldn't help going downstairs and looking toward his window, where a light was shining. He was still reading. But after a while the lamp was turned off, and he went to bed as usual. Uncle Yi had regular habits, unlike her. At this moment someone came in through the main gate of the courtyard. To her surprise, it was Heishi!

"Are you looking for Uncle Yi?" Xiao Sang asked him.

"No, I was looking for you."

"Looking for me? Ha, how strange."

"It seems like I'm not welcome."

"No, you're welcome, you're welcome."

"Let's sit for a while under this tree," he suggested.

Then the former classmates shared an open-hearted conversation.

Heishi loved his mother, but he didn't approve of her attitude to life, although of course he wouldn't interfere. She had a nature that easily went to extremes. When Heishi was very young, his father had left them and before long married another woman. Heishi's mother could never forget about her former husband. However many years passed, while her ex-husband's family remained tranquil and happy, she still wouldn't let him go and sometimes used Heishi as an excuse to seek him out. Then she would be rejected. After these incidents she'd sigh and even ask the young boy: "How did I lose your father?" Two years ago she had overdosed on sleeping pills because she believed herself better off leaving this world, since Heishi no longer needed her and the boyfriend of her youth, Uncle Yi, wasn't interested in her. After being rescued she felt deep remorse for what she'd done, that she'd wronged her son and Uncle Yi. And both men treated her with even more gentleness and care. Now, her desire to live had seemed to rekindle.

"Do you think Uncle Yi still loves your mother?" Xiao Sang asked.

"I've asked him that before. He said he still loves her, but only like a family member. You know, people can change, and not everyone is like my mom. In fact, her youthful love for Uncle Yi came back after the incident with the sleeping pills. It's such a pity that he no longer loves her. Oh!"

"Your father—is he handsome?"

"Yes. The kind of man people turn to look at when he walks down the street. That's why my mom left Uncle Yi and married him so quickly. They were madly in love about a year before there was conflict. I don't look anything like my parents. When I was little, people thought I was a foundling. You see, it's the opposite for someone like me who isn't good-looking—everything goes peacefully."

When Xiao Sang heard Heishi mocking himself this way, her heart suddenly ached for him.

As they talked, the black cat came back into the courtyard and wound around the both of them, seeming especially excited. A few sentences appeared in Xiao Sang's mind. She thought: "Even the cat . . ."

"Heishi, I admire you," she finally said.

"Why?" Heishi glanced at her confusedly.

"You will eventually turn into another Uncle Yi. You should know that Uncle Yi's my idol."

"Thank you, Xiao Sang, but you speak too highly of me. How could I compare with Uncle Yi!"

When he'd said this, he stood and said goodbye. Xiao Sang asked him where they would meet next time. Heishi just said:

"At the street with used bookstores. It will become familiar the more you go there."

After he left, she pondered the sentence he had said . . . "It will become familiar the more you go there."

She felt that the sentence's implications were like a dark cave. She also sensed there'd been people like this all around her, living lives completely different than hers, lives too difficult even for her to imagine. Take Uncle Yi: she'd believed that she knew him, but now the information she'd learned made clear that she only understood superficial things about him. Thinking this, Xiao Sang smiled at herself mockingly. Naturally, how could she fathom a person as weathered by experience as Uncle Yi? This was probably where the fascination of this book *XXXX* came from. It couldn't be fathomed, while enticing you to go deeper, and each step going deeper brought joyful results. The world of fiction that Uncle Yi had guided her into was his soul! Xiao Sang was excited by her discovery. So, could she, like Heishi, become more and more like Uncle Yi? This was exactly what she wanted. A former girlfriend whom Uncle Yi no longer loved had needed to be rescued, and Uncle Yi rescued her. Without letting her misunderstand his intentions, he had helped her find the courage to live. Managing this relationship must be very hard. Xiao Sang felt lightheaded just thinking about it. But Uncle Yi stayed self-possessed, giving the impression of a large tree. Then there was this furtive Heishi. Could Uncle Yi have been like Heishi when he was young? Xiao Sang's eyes rested on the book again.

It was as if all the characters in the book were engaged by, or concerned with, the same thing. A reader could perceive the dense atmosphere, but to grasp or confirm it was impossible. It was like an invisible trap, which Xiao Sang had voluntarily entered. She remembered how, when Uncle Yi had introduced this book, he'd casually told her: "This book suits you. You will be able to read it for a long time. Anyway, you have spare time now." Xiao Sang had gotten used to Uncle Yi's way of speaking, where there were always words within words. After picking up the book she'd vaguely sensed that she wasn't confronting a work of fiction, but instead a few incidents—events that would happen in succession in her personal life. This chapter of the novel described a lover who missed meeting the beloved time after time. That lover sat on a nearby stone bench. Xiao Sang noticed that he was handsome . . . Suddenly there was a knock at her door. It was her friend and coworker, Xiao Ma. Xiao Sang was surprised.

"Xiao Sang, I came to sleep over. I've been wandering around with my boyfriend, but I just sent him on his way. I don't want to waste time on him, but my body won't listen to me. What should I do?"

"I don't know!" Xiao Sang shouted toward the door of the bathroom.

Xiao Ma was already inside taking a shower. It was late at night.

When Xiao Ma finished showering, she came out of the bathroom and saw that Xiao Sang had already gone to sleep—today she was truly exhausted.

Xiao Sang successfully found the Pigeon Book Club by herself. The book club was in an empty room behind the conference center of a city government building. She'd arrived too early, when there was only one person there, Qiaozi, busily brewing tea on the stove. Xiao Sang promptly went over to help.

"Qiaozi, is your mom doing any better?"

"Much better, she'll be able to stand up soon. Did Heishi tell you about her?"

"Yes. I have something to ask you, but first promise me you won't be angry, OK?"

"Of course not. Any question at all."

"Why aren't you on better terms with Heishi? You are so well-matched."

"Thank you, Xiao Sang. You'll be surprised to hear that we dated before, when I was twenty."

"What do you mean?"

"It means that we broke up four years ago. But we're still good friends."

"So that's it. I was concerning myself over nothing." Xiao Sang started to laugh.

Even though this exchange was only a few short sentences, Xiao Sang noticed how Qiaozi's large eyes suddenly, radiantly shone. It appeared that this book friend had loved Heishi in earnest.

"Later I fell in love with someone else, though I broke up with him, too. This proved at least that Heishi and I aren't well-matched. But I promise, he's the best of all the men I've ever met. I don't have a lover now, Xiao Sang, and you're the one I love the most in this book club. When you first joined, I stared at you, and when you spoke my blood ran hot. I don't know why. I want to read books like you do . . . I went home and told my mom about your speech. She was so impressed with you! She is also enchanted by books, she's very empathetic."

Listening to Qiaozi, Xiao Sang gave a quiet sigh, but inwardly she felt a rush of warmth.

At this moment the four men entered. Heishi came in last. When he sat beside Xiao Sang as usual, she glanced at him gratefully. She heard Fei saying that he wanted to talk about his new impressions of the book *XXXX*. As soon as he said this, Xiao Sang felt a kind of emotion blowing against her, enveloping her, but she couldn't decide just then what that emotion was. Fei didn't start talking about his impressions immediately, and instead whispered with Li Hai.

"Xiao Sang, your speech—speak, I love to listen to you the most," Qiaozi entreated her.

"But I'm waiting for Fei's speech."

"You don't need to wait for him. If we wait for him, he won't be able to speak. He likes to speak when it's unexpected. But you, you can always lift our emotions."

"Qiaozi, you're very observant," Xiao Sang said appreciatively.

Then she made her statement. She talked about how, over time, her life had been transformed by the book *XXXX*. She spoke in vague terms, yet the more ambiguously she spoke the more she tried to convey a certain intent. She felt how the others had their eyes fixed on her, so she began to feel moved and raised her voice slightly. She could remember the last few sentences she said.

". . . because of this book, my sense of hearing has become sharper. Within just three months, I've heard many sounds that I never heard before. When I quiet down, they're always there, converging into soundwave after soundwave. I'm surprised there are books like this in the world—not directly conveying information, but instead stimulating your hearing."

Xiao Sang finished speaking. She asked herself: what was she saying?

Then Qiaozi approached her and took hold of her hand. Xiao Sang raised her eyes and saw Heishi smiling at her. He always seemed to have plans in mind. He was catching up with Uncle Yi.

Just as everyone was looking at Xiao Sang, Fei's voice rang out. Qiaozi made a face at Xiao Sang.

"My lover recently changed toward me. Now she pursues me relentlessly. I recognized her early on—long before Xiao Sang met her—but in the end my appreciation of her beauty fell far behind Xiao Sang's. This isn't important, though—what matters is, I'm on the way now. Li Hai and I just figured out a direction in the book's plot. We both feel that we can see where things are headed, especially the part when the animal keeper appears. Could my experience suddenly rise to another level? It's been a year since the last time I had such a pleasant surprise. I'm too lazy. There's an important emotion hibernating inside me . . ." He couldn't continue.

Xiao Sang thought Fei seemed a little pessimistic, but Li Hai didn't see it this way.

"You always say I am a detective, when in fact the real detective is Fei," he said slowly.

Xiao Sang turned to Heishi and softly asked him:

"Why don't you make a speech?"

"I'm waiting," Heishi also spoke softly. "Maybe I'm waiting for the right words? It seems as if they won't come this evening. I admire you, Xiao Sang. I have difficulty expressing myself."

When Heishi spoke this way, Xiao Sang seemed to see him in his youth, as an unassuming figure that now made her heart tighten. She thought: all along, her judgment of people had been oriented to the surface. How deep of an understanding did she have about him and Uncle Yi, these two men so close to her? They were the setting of this book *XXXX*. There was also Qiaozi, who clearly loved her and was so much younger than her, and Xiao Sang couldn't fathom her either . . .

"Xiao Sang has a superhuman ability," Qiaozi said, "which is that she can detonate at any moment. If she wants to, she can tell us about the world of this book. I often wonder: why can't I do this? I hesitate, and so I am excluded. Yesterday I vowed that I would rush straight in, but when I arrived at the scene, I began to hesitate again."

Xiao Sang noticed that when Qiaozi made this speech, Heishi nodded slightly, as if saying: "Yes, yes."

"It's not entirely hesitation," the square-faced man named Yan said. "I can tell that you're a woman who likes to consider the things that happen to her deeply. Your eruption will last a long time. As for me, I read this book as a guide to life. I believe our everyday life needs a guide like this. Do you feel the same way?"

Everyone started to laugh, showing that they felt the same way. Xiao Sang realized that she had the same deep feeling herself, then felt that Yan's literary attainments were extraordinary. She was immersed in happiness to encounter so many like-minded people all at once. This was another example of good fortune falling from heaven into her life. The first example, of course, had been meeting Uncle Yi. She saw Qiaozi smiling at her. The two women spontaneously jumped up and hugged each other. Xiao Sang also saw Heishi smiling at her, although she didn't dare to hug him, so she sat back down reservedly.

"I really like your attitude to things," Heishi said to her.

Xiao Sang was stupefied at first, but quickly felt that she could comprehend his words. She replied:

"I like your attitude, too. You can always make a fool like me be much more careful."

"It seems like we are starting to appreciate each other?" Heishi broke into a smile.

"Probably not just starting today."

When it was time to go, something unexpected happened: Heishi's mother had a fall, so he had to leave hurriedly ahead of the others.

Now Xiao Sang knew how to find the way, like she was suddenly enlightened. She walked alone in a relaxed state of mind through an alleyway she hadn't been to before. Streetlights stood in the alley, and nearly every household had its doors wide open, as if to welcome guests. It was a special alleyway. A girl ran out of one of the houses and right up to her. Oh, to her surprise it was the girl she'd seen the previous time she'd gone to a meeting at the book club.

"Did the book club move here?" Xiao Sang asked the girl.

"The book club was here originally. Aren't you just coming from there?"

The girl's eyes widened in surprise as she looked at Xiao Sang.

Xiao Sang's face unexpectedly reddened. She repeatedly said she was sorry.

"Why?" the girl asked, not understanding.

"Because I said something foolish."

"Haha, haha!" the girl laughed cheerfully. She considered and then said: "Let me walk with you for a ways."

She held Xiao Sang's hand tight, her expression growing serious as they walked together. Xiao Sang could feel the girl's hand sweating and asked her whether she was excited.

"I'm always like this. My uncle said I'm the soul of the book club." She spoke like a grownup.

"Your uncle was right. You are remarkable," Xiao Sang said with feeling.

"I want to read all of the children's books in the world. Will that take me a long time?"

"Yes, you will need a long, long time. You are very happy."

"Are you happy, too?"

"I'm happy, too."

When they'd reached the end of the street, the girl said goodbye to Xiao Sang.

Xiao Sang had myriad thoughts at once. At the entrance to the street she turned back to look and saw the entire alley lit up bright, like it was carrying on a silent conversation with her. She abruptly started to feel anxious, because she'd remembered about Heishi's mom's fall. She sped up, planning to ask Uncle Yi about it when she got back. By now Uncle Yi surely would have news. Throughout this evening's gathering at the book club, Xiao Sang had felt as though Heishi was family. Yes, just like family, like her parents and brother.

"Heishi's mother is fine. She didn't break any bones," Uncle Yi told her. "Was the discussion enthusiastic this evening?"

"It was wonderful, Uncle Yi! I learned so much . . ." Her voice suddenly broke. "I love you, Uncle Yi. You've done so much for me."

"I love you, too, Xiao Sang. Go on home and get some rest. I know this kind of discussion is tiring."

Xiao Sang lay in the dark for a long time still thinking of the incident with Heishi's mom. "She's so lucky," Xiao Sang sighed. She imagined that if she were her, she would want to live—to see her son marry, until her grandchildren grew up. Then there was this unfathomable Uncle Yi. Xiao Sang could remember him telling her that he'd left the North Sea back then because of a failed love. Who wouldn't love Uncle Yi? Naturally, he wouldn't have been the same as he was today—surely he could only be this way after he'd been through many troubles. So, what was he like now? He had a halo, Xiao Sang thought. Would he have met Heishi's mother after he left the North Sea? Back then the beautiful woman had blind spots in her vision, so she didn't see how handsome Uncle Yi was. After many years, she'd eaten her fill of hardship and only then turned back to discover her former lover's grace. By then, Uncle Yi no longer loved her. Xiao Sang tossed and turned in bed for a long time, falling asleep only when the sky was almost light.

Xiao Sang and Xiao Ma agreed to meet after work to go to the tony coffee lounge. Xiao Sang recalled that it had been a long time since she'd been there with Xiao Ma, because her attention had shifted to the Pigeon Book Club.

"Xiao Sang, you shouldn't let him go so easily. I will pursue him, if you set him free!"

Xiao Ma was teasing Xiao Sang, thinking that Heishi was her new boyfriend.

"That's just silly, he and I are only friends. He was my classmate."

"Really? Then you're saying I can still hope?"

"I can introduce you to him."

"No, you keep him. I've met him, he's extraordinary. I almost think that maybe someday you will start to like him. As for him, I can see from how he looks at you . . ."

"Xiao Ma, you're making things up. When did you see us together?"

"At the street with used bookstores. You didn't notice me, because you were distracted."

Xiao Ma was pleased with herself, but Xiao Sang was surprised. How could this have happened? Had she walked past Xiao Ma without seeing her? Xiao Sang tried to remember what it was like at the used bookstore street with little result. The memory was too vague. She only remembered Heishi's mysteriousness. Just then the coffee shop's server startled her.

"Welcome, welcome," his voice suddenly rang out in the dark.

There was only the one candle lit on the table, so their surroundings had become black as a cave, and she didn't know whether there were other customers in the room. The women both wore thin sweaters but still felt a chill. Two large cups of hot coffee arrived. How satisfying! There was an animal rubbing back and forth along Xiao Sang's calves. Xiao Ma said that it was the leopard.

"I started to leaf through this novel you're reading. I couldn't get into it right away, so I can only call it leafing through. That time at the used bookstore street, when I saw both of your captivated expressions, I made up my mind to read it."

"Tell me, are you and that boyfriend making any progress?" Xiao Sang moved closer to Xiao Ma.

"No, though we haven't broken up either. He isn't the kind of man I want to pursue."

"Have you decided what kind of man to look for?"

"Not yet. If he's like Heishi . . . ," Xiao Ma giggled.

"I really can introduce Heishi to you—"

"No, no, don't introduce us. Wait a bit. How can you be so sure of yourself? Hmm?"

Xiao Sang fell silent and became a bit lost in thought. She wasn't that sure of herself, but she was certain she hadn't fallen in love with Heishi. Her heart hadn't pounded, even though Xiao Ma was teasing her. But with Heishi, you only had to interact with him to know he was the kind of person who made a deep impression.

"I've always thought you are the kind of person who'll do well even without a boyfriend," Xiao Ma said.

"Yes. As long as I can think of having a book there quietly waiting for me after work, I'm inspired."

At this moment the leopard leaped onto the table, reached out its paw, and snuffed out the candle. Then it left.

The women's thoughts entered a tunnel. They were thinking about things to do with the book. Or, immersed in its subtle artistry, they might not have been thinking of anything.

Xiao Sang didn't know how much time passed before she suddenly heard Xiao Ma softly calling her.

"Xiao Sang, Xiao Sang, where are you?"

"I'm in the countryside. There's farmland here, and I'm walking along the ridges in the fields. My mood is lifting."

Xiao Sang had just finished speaking when the server lit the candle. At the same time the women saw young people pouring through the main door from outside, chatting animatedly.

"Let's go home," Xiao Sang said.

Outside was a deep blue night sky, the moon larger than usual.

"Xiao Ma, what are you thinking about?"

"I was wondering, Xiao Sang, have you ever missed out on having someone in your life?"

"Of course I have. But that wasn't such a bad thing. What do you think?" Xiao Sang said.

"Hmm, maybe."

"Besides, at my age, it's hard to miss out on anyone any more."

"You're a little pessimistic."

"I'm not sure whether it's pessimism. Could I also still be waiting?"

"I'd like to believe you're still waiting."

After leaving Xiao Ma, Xiao Sang didn't want to go home just yet. Without knowing why, she felt gloomy this evening. She rarely went to the bar, but that evening she ended up there unawares. She ordered a glass of wine.

After she finished the wine, she felt much more at ease. She asked herself: had she been inhibiting herself? No, she answered soberly. Her life was rich and not without passion. It was simply that she hadn't had a boyfriend in several years. She'd been absorbed in reading novels and wanting her standards to rise. There was one strange thing, which was that, ever since she'd begun reading the book *XXXX*, she seemed to feel a sort of mystery taking shape around her. She didn't know yet whether it was the magic of the novel, or if there really was enchantment in her life.

"Your first time here?" a tall man came over to her and asked. He was drinking baijiu.

"No. Thank you, but I don't want any more to drink."

"My hometown is the Changbai Mountains. I don't want to go back, I only want to long for someone in this city."

"Maybe because returning to her there you won't recognize her?" Xiao Sang said, raising her eyebrows.

"Yes." After the man said this, his head drooped, then he leaned over the bar and went to sleep.

Xiao Sang hurriedly got up and left.

She reached the main entrance to her courtyard and saw Uncle Yi outside waving to her.

"Xiao Sang, it turns out I was going to bed late, so I came outside to wait for you. Did you have a good time?"

"Yes. I drank coffee and wine. I haven't felt so carefree in a long time."

As they went upstairs together, Xiao Sang asked Uncle Yi whether he had seen Heishi recently. Uncle Yi said he had seen him, that they had gone together to a sailors' library and talked with a sailor there for a long time.

"Heishi yearns for the sea," Xiao Sang said, as if she had something on her mind.

"You're right," Uncle Yi answered her.

When Xiao Sang lay down on her bed, she thought: some people enjoy the risk of going to sea, while some people might experience homesickness instead. Heishi probably belonged to the latter. What deep kind of emotions did he feel about his hometown? His childhood hadn't been happy in the normal sense, but he had grown up to be the person he was now. Who was he now? Xiao Sang didn't know, but she couldn't stop herself from sighing that she wasn't his equal. Without knowing why, she thought that Heishi and Uncle Yi were gradually entering the book that she was reading. Naturally they weren't the main characters, but instead obscure background figures—for example, Heishi had become a vendor whose face was blurry; Uncle Yi had become a rescue worker at sea. Thinking this over, Xiao Sang laughed aloud. This kind of thing often happened in the book: a character suddenly emerged from the vague background. Xiao Sang knew that readers must have patience, must be good at waiting. Everything would eventually be like rocks emerging from receding water. If a reader hadn't ever had this sense of rocks emerging from the waves, then she (he) wasn't suited to this kind of book. What kind of book? It was the type of book that she, Uncle Yi, and her book friends from the Pigeon Book Club all loved. Before, she had been wrong to think that there were only a few readers on her level—only Uncle Yi, whose standards were even higher than hers. Then Heishi arrived and brought her to the Pigeon Book Club. She only then discovered that there was such an enchanting world within the city. This microcosm seemed broad in its implications. Every single person in it seemingly could cause endless "incidents." So Xiao Sang didn't feel that the Pigeon Book Club was actually discussing the book *XXXX*—instead it was discussing everyone's everyday lives. Wasn't this the state she was pursuing? She and Uncle Yi had been looking for a kind of novel that would melt into their lives. "Melt into one!" she said out loud in the dark. She walked by herself into a dark alleyway where there wasn't a single streetlamp and the sound of slow reading aloud came from the squat houses.

"Should we walk along the edge of the forest? Do you hear the sound of drumbeats?"

"Look, this is the ground where I scattered seeds a few days ago. They've already sprouted."

"What does 'unexpected' mean? It's when you take pains to forget something . . ."

"Yes, in the city, people are sowing seeds everywhere."

Xiao Sang listened as she walked along. She thought: what brilliant dialogue! And how close to everyday life! Didn't dialogues like this frequently ring in her ears on those evenings when she sat in the courtyard reading under the streetlight? Of course, it was usually the workers on the night shift who were speaking. Gradually, the voices reading aloud from books faded and couldn't be heard clearly. Yet their tone of voice could still be distinguished, that tone of voice that seemed to bless Xiao Sang into dreaming.

Han Ma unexpectedly appeared at the Pigeon Book Club. Only she wasn't introduced by Xiao Sang—she arrived with Fei. Xiao Sang saw her and Fei sitting at the table chatting and all at once realized: no wonder Fei and Han Ma had recently come into her dreams about her reading! Fei had said that he took the novel to be his lover, while Han Ma was the sort of young person who would write fiction in the future. Maybe she was already, secretly trying. When Xiao Sang entered the book club, Han Ma came over and sat by her, so that Xiao Sang felt the energy of her youthful body.

"Fei and I met at the sailors' club," Han Ma said unaffectedly. "I never would have thought we'd both be interested in life at sea, though neither of us are sailors. After I got to know him, I wanted to start writing fiction. I want to write the kind of stories that he and I enjoy. I know this won't be easy . . . His obsession with fiction infected me, so that I want to become the kind he falls in love with . . . Xiao Sang, do you think this is madness?"

"No, I don't think it's madness at all. You're born to be fellow travelers."

"Haha, there are so many fortunate encounters in the world!"

"It might not be by chance—"

Xiao Sang thought of her dreams, but she didn't want to keep talking, because it wasn't necessary. Fei's eyes glimmered across from them. He'd become so enthusiastic and forthcoming. He and Han Ma exchanged glances the entire evening.

As Xiao Sang had entered the book club she'd discovered Heishi wasn't present. She was a bit disappointed. Qiaozi told Xiao Sang that Heishi had gone with his mother to the ocean and would be back in a week. "He specifically wanted us not to forget to tell you." Qiaozi made a teasing face.

Xiao Sang only then discovered that Qiaozi and the "detective" Li Hai were sitting together, the two of them seeming to speak in endless whispers regardless of who was giving a speech. It looked as though the Pigeon Book Club's structure was transforming.

Now Han Ma was giving a speech.

"For me the book *XXXX* is like a catalyst. Time passes day by day, and I feel things inside me changing, as if I'm no longer myself. I admire the author's talent, and at the same time I think: if someone like him could cultivate a vision like that, couldn't I give it a try myself? I haven't read as many books as everyone else. My realizations lag behind yours. I came to understand only recently that good novels teach people how to act. Now, oh, once I pick up the book, indistinct patterns float through my mind. Like there's someone standing beside me, prompting: 'Grow up faster!'"

“I’m the one urging Han Ma on!” Fei cried out.

“Han Ma, get started soon. We’re all waiting to read your book!” Li Hai and Qiaozi chimed in with him.

Han Ma sat down, her whole face red. Fei sat close beside her. Xiao Sang thought their expressions were just like drifting on the sea. They were both obsessed with the sea . . .

“I agree with Han Ma’s ideas. Recently my life underwent a transformation caused by this beautiful novel. I’m like Han Ma, I’m also taking action . . . but I’m not sure what kind of action it is. It’s like how a mountain is still a mountain, but also something completely different. Oh,” Xiao Sang sighed.

She realized she suddenly felt sentimental. But why?

“The best novels can train those who take action,” Yan, who had all along been silent, abruptly added.

“Then are you also taking action?” Xiao Sang asked him.

“I think so. For example, when I do chores at home,” Yan responded.

Without knowing why, Xiao Sang felt Yan’s answer to be especially touching. “He’s a remarkable young man!” she exclaimed to herself, and looked at him steadily for something like ten seconds, until Yan uneasily lowered his head.

Xiao Sang thought about how every single person there, herself included, had studied the novel *XXXX*. At this moment they were thinking about how to expend the energy drawn from the novel, because this was now their task. She suddenly remembered Heishi wasn’t there. What a pity! Xiao Sang imagined herself introducing this book to the young people at the department store. She already had plans. She also thought that Xiao Ma and the others would be inspired if she brought Heishi to the department store’s reading group. The next time she saw him she’d suggest this. Xiao Sang looked opposite, saw an intimate look pass between Han Ma and Fei, and was surprised to feel her heart fluttering. How strange, when she wasn’t the one in love. Why would her heart flutter? Was even being in love contagious within the atmosphere of a novel? Oh, their enthusiastic discussion had risen to a peak this evening because of Han Ma’s unexpected arrival!

“Even though I have no definite plan,” Xiao Sang continued, “even though everything is unclear, I will still take action—just like that statue in the book, moving deep in the night when everything else is still.”

After Xiao Sang finished speaking, everyone looked at her appreciatively. This made her confident that she ought to have said these things. Most of the time she didn't have a definite thought progression when she talked about fiction. Even so, she had an impulse from the bottom of her heart, a nameless impetus pressing her to say things . . . Having experienced several gatherings of the Pigeon Book Club, she felt that her book friends liked to listen to her sharing her impressions.

"Li Hai and I have decided to take action together!" Qiaozi excitedly said.

Xiao Sang turned admiring eyes to the two of them.

Everyone stood and got ready to go home. Yan said that he wanted to see Xiao Sang on her way, but she declined. Then Yan made his way to one of the used bookstores. Like the time before, Xiao Sang walked that small alley alone. Now the alleyway turned back into the alleyway from the time she and Heishi had first gone together to the Pigeon Book Club. This made her sigh with myriad emotions—in the blink of an eye several more months had passed. Had Heishi passed through the crisis in his life? She was so hopeful that she could help him. But she reflected that Heishi was the sort of person who seldom needed help; maybe he even wanted to help her. Yes, he'd definitely tried. Otherwise why would he have invited her to the book club? They hadn't seen each other for years then, although he'd been interested in her all along, with what might have been a former classmate's interest. There was also Uncle Yi. What had Uncle Yi said to Heishi about her? Warmth flowed through Xiao Sang as she remembered such wonderful events from the past. Though she was single, she didn't feel at all alone! She had so many precious friends she would never be separated from as long as she kept reading. Everything seemed to be happening in some obscure way, but inside of everything there also seemed to be a skillful plot—not a short-term plot, but one that extended toward destiny in the distance . . . "What is happening?" Xiao Sang unconsciously spoke out loud. She immediately looked left and right. It was OK, there were no passersby in the alley, only the bookstores' soft lamplight scattering onto the surface of the road.

It was still early (the gathering had ended early, probably because some of the members were dating). Xiao Sang couldn't help turning along her way into a unique "plant studies" bookstore. The salesperson let her sit on a round stool to select books. There were so many varieties of books about plants, opening up Xiao Sang's outlook.

"This is an introduction to Xishuangbanna Tropical Botanical Garden." The salesperson handed her a thick volume with pictures. "I think you'll like it. Heishi bought this book, too."

"Does Heishi come to your bookstore often?"

"Yes. I've seen you and him walking past here."

Xiao Sang was fascinated by the pictures of two foxtail palms, so she bought the photograph collection. She heard a pair of lovers by the bookshelf in front of her discussing the plants in their books, then suddenly realized: this was an environment for people in love, and she should leave right away. The salesperson wanted to recommend another book, but Xiao Sang left smiling, waving a hand.

As she exited the alleyway, a question leaped unprompted into her mind: who had Heishi taken to this bookstore? Xiao Sang slapped herself on the forehead and said: "You're making a big deal out of nothing."

On the bus, recalling the sight of Han Ma and Fei together, Xiao Sang's mood relaxed. It was like that dream from the novel appearing in reality. At this moment she heard the male passenger sitting behind her say: "They came together spontaneously. It wasn't by arrangement." A woman answered him, saying: "There's still a good chance. For example, back when we were working in the outskirts of the city."

Xiao Sang returned home. She saw the lights still shining in Uncle Yi's home, so she felt peace of mind.

She wrote in her diary: *Han Ma came to the book club. Heishi went with his mother to the sea. One instance of enthusiastic speech. Bought a photo album about Xishuangbanna Tropical Botanical Garden.* After she finished writing she looked again several times at these sentences, feeling them shimmer. She still didn't know whether she was near or far from the mystery she was trying to solve.

Then she saw a folded slip of paper under the door. Who had slipped it inside?

Recently I've been attacking literature. I feel this is the only way I can be sure of myself.—Xiao Ma

Haha, Xiao Ma had come by. The young woman would soon be well on her way with reading. Xiao Sang persisted in believing that people who were on the path of reading would have good lives. Weren't there these living examples around her? But not everyone could be on this road—it depended on individual nature and was also determined by certain turning points. Xiao Sang decided to help Xiao Ma.

Xiao Sang lay in the dark, thinking of these things that brought her such happiness, and was unable to go to sleep for a long time. Tomorrow she would go back to work. She liked her work. The hours at this job weren't long and it was somewhat demanding, which structured her life. Interacting with all sorts of people during the day was also a kind of training for her. In a few days she would turn thirty-five—life was passing fast! She wasn't sad about getting older. Wasn't she making progress every day? Recently it could be called advancing by leaps and bounds. When was there time to be sad?

During the day Xiao Sang kept busy with her work at the department store. Then, in the evening, she rested and read the book *XXXX* for a while, falling asleep in the atmosphere of the novel. In the blink of an eye, a week of tranquil life passed by. During this week she saw Uncle Yi several times in the courtyard. Each time she tried to make out from his expression the answer to a certain question, but Uncle Yi never let her. He was simply too profound. Xiao Sang couldn't help but suspect that she wasn't skilled enough.

Her day off arrived. Xiao Sang was going to battle through the night again. She finished drinking her tea, blow-dried her hair, and went downstairs with the book pressed under her arm. This time she also carried a comfortable soft chair, because she had read up to the part of the book that brought her the most joy.

It wasn't yet nine in the evening. A few of her neighbors came out of the building one after another, all young people, probably going out to bars. Xiao Sang remembered what happened the last time she went to a bar, when she'd been sentimental. She wasn't sentimental any more. Emotions are so intriguing. The young people appeared cheerful, likely because of their thirst for life.

Xiao Sang sat in the soft chair and began to read by the light of the streetlamp. This chapter was about a few vague circumstances. A woman tour guide led several visitors into a national park. They had walked a long way and were all exhausted, but the tour guide, Xiao Man, persevered, saying that they would soon reach the stone forest, and when they reached the stone forest their fatigue would disappear. Every time Xiao Man told the tourists this, their eyes would flash. Naturally they would persevere. It would be the utmost happiness to see the stone forest once in a lifetime. Xiao Man's guidance was strange: she spoke of the stone forest as beyond marvelous, but why were they not reaching it? How big was this national park? Later on this tourist group met a local indigenous person. The mountain resident pointed behind him and said that the stone forest was right there. Then their eyes began to shine again. They hadn't found the stone forest, but their fatigue was disappearing little by little, and they became more and more spirited. Watching them climb the mountain, Xiao Man was secretly joyful . . . This chapter's title was "Creation." Xiao Sang remembered her speech at the Pigeon Book Club gathering and thought that her experience was similar to that of these travelers. This was creation then. Xiao Sang also felt joyful.

The black cat came over and rubbed back and forth against Xiao Sang's leg. She thought: the black cat is also creating. An evening like this was a night of creation. The people of the Earth were all participating in creation. Xiao Sang was moved by her enjoyment of the book's contents. She wanted to read this chapter again, and to share her impressions with Uncle Yi. Look, now the light was on in his study. He must be reading an even more profound book. Han Ma had said that the best stories taught people how to act, so should she take action? Or had she been taking action all along, just not consciously? Sometimes, unconscious action *was* taking action.

While Xiao Sang read the chapter a second time, the vague details became an outline. They turned out to all point toward the same state. Several workers returned from the middle shift at the machine factory. Xiao Sang heard their whispers in her ears:

"Shh, quiet. Xiao Sang is reading."

"She works hard during the day, when she rests she reads . . ."

"Go around this side, don't get too close to her."

They quietly went inside the building. The black cat followed them for a few steps, then came back. It was thinking that Xiao Sang would give it dried fish pieces. Xiao Sang unconsciously reached into her pocket, feeling for the dried fish. The black cat gently stretched its neck to reach her palm. At this moment Xiao Sang read the sentence: "Someone climbed up from the mountain ravine, waving toward the travelers." Listening to the pleasant sound of the cat chewing the dried fish, she told herself: "What a captivating night!" She wanted to go talk with Uncle Yi about this chapter, but held back. She would think independently and experience it by herself.

Late at night the light in Uncle Yi's study went out. Xiao Sang remembered that on Monday she would be going on a business trip to the city Hui. More than two hours of traveling, and she could read on the plane. These circumstances would be rapturous. Today when she'd gotten off work and come home, she'd told Uncle Yi about this trip, and he was happy for her. He'd even picked up a notebook and recorded her flight number and the hotel where she would be staying. Xiao Sang had found his gesture touching.

Xiao Sang had just stood up when Uncle Yi came out of the building.

"Haha, so you haven't gone to sleep yet."

"The weather is so nice, I wanted to go for a walk around the neighborhood."

"I'll walk with you. This evening I was brilliant in combat."

"That's good."

Xiao Sang placed the book on the chair and walked happily with Uncle Yi out of courtyard.

"I haven't seen Heishi since he and his mom came back from the ocean," Xiao Sang said.

"I've been thinking we three should get together. How about going rowing in the park? That park behind the mountain is a bit further from the road, and there aren't many people there."

"Yes! I'd really like to."

"I'll make a date with Heishi. He's been working too hard recently. You must have noticed how he does things meticulously."

"Mm-hmm, I have. Maybe it's your influence on him."

"No, I can't compare with Heishi. I'm often influenced by him," Uncle Yi laughed.

When they passed a bar, a man came outside and warmly greeted Uncle Yi. Xiao Sang could tell from his face that he was young.

"I never knew you went to bars," she said.

"When I was younger I would go sometimes. Since getting older I rarely do. The last time I went was more than a year ago. I met this young man at the bar, and we got along pretty well."

"I'd like to see you when you're drinking."

“A pity it’s so late now, otherwise I could let you.”

“How is Heishi’s mom?”

“You could say she’s adjusting well. She’s even started reading novels under Heishi’s influence.”

“Heishi is wonderful! Whoever marries him will be happy.”

“I think he should get married, too. Do you know someone suitable I could introduce him to?”

“Not just now. There was someone, who’s very pretty, but she wouldn’t accept my introduction.”

“Why not? It’s not often you come across a young man like Heishi.”

“I don’t know why not,” Xiao Sang said indignantly.

They were both silent. Each was thinking their own thoughts, or it could be that they weren’t thinking of anything, just enjoying the companionable walk. For Xiao Sang, Uncle Yi was the person she was most willing to be around: someone from the older generation and also her best friend, who was even more understanding than her parents. She’d never tire of being with him, having endless heart-to-heart talks and looking ahead to the future. He always encouraged her to improve. They quickly came to the city moat, where Uncle Yi said they should go back home. So they turned around and walked back.

“Uncle Yi, I want to ask you something, but only if you say you won’t be angry with me,” Xiao Sang said.

“Of course I won’t be angry, because it’s you who are asking.”

“Why did you go to the bar that time more than a year ago? What did you and that young man talk about?”

“Oh—it happened like this. There was a personal issue that made me unhappy, so I wanted to go to the bar and relax a bit, and I met the young man there. He’d already had a lot to drink, but he wasn’t completely drunk. He grabbed on to my sleeve and kept pouring out words, confessing that he didn’t want to live. That evening the young man and I stayed there for a long time. By the time we said goodbye, my unhappiness was mostly gone. I hadn’t gotten drunk, but I’d returned back to normal.”

Xiao Sang felt that this sentence of Uncle Yi’s was very telling, but she didn’t want to bother him with more questions. So she fell silent. She thought secretly: so it turns out Uncle Yi also had times when feelings of melancholy overwhelmed him. When they headed upstairs, she finally said:

“Uncle Yi, I sometimes imagine that I could share your burdens.”

“Thank you, Xiao Sang. But I don’t really have any burdens.”

They said good night to each other on the third floor.

Xiao Sang wrote in her diary: *Going to the bar to dispel depression! What had happened?*

The incident with Uncle Yi unsettled Xiao Sang so much she had no desire to sleep. She kept supposing . . . Maybe it was about that beautiful woman with a complex soul? But she instinctively knew that wasn’t it. Uncle Yi’s manner had been calm when she’d run into the two of them. What burdens did he have then? He had retired early, spent his later years in leisure, and was enchanted with reading. In Xiao Sang’s understanding, at least seven or eight other young people had been influenced by Uncle Yi and held him in esteem. Especially Heishi, who was like his biological son and must be his greatest comfort. There was also Heishi’s mom, who now had her heart set on him again. Xiao Sang told herself: “If I am to solve the mystery in Uncle Yi’s life someday, I will need a detective’s eyes, like Li Hai. No, I can’t. This is my shortcoming.”

She picked up the book and turned to the part she had read in the evening. There were two lines of dialogue that jumped out at her.

“When we looked for them, they were also looking for us.”

“Their scent is in the wind, they have never left us.”

She liked these two lines of dialogue, without knowing why. Maybe because of that mystery Uncle Yi had revealed? His thoughts were so deeply hidden, and naturally she wasn’t his equal. Besides, in a few more hours the sky would be light, so she should sleep. She counted for a long time, then finally fell asleep. But she slept fitfully and kept hearing herself talking in her sleep. Since she had forgotten to close the curtains, she saw a ball of light through her haze, a warm halo that gave her a feeling of confidence. She felt that she could recognize something well-known, so affectionate, so evident . . . “Hello, it’s been a long time. Why didn’t I ever realize it was you?” she heard herself sigh.

On the plane, Xiao Sang lived out her desire to read in flight. The department store’s manager had rewarded her by letting her take business class. The seats were so much wider than in economy! Afraid to waste time, she opened the book as soon as she boarded the plane. Her seat was by the window, so she watched the mountains and seas of clouds while she sank into the world of the novel. After a while she sighed: “How enjoyable!” At altitude it seemed like there might even be hope of solving Uncle Yi's mystery within a mystery, but Xiao Sang didn't dare to draw any conclusions yet. The book depicted the love between a single mother and a middle-aged pilot, with twists and turns, until, at last, the woman chose to forsake him. But her abandonment wasn't cause for sorrow. She went looking for a new goal like a bird that had won its freedom—maybe some new hobby, or devoting herself to ascetism, or maybe even waiting for a new love to come around . . . Could Uncle Yi also be waiting? Who was he waiting for? Could it be that he hadn't made up his mind whether or not to marry Heishi's mom? Xiao Sang considered this and decided that he shouldn't marry her. But Heishi's mom would be so disappointed if she were to find out that Uncle Yi had another love!

The two hours of plane travel passed without Xiao Sang satisfying her craving. The store's manager had sent her to Hui to order embroidery products, so she was going to look at samples. She took a taxi to the Mount Tai Hotel, which was mid- to high-end, an especially tall building. The room she'd reserved was on the thirty-fifth floor. She had reserved on such a high floor in order to read in the sky above the city.

Xiao Sang freshened up and went downstairs carrying her handbag to find somewhere to eat. She'd heard that Hui had a good food scene and hoped to try the local cuisine.

She came to a dining street—a broad, chiseled stone road lined on both sides with restaurants.

She went into a restaurant that sold local food and ordered pickled vegetable fish and salted duck. All at once she felt very hungry and ate until her forehead ran with sweat. The female server recommended that she try a little of the local liquor, saying it could take away the fatigue from her journey. The alcohol content wasn't high, but after Xiao Sang drank a few sips she had the sensation of being drunk. She heard the server pointing out a tall building from the window and saying to her:

"Look, that's your room, high up . . . I never imagined someone could stay so high. This hotel's name means 'high,' isn't it 'H'? If there's a power outage, how will your husband climb up there?"

Xiao Sang looked at the monstrously tall building with blurry vision, discovering that it was shaped like a tripod standing in the busy city center. The windows were all dark. Could there be no guests inside? She said in a lowered voice:

"Don't worry, I don't have a husband."

"Don't have a husband?" The server clapped her hands with excitement. "There are always your parents, though?"

"Yes, they live with my younger brother."

"Haha, you're lucky, all on your own with no attachments—you can go wherever you want!"

After the server left, Xiao Sang couldn't help but drink another few large sips of the liquor—she suddenly wanted to experience Uncle Yi's state at the bar. She craned her neck to identify her room in the hotel. But it was a futile effort when the windows were all dark. Could the power really be out? Xiao Sang thought of her distant parents and brother. Ordinarily she seldom thought of them, but at this moment, because of this strange liquor, she saw each of their faces. They were bent over, fumbling around looking for something on the floor of their home . . . Xiao Sang leaned over the table and started to cry.

"Miss Sang! Miss Sang!" the server shook her and said, "someone's calling you on the phone."

The server pulled her over to the telephone. She picked up the receiver, and to her surprise it was Xiao Ma!

"Xiao Sang—" Xiao Ma drew out the syllables cryptically, "I've entered into the book."

"How did you know I was here?!" Xiao Sang shook, and the receiver almost fell to the ground.

"There are no walls impervious to secrets. I just got off work."

"Damn it, why won't you just tell me?"

"I found out from my rival where you were."

"Rival?" Xiao Sang completely sobered up. "Who? Not Heishi? Stop messing around!"

The telephone exploded with wild laughter. Xiao Ma said, "You'll never guess!" and hung up the phone.

Xiao Sang paid the check and slowly went back to the hotel. With a warm wind on her cheeks, she felt her thoughts were unusually clear. She wondered: who would know her movements? The department store manager knew that she had come to Hui, but not the plane itinerary or specific hotel. Could it have been Uncle Yi? Xiao Sang's mind suddenly expanded. Uncle Yi had asked her the address of the hotel where she was staying and recorded it in the notebook. Xiao Ma might be familiar with the neighboring streets . . . But what did calling Uncle Yi her "rival" mean? On the surface, Xiao Ma seemed to be joking, saying that she herself loved Xiao Sang and that she believed Uncle Yi loved Xiao Sang—and so he was her rival. She was talking nonsense! How could she talk this way about an elderly person? Even though Xiao Sang was sure Xiao Ma had been joking, she still wondered: could Uncle Yi have fallen in love with her? No, he couldn't. Xiao Sang had never had this strange idea before, because ever since she and Uncle Yi first met many years ago (he wasn't too old then), her relationship with him had settled into place. He was her beloved uncle, someone even closer than her parents, who could even be described as her soulmate. She lived in his building, luckily. Love? She surely loved Uncle Yi, and he also loved her (once Xiao Sang thought of this she was moved), but it wasn't the kind of love that Xiao Ma meant. She remembered bringing Xiao Ma to Uncle Yi's study several times before. Each time Xiao Ma sat primly in her chair, so still that Xiao Sang hadn't known whether she was in a daze or sunk in thought. Uncle Yi liked Xiao Ma and had told her that Xiao Ma was "highly gifted." Could it be then that Xiao Ma had taken a liking to Uncle Yi, so that once Xiao Sang left, she went looking for him on the pretext of needing to call Xiao Sang? Oh, she shouldn't think about such nonsense. The liquor must have affected her judgment.

The hotel was dark, with a row of people standing outside—there really was a power outage. Xiao Sang couldn't go upstairs.

"Excuse me, are you Ms. Sang?" a young man stepped forward and asked her.

"Yes. Excuse me, you—"

"I'm a friend of your friend Fei. I work at a company here. Fei asked me to take you to the Pirate Movie Theater to watch a film. Look, the electricity at the hotel won't come back on for a while. We might as well leave now."

"All right. I'm so grateful to you. Let's go."

Xiao Sang thought it unusual that everywhere else was lit up, and the power was only out in that tall building. She asked this man, surnamed Ning, why the power was out only in the hotel. Ning told her that Mount Tai Hotel was just like this, probably to try the guests' patience. She was puzzled, but didn't want to pester with questions.

They walked a short while through the well-lit main streets and arrived at the Pirate Movie Theater. The movie they were going to see had been adapted from a Japanese detective novel. The story suited Xiao Sang's mindset. Her heart was full of gratitude toward Fei.

The movie was very good, more intense than the novel. Xiao Sang immersed herself in the plot from beginning to end, completely letting go of her earlier distress. When they emerged from watching the movie, Xiao Sang asked Ning how he'd found her, but Ning said it was a secret. Then he waved and said: "Look, there's electricity!" The hotel's power was back on again.

Xiao Sang returned to her room, sat down, and drank a cup of tea. She walked over to the window to look at the night scene. This city at night was beautiful. Strangely, as she went to stand in front of the window, the neon lights and illuminated windows surged toward her, finally stopping at a spot five or six meters away from her. In every large patch of electric light there was the black shadow of the gigantic building. These shadows seemed to be threatening her. Xiao Sang stepped back in alarm, retreating all the way back to the bed, where she sat down. After a while she finally, slowly walked over and pulled the curtains shut. She reflected on how she'd come to an unfamiliar city, yet the things she had left behind in her own city had followed her, like the shadows of the building in the lights. Was this a good or a bad thing? Oh, she shouldn't pay attention—better to read.

She picked up the book, lay down on the bed, and began to read. She'd planned to sit in front of the window and read within the city's night scene. Now, even without looking out of the window, she sensed the buildings eying her like a predator. She also felt that it was all inside her mind, a few mysteries she'd never truly solved . . .

The chapter that she was reading now happened to be about a journey, too. There was a middle-aged man who referred to his trip as "the longest journey in my life." He went to the top of the city wall, looked down, and saw the moat. He felt foreboding—thinking that he couldn't cross the barrier of the river. He hurriedly came down from the wall. Returning into the city, he ate by the side of the road at an outdoor restaurant. Someone with a familiar face approached and looked him up and down attentively, then asked:

"Is this the longest journey in your life? Where will the next stop be?"

"I don't know. I haven't decided yet. This is a predicament," he answered.

That person nodded solemnly, as if to indicate approval, and then left.

When Xiao Sang read up to here she had a sense of enlightenment. Originally she'd always circled the center, instead of ever entering it. After drinking at the restaurant, she'd neared that center slightly. Then she felt afraid, so she cried. She was hopeless. Now she heard herself saying, "The longest journey is about to start." Enchanted by her own voice, she continued to read.

Reading, reading, until she became dazed, probably from being too tired. Only she still couldn't sleep. Today everything that had happened was so unusual it left her very excited. Then what had happened? She tried hard to recall, but couldn't remember a single thing. She thought that must be a good thing; she could wait and see.

Xiao Sang returned from her business trip. As she ate lunch in the department store, Xiao Ma wandered over to her.

"Did you get my address from Uncle Yi?" Xiao Sang asked.

"Yes. I tricked him by saying I had an urgent issue and needed to find you . . . I was trying to confirm, to see whether he had your address. Ah, he really did." Xiao Ma hung her head.

"Xiao Ma, are you in love with Uncle Yi?" Xiao Sang asked in a lowered voice.

Xiao Ma looked at her blankly. After a while she finally whispered:

"Xiao Sang, let me have him. There are so many people who like you, just leave this one to me."

Xiao Sang looked indignantly at this friend and colleague and emphasized, one word at a time:

"Xiao Ma, you're mistaken. Uncle Yi is my best friend, but it's not the kind of relationship you assume."

"Then I still have a chance? So you don't love Uncle Yi! God, I'm going to faint!"

"I won't say anything else. You're on your own."

Xiao Sang left the cafeteria by herself, without turning her head to glance back at Xiao Ma. She felt exasperated.

That evening, Xiao Sang didn't open the novel and instead lay down on the bed. But she tossed and turned and couldn't sleep, thinking of the relationship between Uncle Yi and Xiao Ma. She believed from the bottom of her heart that this was a very good thing, only she couldn't get past Xiao Ma telling her in such a vulgar way. Dear Uncle Yi, finally there was someone in love with him, and it was her close friend! Wonderful! Xiao Ma was extraordinary! Maybe she had fallen in love with Uncle Yi from the first time she saw him. He was undemonstrative, but young women would like this. Xiao Sang hadn't thought about this side of Uncle Yi, because he was too familiar and from the beginning theirs had been a caring father-daughter relationship. She didn't have Xiao Ma's enormous curiosity . . . Thinking this over, she no longer blamed Xiao Ma. Vaguely, though, she felt a sense of loss. Why? Because over many years Uncle Yi hadn't fallen in love with her and instead had now fallen in love with her girlfriend? But did Uncle Yi actually love Xiao Ma? It was possible. Hadn't he told Xiao Ma her address? But did telling her the address show he had feelings for her? Hadn't Xiao Ma tricked him by saying she had an urgent issue and needed to find Xiao Sang? Xiao Sang imagined the scene that could have taken place when these two were together—an enchanting thought. She knew that she wasn't able to attract the opposite sex like Xiao Ma did. But if Xiao Ma's longing were only one-sided, in that case Xiao Sang thought that she might be able to help her. After all, if a young woman loved Uncle Yi madly, he could hardly fail to be aroused. "I don't have a husband." Xiao Sang reminded herself of what she'd said to the server in the restaurant. In recollection, these words sounded a little desolate. Still, memory is oversensitive.

At midday during lunch at the store, Xiao Sang sat there pretending to be fuming. Xiao Ma again had the cheek to come up to her. She looked timidly at Xiao Sang, then finally said in a quiet voice:

"Xiao Sang, I'm sorry, I know he's the most important person to you. Just pretend I was talking nonsense, don't take it to heart. OK, Xiao Sang? Please answer me."

Xiao Sang snorted with laughter and said:

"You're terrible! If you'd been talking about Heishi, I wouldn't be angry. But how can you talk nonsense about Uncle Yi?"

"I'm losing it, Xiao Sang! I'm really in love with him. Last night I dreamed about him again."

"You're crazy. How strange you haven't made him swoon yet!"

"Good Xiao Sang, show me, how can I pursue Uncle Yi?"

"Pursue him? How would I know? Hmm? You love reading books. Isn't that a ready excuse?"

"I get it! I understand . . ."

Xiao Ma jumped up and left the cafeteria. She was so excited she didn't know what was what. Xiao Sang watched behind her and thought that by appearances Uncle Yi hadn't fallen in love with her yet, but he couldn't withstand such a ferocious onslaught.

"Han Ma, has your romance with Fei been making progress recently?" Xiao Sang asked jokingly.

"I'm going to be married soon, Xiao Sang," Han Ma answered. "Because of him, I started practicing to write fiction. Isn't this the greatest reason to get married? When are you going to get married?"

"Me? But I still don't have a lover." Xiao Sang's whole face turned pink.

"How's that? Everyone can tell. Haha, Xiao Sang . . ."

"Tell what? Don't talk nonsense." Xiao Sang was a little unhappy.

"I'm sorry, I'm so sorry, Xiao Sang! Because I'm getting married myself, I just thought you should be getting married, too. I must be oversensitive. Don't be angry, you're my dearest friend."

On the way back home Xiao Sang kept thinking that today there were two people who'd apologized to her. Was she so rigid? Or was her way of looking at problems different than everyone else's? Of these two women, one had thought mistakenly that she loved Uncle Yi, and one had thought mistakenly that she loved Heishi. When in fact there was no such thing. She hadn't made out that these two men loved her either. Those around her, though, seemed to be able to tell. What was going on? As she rode the bus her head rumbled chaotically, as if it might explode. Only she still hoped that Xiao Ma would pursue Uncle Yi. That might be the happiness of Uncle Yi's lifetime. This pure young woman was a flame . . .

While the bus was waiting at a stoplight, she suddenly discovered Heishi walking along the sidewalk.

"Heishi! Heishi—" she called.

Heishi made a signal for her to get off at the next stop.

Xiao Sang's spirits rose so quickly that she was amazed at herself.

"Heishi, I haven't seen you for such a long time. I've really missed you though," Xiao Sang said teasingly.

"I've missed you, too. I was just thinking of when to invite you to the coffee lounge. Then all of a sudden you appeared. How strange. Ha!"

Noting his enthusiastic appearance, Xiao Sang couldn't help but feel a little unconvinced. However, she soon let go of her mistrust.

There was no one else in the lounge this time, so they were the only two customers. Heishi spoke in the server's ear, and the lights turned on in the room. They chose a table by the window where they could see the passersby on the street.

"Heishi, this is the tony coffee lounge, but now you've made it into an ordinary coffee shop," Xiao Sang said, laughing.

"Am I too conservative? I thought maybe you would prefer it this way."

As Heishi spoke he looked Xiao Sang in the eye. She felt her heart fill with joy.

"Your mother, is she better now?"

"Yes, much better! Thank you. Actually, I'm grateful to my mom. I understand love because of her . . ."

"Heishi, you're the best!" Xiao Sang gave him a thumbs up.

"Do you really think that, Xiao Sang?" A trace of melancholy flared in Heishi's eyes.

"I said what was in my heart, Heishi. People like me can't compare with people like you. I went to Hui by myself on a work trip, sat there drinking a bit of liquor alone, then suddenly felt like I was a disappointment and just started to cry. Oh, Heishi, you see, it's awful that I'm telling you this kind of thing." As Xiao Sang finished speaking she felt astonished at her excitement.

Their coffee arrived, a large cup for each of them. Xiao Sang thought the coffee this time was even better than before, simply transporting! She couldn't say anything, but kept pointing at the coffee.

"The owner of this coffee lounge is my mom's colleague," Heishi said, smiling. "I was surprised by what you just said. I've always been afraid that only Uncle Yi could communicate with the souls of young women like you. I'm not skilled enough. But I like listening to you, you're extraordinary. Even though we were classmates, over the years you've gone far, far ahead of me. I hurry but I can't catch up."

As Heishi was speaking Xiao Sang watched him, thinking to herself that he had matured into a man who could understand other people's minds, like when he'd said he was grateful to his mother. Without meaning to, his mom had created an environment like this for him . . .

"When did you get to know Uncle Yi?" Xiao Sang asked.

"About twenty years ago."

"Ha, eight years earlier than me! Could it be a coincidence? You and

I, at different times, became acquainted with someone from an older generation who we revere—"

"But I don't really see Uncle Yi as being from an older generation. It's the same for you, isn't it?"

Xiao Sang carefully thought and then answered:

"Sometimes, yes. But what does it matter, he's the person dearest to me."

"Of course it doesn't matter." Heishi looked a bit uncomfortable when he said this.

"You rarely go to Uncle Yi's home—I haven't run into you there once. Why not?" Xiao Sang finally asked.

"I don't know. It seems to be logical enough, Uncle Yi and I always meet in this coffee lounge. But we sit in the room behind the counter. One time I saw you and your friend from over there."

"Oh, you two are mysterious. I have the sense that the world has suddenly become very, very complicated. It's like that book we're reading." Xiao Sang's eyes widened.

"We read books because we want to read ourselves. Xiao Sang, I think your insights are much better than mine—so acute, so layered . . ."

"No, no!" Xiao Sang interrupted him, "You're the perceptive one! I'm crude in comparison. Fortunately Uncle Yi tolerates me, so I'm not as superficial now. Didn't I just tell you about when I drank and then cried? I felt like I was so coarse, so naive."

Heishi's eyes suddenly shone bright, just like Xiao Sang had seen at the Pigeon Book Club. Her heart warmed, and she grew excited.

"You just said we want to read ourselves. That's really well put! Ever since I met you, ever since we discussed this magnificent book at the Pigeon Book Club, ever since we discovered that we're both close to Uncle Yi . . . What am I saying? Am I being incoherent?"

"Xiao Sang, I like listening to you so much." Heishi gave a heartfelt sigh.

"Actually, it's not that I speak so well—it's that you have keen ears. You hear all of those things that I'm not able to express."

"Let's keep flattering each other," he said cheerfully.

Xiao Sang's eyes swept the room as she tried to find the leopard. Heishi told her that the leopard had never appeared in the lamplight. Listening, she blinked in confusion.

"I think it's about to evolve into a human being," Heishi said in a quiet voice. "It's just like us, isn't it? Sometimes, when the lights aren't on in the room, it walks the dark floor. I've heard it crying."

"Heishi, I have so many things to ask you."

"Ask away, ask away."

"I won't ask now, I'll save my questions for later, when time allows. We'll meet more often after this, don't you agree?"

"I was thinking that, too. But I also worry that you will get tired of me if we meet more often. After all, I don't have Uncle Yi's accomplishments. When we were classmates, you never paid attention to me . . ."

"But you didn't pay attention to me then, either. We were both just kids. No one showed any interest."

"It's not like that. I was interested in you."

"What?"

"I'm telling the truth."

The sky was already dark on Xiao Sang's way home. With the lights coming on, she felt that the city was especially beautiful at this moment. Heishi saw her all the way to a place a few steps from her home. She invited him to go to Uncle Yi's, but Heishi declined, saying he still needed to go back to the office to do some work. He added that speaking with Xiao Sang so much today had made him extremely happy. After saying this, he turned around and hurried to the bus.

Feeling contented, Xiao Sang also felt faint excitement at the bottom of her heart. So Heishi had also looked forward to meeting with her. But why was he so reserved, so cautious? Could there be barriers between them, resulting in their not being able to have an intimate connection? She suddenly remembered what Xiao Ma had said about Heishi. She'd said Heishi looked at Xiao Sang with adoring eyes. Xiao Ma had a very high emotional IQ, only her words couldn't entirely be believed . . . Heishi was always equivocal, but whenever Xiao Sang was with him she felt especially comfortable, even had—passion. He truly was the kind of friend who is difficult to find. Was a romantic relationship so important? Xiao Ma liked making much ado about nothing.

Xiao Sang raised her eyes and glanced upstairs. Ha, Uncle Yi was already asleep. She couldn't help thinking that it would have been good for Uncle Yi to hear her conversation with Heishi. They both loved him, revered him! That kind of relationship was rare in this world. Xiao Sang also wondered if maybe Heishi's relationship with Uncle Yi was even deeper, even closer than her relationship with Uncle Yi. After all, Heishi's mom was Uncle Yi's former lover. Once she thought this, she felt slightly jealous of Heishi, while also being amused at her jealousy. As Xiao Sang passed Uncle Yi's door, she abruptly moved to place her ear against it. She seemed to hear someone pacing inside, so she hurriedly shifted away. She went upstairs covering a smile, saying to herself: "Madness, it really is madness."

She entered her own door and fell onto the bed laughing her fill. At what? Naturally at these two remarkable men in her life who were both fond of her. She was no longer a young girl, yet there were highly interesting men who so obviously liked her. Their appraisal of her was better than she could have expected. This was so heartening! This proved she wasn't so awful . . . Just yesterday she'd given her father, mother, and brother a phone call. They loved her, and missed her. Yes, if someone invested themselves body and mind in literature, then they wouldn't be irredeemable, no matter how awful they were. Didn't she have so much in her life that supported her? Just take her classmate Heishi. Even though he hadn't fallen in love with her for now, it wasn't completely impossible. And she herself might someday exceed the bounds of fondness for him, developing a different feeling . . . At this thought, Xiao Sang pinched her leg and said aloud: "Am I daydreaming?"

Before Xiao Sang fell asleep, she was feeling very pleased about the affections of these two men around her. A line of dialogue from the book *XXXX* resounded in the dark:

"I knew you were always there—by the small forest where I went so often. But why did you never come over? You never once . . . something was blocking you."

Now Xiao Sang was finally satisfied with herself. She decided to continue to explore—in the book and also in life. These beautiful mysteries, she wished for them to consume her youth. She was almost asleep when she suddenly thought back to Xiao Ma's love for Uncle Yi. Such a loveable young woman. It would be good if Uncle Yi could love her. How would things develop? She was overwrought about her friend. Thinking it over, she finally felt tired, then fell into a dreamworld.

Xiao Sang received the highest annual bonus. The department store manager congratulated her, and said to everyone:

"Xiao Sang never disappoints. People who read can work!"

While she was having dinner at the store, Xiao Ma ran right over to her.

"You've earned so much money, you'll have to treat," she said.

Xiao Sang wanted to invite her out to eat seafood, but Xiao Ma said she would rather go to the tony coffee lounge. Then Xiao Sang understood that her friend had many things in her heart to share and would immediately pour them out to her.

It was again a pitch-black, cool environment. Xiao Sang hadn't told Xiao Ma about Heishi inviting her here. She worried that Xiao Ma would make a fuss if she knew. The two of them had just sat down when the leopard arrived. It stood, placing both of its front paws on the table, prepared to listen to these close friends' heart-to-heart.

"Xiao Ma, you must have major updates?"

"Hmm, I have results, but they're all academic. I visited Uncle Yi twice, both times to ask him to teach me the secret to reading novels. Uncle Yi spoke so well and with such free enthusiasm. I don't mean that kind of outward enthusiasm—I can't describe it."

As Xiao Ma spoke, Xiao Sang sensed that she was much steadier than before, and her intuitions were accurate. She'd said "but they're all academic"—wasn't that an indication of Uncle Yi? Xiao Sang was familiar with Xiao Ma's personality, and she must have communicated her adoration to him, now that she had gone to his home twice. Xiao Sang didn't know what she should say to her friend. She didn't know how to give her advice, or whether or not to encourage her. None of this seemed suited to someone like Uncle Yi. However, Xiao Ma didn't need her advice or encouragement—it was as if she'd become another person all at once. She'd invited Xiao Sang to come here only to be immersed in an atmosphere connected to Uncle Yi. She lowered her voice to talk about fiction and about her impressions of Uncle Yi.

"Then have you considered how things will develop in the future?" Xiao Sang asked, intentionally not using the plural "you."

"No. I don't think about that kind of thing. I love Uncle Yi."

"Xiao Ma, you seem to have matured overnight!" Xiao Sang exclaimed with surprise.

"Because you and Uncle Yi are teaching me! Even though he hasn't fallen in love with me yet, I feel so happy at his side. I never felt this with my previous boyfriends."

At this moment the leopard placed its neck against the tabletop and made a strange sound. Xiao Sang remembered what Heishi had said. Could it be crying? When true love occurs, do people cry? She had cried once in the restaurant in Hui. Why was that?

"Xiao Sang, I'd be fine if I were like you," Xiao Ma said, stroking the leopard.

"How is it fine being like me? No one loves me, and I haven't fallen in love with anyone. I actually envy you."

"When I sit in Uncle Yi's study—that place is like paradise—I have a strange sensation that if I were you, Uncle Yi would fall in love with me. Don't be angry, I'm only telling you what my intuition says."

"So you're telepathic . . ."

Xiao Sang said this and couldn't continue. She felt impetuous, and not only because of Xiao Ma's ability to make people fond of her. She wondered: would there be some difference in her when she returned home from the coffee shop, if she came across Uncle Yi? Oh, Xiao Ma, Xiao Ma, what kind of spirit are you? The scene when she'd gotten the phone call from Xiao Ma in Hui repeated before her eyes.

"My love for Uncle Yi is partly also love for you. I've heard your conversations, and my heart yearned for that state. I've lived in a slapdash way for so many years."

"I'm slapdash, too," Xiao Sang said, "only I've decided to change. Xiao Ma, I can't give you advice. I know you don't need it either. Let's live in earnest."

"Haha, you're so serious, you've almost become a character in a novel."

"We always live inside of stories."

On the way home, after saying goodbye to Xiao Ma, Xiao Sang felt her mood gradually brighten. "Of course I can face things calmly!" a loud voice inside her said. Suddenly, the uncertain dejection from when she had been in Hui dispersed like mist or clouds. She felt that this time it was Xiao Ma who'd enlightened her. Xiao Ma was better than her at going deep into human emotions. Still, Xiao Sang didn't believe that Uncle Yi's feelings for herself contained an element of love. He'd been proposing that she and Heishi go rowing together with him in the secluded park to talk freely about literature.

Uncle Yi's window was dark as a cave, so he must already be resting. He didn't often stay up late, because he felt he was no longer young.

Xiao Sang thought about how Uncle Yi had brought nearly all of the bright colors into her life, especially recently when she had experienced so many things that excited the heart, each one related to him.

Reading the latter half of the book, Xiao Sang sensed how there were some clues that had already become apparent. But she also thought that her strength didn't match her ambition. She didn't know how to connect these clues with her emotions accurately. She felt herself gradually approaching what might be a soul-stirring state. How good! Living in earnest would be happy . . . Wouldn't it be? Hadn't she been improving herself according to plan up to now?

"Aunt Bian, your eyes are so beautiful."

"I've always wanted to see that thing, now at last—is what you're saying true?"

"Of course it's true. What you want to see is already in your eyes."

Xiao Sang felt that this dialogue from the book was also her daily life, although she couldn't yet articulate how. The deeper she entered in, the more enticing it was for her. She hoped she would one day become like Aunt Bian. Later she went to sleep bringing this kind of longing with her. After she'd experienced such an emotional shock, her sleep was particularly tranquil.

After the time Xiao Sang had coffee with Heishi, she went more than three weeks without seeing him. She'd asked Uncle Yi and learned that he had seen Heishi during this period. So Xiao Sang felt a bit discouraged. Uncle Yi noticed her mood and hastily told her that Heishi had asked about her.

"He said that he'll come looking for you as soon as he's not so busy."

"But I don't want him to come looking for me. I'm only worried about him," Xiao Sang said.

"He's the one who wants to come looking for you, it's not me asking him to," Uncle Yi said, smiling.

Xiao Sang was somewhat annoyed about forgetting herself in this way. She was obviously concerned about her friend. Why couldn't she say so without this affectation? Her annoyance didn't last very long, though, because Heishi came over that evening. He arrived late again like the last time, when Xiao Sang was about to sleep—the next afternoon she had to work overtime, so she couldn't stay up all night reading.

"Xiao Sang, Xiao Sang!" he shouted toward her window.

She was astounded—how had Heishi become like this? She answered him, flew downstairs, and stood before him. She thought that she should be straightforward in response to his directness.

"Heishi, you look handsome in your work clothes."

"Thank you, Xiao Sang. I just worked overtime. I was originally planning to head back to the dormitory. Suddenly I just came to your place here. Let's sit down on this bench."

"Why did you think of coming to see me?" Xiao Sang asked him, smiling.

"I'm not disturbing you too much, am I? After all, it's so late."

"Haha, seeing as you ran over in the middle of the night—we aren't just ordinary friends."

"I'm so happy that you're thinking this way! My mom started playing ping-pong recently. She's naturally good at it."

"Heishi, I get the sense that your mom is pretty happy now. She has you and Uncle Yi. It's difficult for most people to have such luck. Now she's retired, and you went to the ocean together. How wonderful!"

The black cat came over again. Xiao Sang realized that she'd forgotten to bring dried fish pieces.

"One day at the tony coffee lounge I heard the leopard cry."

"So did your friend fall in love with someone?"

"That's how you think of it, too. I don't know. Do you think Uncle Yi would be moved if a good woman fell in love with him?" Xiao Sang asked probingly.

"Of course he would. But it must be a woman who is extraordinary in all respects. That's what I think. As a man, and one who has rich emotions, he'll have to be moved. Only Uncle Yi has more self-restraint than most people."

"You're making me confused. Let's talk about something else. When you were on the ocean, did you think about things on land?"

"I thought entirely about things on land. I also thought of you, I imagined you giving a speech at the Pigeon Book Club. I said to myself, I didn't attend and so I missed Xiao Sang's passionate, uninhibited speech. What a pity."

"Thank you. The day I was at the book club I also thought of you quite a few times. Afterward I went to a bookstore, where the store employee also mentioned you. Then I bought that book that you'd bought. It seems like you are everywhere. Why?"

"It shows I've made a deep impression on you. That's good, I'm delighted," Heishi said in a low voice.

"If Uncle Yi weren't already asleep, I would call him down and we could go out together for a drink."

"I would like that, too. Maybe I should get going. Take the day off tomorrow. I hope you sleep well."

Xiao Sang saw Heishi to the entrance onto the street, watching him walk into the distance then turn around again and wave to her. She asked herself with a sudden, forceful surprise: "Is this love?" It didn't seem to be, but she also felt it was almost love. Naturally, it was possible that she was being oversensitive. No matter what, Heishi was already one of the important people in her life.

Xiao Sang returned home and remembered something. Heishi was familiar with her through Uncle Yi long before the first time they'd met and gone to the book club. He thought too highly of her, so he hadn't sought her out for many years (he had said that he was interested in her at school). Then what had Uncle Yi said about her in front of him? Why had Heishi only suddenly come looking for her this year? Was it connected to Uncle Yi? Oh, these things were bewildering, just like in a novel. She didn't want to keep making meaningless guesses. In sum, this time Heishi came to see her and even called loudly to her from downstairs, which made her feel unusual warmth. She hadn't been called for by a young man, like she was his lover, for a long time. Although happy, Xiao Sang was still somewhat dissatisfied: why didn't Heishi come to see her more often or arrange to meet with her somewhere? Was there something impeding him? When they were face-to-face, wasn't he excited? That didn't seem like pretending.

Before going to sleep Xiao Sang pondered what Heishi had said about Uncle Yi. More "self-restraint" than most people! Wasn't this exactly what Xiao Ma liked? Did she have hope? She would bring Uncle Yi the vitality of spring. Later Xiao Sang had a dream in which Xiao Ma and Uncle Yi had married. The couple stood in the courtyard, grinning. Xiao Sang watched them from the window, feeling extremely excited. But in the excitement there was also a touch of disappointment, only such a little bit . . .

"Xiao Sang, today you'll work overtime?" Uncle Yi asked her.

"Yes, but how did you know?"

"Xiao Ma told me. When Xiao Ma and I meet she always reports to me on your situation."

"Uncle Yi, I think she's in love with you," Xiao Sang said abruptly.

"Oh?" Uncle Yi stared at Xiao Sang.

Xiao Sang's face suddenly reddened. She regretted what she had said. Why did she regret it? She didn't know.

She said she was going out to buy a few things, rushed in front of Uncle Yi, and hurriedly left the courtyard. Out on the street her mind was in chaos as she thought: she wasn't a matchmaker, why would she disrupt Xiao Ma's pure relationship with Uncle Yi? This affair didn't need her involvement. She shouldn't insert herself, even though she was Xiao Ma's close friend. But she'd made a mistake in a moment of impulse. What would Uncle Yi think of her from now on? She hurriedly bought a bag of dishcloths at the supermarket and dashed back. Returning to the courtyard, she found to her surprise that Uncle Yi was still sitting on the bench.

"Xiao Sang, I borrowed this book from the library. I think you can read *XXXX* alternately with this book. It's also a brilliant book."

Uncle Yi handed her the book he was holding. Xiao Sang smiled uneasily. It was as if she were relieved of a burden. Uncle Yi was himself after all, and she couldn't offend him. She was still too inexperienced.

"I'm happy to see you maturing along with that book."

"How could I not mature, with you always beside me?"

They went upstairs, joking with each other, and each returning to their own home.

Xiao Sang opened the book that Uncle Yi had given her. The first sentence was: "He finally came back from outside." Her hand holding the book trembled slightly. Why was she moved?

That afternoon Xiao Sang finished her overtime at the department store and was just about to return home when Han Ma came looking for her. Han Ma invited Xiao Sang for a drink at the bar, to which she agreed with pleasure.

They both drank wine, slowly, with restraint.

"When will you marry Fei?"

"Right now I'm hesitating."

"What's the matter? Don't you want to get married?" Xiao Sang was surprised. "You two are like a match made in heaven!"

"You're right. But there's more than one match, there are two . . . Fei is a born romantic, he has another lover. It's his former nanny's daughter, a music teacher."

While Han Ma spoke her eyes kept staring at a certain point in front of her. Xiao Sang asked her:

"How will Fei choose? Will he marry you or marry her?"

"He says me. He also said he can't break off the relationship with her because they grew up together. And she's divorced."

"And you, in the bottom of your heart, do you want to get married or not?"

"I want to, I want very much to. I love Fei. The main thing is that he inspires me. I already can't leave him. I think I'll still marry him—maybe I can manage a three-person relationship. I'll give it a try."

"Han Ma, you're right, you give it a try. I'm not worried about you at all. You have the courage to handle this kind of problem. You're brave and calm, otherwise why would I believe that you have the potential to write fiction?" Xiao Sang said excitedly.

"Xiao Sang, I love you, you're the only one who understands me. Congratulate me, drink up!"

"After all, that woman is Fei's history." Han Ma thought a bit and added, "Fei didn't marry her before because he wasn't sure yet. Then she married someone else in a fit of rage. It was a little rash, yes. Maybe I'm a better fit for him."

"Since your love for each other runs deep, just get married and see."

"It's hard to say who's a better fit for whom. It has to pass the test of time."

"If you think too much, then you won't be able to get married."

"Hmm. Xiao Sang, you seem to be my backbone."

To their right a young man was leaning over the bar crying. Xiao Sang whispered to Han Ma: "It must be loss of love. True love is so hard to find." Han Ma whispered to Xiao Sang: "I've already decided."

"Come then: to the future bride and novelist—" Xiao Sang raised her glass.

After several seconds the young man who was crying stood up and totteringly walked toward the two women. He said to them in a loud voice: "Love is poison!"

Xiao Sang also stood, took the glass from his hand, and said to him: "You're wrong. It's your sense of inferiority that's poisoning you!"

The young man, dazed, stared at Xiao Sang for a moment and then stammered:

"Thank you, thank—you!"

He turned toward the bar counter, paid his check, and left.

"I love you, Xiao Sang," Han Ma murmured. "I'm so fortunate to have become friends with you."

However, Xiao Sang thought to herself that Han Ma could have such wonderful love at first sight because of the heat of youth. And I am already a bit old. She envied the young woman, admiring how she could be engrossed in her emotions despite everything. Her attitude was brand-new.

"Prepare yourself," Xiao Sang said.

Han Ma had tears in her eyes as she nodded hard. They parted at the door of the bar.

A loud voice inside Xiao Sang said: "I'm not at all sentimental about her! A pretty young woman rushing toward her happiness. How courageous!" She thought how maybe in a flash happiness could slip through people's fingers. Hadn't Heishi's mother lost Uncle Yi? But now she'd returned to Uncle Yi in a way, which was good. Uncle Yi wouldn't let anyone who loved him be disappointed. Naturally this included Xiao Ma. Xiao Ma's recent transformation was an enormous relief to Xiao Sang. Next the path of Xiao Sang's thought turned back to Heishi. She thought warmly of this best of friends. She also thought of Qiaozi with her frank enthusiasm. Unconsciously, Xiao Sang compared herself to Heishi's former lover. She said to herself: "My youth has passed. Could Heishi still be interested in me? If he can, why would that be?" Maybe not for any reason, maybe only because of the return of a dream from many years ago . . . Thinking this over, Xiao Sang was suddenly, violently surprised, feeling it was wrong. No, she couldn't think of herself as an object of romance, as if she'd returned to her youth. It was only his having taken notice of her in their school years; that didn't count for anything. She shouldn't make anything more out of those youthful feelings.

It wasn't very late yet when Xiao Sang returned home. She opened up the book that Uncle Yi wanted her to read. How strange, this book's beginning was about a young person's feelings. He ran hot with passion (most of the time it's warm-hearted) and was responsible, both qualities which made Xiao Sang think of Heishi in real life . . . She was startled by the first chapter's characterization. What was happening? Could she have gone too far, into infatuation? Or was Uncle Yi casting a spell? She put down the book, went to the window, looked outside, and saw that the courtyard was still. There wasn't anything out of the ordinary. Yet there was a disturbance at her door.

It was the black cat! Xiao Sang gave it dried fish, which it ate and at the same time made a *wu wu* sound, with a contented look. Xiao Sang loosed a breath: the cat wasn't crying, which proved that there wasn't love in this room. She stroked the black cat and started to laugh. "Oh, oh . . . ," she said.

Once the black cat finished eating, it unceremoniously went back outside—it still had work to do.

Xiao Sang closed the book and sank deep into thought. Had Uncle Yi eagerly recommended this book to her because he also felt that the boy in the book was similar to Heishi's personality? Uncle Yi must have met Heishi in his childhood, but Heishi had said it was twenty years ago. How mysterious. Without knowing why, before Xiao Sang's eyes a tableau appeared of Uncle Yi and a young Heishi running along the ridges between fields. There were unexpected tears in her eyes. She felt deeply that their relationship was dearer than an ordinary father and son . . .

Suddenly Xiao Sang heard the black cat below crying. God, it was that kind of caterwaul.

She covered her ears and went to the bathroom to shower, finished her shower, and came out. Outside the window, quiet was already restored. The black cat's unusual visit had surprised her. It was the first time, and the cat was in love.

Xiao Sang lay down on the bed, but for a long time she couldn't fall asleep. There was some atmosphere that was slowly gathering around her. What was it like? Foggy and warm. She'd experienced this in her parents' care when she was young.

The next day at the department store Xiao Sang saw Han Ma again. Han Ma was glowing and extremely pretty. The customers all valued her as a shopping guide. Xiao Sang couldn't help thinking: our store really is a place for undiscovered talent.

There was also an unprecedented surprise: when Xiao Sang got off work, Heishi came to meet her. He wanted to go with her to the book club. Xiao Sang felt excited and also a bit embarrassed in front of her colleagues. She saw that Xiao Ma was even more excited and kept trying to catch Xiao Sang's eye.

This time Xiao Sang found herself again entering that alleyway from the first time she'd gone to the Pigeon Book Club. It was still early, and the setting sun shone into the small alley. Everything was so cozy and nostalgic.

"I'm going to buy a photo album of Xishuangbanna Tropical Botanical Garden to give Uncle Yi," Xiao Sang said.

"That bookstore isn't in this alleyway," Heishi said regretfully.

"How strange! It seems like every time I come it isn't the same alleyway. Heishi, is there something wrong with me?"

"This shows that you have entered into fiction. I am fortunate to be with you at a time like this."

"Then, Heishi, do you dare to kiss me?" Xiao Sang asked.

"No, I don't. Because I'm not the one you're in love with."

"It isn't you? Then who is it? Last night that cat came to my home, then later it cried. Who can it be?"

"I don't know."

The two of them faced each other for several seconds, then they laughed in unison. Next they saw Fei and Han Ma, Han Ma tightly embracing Fei's waist.

"What day will the wedding be?" Xiao Sang asked.

"We decided not to have one. We'll move right in together," Han Ma said.

"Congratulations to you both," Heishi said. "I envy you."

"Heishi, you must take hold of your own affairs. True love slips away in the blink of an eye."

Han Ma furrowed her brow slightly when saying this, seemingly worried about Heishi.

The two couples entered the book club together. Qiaozi was pouring tea for each person, with Li Hai helping her. Xiao Sang wondered to herself: was Qiaozi already together with Li Hai? At this moment she discovered another new person at the table, a young woman whose appearance was a bit humorous. The girl said to Xiao Sang:

"You can call me Yang, it's what everyone calls me. I didn't come to the last few gatherings because I'd gone to the mountains to study. I'm an old friend of Fei and Li Hai."

Xiao Sang smiled and nodded, her heart warming. She wondered: could the book club produce a new pair of lovers? Could everything be a coincidence? Now Heishi sat down opposite her. Xiao Sang looked at him, finding that he appeared a little distracted. She did her best to recall Heishi from their time as students, but really, other than his broad shoulders, any other details were dim. No wonder he had never believed that his relationship with her could possibly develop further. This evening he looked especially young, even younger than the several other men seated, and completely unlike his middle-aged manner the first time she'd seen him. Xiao Sang recalled what she had just proposed to Heishi on the way there and involuntarily her face turned pink. She felt that Heishi was also thinking of what she was thinking. So he'd sat opposite her, afraid that other people would misunderstand. But he was still in a daze and hadn't entered into the discussion yet.

"Heishi, last time you spoke about the struggle of breaking through life's nets. Have you reached a conclusion now?"

It was Fei asking him this. Xiao Sang wondered: had Fei noticed Heishi's forgetting himself?

"Hmm, I've been thinking about this question all along," Heishi calmed down and said. "Not only thinking, I'm also personally putting some things into practice . . . The solution is in books, where I'm slowly approaching it."

"Also in your life, Heishi," Fei said, at the same time glancing at him with sharp eyes.

"Of course, of course, who can escape your circle, Fei!" Heishi said, laughing.

"You're posing riddles, that's not fair!" Xiao Sang called out, pretending to be dissatisfied.

"I'm sorry, I'm sorry, Xiao Sang. I've discussed chapter 36 of this book with Fei. I called that atmosphere an invisible net-shaped thing, a kind of dark and powerful object. But in fact that object is also tender . . . Oh, I don't know how to describe it. Is it a net? Do I need to struggle to break through it? I still can't decide. Probably it isn't time yet. I'm not like Xiao Sang, who's good at communicating emotions—I'm too slow."

Xiao Sang blinked, as if understanding and also not understanding Heishi's speech. The strange thing was that she'd also had this kind of experience. For example, that time in the city Hui, when she'd encountered a kind of dark and tender net, and then afterward she'd cried. She hadn't struggled through that net yet. That meant there was a similar thing that had happened in her and Heishi's lives.

"In my life there's also the question of a dark net," Xiao Sang said. "Like Heishi, I'm not sure of what it actually is. It often approaches . . . then I have complex feelings and am dissatisfied with myself. The past few days, when I read that chapter, I suddenly felt that maybe this is something like love? A kind of affection that I can't define, but that already silently exists? It quietly attacks me from the dark, disrupting my thoughts, and not allowing me an escape route. Ah, at such times you become so dejected. You want to confirm, but you don't get an answer—all of the answers seem to be, but are not, and night has already fallen."

Xiao Sang finished speaking. She felt that she wasn't finished yet, but couldn't think of any better words to say either. Heishi was looking at her, not moving, as if he were trying to absorb something from what she was saying.

"What are you thinking, Heishi?" Xiao Sang asked him in a loud voice.

"Me? I wasn't thinking about anything."

Everyone started to laugh. There was still an expression of intoxication on Heishi's face.

"Ah, very good," he sighed.

"What?" Xiao Sang pressed him.

"I was talking about myself. This novel is magnificent. Xiao Sang's reading is also magnificent. I try my best to attain this state, but am still far short. I often wonder: why does this book have so many readers? Now I begin to understand. We sit here, circling around something . . . Like Xiao Sang said, night has already fallen, so we sit here. That net is in our hearts."

Once Heishi finished speaking, Li Hai started to applaud.

"You two, you both spoke so well! I believe that what you are describing is the most hidden and deep learning. I have been doing detective work and am interested in this more than anything. I need to go home to think it over."

Once Li Hai sat down, Qiaozi kissed him on the cheek. Xiao Sang opened her eyes wide, saying to herself: "Another couple!" She felt that this was a bit rash. She also sensed the girl Yang secretly observing her, so she tried hard to calm down.

When it was time to go home a new situation arose. Xiao Sang had always gone the same way as Heishi, and this evening she also hoped to leave with him. But without her knowing why, this evening, the others came and joined her and Heishi, except for Fei and Han Ma who left alone. They all laughingly held on to Xiao Sang from both sides, which separated her from Heishi.

Xiao Sang stepped along as if in a dream, steeped in the collective warmth. She heard Heishi in front of her speaking in a loud voice, like he was drunk. Qiaozi held Li Hai and questioned Heishi back and forth.

"Heishi, it wasn't long ago that you went to the ocean. Did the ocean answer the question at the bottom of your heart?" she asked.

"It must have been answered, but it was answered in the sea's way, sweeping and obscure, so I didn't understand what I heard."

"Li Hai and I both envy you," Qiaozi said.

"What do you envy about me? I don't deserve your envy."

"I envy your good luck. You don't know what you have!"

"You're both being unfair to me."

Xiao Sang walking behind them could hear all of these words, but couldn't guess their meaning. She told herself: "They don't seem to be talking about me . . . No, it still seems like partially they are." Heishi was the one whom Xiao Sang could fathom the least. He had a look as though everything had nothing to do with him. It was also possible that they were talking about Heishi and another girl.

"Xiao Sang," Yang said to her, "your speech today touched me. Do you always reflect on the most complicated questions like this? How enchanting. Now it's night, but I'm not at all pessimistic. Why not?"

"The night makes our souls even more lively," Xiao Sang heard herself saying, her voice soon drowned by Heishi's laughter. Why was he so overwrought? At this moment the boy Yan at Xiao Sang's left side spoke.

"Xiao Sang has never been pessimistic—this is why we like you. Ever since you joined the book club, we've all been ready for a fight and eager to elevate ourselves. Heishi has done this great, good thing—that he hasn't hidden you away."

"But the first time I came to the book club I had just met Heishi. We hadn't seen each other since our college graduation."

"It didn't seem like that at all. I always thought you were lovers—I think so now."

"Oh, there's nothing I can say. Only that I'm very happy," Xiao Sang sighed. "Now my feelings are also approaching chapter 36. You friends surround me, so I am happy."

Xiao Sang thought: what was she saying after all? Was it self-defense, or communication? Or was it nearing that net? Oh, a net that left people both fearful and loving. On nearing it, emotions like that would be roused. That wasn't sentimental, not a bit, well, naturally a little bit, but more positive, more powerful . . .

This evening the alleyway seemed particularly long, but everyone finally reached the street entrance where it forked. They dispersed noisily, and Heishi saw Xiao Sang onto the bus.

"Heishi, do you like your everyday, ordinary life?" Xiao Sang asked impulsively.

"I do like it. I think I have more passion than in the past several years, as if I'm always hoping for something to happen. Of course it could be that nothing will happen. Just the state of expectation is beautiful, though, isn't it?"

"You were just laughing so loudly. Was that because of expectation? I've rarely seen you open up so much. Uncle Yi wants us three to go rowing in the park. Will you come?"

"I really want to. But recently I'm always working overtime, I can't get an entire day off."

Xiao Sang's bus arrived, so she boarded and sat down. After the bus had driven a long stretch of road, she turned back and saw Heishi still standing in the same place. What was he thinking about?

Before Xiao Sang fell asleep she sensed the net again. She woke violently with surprise, pulled a coat over her shoulders, and ran downstairs.

In the courtyard Uncle Yi was coming in from outside.

"It's so late, and you aren't asleep yet," he said.

"You aren't asleep either. Is this a sleepless night?"

"I'm coming back from walking by the river, where I ran into Heishi. He was also out walking. So we took a stroll together. Your meeting must have been successful, I haven't often seen the young man so excited. Heishi is introverted, careful, and unlike his mom thinks things over thoroughly. Because he was overwrought, I went with him for a little drink to calm down. I always feel like he's holding himself back, and I don't know why."

The two of them went upstairs talking.

When Xiao Sang fell back asleep, warmth rose in her heart. She seemed to think it was the three of them walking together. Uncle Yi was in the middle, she and Heishi on both sides arm-in-arm with him. Gradually, they walked to the riverside.

Han Ma finally moved in to live with Fei. The two of them rented a small, secluded courtyard in the suburbs and went to work every day, each on their own bus. Their honeymoon was only one week off work. Every afternoon and evening that week Han Ma would contend with her writing upstairs in their small house. As for Fei, he gardened in the courtyard. Fei was going to plant a circle of red rosebushes by the enclosing wall of the courtyard to reward Han Ma with joy and to inspire her when she came out for walks. He truly loved her so much. He thought she was refreshing, grand, inspired, and also simmering with energy. "I'm cultivating an author," he said, half-joking. Their lives were exceptionally simple, their home organized very neatly. They often went to the nearby restaurant to eat.

Han Ma was extremely invested in her and Fei's love. But she wasn't an inexperienced young woman with regard to her affections. This was something that Xiao Sang had perceived and so wasn't anxious about her. Han Ma even had a premonition that, if this time of ardent love passed, Fei's affections could start to change and no longer be as dedicated as they were now. Han Ma also believed that she would never have regrets. Ever since the day she'd met Fei at the sailors' club, his deeply emotional vision was engraved on her heart. She felt it was inescapable for her. She didn't try, and thought she shouldn't try, to consider how long their fated love would last. She would grasp life firmly; otherwise the things that she wanted to do would just not happen. With Xiao Sang's encouragement, the intention to write emerged in Han Ma, and Fei was the lover who would do the most to facilitate this. How fortunate! Han Ma was often faint with happiness. Why had heaven given her such good luck? She knew her husband was no ordinary person—he was a high-level reader, and even Xiao Sang admired him. Han Ma wrote for a while, read for a while, and then couldn't help going to the window to watch Fei. In her eyes, the entire length of Fei's body attracted her—even the sweat on his forehead was loveable. She wanted to pick up a towel and run down to wipe his sweat away. But no, she must keep track of time. So Han Ma sighed, then sat down to continue her contemplation and reading.

The morning before the day of their return to work, Fei walked into Han Ma's study and sat down. She sensed that there was something on his mind.

"Fei, just say what it is. It doesn't matter," Han Ma said frankly.

Fei said that Yue, his nanny's daughter, had prepared a wedding present for them, and she wanted Fei to go by himself to pick it up. He didn't know whether Han Ma would agree to this.

"Why wouldn't I agree? There is not a single reason not to. Yue knew you before I did."

Hearing her answer, Fei was a bit astonished and looked at her gratefully.

"Go after we eat. I remember you haven't seen Yue for a long time."

After Fei left their home, Han Ma returned to the study. At first she was somewhat restless. She walked around the room repeatedly. Then she finally forced herself to calm down, sit at the desk, open up the book *XXXX*, find the chapter that she wanted to read, and begin to take notes.

Since Han Ma had been prepared for a long time, she wouldn't yield lightly. She'd been very stubborn from childhood. This chapter was about a man forsaking love. Han Ma tried by every means possible to imagine such circumstances. She said to herself: "Forsake? Isn't that just like experiencing death?" She felt that she could partly understand this, but in the end could not understand entirely. What was the death of affection like? Han Ma thought this over and finally couldn't stand it.

She gave Xiao Sang a call and arranged to go with her to the tony coffee lounge in the afternoon. She made herself up a bit and set right out.

"Han Ma, I've really missed you," Xiao Sang said from the heart.

The two women sat in the dark of the coffee lounge. Not long before they had sat here like that, and those past events appeared before their eyes.

Xiao Sang held Han Ma's hand and felt her tremble slightly. She exclaimed to herself: "Han Ma always moves ahead, even when there is no way forward."

"Everything is beautiful, is going well. I almost don't dare to believe it's real," Han Ma slowly said.

Large cups of hot coffee arrived. Neither made a sound as they drank. After a good while, when Xiao Sang took hold of Han Ma's hand again, her palm was hot. "Han Ma, oh, Han Ma," Xiao Sang whispered to herself.

"I've never loved so deeply as this. Xiao Sang, you must have had experiences like this?"

"I have. But that's already in the past. Now I don't, but I'm hoping," Xiao Sang answered calmly.

In a while the leopard arrived. The leopard rubbed back and forth among their legs, crying, *wu wu*. The women were both a little flustered. However, the leopard didn't stay long before going.

"I sit in the study upstairs, while he's busy in the garden, and the rhythm of our feelings is synchronized . . . I hope so much to always keep sitting that way. But no, people need to subsist. I also have greater dreams, apart from love. Fei has become the right person to help me live out my dreams."

Her voice was raised. Xiao Sang thought that she was becoming overwrought.

As Han Ma spoke loudly, she felt the haze completely disappear. She talked about her reflections on literature up to this time, and her increasingly staunch pursuit of it. "If I weren't writing stories, I couldn't keep living," she declared. It was as if a weight on Xiao Sang's mind had fallen away. She was glad for her young friend and believed she could overcome every obstacle.

"Han Ma, you've set out on the way so quickly!" Xiao Sang also raised her voice.

"It's so strange: first I fell in love with literature, then I fell in love with Fei! It seems like the two are one?"

"It's not strange at all, Han Ma. What is literature? It's love. So you should love."

“I’m deeply grateful to Fei. He really is an expert . . .”

“Han Ma, I’m happy for you! Have you read that new book I recommended to you? Uncle Yi recommended it to me. It’s a really good book.”

“I’m reading it now. Recently I feel something taking shape inside of me. I’ve already written some, and I want to keep writing. I must keep writing.”

“You should hold on to that tightly and ignore everything else.” Xiao Sang’s eyes suddenly shone with flame.

“I will, Xiao Sang. I’ve prepared.”

When they parted Xiao Sang held Han Ma’s hand tight and felt it burning, although her face was still sort of pale. Xiao Sang imagined the immense vibration of the spirit that this young woman was experiencing. Her composed response also made Xiao Sang respect her. She followed with her eyes as Han Ma walked toward the bus and steadily boarded it. “I was far less advanced than her, when I was that age,” Xiao Sang said to herself.

Xiao Sang considered Han Ma the most talented among all of her friends. She wanted to surreptitiously protect the girl’s talent, yet she’d already noticed how Han Ma didn’t need her care, and that she could protect herself. “She has a rare quality—there is significant chance of success in her undertaking.” Without knowing why, when Xiao Sang said this sentence in her mind, her eyes stung a little. “I’m too sentimental, so I innately have the makings of a reader,” she said. She foresaw that eventually this young woman would become invincible.

Just as Xiao Sang was setting out for an amble in the park, she heard Heishi calling her.

“Xiao Sang, come have another drink. Not coffee this time, let’s drink the Longjing tea that you like.”

“Oh, you’re here again!”

“You’ve forgotten, my mom’s coworker owns this shop.”

“Then you’ve been sneaking a look at Han Ma and me?”

“I couldn’t see, it’s so dark in there. I only saw you when you came out. This is the second time I’ve seen you and your friend here together. I like Han Ma, too. I’ve respected her ever since that day you told me about how she loves her job at the department store. She and Fei really are an excellent match. Of course, dazzling love will always throw thick shadows.”

"You're so insightful."

"I don't think Han Ma will have problems."

"You always have such a good sense of things. Have you and Fei known each other for long?"

"Yes. Fei treats people honestly. But that's also the problem."

"Hmm. I think that truly falling in love with someone can be bitter. You have to be ready to endure any blow."

Heishi didn't respond to Xiao Sang's emotions. He seemed absent-minded. Only at this moment did she notice that the entire coffee shop was lit up. She thought: Heishi is so attentive and considerate. If he could fall in love with her, he probably wouldn't let her suffer any blows. But after Xiao Sang realized how absent-minded Heishi was, she rejected that possibility. Dissatisfaction with him rose inside her. He'd asked her out for tea, but was being half-hearted about it; there must be some reason. She didn't have the spare time to figure out his reasons. But Heishi, sitting across from her, suddenly started speaking.

"Were you joking the last time at the street of used bookstores, when you asked me whether I dared to kiss you?"

"I don't know," Xiao Sang answered angrily.

"I said I didn't dare, because I could only say that. What else could I say? For example, my bringing it up now, it's selfish, isn't it?"

"Yes," Xiao Sang again spoke in anger. "You shouldn't have invited me for tea. You're not making sense!"

Heishi sighed, paused for a moment, then said:

"I always do unreasonable things. I just saw you and Han Ma standing at the entrance, then she got on the bus, and I got excited and couldn't help calling out to you. Still, we're the best of friends, so can you blame me?"

Xiao Sang snickered, then abruptly moved over to embrace Heishi and press a kiss on his forehead. Heishi's whole face flushed red. She immediately let go and returned to her seat.

"Oh, Heishi, Heishi, I can't figure out your shifting moods. Since we're the best of friends, and maybe will be lifelong friends, why aren't you more straightforward with me?"

"I can't be straightforward, because you're so, so good. Everyone loves you. How can I have you all to myself?"

"This is nonsense!"

"That's really how I feel, Xiao Sang."

"I need to go home, Heishi."

"I'll see you onto the bus."

"No, I don't want you to."

Xiao Sang stood, stepped quickly outside, and almost ran to the bus stop.

After she dizzily returned home, she kept asking herself: "What happened? What happened?"

After taking a shower, Xiao Sang thought: nothing had happened. She felt that she might be anxious, worried about getting older, so she'd acted crudely. She didn't like herself acting this way that didn't match her personality. Then she sat down and wrote in her notebook: *Today something ordinary happened with H. Actually, it was nothing*. When she'd finished writing, she was no longer flustered. She looked out the window, saw Uncle Yi feeding the black cat, and then thought about how the cat had grown up eating the small dried fish she and he gave it. Her heart all at once grew warm, and she wasn't angry with Heishi, instead reflecting that she was the one not making sense.

"Uncle Yi!" Xiao Sang called.

"Is something going on?"

"I'll be right down."

She immediately ran downstairs, starting to get excited again.

"Uncle Yi, Heishi just invited me out for tea, but he seemed off. You've known both him and his mom for a long time. Have you ever noticed him acting strange?" Xiao Sang reflected as she said this that she'd finally decided to speak up.

"Heishi is the least strange person I know. Maybe it's just that he considers the whole of things and has difficulty being decisive."

"Hmm. That does seem like him. Thank you, Uncle Yi. I'll think about how to understand him better."

Xiao Sang went back upstairs by herself without talking longer with Uncle Yi. She had a phone call from Han Ma, and felt her admiration for this young woman from the bottom of her heart. Today's rising and falling emotions had tired her, so she lay down. She lay in her room reflecting. If the least strange person encountered a complicated situation, they might also seem strange. So, what complex scenario had Heishi encountered? What always made him hesitate? Was it the "net" that he had spoken of? An invisible net that both seduced and repulsed him? Xiao Sang couldn't think of a solution and so turned to think about the new book that Uncle Yi had recommended to her. Every character in the book was simple at first sight, but the further she read the more complex they were. Almost every one had complicated emotional histories, so that their actions also seemed strange. Uncle Yi must be using this book to share with her some most universal truth. Xiao Sang also reflected that if she weren't so impetuous, weren't so brash, maybe her good friend Heishi would open the doors of his heart to her one day. After all, he had a long history of friendship with Uncle Yi and so was indirectly her old friend. Was she still having a lovely dream about three people traveling the same road? Three traveling the same road—excellent! These two men were the ones she loved most, most appreciated . . . Xiao Sang decided to treat Heishi with patience and understanding after this. She wouldn't be angry with him—see, he'd helped her so much. She remembered Heishi's deep-level understanding of Fei, how he simply left her in the dust. She had no reason to be angry with him. She was the strange one herself.

Han Ma returned to her small house from the coffee shop and went upstairs to continue her reading. Once she got started she read and took notes, as if intoxicated. Without her noticing how much time had passed, the sky was already dark when she thought of going downstairs and to the bamboo noodle house to eat. She walked into the bamboo building and smelled the thick aroma of cooking. The husband and wife were stir-frying.

"Miss Han, how come there's only you today?" the woman asked.

"My husband had something to do in the city." Han Ma responded to her with the answer she had prepared earlier.

She silently finished eating her noodles, said goodbye to the wife, and then returned to her study.

Han Ma told herself: "I love him. This doesn't mean he has an obligation to keep me company all the time. It's me who wants to love him. He and I appeal to each other—our goals are the same. This is a rare thing to have!"

She was agitated after saying these sentences to herself. She dialed Xiao Sang's phone.

"Xiao Sang, I'm trying hard to be an independent person. I only just understood what real independence is."

"Han Ma, that's very good. I haven't been wrong about you."

"Xiao Sang, I can't help wanting to share what I've learned with you. See you tomorrow."

Now Han Ma felt peace of mind. She sat down and wrote a passage in a hazy mood. She thought: this isn't a proper story yet, but from here it might develop into one. Then she went to the kitchen to brew tea for herself and Fei.

She brought the water to a boil, meticulously prepared good tea leaves, and first steeped a cup for herself. She would wait to brew Fei's cup until he came back. She sat down and slowly savored hers. It was very good tea.

After a while the phone rang.

"Yue and I want to go see a movie. Afterward I might be back a little late," Fei said.

"OK," Han Ma answered briefly.

She continued to sip her tea. She thought of everything Fei did for her, and told herself gratefully: "He will never be false. Everything is so clear." She thought about how hard it was to meet someone like Fei who was so congenial in spirit. He thought that he wasn't suited to writing himself, because he lacked a certain decisiveness, yet he took such an interest in Han Ma's writing and was even more anxious about it than her. This would have been impossible for most people; Han Ma knew that it came from Fei's soul. She remembered how a friend had asked her, "What kind of partner is the most ideal?" This question—at the time she'd blurted out: "Two people reading one book together." Now she'd achieved her dream. Oh, those days, what wild joy! They would discuss that book for hours in a row, talking and talking until they fell asleep together . . . After they woke up, they'd continue their conversation.

It was already after midnight when Fei returned home. Han Ma heard him drinking tea, then going into the bathroom to shower. After showering he entered their bedroom and lightly got into bed. Han Ma hurriedly shut her eyes tight and pretended to sleep.

"Han Ma, I know you're awake," Fei said in a quiet voice in the dark.

"I was waiting for you." Han Ma also spoke in a quiet voice.

Han Ma embraced Fei, seeming to have seen the pensive expression on his face.

"We have to go to work tomorrow. You should sleep," Fei said.

Holding her husband, Han Ma finally went to sleep in relief. After another good while, Fei also slept.

The next day Fei was leaving the house for work first. He went upstairs to Han Ma's study, and with a glance saw her newly written scenario. How beautiful! Did Han Ma know how beautiful the sentences that she had written were? Fei recalled what had happened yesterday and was filled with gratitude toward his young wife. "Han Ma, Han Ma, what stuff are you made of? How did you fall in love with a rotten man like me?" he said to himself.

"Han Ma, Han Ma!" he shouted as he ran downstairs.

"You've almost succeeded, Han Ma!"

They kissed beside the red roses.

"My goodness . . . ," Fei murmured in recollection.

"No, I haven't succeeded yet," Han Ma said calmly. "Thanks to you, I'm feeling my way along. Just having you at my side, I have hope of success."

"Then, do you have any regrets?" Fei looked her in the eyes.

"Nonsense. You still don't know me. But eventually you'll understand me."

Han Ma met Fei's eyes, and he laughed, ashamed.

They both went back inside and got cleaned up, then went together to the small bamboo restaurant to eat.

On the way, Han Ma said to Fei that his having married her was truly unfortunate because she wasn't even able to make food for him. He still went out to eat every day like a bachelor. Fei answered his wife: "We have spiritual food. Not everyone has that."

The owners of the small bamboo noodle house made minced-meat noodles that were especially tasty. The man only had one eye, but appeared full of spirit. Everyone called him Lao Yao and called the woman Xiao Fei.

It was late, so their customers had all finished eating and returned home. The husband and wife sat down and rested a while.

"Han, Fei," Lao Yao said, "What strange things have you come across living in this suburb?"

"None." Fei was surprised and stopped eating his noodles.

"There are a man and a woman who always circle these few buildings around here, especially when the sky is dark. Sometimes they also come in the morning. They've never run into each other. The locals say that they are searching for each other. Neither is very young, but of course, they aren't old either. Everyone says they must have been lovers before." Lao Yao looked a bit uneasy when he'd finished speaking.

"Sometimes I worry about them," Xiao Fei continued. "Why haven't the two of them ever run into each other? Since they were lovers and are searching for one another, how can . . ."

Fei and Han Ma slowly ate, looking back and forth at the other, but neither of them wanted to answer.

After a few minutes Lao Yao and Xiao Fei quietly retired into the back room.

Fei and Han Ma finished eating and left. Outside there was a slight north wind blowing, so it was a little chilly. Fei held Han Ma close.

"They seem to be criticizing me . . . ," Fei said in a low voice.

"Not very likely. They aren't meddlers," Han Ma comforted him.

"Of course they aren't. And I like them. Han Ma, I plan to ask for tomorrow afternoon off to go visit your department store."

"You're welcome there."

They returned to their small house, comfortably finished drinking tea, then each went to their own study. Han Ma was halfway upstairs when she said in a loud voice to Fei downstairs:

"Fei, I'm enchanted by our simple little lives!"

"Then we'll just continue on!" Fei answered her, also in a loud voice.

The north wind outside the building became fierce, but the small home's walls were thick, and they didn't sense it at all sitting inside. Han Ma felt that this evening she especially wanted to write things that went beyond what she could anticipate. Yet after she sat down, her mind went blank. She was in a daze, then she started to read the novel Xiao Sang had recommended to her. It was an astonishing book. Xiao Sang had said that Uncle Yi from her building had recommended it to her, which showed that he was no ordinary mentor. Han Ma thought that Xiao Sang must be happy. Just think, Uncle Yi, Heishi, such unusual people, so often near her! She read up to the fourth chapter. This chapter was about a girl whose father and mother had died, and who lived a quiet life with her grandpa. One day the grandfather said he was going back to visit his hometown. The girl wanted to go with him. They took a train somewhere, disembarked, then the grandfather looked left and right and said that his memory was wrong. This wasn't his hometown, it was some town he'd never been to before. Hearing her grandpa say this, the girl was immediately very agitated. She suggested that they stay at a local hotel. The hotel was cheap, so they each got their own room. When they went downstairs to eat, the grandfather was in poor spirits. His mood was increasingly low, and he said he would never be able to return to his hometown. But the girl believed in her heart that this *was* her grandpa's hometown. She resolved to help him recognize his birthplace little by little. At the end of this chapter, as the curtain of night descended, grandfather and grandchild were walking toward dots of lamplight coming from the tile-roof houses at the foot of a mountain.

"Hometown?" Han Ma asked herself. "Who can say exactly what kind of place that is? Just like how I can't say exactly what I will encounter ahead of me."

Han Ma especially liked the characterization in the novel of the old man fixed to his dim memories and the girl always having an impulse toward risk. But their actions were also synchronized. The entire evening Han Ma thought about what it was that had happened in this chapter. She didn't write fiction—she immersed herself in fiction written by someone else. All of a sudden she hallucinated as if she had written this novel herself.

"Fei, Fei!" she shouted as she went downstairs. "Where is your hometown?"

"To the south, near Guangdong Province. Haven't I told you before?"

"Can you be sure?" Han Ma asked, taking hold of his hand.

"Me?" Fei's eyes swiveled as he said, "No, I can't be sure. That's too big of a question."

The two of them held each other tight through a night of north wind. Han Ma shut her eyes, and into her mind came those ghostly tile-roof houses and also the dots of lamplight. "Eight years later . . . ," she was vaguely saying.

What was Fei thinking about? He was thinking about a lot. He had been as eager to marry as Han Ma, because he felt this was a chance that wouldn't come again in his lifetime. Oh, the woman! He didn't know how to predict his future with her. No, he wouldn't try—trying to predict their future beside her was disgraceful. One might say they had married confusedly, that he'd resolved with her to take care of each other because there was no other alternative. He'd heard her whispering. He thought: maybe, before eight years had passed, they would no longer be living together. And who can see that hometown at the bottom of the heart? Han Ma was too intelligent. A day would always come when she would know that she no longer needed him. Wasn't that making a prediction? How shameful. He remembered Lao Yao's story at the bamboo restaurant . . . Han Ma, wait for me.

Xiao Sang saw Xiao Ma enter the courtyard gate downstairs. She thought: Xiao Ma is going to visit Uncle Yi. But in a while there was a knock on her door, and Xiao Ma came in.

"Xiao Sang, Xiao Sang," she said excitedly, "why is progress so slow with you two?"

"What progress? Who do you mean by 'you two'?" Xiao Sang asked, furrowing her brow.

"Oh, don't pretend. Of course I mean you and Heishi. You must make faster progress, I'll only have hope then."

"Don't be silly," Xiao Sang said sternly. "How can you stretch interpretation this way? You are yourself, I am myself. What does your affair have to do with me? Besides, I basically don't have any affair going on."

"Oh, good Xiao Sang, then why do I always feel that Uncle Yi's heart is set on you? Then there's Heishi—if I were blind I would still know his intentions! One day I stopped him on the street and asked him . . ."

"Wait, you know Heishi?"

"Why can't I know him? I won't snatch him away from you! I asked him whether he loved you. He heard me, but at first he tried to look oblivious, as if he didn't know what I was saying. So I repeated my question, and then he said he didn't want to answer. What's going on with him?"

Hearing Xiao Ma's words, Xiao Sang laughed coldly, then went to brew tea for her. Xiao Ma followed Xiao Sang into the kitchen.

"Could there be something wrong with both of you?" Xiao Ma kept pursuing the question.

"Why are you talking like this—like wind through an empty cave? Are you not making good progress with the man downstairs?"

"I can't say it's rough going. Uncle Yi and I have become good friends, he's my most valued friend. But, but, there's a boundary between him and me, not like between him and you. I can't say what this really means." Xiao Ma lowered her head.

"Hell, how would you know whether there are boundaries between Uncle Yi and me? Do you have a sixth sense? Oh, Xiao Ma, Xiao Ma, you love Uncle Yi. Why do you have to drag me into it?"

"But I feel like this isn't just between me and him. Am I losing my mind?" Xiao Ma said worriedly.

"Yes, you are a little oversensitive."

After Xiao Ma had drunk a sip of tea, her mood quieted a bit.

"Didn't you say that you feel happy when you're with Uncle Yi? Why are you so irritable?" Xiao Sang asked.

"Because, because when I'm given an inch I take a mile!"

Xiao Ma said this and just laughed out loud. Xiao Sang, though, was a little confused and anxious about whether her friend really was losing her mind.

"I'm sorry, Xiao Sang." Xiao Ma stopped laughing. "I'm awful. I've never met a man as . . . as fascinating as Uncle Yi, so I just make a mess of it. That's my problem. Uncle Yi is always the same, he'll never get impatient with a young person like me. Now I can understand why you've had such a long friendship."

"All right, Xiao Ma, I'm glad for you. I also hope you'll succeed someday."

"Maybe I shouldn't have this idea of 'success'? I'm so confused. I've always been pretty selfish."

"Who isn't a little selfish? You're just confused. In any case Uncle Yi is always considerate."

Xiao Ma glanced gratefully at Xiao Sang. Xiao Sang's face unexpectedly flushed at her look. She hurriedly made a joke.

"Uncle Yi is right downstairs, his ears would burn if he heard us talking about him like this."

"Xiao Sang, you must be so happy," Xiao Ma said with feeling.

"Surely. Work, reading, friends—I have the best of these three things. But the same as you, sometimes I also have an idea about 'success,' because I'm selfish, too. Now you've set an example for me. Thank you, Xiao Ma."

"I hope from the bottom of my heart that you will succeed. Look, I'm at it again, I'll stop. This tea is really tasty."

"My younger brother bought it from the West Lake Tea Company for a high price. My brother will do anything for me."

"You come from a gentle place, so your nature is gentle."

"Actually it isn't. Sometimes I'm careless and flippant." As Xiao Sang spoke, she slipped into reminiscences.

"I know you're thinking about the business with Heishi. Let me ask, don't you have any romantic feelings?"

"I don't think so. Besides, he doesn't love me either."

"He doesn't love you! Wait, let me think, there's something wrong here! Haven't you ever thought that there could be a barrier to Heishi's feelings for you?"

"What barrier? If, like you say, he's secretly in love with me, then who could stop him? Is he someone who can be held back by other people? Don't speculate—there's nothing there."

"I still think there's something wrong here. I also don't think anyone can hold Heishi back, except for one person: that is himself. My intuition tells me there is an obstacle he can't get past."

"Enough, enough, you'll turn into Sherlock Holmes soon," Xiao Sang said as she poured more tea for Xiao Ma. Her hands shook slightly.

"Let's not talk about such boring things any more," she added.

Xiao Ma fell into thought as she drank her tea. When she finished, she stood and said she was going home.

At the doorway, when they were saying goodbye, Xiao Ma said to Xiao Sang:

"Nothing is simple, but we also shouldn't see everything as disconnected."

Her words surprised Xiao Sang greatly. She thought that today she saw Xiao Ma with new eyes. This probably was Uncle Yi's subtle effect on Xiao Ma. Her dear friend had now moved on ahead of her.

Xiao Sang's reading that evening didn't go very smoothly. In the book she read about the deep and lasting entanglements of the human world. Originally there was a simple relationship among several characters that, with one misunderstanding after another, seemed unexpectedly like it would enter an impasse. Even though Xiao Sang was reading fiction, she felt a jittery sensation in her flesh. This was because her thoughts kept being pulled away by those ambiguous words Xiao Ma had spoken. Had Heishi fallen into such entanglements? What had he encountered in the dark passageways of history? Xiao Ma really did have a certain superhuman ability: connections could be found among all the things she'd spoken about. But why was Xiao Sang oblivious? They had been talking about Heishi. What was Heishi like in Xiao Ma's mind's eye? Xiao Sang regretted that she hadn't caught her close friend and asked her the questions that she had. But wouldn't it be harmful to Heishi if she'd done that? How could they so rudely comment on a good friend behind his back? "Oh, Xiao Ma, maybe you're mad, or maybe your words weren't just wind through an empty cave. No matter, you've made it so I can't read."

Xiao Sang knocked on the door, and it opened immediately. Uncle Yi let her into his study. He wanted to pour her tea, but Xiao Sang shook her head, saying she'd just drunk some. Her mind was a little chaotic, and she didn't know what to say.

"Is something bothering you?"

"I wanted to ask you: what do you think of Xiao Ma?"

"She is a loveable woman and has special talents."

"Do you think that she can see into people's thoughts? Yours, for example?"

"I don't know. It's possible. She loves literature, and literature can strengthen people's ability in this regard."

"I'm so disappointing in comparison to her—far short of her."

Uncle Yi laughed and quickly followed:

"You aren't a bit disappointing—you're in another category."

"You encourage me. But I really am a little slow. Aren't I?"

"No, I think you belong to a type of person who is fairly sensitive. But what did you actually want to say?"

"I wanted to say—I wanted to say, no, I don't know what I wanted to say."

"Is it about Heishi?"

"It seems to be, and also seems completely unrelated . . ."

"Xiao Ma thinks that Heishi has fallen in love with you. Couldn't this be a good thing?" Uncle Yi said.

"I think things aren't so simple. Xiao Ma may not be able to see through Heishi at a glance. He's the most difficult person to understand. Maybe this isn't to his advantage."

Uncle Yi went silent. After a while he finally said:

"I never thought that Heishi had given you this impression. He really is enthusiastic, the kind of person who is rarely met in a lifetime. Of course, I think you are also that kind of person. You three, including Xiao Ma, are all vital."

"You're mistaken. I didn't mean to say that Heishi is bad. He's like you, he's my best friend. I can't put it into words. Wait a minute, what was I just saying? I'm trying to say that Xiao Ma's judgment isn't accurate this time. She has unusual intuition, but when it comes to Heishi it doesn't work . . . Heishi's deep and avoids revealing himself. Could he let her see through him?"

"You're right, maybe she can only see through me."

When Uncle Yi said this, they both started to laugh at the same time. After laughing Xiao Sang felt a little embarrassed again.

"Uncle Yi, I'm sorry. Today I'm a little incoherent."

"Probably because you're uneasy in your mind. I watched Heishi grow up, because of his mother, so I enjoy him a lot. He surpasses other people in some ways." While speaking Uncle Yi was looking at a row of books.

"Is Uncle Yi playing matchmaker?"

"I'm just stating the facts is all."

"And Xiao Ma?" Xiao Sang challenged. "Because of you she's gone mad over at my place several times now."

"Don't you think she's too young for me? I'd like to keep the status quo with her."

"I should go home. This evening we've been talking madly."

"Don't worry, Xiao Sang. Someone my age, I forget once I turn around, as if these things haven't been said."

After Xiao Sang returned home she sat down in a daze. She was a little regretful. How could she run to Uncle Yi's on an impulse and say so many things that shouldn't be said? She felt that she'd been rash and shallow. It was no wonder that over so many years Uncle Yi hadn't fallen in love with her and would recommend her to Heishi . . . She also thought that Uncle Yi might fall in love with Xiao Ma after this . . . And Heishi? Why did she not sense that Heishi had feelings for her that exceeded friendship? Did he truly have a barrier inside him? What barrier? Had Xiao Ma really been able to see it? She didn't want to ask Xiao Ma, because if she did Xiao Ma would believe that she was in love with Heishi. And she actually, really wasn't.

Excited and dejected, Xiao Sang turned over her thoughts about what had happened today and also remembered some events from the past. There'd been so much intimacy between her and Uncle Yi that she could say there was nothing that they didn't talk about. Ever since Xiao Ma had gotten involved, though, Xiao Sang had pulled away from Uncle Yi slightly. Because Xiao Ma truly loved him, and Xiao Sang didn't want her to misunderstand her friendship with him. Naturally there were some times, when it was late at night and quiet, that she felt that taking pains to distance herself from Uncle Yi was a kind of loss. Wasn't Uncle Yi still not officially in a relationship with Xiao Ma? Yet she, as a close friend, ought to create opportunities for Xiao Ma. In Xiao Ma's eyes, the two men's feelings for Xiao Sang were both love. How could such a good thing be real? At least Xiao Sang herself hadn't realized that there were hints of being more than friendship. Hadn't even Uncle Yi said she was sensitive? If they had that kind of affection for her, why hadn't she perceived it?

Thinking, thinking in this way, Xiao Sang finally went to bed late. In a haze she had the same dream again where she was arm-in-arm with Heishi and Uncle Yi on each side, walking along a broad road by a river, talking enthusiastically . . .

Fei decided on a day off to go with Han Ma to the sailors' club to hear a captain make a speech. After hearing his proposal Han Ma hesitated a bit, then agreed. Originally she was thinking of spending Saturday hard at work at home, settling into her writing pattern. But she thought there was a subtext to Fei's suggestion. He wanted to go there to relive an old dream. Why? She was a little uncertain and vaguely apprehensive. Han Ma reflected on how she'd almost overcome the barrier of the love triangle and could face it unperturbed. But she still felt that she and Fei weren't in sync. He loved her, but sometimes he would reveal a remorseful mood to her. Meanwhile she believed that he didn't need to be remorseful. She knew that Fei was still attached to his former girlfriend, but this only showed that he had strong emotions. She didn't like people who just clean forgot a lover once they turned their head. On the whole, Han Ma felt that her newly married life was rich, tranquil, and stimulating. For a long time she'd been seeking this kind of life, and now it was realized.

They arrived a little early, so they strolled in the club's small garden. The scenery before their eyes was so dear to them, but they also seemed not to have seen it in ages. There was a pair of very young lovers sitting by a flower bed talking in quiet voices, making them both think immediately of the days before their marriage.

"I feel a bit old next to them," Han Ma said.

"I like this older Han Ma. Before you I'd never met a girl like you. You gave me a sense of urgency. I felt like I might fall behind you, far behind."

"Impossible, Fei. You worry too much. Your emotional world is so rich, which is what attracts me to you. In you I see my own direction becoming firmer step by step. I still don't completely understand you. I think love doesn't require too much understanding. Fei, relax—there's no use being nervous. See how relaxed I am."

People came along in twos and threes. Fei and Han Ma went into the auditorium with the flow of people.

The captain onstage was a retired older man with snow-white hair, a red nose, and large eyes that he seemed unable to keep open. Han Ma didn't pay attention to what the elderly man was saying. She was thinking about her writing. Fei held her hand tight, so that she could feel his pulse. The captain seemed naturally optimistic and kept telling jokes, with the audience down below becoming one in their laughter. Han Ma wondered: why wasn't Fei laughing? Her thoughts returned all at once to Fei. That day, by the lawn outside the auditorium—Fei pulling her by both hands, looking at her with steady eyes. That instant was a freeze-frame in Han Ma's memory. At that instant she'd decided that she and Fei would care for each other for a long time. She said in Fei's ear: "I want to go outside to look around."

Han Ma reached that place beside the lawn. Yes, it had been here, here was the large, peculiarly shaped rock that was their witness. That day it had seemed like everything around them was aflame—the sun, the clouds, the grass, the white shirts and colorful skirts of the young people in the distance, the milky-white ground lamps—and all were burning. Han Ma squinted, feeling the heat of the Earth. She and Fei kissed repeatedly. As if these kisses would confirm their resolve . . . This scene had taken place less than two months ago.

"Ms., do you want to understand the emotional life of sailors more deeply?"

Someone pushing a magazine cart paused beside Han Ma.

She bought *A Record of Life at Sea*. There were many pictures inside the magazine, which interested her.

She read the magazine for a while on a bench by the path, then saw Fei coming toward her.

Fei's eyes were red—he'd been crying.

"What's wrong, Fei?"

"Oh, it was so moving! The old captain talked about himself and his wife, about sorrow at sea, that kind of desperation, that helplessness . . . Han Ma, let's go back. It's getting cold," he said.

Han Ma wondered: why did Fei feel like the weather was getting colder? She raised her eyes, looked into the resplendently sunny blue sky, and felt a bit apprehensive about whether Fei was getting sick. He'd gotten so sentimental all at once, which she hadn't expected. She felt that he seemed changed into another person. Maybe, though, he'd always been like this?

They soon returned home. Fei embraced Han Ma and gently said:

"The captain's words made my heart freeze like a piece of ice. No, I won't think about him. I want to forget his story. Han Ma, if someday you are going to leave, will you tell me beforehand?"

"I haven't thought of leaving. How could I leave? Impossible."

"It's possible. Everything is possible."

Han Ma didn't want to pursue Fei about the old captain's story. She thought she could already guess. It must have been about love unchanging unto death. Could she herself be unchanging unto death? She didn't know and was unwilling to think much about it. Fei might feel inferior in contrast to that elderly captain's state, but there was no need for that. People are different from other people; Fei's state and the captain's were different. It was hard to say whose was better, higher . . .

That night, after the ecstasy of sex, the two of them searched for each other in the dark. Han Ma suddenly experienced the scene that Lao Yao from the bamboo restaurant had described.

"My mom has a new boyfriend," Heishi told Xiao Sang, his face reddening. "He's a few years older than me, my mom's ping-pong partner. What do you think about that?"

Xiao Sang could see that Heishi was excited. He was a son who understood his mother's heart.

"It must be wonderful. Your mother is passionate, beautiful, and able to attract younger men."

"Thank you, Xiao Sang."

"What for? Just because I said something nice about your mother?"

"Also because of your patience with me. When I speak I get tongue-tied and give people the impression that I'm stupid. You always put up with me. A few weeks ago I got to know your friend Xiao Ma. Her personality is the exact opposite of mine."

"Oh—" Xiao Sang dragged out the sound, as if unwilling to talk about her close friend.

"I sensed her enthusiasm, and she loves Uncle Yi. Only sometimes she takes her judgments to be fact. She's still a mystery to me at the moment."

"What about me, am I also a mystery to you, Heishi?"

"No, you are distinct, you're right there. If I think: 'Xiao Sang,' you just appear. But Xiao Ma isn't like that, she's full of uncertainty."

"That is to say, you're sure of me." Xiao Sang dejectedly turned her face to look out the window.

"No, I'm not sure of you. I'm saying stupid things again. What I mean is, I can sense you there at any time."

"You're not at all passionate like your mother."

"I don't know. My mom and I aren't very much alike. But you can put up with me . . . When I was about to get off work I thought to myself: I can go for tea with Xiao Sang again, that's really great."

"Yes, there are friends, especially ones like you, who really are worth enjoying." Xiao Sang became inspired.

The two of them had met again at the tony coffee lounge after more than a week of being apart. In Xiao Sang's eyes, Heishi looked handsome in his work clothes, emanating vigor and steadiness. She wondered: had he been listening to Xiao Ma's silly teasing, changed his view of her, and come to meet her for that reason? According to Xiao Ma's way of thinking, Uncle Yi loved Xiao Sang, and if she could make Xiao Sang and Heishi a couple, Uncle Yi would take notice of her. Now that Xiao Sang had even said that she didn't love Uncle Yi, Xiao Ma could tell Heishi this, ridding Heishi of any apprehensions about pursuing Xiao Sang. Oh, Xiao Ma, you're so bizarre! Xiao Sang sighed to herself. She raised her eyes to look straight at Heishi, but Heishi's eyes were a little misted over like before. “No, he doesn’t love me,” Xiao Sang thought. “He sees me as an understanding friend and wants to tell me the things in his heart.”

“Heishi, today will you tell me about what’s on your mind?”

“Tell you what? I have nothing to tell you, everything in my life is fine. I’d rather listen to you, that was why I wanted to meet with you.”

“So that’s how it is.”

“I read in another novel about how there was someone who kept thinking about one thing, and as a result that thing developed in the direction of his thoughts. I think there was a condition, which is that this person is someone who has a goal in life and is sure of himself. My mother, for example: now she’s become more stable under Uncle Yi’s influence, so she’s finally found love. I think that for her it isn’t too late at all. But before, no matter how hard she tried, things never went the way she wanted them to.”

“I’m so happy for your mother. And you, Heishi, are you also someone who has a goal and is sure of himself?”

“To a certain extent you could say so.” Heishi averted his eyes uncomfortably.

“Your saying so pleases me. It seems as though like meets like—we’ve both been deeply influenced by Uncle Yi to become the way we are today. You’ve worked a lot toward your goal, haven’t you?”

“I have, although for the most part it’s been wasted effort. But I was willing to work at it. I would regret it if I didn’t. My mom said I have an old soul.”

“You are thorough and you worry too much. In fact, a little carelessness in life is a good thing. Of course, I’m someone who doesn’t want to be careless either. I don’t know whether this is a shortcoming. And I’m an old soul, too, in comparison to Xiao Ma. Today, hearing you say these things, I’ve gone a step further in understanding you. I do feel pleased. So, have you made progress toward what you’ve always been thinking of?”

“There’s been some progress, I’m on the way. Listening to you always inspires me.”

“It’s the same for me. I like to hear everything you tell me. You just told me the happy news about your mother, and I’m touched. She’s so fortunate to have a son like you!”

"You think too highly of me, later on you'll be disappointed."

"Why would I be disappointed? I don't think too highly of you. When I think 'Heishi' in my mind, you are distinct, neither high nor low. Look, the leopard has come out during the daytime!"

The leopard circled the table once, rubbing against their pants legs, and then left. They looked at each other and laughed, both red in the face.

"See, the leopard doesn't only belong to the night like you said," Xiao Sang said reproachfully.

"So I need to ponder its thoughts more carefully."

"Ponder and you will have results."

When Xiao Sang finished this statement, she noticed that a diamond-like radiance shone in Heishi's eyes again. She sensed at that moment that he was very much like his beautiful mother. "Heredity has great power," she told herself, as in a flash she remembered his mother's passion. However, she still couldn't be sure of the object of Heishi's passion. When she glanced toward him again, his eyes had already recovered their normal look.

"Have any major events happened in your life this month?" Xiao Sang asked.

"Some major events may still be brewing. Sometimes I rouse myself and am no longer as dissatisfied with myself as in the past. I have the distinct feeling that I've gone a step further in understanding the characters in the book we've been reading. Next time we go to the book club I will tell you more."

"What if the opposite of what you expect happens?"

"In that case, I think I could endure it. I was an obedient child, there were many things that I endured without making a sound."

Hearing this statement Xiao Sang's eyes stung, although she hurriedly controlled her emotions. She looked out the window at these same pedestrians, the same traffic, the McDonald's across the street. How many times had she and Heishi sat opposite each other like this? She hoped she wasn't imagining that she was the object of his affection. But things in this world are hard to predict. Who could be like the character in the book Heishi spoke about?

"Reading novels is wonderful," Xiao Sang said.

"Talking with you about novels is my greatest joy. Because, you know, sometimes I can't keep up, since your views are so advanced. That kind of discussion takes courage."

"You're the best audience, though—you can hear those ideas that I can't say. Now I'm thinking about whether you and I could go traveling at sea. Of course I don't mean . . . what I mean to say is as travel companions, each taking a different book or the same book, to discuss along the way."

"I will consider your proposal seriously."

On returning home, Xiao Sang couldn't calm down for a long time. Was her friendship with Heishi reaching a turning point? Heishi was still speaking evasively, but she could sense his enthusiasm. He had met with her, it seemed, not in order to tell her something; he just wanted to see her—but, but what else? He hadn't explicitly indicated that he loved her, so she shouldn't think too much of it. Xiao Sang laughed lightly. She thought of the many possibilities depicted in the Japanese detective novel . . . cracking the case of Heishi's soul was beyond her. She should stay where she was, patiently waiting for some mystery to unfold. Her feelings for her good friend were a bit closer to love now, but not quite. Neither had opened up their souls yet. She walked to the window, heard Xiao Ma below talking in a loud voice, and rapidly moved away.

"Where I lived before I would hear the train passing by my head all night. Single-parent households are difficult, but my mom protected us like a mother hen."

Xiao Ma and Uncle Yi were walking out of the courtyard. Xiao Sang said enviously to herself: "This will be out in the open soon. Xiao Ma has such a practical spirit. Uncle Yi, what are you waiting for?" She intended from now on to distance herself somewhat from Uncle Yi—a self-sacrifice for her dear friend Xiao Ma, as she ought. When Xiao Sang thought of this "sacrifice," there was a faint pain in her heart. For a long time Uncle Yi had been the closest person to her, much closer than her parents. And now her relationship with Heishi was in an ambiguous place . . .

Her phone rang.

"Next Friday let's go to the book club. I'll wait for you at the bus stop where you get off. Don't forget," Heishi said on the phone.

"Heishi, you're terrific. Thank you."

They had just parted. Then he'd called her. Was this the sign of a turning point? Xiao Sang's heart blazed, and she remembered what had happened with Heishi's mother. Was Heishi like his mother after all? There had been such extended waiting in his life, until finally his mother's happiness arrived. Xiao Sang remembered how she had lost her temper at him, and now she felt ashamed. "He is Uncle Yi's student. I've only learned some trivial things," she thought.

The next day at noon when she was having lunch at the department store she came across Xiao Ma and quietly asked her:

"Have you made progress?"

"I don't know. I've said that I don't care. Maybe he loves me a little bit."

"You're so calm."

Xiao Sang was thinking: even Xiao Ma had become calm. It seemed love truly could alter a person. Would there be a day in the future when Xiao Sang herself would alter for the person she loved? She thought: I'll have to wait until it happens to know.

The night before Han Ma took up her pen to write the fragment of a story, she had a dream. Fei was working overtime at his unit that evening. Han Ma read for a while, felt a little tired, and remembered how she had taken part in a tree planting during the day. She went to bed earlier than usual and fell right asleep. Through a haze she heard someone calling to her from the living room. She fumbled around to turn on the light at the head of the bed and pressed the switch, but the lamp on the bedside table was out. She felt around again to turn on the overhead bedroom light, but it was also out. It was a woman calling her. Han Ma could gradually hear more distinctly that it was Xiao Fei from the bamboo restaurant. Han Ma answered as she went into the living room. The light in the living room wouldn't turn on either. There must be a power line outage. Xiao Fei wasn't in the living room though. Where was she calling to Han Ma from?

"Xiao Fei, Xiao Fei!" Han Ma called out twice.

"Han Ma—I'm where we agreed to meet. Let's go together."

The wind was blowing Xiao Fei's voice in from somewhere far in the distance. Han Ma realized that she was far away and that she couldn't find her, so she sat down on the sofa in the living room to wait. She waited for a while, but she didn't hear Xiao Fei's voice again. Looking out through the French windows, Han Ma could see the reflection coming off the water in the pond. She grew a bit anxious—a rare feeling for her. She asked herself again and again: "Did something happen to Fei? Did something happen to Fei?" What she worried about most was a traffic accident. Han Ma didn't know how long she sat there before she suddenly remembered that Fei would be sleeping at the dormitory at his work unit and wasn't taking the night shift bus back home. Han Ma muddled back to the bedroom and tossed and turned for a while before falling asleep.

The next morning, after she got out of bed, she discovered all of the lights were working and that the shawl she'd left on the sofa in the living room wasn't there. She could remember herself walking out of the bedroom wearing the shawl, but now it was hanging in the wardrobe. So it must have been a dream. There was no need for her to be anxious about Fei; she was only making herself anxious. Establishing a small family was probably always anxiety-inducing.

When Han Ma got off work, she ran to catch the bus.

Pushing open the courtyard gate, she saw Fei busy in the yard, and the weight on her mind finally lifted. She didn't tell him about her dream.

"Did you sleep well?" Fei put down the hoe, kissed Han Ma on the cheek, and asked.

"Yes. You?"

"No. There were a few mosquitos in the dormitory bothering me so much I couldn't sleep. I kept thinking about you."

"Then let's have something to eat soon and go to bed early this evening."

"No, no, you still need to write in the evening. Now is the key time."

Han Ma's eyes almost welled with tears when she heard this.

She wrote two sections of a story one after the other. It wasn't about love, but instead about someone trying to survive in a foreign land. She was trying to capture a tone of voice, trying to fix the intent of the sentences under her pen, even though it couldn't ever be definite. Now she wanted and wanted to write and write. Only Fei was fully aware of her longing, so he'd said it was the "key time." She read over the sections she had written several times, then went downstairs to him. He hadn't gone to bed yet.

Fei raised his eyebrows and took Han Ma's notebook. It seemed to Han Ma that he only swept his eyes over it.

"You'll be on your way soon, Han Ma," he said.

"I also felt that this time was a little different."

"Not just a little, it's very different. You are maturing."

"Fei, I want to ask you a question."

"Go ahead."

"Why don't you write yourself? For a long time I've wondered: why don't you write?"

"Haha, do you think I haven't tried? My language isn't any good. It's so inferior to yours, it falls short. I'm the kind of person who nurtures authors, aren't I?" Fei made a face.

"Let's go to sleep, Fei. I'll bore you to death if we keep on talking about this."

Once they got into bed Fei started to snore lightly. Han Ma gently drew back the arm that was embracing him. In the dark she felt surges of warmth through her heart. She couldn't distinguish whether it was her passion for writing or love.

Han Ma was thinking deeply. She couldn't foresee the future development of her relationship with Fei. She would never ask Fei about how he was handling his former lover Yue. She thought that she should approve of their relationship, even if it were still intimate. As a woman, she understood another woman's loneliness. Further, the woman loved Han Ma's husband, and Yue's love had never altered. This was a knotty problem. Han Ma's feelings would sometimes involuntarily be affected, but she had focus and wouldn't be easily defeated.

The day of the typhoon Fei had disappeared for an entire day without calling Han Ma or telling her beforehand. She knew he didn't want to lie, and this kind of thing was too difficult to explain. Han Ma also knew that this sort of thing would happen frequently. She had to force herself to get used to it.

Han Ma was at the department store then. The wind blew the store's signboard into the street. Blackness pressed in everywhere while the employees waited inside. Fei had left the evening before and hadn't returned for the night. First thing in the morning, Han Ma had gone to the department store. She'd only been there for a short while when the typhoon started to blow. The same as the last time, a voice sounded in her heart: "Did something happen to Fei? Did something happen to Fei . . ." Her soul grew tense as she kept thinking that Fei would be out walking the streets.

"Han Ma, are you cold? I have some extra clothing. Do you need it?" the store manager asked her.

"No, I'm not cold, I'm just a little nervous. I've never seen such a severe typhoon."

"It will pass. The weather station said there would be major damage."

The store manager patted Han Ma on the shoulder and went back into the office.

Han Ma sat between the shelves, determined to concentrate her attention on the developing story. Fiction brought her life so much joy! Perhaps her writing could help other people, too. If there was someone in her current situation, she could just tell this person through the story that everything wasn't as terrible as most people imagined it to be. There would be ways for things to resolve naturally, if only people were a little more patient and had mutual trust . . .

There was a woman crying hysterically outside of the shut doors of the department store. Han Ma told herself: "I won't ever get hysterical."

"Han Ma, can you go to the book club on Friday?" Xiao Sang was asking her.

"I'll definitely go, along with Fei."

"I'm going with Heishi. He's going to make a brilliant speech!" Xiao Sang said excitedly.

"Xiao Sang, I admire Heishi the most out of all our friends at the book club, other than Fei."

"So, did you begin writing fiction?"

"I'm writing a short story. Living with someone like Fei, I constantly erupt, and now I have no escape route. You can see how miserable I am."

Xiao Sang smiled. She was imagining the happy scene of when this couple was together.

"Han Ma, you really have vision."

"I also feel that my vision is good. He has the heart of a newborn," Han Ma said proudly.

At this moment Han Ma pushed her soul's small panic about Fei to the back of her mind. The days and nights talking with him about literature appeared in her memory, even now making her face flush and her heart leap . . . If it weren't for him, she would still be hesitating on the margins of literature. Starting from her youthful reading of fiction and poetry, she'd adopted a way of putting herself body and mind into the books, as if she were intoxicated or mad. Up until the day she met Fei, when she finally discovered that the best stories were full of dim windows, one after another. Fei aroused her enthusiasm to open those hidden windows, to explore the unfamiliar universe beyond the windows. A transition in Han Ma's reading took place then.

"Are you thinking about him?" Xiao Sang asked.

"I'm always thinking about him, because he and my literature are connected. Isn't this convenient?"

"It's wonderful! Han Ma, this is simply, it's simply—I don't know how to describe it. I need to go clean up things now. I won't disturb your profound reveries."

Han Ma moved her chair to a dark place and listened carefully to the sound of the rain outside. Now she no longer felt afraid. In nature there were clear days and also typhoons. It had been this way since ancient times. Just a moment ago she'd thought of a plot for her story. She recorded it in a tiny notebook. Maybe when she returned home Fei would be there, and then she would enjoy it together with him.

Over by the shelves her coworkers, two young women, were pouring out their love stories to each other in low voices like pigeon coos. Han Ma seemed to listen without listening, sighing: How moving! Then confidence rose in her soul. The world wouldn't lessen her sense of wonder because of a typhoon.

"Han Ma, so you're hiding here! I was looking for you at the store first thing in the morning."

It was Xiaoyue, who worked in the large bookstore opposite. He also participated in Xiao Sang's reading group. It gave Han Ma a feeling of warmth to see him. On the surface Xiaoyue appeared withdrawn, but he was like a flame if he were talking about literature. He was also good at communicating with people and familiar with what readers from all parts of society preferred. Ever since he'd joined the reading group with Han Ma and the others, he'd been supporting Xiao Sang in elevating the group's reading level. Han Ma especially admired Xiaoyue's communication skills and his ability to apply book knowledge to reality.

"Xiaoyue, it's good that you're here! I've been thinking, you should join the Pigeon Book Club. You represent a new influence, and the book club needs you," Han Ma said excitedly, her eyes smiling.

“Of course I’ll join. I’ve heard about your husband—like a character from a legend! I’ll admit to you, honestly, that I feel a little inferior to him. I can only count as a student.”

“You don’t need to be modest, I’ve noticed your excellent skills. You should come.”

“I definitely will. There’s something else to discuss with you: tomorrow evening at the reading group here at the store, I want to talk with everyone about the experience of one of our readers maturing. After I’ve given the talk, I’d like you to add some comments. What do you think?”

“That’s great, I like the topic. I’ll definitely put all my strength into it.”

“Besides that I also wanted to speak with you about something off-topic. Please don’t be angry. Han Ma, I’ve known you for just a short time, but I feel like you’re an old friend and someone I can reveal all my thoughts to. You have an exceptionally broad vision, so you don’t make something out of nothing, but you also understand what’s happening on the inside. That’s hard to achieve.”

Xiaoyue finished speaking and said goodbye. Han Ma watched him moving away, thinking: here is another good friend. She reflected that she had found more friends ever since she’d formed ties with literature. Xiaoyue was younger than Fei. He’d said that Fei was like a character from a legend and that he felt a sense of inferiority around him. This showed how Fei fascinated the world of readers . . . Xiaoyue hadn’t been exaggerating. Han Ma recalled her first meeting with Fei, bits and pieces appearing one by one in her memory, where they were still able to stir her spirit. Had this book friend Xiaoyue, this young man with deep experience in human relationships, come over specially to express his respect for her?

The wind outside gradually lessened, while Han Ma’s soul became brighter and clearer. She thought back on the plot for the story she had taken notes on today, then from the bottom of her heart a burst of enthusiasm was suddenly born. She called this enthusiasm “imagining Fei.”

“Han Ma, let’s go have something to eat. What are you smiling at?” the store manager waved to her.

“The typhoon will pass, and we haven’t sustained major damage, so I am glad.”

"You are such a dear young woman. I love you."
"I love you, too, manager."

On Friday afternoon Xiao Sang got off work, rushed to the cafeteria, and bought two steamed rolls that she ate as she walked. She wanted to save time to dress up a bit. She put on her favorite casual clothes and a pair of attractive slip-on shoes. She slid out the door as quickly as possible, afraid of running into Xiao Ma.

She rode two stops then got off the bus. Heishi saw her first.

"Xiao Sang, your clothes and shoes are really pretty," he said appreciatively.

"These are just my ordinary home clothes. I can't wait to go to the book club to hear you share your views. Heishi, have you seen Xiao Ma recently? I'd like to know."

"I saw her once, a few days ago, at the supermarket. She looked like she was in a good mood."

"That's good news. Maybe her affair has been progressing."

"Her affair—do you mean hers with Uncle Yi?"

"What else could it be? You've known about it from the beginning."

"I did know a little about it, but I feel like some parts are uncertain . . . There are some things that are hard to define."

"Is that because the people whose affair it is don't want to define them?" Xiao Sang glanced at him probingly.

"Not entirely. Maybe the time hasn't come yet."

The used bookstore street was crowded this time with people coming and going from every store. Xiao Sang discovered many sailors mingled with the stream of people. She didn't know why the sailors almost put her into a trance. Heishi, beside her, said that it was still early, so he would take her to see a "ship captain's wife."

Then he pulled Xiao Sang into the low building of one of the bookstores along the street. The bookstore's ceiling was also low, so all of the customers were sitting on short stools browsing through books. They appeared to be mostly regulars. A small, thin hunchbacked old woman came toward them.

"Heishi, is this your fiancée?"

"Her name is Xiao Sang. She's my best friend." Heishi's voice was calm.

Xiao Sang discovered that all of the books here were about medicinal herbs. She picked one up and sat down to page through it, at the same time listening attentively to Heishi talking with the elderly woman.

"Aunt Fang, have you met with Uncle Lan again recently?"

"Once recently, but only for a short time. He remembered something that he wanted to tell me. We were at the beach, and when he finished explaining he hurried back on board his boat."

"How wonderful!"

"Then get married. When you do, you will know how wonderful marriage is."

"I've been considering it, Aunt Fang."

Leaving the herbal medicine bookstore, Xiao Sang asked Heishi about the incident with Aunt Fang. He told her that Aunt Fang's ship captain husband had passed away more than twenty years ago, yet she still met him frequently at a certain place. Heishi had known Aunt Fang for many years, so she was willing to share this secret with him. "It's not actually a secret. Didn't you hear what she said?"

"Then, Heishi, do you believe this from your heart?"

"I believe it from my heart. What form it takes isn't critical."

While they were speaking the two of them had already reached the book club. The others were all there in the room, including the young woman named Yang whom Xiao Sang had seen only once before. Fei was saying something to Han Ma in a low voice. As if in agreement, all eyes swept toward the newly arrived Xiao Sang and Heishi. Xiao Sang went over to help Qiaozi pour the tea. She no longer felt that slight anger at everyone's close attention; instead she was a little proud—feelings could change so quickly. What did it matter, even if they guessed wrong? The important thing was to catch hold of immediate impressions. Now, in the half-lit book club, in friendly view of everyone there, Xiao Sang felt her heart especially able to communicate with Heishi.

"Heishi, about that kind of invisible net—have you found an answer in the book?" Fei got straight to the point.

Fei was the sort of person who had perspective on the whole situation. He could comprehend everyone's mood all at once.

"Book friends, today I want to tell you about my most recent impressions from reading. Maybe this won't be helpful to all of you, but I long to speak and also to sort through my emotions while giving this account. I have read *XXXX* until it's become familiar, and now I've reached a conclusion. Recently, I suddenly realized what this beautiful novel was revealing to me: human adaptability in real life. There was a time when I was quite depressed, and even though I had dreams, I saw those transparent nets everywhere, seemingly trying to trap me hand and foot. When I encountered nets in my life, my instinctive reaction seemed to be to avoid them. But this novel showed me another, less familiar plan of action. Feeling perplexed, I would contemplate the phantasmagoric lives of the characters again and again. I started to ask myself: Is avoiding these weblike things really what I want? Must they infringe on my will? Then my principles were shaken, compelled by curiosity and also by enthusiasm from the bottom of my heart. I tried to conduct an experiment: to go into the nets of life and the nets of emotions, to become one with the nets, and, in expressing myself, to gradually observe my experiences. Now that I'm on this path and have so many new experiences, I'm more patient than in the past. I'm not anxious to know the outcome. Everyone knows this to be true: the outcome isn't the most important thing. Since I'm attracted to that kind of life, why shouldn't I devote myself to it? One needs to take action, only then will there be genuine understanding of one's own heart. If you are always worn out by the nets of life, always dodging left and right, your heart will eventually harden. Now I even envision: there may come a day when all of the nets, conversely, become the impetus for my actions and no longer an obstacle. Why not? Anything is possible. I have encountered this both in the novel and in life, but before this I didn't know that I must experience it or envision it boldly."

Once Heishi finished speaking Fei started to applaud. The others had expressions of confusion on their faces at first, because they couldn't keep pace with Heishi's ideas. But when he ended, each one of them understood some of it. They didn't understand completely, so they were also carefully pondering his words. Xiao Sang was the only exception. She felt that everything Heishi had said was what she wanted to say. Whatever Heishi had meant, he and she had the same type of longing in their hearts. So Xiao Sang gazed into Heishi's face, hoping to exchange glances with him. But sitting opposite her he seemed timid and didn't look toward her.

"Heishi is flying ahead!" Qiaozi said loudly.

Then she lowered her voice and whispered with Li Hai.

"Heishi doesn't usually make long speeches, but today this was like thunder in my ears! Your experience of the novel *XXXX* is exceptional. I'm beginning to worship you. Will you accept my worship?"

It was Yang. She walked up to Heishi and embraced him.

"If I really imagine what is written in the novel, I will have a spectacular romance with Heishi!" she said.

Xiao Sang saw that everyone was smiling, except Heishi. What was he thinking about? Was he still immersed in the words he had spoken? Xiao Sang heard Fei giving a speech, and he spoke very well, but she was absent-minded throughout. She kept trying to exchange looks with Heishi, but he, just like certain times before, appeared to be in a trance. What was actually going on with him?

"What Heishi has discovered is something foundational about this outstanding novel," Li Hai said loudly.

"This is what deserves to be called detection!" Yang made an exaggerated gesture.

Then she approached Xiao Sang and said in a lowered voice:

"Xiao Sang, will you still not make a move? If you don't, I'll make my move. I've been secretly in love with Heishi for a long time. This evening his speech made my enthusiasm peak."

"Yang, you don't need to ask me. I think you have a chance," Xiao Sang answered, smiling.

After she said this, she heard that Heishi was speaking.

"In fact, it's life that has been pushing me forward in my reading. I become more fond of every passing day. While I was reading this book, Xiao Sang joined the book club, and her method of reading jarred me. For a time I kept asking myself: Why can't I read like her? Why do I always consider those invisible nets as barriers and not as the impetus for life and for reading? I strove to clarify my thoughts and emotions, but this only left things in turmoil. Thank you, Xiao Sang. From an even higher level you enlightened me just in time. And Fei, you were always compelling my breakthroughs."

This surprised Xiao Sang, who hadn't expected Heishi's speech to take this turn. She felt that he always unexpectedly understood the voices calling to her, and he comprehended things she wasn't even aware of herself. They might be lost forever, if Heishi hadn't discovered them. Just think of how intriguing reading is! She and Heishi were joining hands to accomplish this kind of reading. It made her heart beat fast. So many things had happened while she wasn't paying attention. Xiao Sang raised her eyes and saw Yang making a face at her.

"I was wondering," Xiao Sang said thoughtfully. "That being 'devoted to life,' which Heishi and I have both discovered, isn't at all like the devotion to life described in Goethe's *Faust*. There's a major difference between what we've spoken of and what Goethe spoke of, isn't there? Many years have passed, and we are seeking a new path . . . only I still can't see it clearly."

"You're so very right, this is completely new—not the same as Musil or Goethe," Heishi answered.

"You both have had such an impact on me! I can't wait to write—oh!" Han Ma said.

Xiao Sang's face flushed with excitement as she looked toward young Han Ma and their eyes struck sparks. Xiao Sang's knees trembled slightly. She thought: she and Heishi were approaching the same miracle . . . Why get tangled up in minor trivialities? Had she been too pedantic before? One would never make mistakes, of course, if one never took action. Of course, taking action didn't mean being rash; it was important to be cautious and deliberate. Just because she'd done poorly before didn't mean that from now on she would do well, but this didn't matter . . . So . . . Her thoughts broke off.

That evening the discussion was more animated than ever before. Each of them tried anxiously to say what they had learned from classical literary models and contemporary developments in literature, about the emotional outlets available to modern humankind. So the occasion grew a bit chaotic, and time quietly slipped away. Finally, the owner of the Pigeon Book Club came to urge everyone to go home.

It was already late at night. For some reason the shops along the used bookstore street had all closed early. The sound of young people's animated conversation rang out in the street. They formed four pairs in all: Han Ma and Fei, Heishi and Xiao Sang, Qiaozi and Li Hai, and also Yang and Yan. Xiao Sang thought: finally we are all paired off. This is a bit of an unexpected coincidence, but also like the result of hard effort. After walking for a while, they parted, pair by pair.

"Xiao Sang, what did you think of this evening?" Heishi asked.

"I'm too excited, I don't know what to think . . . Heishi, I want to thank you even more for introducing me to the Pigeon Book Club."

"So, you haven't changed your proposal about going to sea to discuss books?"

"That is a dream—a dream I've had for a long time. Do you agree to my proposal?"

"I'm still thinking over the details. Because this is also my dream."

Then neither spoke. Xiao Sang wondered how they were still walking through the same alleyway, when they'd already turned a corner. They were in silent conversation with mighty specters. Suddenly the door to one of the bookstores opened a crack, and at the same moment they both saw shadows leaping in the dazzling lamplight. Could those be the specters? Xiao Sang was a little nervous at this thought. But then she relaxed, seeing Heishi's calm, self-possessed demeanor. If they could dance with the specters, oh, that would be to experience extreme joy. By the time she thought this, they'd reached the main street. What a coincidence, the night bus was just arriving.

"Xiao Sang, tonight you should think about your dream," Heishi said.

"I will. You, too—"

Heishi nodded firmly.

On the bus Xiao Sang told herself: "Haven't I already embarked? Ahead is the ocean. In taking this kind of action, you cannot predict the outcome from the beginning. Yes, predicting the outcome isn't important at all." Her thoughts continued from where they'd broken off in the book club, and she felt another burst of excitement.

That night Fei and Han Ma came out of the book club and turned into a dark alleyway. The alley opened out onto the riverbank. They planned to take the bus back from there. Once they were on their way Han Ma sensed that Fei was crestfallen, so she sounded him out.

"Fei, what do you think of Heishi's new point of view?"

"I've already said, he spoke incredibly well. Heishi has an unusual skill—he's the type of person who embodies his beliefs, so his understanding runs deep . . . His words left me ashamed, because I can't reach that state he spoke about. I am someone who drifts with the waves."

"But, Fei, I like you the way you are."

"That's because you haven't had any difficulty yet. You haven't confronted choices. You can probably tell that I'm not a responsible person. I have as many bad points as good ones."

"It's just as well that I fell in love with your good points. That was fate. Of course, I also appreciate Heishi's depth. The state he experienced is the one today's literature should pursue. He's quite gifted to be able to read at that level. It's the same with Xiao Sang. Fei, be inspired. Everyone has good points and bad points—that's not a reason to be depressed."

Ahead was the river, flashing with strange white light, piercingly bright. Han Ma was in high spirits after listening to Heishi and Xiao Sang's speeches, but Fei's mood was downcast.

To reach home they still had to walk a stretch of road after getting off the bus. There were no buildings on either side, only some shrubs. They'd heard that sometimes stray dogs would scurry out from the bushes here and bite people. Han Ma somewhat nervously looked ahead and behind as she walked. All of a sudden she discovered that Fei wasn't beside her. What had happened? She shouted, but he didn't answer her. Han Ma sped up, almost running. She wanted to get back home—once she was back home she would find out what had happened. Maybe Fei was playing a trick on her, to test her courage. Running, and running, she unexpectedly collided with someone. It was Xiao Fei, and up ahead was her bamboo restaurant.

"Han Ma, come with me quickly into the bamboo building. Fei is inside waiting for you," Xiao Fei said.

In the lamplight Fei looked all at once ten years older.

"How did you get here?" Han Ma asked.

"It seemed like there was something pulling me into the wasteland. I fought with it, wrestled it. Then I suddenly saw the bamboo restaurant and just rushed inside. You can tell that every road leads to my beloved."

Fei started to laugh, an ugly laugh.

The two of them returned home in silence, then silently went to sleep holding each other. But Han Ma was surprised not to have a single dream.

The next day at noon Fei and Han Ma ate Yangzhou fried rice at the bamboo restaurant. They had just finished when Lao Yao came over. Lao Yao sat down beside their table and said:

"This morning the young couple playing hide-and-seek around here traveled far away. I saw them get on a long-distance bus, both with large rucksacks on their backs, joyfully, like they were going on a holiday."

"They've found each other. Thank heaven and earth," Fei said.

"Maybe they're changing locations to continue their search." Lao Yao's sole eye winked.

"Lao Yao, tell us about you and Xiao Fei," Fei pleaded with him.

"We never played hide-and-seek," Lao Yao answered frankly. "When I met Xiao Fei at a shabby little hotel, she'd already tried to find herself a job in three different provinces. She was tired of wandering and had almost used up her money. I had my trade, but I didn't have a good network. A large restaurant in the capital fired me. You could say she and I arrived here outside Meng as itinerants. We didn't pity ourselves—instead we held on to common ideals. Later we started this little bamboo restaurant, where we work night and day."

As Lao Yao spoke Xiao Fei had quietly walked up behind him and stood there with a smile on her face.

"So, Fei, you and Han Ma are also forging ahead, night and day?" Lao Yao abruptly changed the topic. "People with ideals have no time to play hide-and-seek, right?"

"Exactly!" Fei and Han Ma said in unison.

"Xiao Fei and I are a like-minded couple: one of us thinks up an idea, the other adds flavor to it . . . We're always thinking up ideas and trying to do our work even better."

Fei's mood had improved by the time they came out of the bamboo restaurant.

"Han Ma, are we all right?" he asked.

"We're excellent, much better than 'all right.' Have you read the short story I wrote? Is it all right?"

"I've read it, and I wanted to tell you it's excellent. You haven't finished yet, the next part will be even better!"

"See, we're also night and day . . . Who has time to play hide-and-seek?" Han Ma laughed aloud.

"Oh, oh, Han Ma, Han Ma . . . ," Fei murmured.

"We live in each other's hearts. What use is there in searching?"

They each went to their own study. Fei sensed that time was more and more pressing for him. He must be a help to Han Ma, must increase how much he read, must take notes constantly . . .

Han Ma immersed herself in the world of her story, which was still not too familiar. She could tell that she was a new hand at this, because she was bewildered from time to time. But one thing was clear, that there was something attracting her, making her leap at the attempt and press onward toward *there*. This wasn't ordinary excitement, but also not unexciting. It was instead an activity, an effort to pull forward and an effort to suspend. When Han Ma finished writing a passage and stopped, she suddenly understood what Fei had said. He'd said he wasn't suited to writing because by nature he drifted with the waves too much. He believed Han Ma was the one who ought to write because she possessed such a high degree of self-discipline and could constantly renew the meaning of language. The night deepened. Fei was calling to her.

"Han Ma, you are the pioneering type," he said excitedly.

"Maybe it's because of love that I finally feel confident."

"Even without me, you'd still . . ."

"No, it's not like that. I remember clearly. We're just like Lao Yao and Xiao Fei."

They looked out the window together and saw the lights still on in that bamboo restaurant.

"They are also conducting creative experiments, with food," Fei whispered in Han Ma's ear.

"Fei, I'm so happy. Ever since I was little I believed that I could do something, but I didn't expect happiness would come so soon . . . This all is because I have you. We are one person, in a literary sense, aren't we? Before, when I didn't have you yet, I was always searching for you. Later I found you, then I moved forward in my undertaking. This is no accident. I always tell myself, I've gotten the best."

"Oh, Han Ma, Han Ma . . . ," Fei couldn't speak.

They embraced each other standing in the living room. Both heard the sound of car wheels coming from the city center of Meng. There was a procession passing by on the main road.

Fei's heart ached for Han Ma. He couldn't speak out of shame.

But Han Ma didn't think of herself as pitiable—she was proud to have a partner like Fei. Her concern at this moment was: how could she finally make Fei understand the true condition of her feelings? Why did most people find it hard to overcome the "possession" complex of love? Thinking this over, Han Ma just smiled in the darkness. To be sure, for some time now she'd no longer felt bewildered when Fei left her from time to time. Everything could change, just like in fiction. She was slowly becoming the person she wanted to be.

"You really don't need to . . . Fei, things aren't the way you imagine at all. At first it was a little hard, then I gradually started to adapt. I've loved a few people before, but never as deeply as I love you. Are you listening?"

"I'm listening, Han Ma. I ask myself every day how in the world there could be a woman as good as you. And me, I'm just a leftover lump of coal. I think I should take the initiative to leave you, but I can't do it."

"Why do you want to leave me? Because of your comical self-esteem? You can't say it's because of me. You're the person I need the most—care about the most. If you pick up and leave, I don't know if I'll still be able to write."

The wind through the wilds of the city outskirts blew with such mercilessness that the doors and windows shivered. Difficult communication leaves lovers exhausted, so they finally muddled off to sleep. Han Ma's thought before falling asleep was: "Fei doesn't believe that I understand him, because women like me are rare." Fei's thought was: "She's so good, and I've hurt her so badly!"

During the night Fei had a nightmare and cried out. Han Ma hugged him tight, gently patting his back. She heard him faintly say: "Is it you, Han Ma? Have we already crossed over?" "Yes, we've already crossed over," Han Ma answered. She heard Fei make a slight snore. But she stayed awake, thinking about her story, thinking of the brightest, most resplendent phrases. Returning to reality, she said to herself: "Fei can't forgive himself, even if he understood my understanding of him. Because he thinks he hasn't been fair to me. This is a knotty problem. If there's love, how can there be talk of fairness?" Staring at the dot of moonlight at the window she kept thinking, "It's me who's willing to love him and not leave him. He won't leave me either. If it weren't for me, he and Yue might have gotten back together after their setback. Maybe I've been too selfish. I would be genuinely selfish if I didn't try to understand Fei and interfered in his relationship with Yue. New love has emerged, but that doesn't mean old love has disappeared completely. I know Fei isn't that kind of person. This may even be why I like him. Their love accumulated over more than a decade. Maybe my love isn't as deep as hers, definitely not as . . ."

She didn't shut her eyes all night.

Xiao Sang decided to call Heishi to talk about their trip to the ocean. She thought: why be shy?

"Heishi, have you decided about going on a trip to the sea?"

"I think it's still a little too soon. I need to plan carefully. It's not because I have misgivings, only that certain conditions haven't developed yet. But I really want to go with you right away."

"You're speaking diplomatically . . . Oh, I'm sorry. Maybe I'm thinking about this too simply? You see, I've read so many novels and am still a simple person."

"Believe me, I'm planning for it. I just need to wait for a while first."

After putting down her phone, Xiao Sang sat at the table in a daze for a long time. Heishi's answer wasn't exactly a dash of cold water, but his behavior was incomprehensible. Could it be, like Xiao Ma had said, that there was some obstacle? Xiao Sang was unwilling to make wild guesses. She could also wait. Once Xiao Sang thought this, her mood improved.

"Xiao Sang, has there been any progress with your affair?"

It was Xiao Ma, who had come up from Uncle Yi's home on the third floor.

"What affair?" Xiao Sang countered rigidly.

"Your affair with Heishi. He pretended not to be interested in my relationship with Uncle Yi, but I know what he's thinking. Xiao Sang, this is all because of you."

"Xiao Ma, don't keep going around in circles, all right? I don't understand."

"By the way, I learned that Heishi and Uncle Yi's relationship is closer than father and son! Poor Heishi. If this chain isn't broken someday, he won't dare to declare his feelings to his dear . . ."

"Don't talk nonsense!" Xiao Sang howled.

She'd frightened Xiao Ma, who spun toward the door, then opened it and marched away.

"Damn it, she's chasing after shadows . . . ," Xiao Sang said to herself.

"Can Heishi be as crazy as her? Closer than father and son—does that mean 'engraved on each other's hearts'?"

Xiao Sang felt like her brain was going to explode. She took a cold shower, hoping to wash away these confusing thoughts. Coming out of the bathroom, she decided never to ask Heishi. Xiao Ma was only guessing, and if Xiao Sang inquired about it, it would hurt Uncle Yi—the person she loved the most—deeply. Let this be an eternal mystery, a beautiful mystery. What Heishi did was right. Thinking of Xiao Ma's intimation, Xiao Sang respected Heishi even more. And when she thought of Uncle Yi, waves of warmth poured from her heart—her relationship with him surpassed that of father and daughter! Xiao Sang wrote in her diary: *I, Xiao Sang, an ordinary woman—that I should be so fortunate!*

After Xiao Sang finished writing this sentence, she decided that, even if Xiao Ma were guessing wrong, even if Heishi was being oversensitive, she would maintain her current approach. The deep emotion this uncle who had helped her mature, who had cultivated her attainments, felt for her was irreplaceable by anyone else. Although she knew Xiao Ma wasn't the jealous type of woman, and might even mean her and Heishi well, Xiao Sang could not tolerate anyone talking about dear Uncle Yi this way in front of her.

More time passed, and Xiao Sang finally calmed down. Thinking more carefully, she felt that she shouldn't be so angry with Xiao Ma. After all, Heishi had never disclosed his true feelings. Maybe his reason for not revealing them was the same as her own. Surely he wouldn't divulge them to Xiao Ma, which meant that he would let her suspicion become an eternal mystery in order to safeguard the people he loved the most. But Heishi wouldn't lose his temper at Xiao Ma either, because he was cultured when it came to his emotions, not coarse like Xiao Sang. Xiao Sang thought this over and involuntarily let out a bitter laugh: why couldn't she just let go of her weaknesses? This was where the distance between her and Heishi lay. Their environments had been different growing up, so they'd become different people. Still, there was no use in feeling dejected: she and Heishi also had many points in common. As to what their future relationship would be, let nature take its course. For now, Heishi was attractive to her, especially his views about life, which deeply enchanted her. Now she even knew a little about what he was waiting for. He was waiting for a certain enigma in life to spontaneously reveal its answer. He'd said at the book club that he no longer waited passively, but instead was devoted to life. All in all, no matter whether the mystery in Heishi's heart was or wasn't related to her, Xiao Sang was willing to wait together with him. Hadn't he already answered her travel suggestion, and wasn't he in the process of planning? She should believe her sincere friend.

After Xiao Sang had cleared up her thoughts and emotions, her mood changed for the better. She went downstairs, planning to go to the bar to celebrate herself. She thought of how she'd entered into a life of passion, yet, often, she felt she had reached murky dead ends, without noticing that ahead "dark willows, bright flowers, a village appears."

Once Xiao Sang entered the bar, that tall man came over to welcome her.

"Has your lover gone away again?" he asked.

"You've guessed wrong, it's actually that he and I are hesitating," Xiao Sang said cheerfully.

"Haha, hesitating, hesitating, this shows the depth of both of your feelings!"

"Why?" Xiao Sang drank a sip of wine and asked curiously.

"That's my experience. My girlfriend and I may hesitate for a lifetime."

"You're an unusual man."

Xiao Sang thought secretly: "At my age, passion no longer just bursts forth like it does for Xiao Ma. It's like the dark bottom of a river."

The tall man suddenly started to sing a folk song into the air. It was a strange kind of song: wild, cruel, defiant. His uninhibited voice toppled Xiao Sang over with admiration. It seemed as though everyone in the bar turned their faces toward him.

Someone spoke softly in Xiao Sang's ear—the bar server.

"This man, his lover passed away not too long ago."

Xiao Sang listened, the tide of her emotions rising and falling. "Beautiful . . . ," she murmured in a low voice, almost in tears.

Walking the road home, Xiao Sang kept whispering to herself: "Don't let go of those bright points in life . . ."

After Xiao Ma left Xiao Sang's home, she kept reproaching herself for being so rude. "Damn it, damn it! I look so selfish! No wonder Uncle Yi doesn't love me the way he loves Xiao Sang! I'm so small, always thinking of my own schemes and not taking other people into account."

She confusedly walked toward her rental apartment, thinking that she would cry for a while and then be better.

Xiao Ma had moved out of her mother's house and leased a small unit. She wanted to be independent and not be interfered with by her doting mom. She'd often felt like she was bound hand and foot, even though her mother was a good person. Xiao Ma opened the door with her key, fell onto her small, well-crafted bed, and lay for a long time without moving. "Originally he liked me some, and my relationship with him was like embracing to keep warm, then today this happened by surprise! Oh, I don't know my limits, I think too much of myself. Why can't I change my bad habits?" Xiao Ma also wondered how Uncle Yi would treat her if he knew she'd made up this scheme behind his back. Regardless of what she imagined, she knew intuitively that Uncle Yi wouldn't be angry at her. At most he would put her in her place with a laugh, taking her to be a child who needed protecting. But how could this kind of relationship to each other ever make him love her? When Xiao Ma realized this, she made a vow to herself: she would never say anything again about who Uncle Yi loved to Xiao Sang or Heishi. And if she transgressed, she would bite off her tongue! After promising this, she felt a little more carefree. Xiao Ma sat up and opened the new book that Uncle Yi had given her. It had Uncle Yi's inscription: *I hope Xiao Ma will soar!—Uncle Yi.* Usually she placed the book under her pillow to let it accompany her into her dreams.

This chapter was about unrequited love. Xiao Ma thought that the protagonist was like Heishi, and also a little like her. She muttered: "What's wrong with one-sided love? Isn't everyone in unrequited love? This is grown-up love, after all . . . I just want to be in a one-sided affair, to love for a lifetime! This way . . ." She suddenly blushed. The character in the book finally declared his feelings to the object of his affection. However, he was surprised to discover that the other was also in unrequited love with him. It wasn't a happy ending, though, probably because their temperaments were too similar. Xiao Ma reflected that she loved Uncle Yi because he was a type of person she didn't know well; although unfamiliar, everything he did shook her to the core of her being. Now she denied that she'd ever been in love before, since that hadn't been true love. Was it true love now? "I don't know, I am studying with a teacher," she said to the book. Then she thought about how she was not only learning from Uncle Yi, but also from Xiao Sang and Heishi, and she wanted her sentiments to draw close to theirs. She couldn't hope wildly that Uncle Yi would just fall in love with her—that was impossible. But he liked her, and, provided he kept being fond of her, she had hope. Why did Uncle Yi like her? It must be that her sensitivity to life, toward literature, attracted him. Xiao Ma resolved to try harder, but not to be impetuous any more. Her carelessness annoyed people. It was childish, base behavior.

"It's me, Xiao Sang. I won't ever say such stupid things again, believe me," Xiao Ma said over the phone.

"Forgive me, I shouldn't have lost my temper. Sometimes I get a little unsettled," Xiao Sang said on her end of the call.

"It's you who should forgive me. You're still my dear friend, aren't you?"

"Of course I am. I will always be."

After Xiao Ma set down the phone, tears flowed from her eyes. "Such a good friend, so lofty!" she thought. She remembered how that afternoon she and Uncle Yi had reviewed the final chapter of *XXXX* together. Afterward Uncle Yi went to the kitchen to make her rice with string beans, which were in season, and she'd gone to the kitchen to help. Their hands often touched while they washed the vegetables and cooked, which for her was like an electric shock, while Uncle Yi remained calm and kind, just like he was her actual uncle. "He doesn't love me at all," she thought, "but he's fond of me. This is because I'm not mature enough or good enough. I don't suit him. So he's only fond of me, as if I were his niece. But he likes me a little more than simply a niece, he's said that I have amazing literary intuition . . . I need to demonstrate my special talents in this area, then it will be enough to win his heart." Thinking this over, Xiao Ma felt a sense of urgency, so she washed her face and sat down to read the book that Uncle Yi had given her.

She read until late at night, then took a shower and lay down on her bed to keep reading until she went to sleep.

The next day she woke up on time and went to work at the department store. Her spirits were revitalized. "Being in love is truly good," she said to herself. She was even more patient with the customers, her brain more agile and clear. She raised her eyes to glance toward Xiao Sang, who she saw was working methodically, her capable, steady demeanor on full display. That demeanor was why Xiao Ma studied her now, not to further her surreptitious scheme from before.

At lunchtime Xiao Ma timidly approached Xiao Sang. Xiao Sang smiled at her pleasantly.

"Yesterday I cried after I got off the phone with you," Xiao Ma said.

"Ha, you're becoming sentimental, but I'm also touched by what you're saying. I must do everything I can to help my Xiao Ma."

"Uncle Yi said you've been going to his home less now. Why?"

"Because he introduced me to so many friends. I'd be too busy even if I had three heads and six arms."

The dear friends regained their intimacy of former days. They both felt it strange that they hadn't exposed the entire secrets of their hearts to each other—so why did they suddenly understand each other? Xiao Ma thought to herself: this is culture and sentiment. She must observe everything Xiao Sang and Heishi did from now on. They had what she lacked but was making the utmost effort to pursue.

"Xiao Ma, you look so pretty now," Xiao Sang said significantly.

"Sometimes I want to tell all of my friends: I'm in love!"

They kept hugging and smiling.

"Xiao Sang, for the past few days I've been having a dream," Xiao Ma said.

"Can you tell me about it?"

"I want to study reading with Uncle Yi, then wait until someday in the future when I can try to teach fiction at the Youth Literary Research Institute. Do you think I have any hope?"

"Of course you do! Uncle Yi said you're naturally very talented. Besides, besides—" Xiao Sang stifled a laugh with her hand.

"I know you're going to say that I have such an excellent teacher in Uncle Yi. Ha, I'm so fortunate! I've had good luck, to become your dear friend, and through you to meet him. Uncle Yi is our secret weapon."

"Mm-hmm," Xiao Sang nodded seriously.

Xiao Sang and Heishi still couldn't decide on a date for their sea voyage, but she was going on another trip. She would return to her hometown in the north to visit her parents and her younger brother's family. Four years had passed since her last visit, so she felt apologetic to her parents. Influenced by Heishi, Xiao Sang was even ashamed.

The day before her departure, she sat with Heishi for a long time on wooden chairs beside the river. Their exchanges were more frequent now than before—they met every week. Xiao Sang's visit to her family was going to be a two-month vacation, which was a long stretch of time for the both of them. Xiao Sang had come up with a plan, which was that they could communicate by letter. She thought that Heishi would have to reveal something in his letters, regardless of whether it were good or bad news.

"I've told you so much about my mom. Tell me about your parents," Heishi said.

"They're a simple, plain couple. They've always been loving toward me, but I've sort of neglected them since I've gotten older and no longer needed their blessing. You can tell how selfish I am."

"They're free from worrying about you. They know you're doing well off in another part of the country, living your life to the fullest, and they must be anxious that their nagging would bother you."

"Maybe, maybe. But I really am awful."

"It's all right. Aren't you going to see them now? Your parents will beam with joy once they see you. When I was at college, and just imagining your family, I thought it must be full of warmth."

"My parents worked as geological prospectors, and back then they hadn't returned to the capital. You're quite the dreamer to imagine my family environment based on nothing!"

"We boys were playing soccer, and you were sitting by the playing field reading a book. I can still remember that scene today."

"Heishi, you've taught me the most important thing."

"I was thinking: let's wait until you return, and, if you haven't changed your mind, we can go on the ocean voyage."

"I think you are the one who's more likely to change your mind. Let's wait and see."

At the riverside a ferry approached the shore. Its steam whistle startled Xiao Sang so that her eyes filled with tears. "And when did my emotions get so dried up?" she asked herself.

"I've been to the capital a number of times. My father's new family lives there, and I have a cute little sister," Heishi said.

"You don't hate your father?"

"I did a little bit when I was younger, then later that changed."

"Because later you met another father," Xiao Sang finished for him, "the most outstanding of all fathers."

Heishi, looking at Xiao Sang appreciatively, didn't speak.

"Look at those people supporting one another, coming over hand in hand." Xiao Sang continued, "I often think that learning to read literature was the turning point of my life. I seemed all of a sudden to have become a new person."

"But in my eyes you've always been a new person, while I'm the old one. Do you still remember that day? That day I'd planned to invite you to the Pigeon Book Club, but I was worried you would decline. I was so nervous that my legs almost went limp, though I purposely kept up the appearance of not caring. You're so good, you agreed right away," Heishi recalled.

"You must have heard many things about me from Uncle Yi? Oh, I shouldn't question you. I knew nothing about you then. You could say—haha—I was in the light, and you were in darkness."

"You had such poise. Your calmness is my favorite thing about you."

"Are you saying that we have the opposite temperaments?"

"Not entirely." Heishi, too, started to laugh.

Although they still weren't entirely clear about each other's situations, this long talk by the river brought their youthful hearts closer. They were both overwrought, despite their restraint.

"If we go to sea, I will bring *XXXX*, because this magnificent book brought us together. I was overcome by reading this novel," Xiao Sang said impulsively.

"I have the same vision. We've talked about the nets, now we'll enter into them, and we'll be inspired, because we'll have some assurance about ourselves. Isn't this what we talked about that time, that we are neither like Goethe's *Faust*, nor like Musil's characters?"

"Yes, exactly. Heishi, I'm ready now. We won't become a decadent school just because we're devoted to life. That would be unworthy of Uncle Yi's hopes and also unworthy of this magnificent novel. Now, ha, I will leave Meng and go to the capital. I've gotten used to living in Meng, where each day passes so compactly: work, reading, friends. I don't have the chance to be sentimental, since every day I'm forging ahead.

We've known each other—I mean that we've been reacquainted—for six months? What a strange feeling! We'll soon be a year older together."

As Xiao Sang said these words, she noticed that Heishi's expression seemed sad. Of course, she could be imagining things. She thought so. In the distance another group of people disembarked from the ferry. They walked quickly because they were eager to devote themselves to life. Ordinarily Xiao Sang would have been the same as them. But suddenly she faced a reunion, her visit to the family she hadn't seen in such a long time. Facing Heishi, a blank space appeared in her mind. She would be gone for two whole months, and things would surely happen here. What would happen? She suddenly shivered.

"I want to cancel this visit to my family," she blurted.

"Why? This visit will be a very good thing for you. Look, you haven't left yet, but I'm already thinking about how to write you a letter. There's also Uncle Yi, who's gotten so used to seeing you daily—you're very important in our lives. However, your parents and your brother are also important. We must be patient through the empty days without you. Two months will pass quickly, then you'll be back."

"You're exaggerating, Heishi. You say 'empty days,' but I think your days will be full."

"That's how it is, when you're here," Heishi said in a low voice.

Xiao Sang didn't press him further. She didn't want to seem weak. Wasn't it just being gone for two months? If something was going to happen, then let it happen. She knew there would be book club gatherings here as usual; the relationship between Uncle Yi and Xiao Ma might change unexpectedly now; Heishi might meet a new girlfriend, or rekindle a former affection for some woman . . . Anything could happen, but the sky wouldn't fall.

Heishi looked a little uneasy as he watched Xiao Sang board her bus. His eyes were like a little boy's. Xiao Sang turned around and took an inside seat.

Returning home and seeing her luggage packed, her mind grew chaotic. She finished a cup of tea and forced herself to open *XXXX*. The character in the book sat in the cabin of a plane flying across the Pacific Ocean. He was thinking: "Space isn't a vacuum at all." His connection to the Earth was the same as usual, while everything meaningful remained below on that small patch of ground. After Xiao Sang read up to here, she wrote in her diary: *Once I have some distance, I will reflect seriously on this year of my life.* It had been six months since her "chance meeting" (in fact it was no chance meeting) with Heishi that day on the bus, when he brought her afterward to the Pigeon Book Club. Over those six months her relationship with him had meandered. Now it seemed to have developed into a relationship somewhere in between good friends and a couple. Going a step further, maybe they would become lovers; or, taking a step back, still be friends. Without knowing why, Xiao Sang felt dissatisfied with herself because of these ambiguous possibilities. She'd always thought that taking the initiative was up to Heishi—he was the one keeping the attachment between them from going any further—and there were many circumstances that proved this. She felt slightly wronged and blamed him somewhat. Now that she was leaving, if Heishi's manner transformed (she always believed that it would transform), their situation would eventually become clear. But even if it were proved that Xiao Sang's hopes were futile, she also believed that she wouldn't be defeated. That would only show how things between them just weren't suitable. As for Uncle Yi thinking that the two of them were well-matched, that was because he was an outsider, and one who deeply loved both her and Heishi. But if Heishi's manner transformed in a positive direction? Then she would have to be observant and not let it go to her head . . . Her thoughts turned back to Uncle Yi. Xiao Sang went to his house less frequently since Xiao Ma had fallen in love with him. He still treated her with kindness. Perhaps he believed that she and Heishi were together, or that her new friends at the book club were occupying her time. Yet there was such a sense of loss in how much she wanted to revive her past relationship with Uncle Yi. For him to attain happiness, she was naturally willing to make some sacrifices. It was also repaying his past kindnesses. What's more, Xiao Ma was such a loveable young woman, she would bring more joy into Uncle Yi's life.

Xiao Sang lay in bed thinking through these issues, conscious that a major transition in her life would soon come. It was possible that her two months away from Meng would allow the solution to a certain enigma to appear. From this perspective, her absence was a good thing. It could prompt many vague signs to reveal their significance. The discussion from the book club gathering when she and Heishi had talked about the nets of life reappeared in her mind. Now she genuinely sensed the dragging of those dark, invisible nets, but she accepted their pull with pleasure. She thought: even though she didn't know much about Heishi's personal life, she could tell that he existed at this moment in similar circumstances to her. That meant it was reading that brought their two hearts closer, while reading also pointed their way out of murky obscurity.

Xiao Sang was airborne again, the plane bearing her leaving Meng behind, and ahead her destination was the capital. The journey brought her many conflicting emotions, because it was unlike any time in the past. When she opened her book, her heart remained with the city of Meng, so everything she read reminded her of Meng.

In a haze she saw Uncle Yi walking through the entrance of the courtyard with a smile on his face, appearing to be only a little over fifty years old. Next Xiao Ma came in behind him, her cheeks like fresh apples.

"Xiao Sang, Xiao Ma and I are getting married," Uncle Yi told her.

"Oh, how wonderful, Uncle Yi! I'd been hoping that one day . . ."

Xiao Sang's voice choked with sobs. She didn't know why she wanted to cry.

Xiao Ma came over to hug her, and the two women started to cry together.

"You both, this is . . . this is . . . ," Uncle Yi said, standing awkwardly to one side.

Xiao Sang woke up crying. She felt her face with her hand, and there really were tears. The flight attendant came over to give her lemon tea.

Xiao Sang drank the tea with a flushed face, wondering: "Did I cry out loud?"

She didn't understand why her emotions had been so overwrought just now. Could she already be so close to being in love? Probably not—there'd been no reliable signs in evidence. Was her personal life just a mess, or a building up of achievements? She didn't know and also didn't want to judge. Yesterday she had written in her diary that she would reflect seriously. What kind of reflection? She couldn't hope to reflect while sitting at home; maybe she should devote herself to those nets more single-mindedly. Maybe this devotion was reflection? Yes, that was what Heishi's speech that day had meant! Xiao Sang was enlightened and had some new ideas. She hurriedly found her notebook and jotted down these impressions. She planned to expand on her thoughts in her speech the next time she went to the book club. She told herself mockingly: "You're already gone, but it's like you haven't left yet." She glanced down through the window to where great stretches of the plains were coming into sight. She had already entered another world.

Xiao Sang saw her father and mother craning their necks and looking around at the exit, both a little older and also a little thinner than before. Four years had passed.

"Dad! Mom!" she shouted loudly.

"Sangsang, Sangsang . . ."

Xiao Sang's mother flung herself at her with a hug, while her dad took the suitcase from her hand.

Xiao Sang felt her mom thinner and smaller in her arms, so her eyes reddened.

The family finally calmed down once they sat on the bus. Xiao Sang's mother didn't speak, only looking at her daughter without turning her eyes away, seemingly afraid that she would suddenly disappear. After a long time, she finally squeezed out:

"Sangsang, are things still all right there?"

"They're still all right, Mom. Everything is going well. I plan to invite you to live there from now on."

Xiao Sang was surprised as she finished speaking—she hadn't known she would say this. Then she was pleased with what she'd said. Was she entering a new net of life? She must be brave.

Neither her father nor mother responded to her proposal. Xiao Sang knew that they were feeling somewhat estranged from her.

Her parents' home looked the same: the old furniture, the clean wood floor, appearing both casual and comfortable. It was a two-bedroom house, and Xiao Sang placed her luggage in the bedroom where she would stay. The sheets and blanket on the bed were new. The slip-on shoes, bathrobe, towel, the tote bag for going out were all new. Xiao Sang thought: Mom must have been looking forward to today so much. Still, her parents seemed reserved around her, as if undecided about something.

"Mom, Qingqing isn't back yet?" Xiao Sang asked.

"He and his wife went to work and aren't back yet. The little one is at nursery school. They'll be here this evening to welcome you. Sangsang, take a shower and then rest for a while. Your dad and I will be busy in the kitchen."

"No, Mom, I shower in the evenings. I'll join you in the kitchen."

The tiny kitchen couldn't fit three people inside. Her father went to the living room to read the newspaper.

Xiao Sang sat on a low stool helping to prep the vegetables and shell the peas. Her mother was making lamb with aster.

"Qingqing's family lives just upstairs. Chun is a very capable daughter-in-law, and keeps their household in good order. So your dad and I have nothing to do every day now. Every morning he goes to the teahouse with his old colleagues, and I am just at home. Sometimes I embroider, and sometimes I help knit sweaters for your niece. I'm becoming unsociable—I don't like commotion."

Xiao Sang heard her mother's voice emanate loneliness. She remembered how her mom had been an avid reader. Whenever she had free time she'd read novels. Sometimes when there was no time during the day she would read in the evening, all the way until late at night. How had she changed? Because Xiao Sang had been away from home for so long, she didn't know when her mother had started to change either. Her heart ached a little, and she felt a little flustered.

"Mom, do you still read novels?"

"I haven't read for a long time. There's no one to talk with me about literature. Your dad doesn't read any books at all. Qingqing is busy all day with work, and when he comes home in the evening he's still busy with work. Ah."

Xiao Sang furrowed her brow and didn't know what to say to make it better.

"Sangsang, when we were on the bus you said you wanted to invite us to live with you. I didn't answer you, because I don't think it's suitable. Here I can help take care of our granddaughter. What would I do there? I'd only get in the way of your personal life. A nagging old woman, a housewife, who doesn't understand anything . . ."

"Mom . . ." Xiao Sang had tears in her eyes.

Xiao Sang hurriedly changed the topic and started to ask about her niece Yangyang.

"She's wonderful, and so patient when she does things. She can help me thread my needle. Wait until this afternoon, you'll see her then. She's much sturdier than the last time you came home. She's about to go to elementary school. By nature she's like me, not like her dad or mom: she's a bookworm, the same as I used to be."

A smile appeared on her mom's face only when she spoke about her granddaughter.

Xiao Sang remembered that when she was little there'd been so many books around the home. Two bookcases were placed side by side against the wall with her mom's books on them. There'd also been two low bookshelves holding children's books and picture books. Xiao Sang's love of reading was due to her mother's influence. Her parents' worksite would change, but those bookshelves always followed them when they moved into a new home. The last time she'd come home she had discovered the two bookcases were gone, replaced by two display cabinets with her mother's embroidery placed inside. Xiao Sang had wanted then to ask her where they'd gone, but she'd just ended a romantic relationship and was upset, so she'd forgotten about the bookcases.

While her mother was busy in the kitchen, Xiao Sang gazed at her back. She seemed to see an elderly woman walking through wilderness at dusk, the road before her narrowing, the sky growing darker . . . "It's my fault," Xiao Sang wanted to say.

Her father didn't say much when they sat down to eat at midday. He'd always been like this. He just urged Xiao Sang to eat more meat, saying she wasn't robust enough. Xiao Sang talked about family matters with her mom while he focused on eating. When they'd finished, her dad finally said:

"Xiao Sang, you used to be the family's treasure."

"Dad, I know you blame me. I came back this time to try to make up for my negligence."

"No, no, how could I blame you? Since you don't want to take a nap, let's go to the exercise park this afternoon for a walk, all right?"

"Yes, Dad, I've been looking forward to talking with you."

After saying this Xiao Sang felt a bit uneasy.

They rested for a while, drank tea, and then father and daughter went downstairs together. Walking the familiar neighborhood, Xiao Sang responded distractedly to several elderly people who greeted her.

They'd gone into the park and sat down together on a bench by the lake when her father finally said:

"Sangsang, there's been a major change in the years you've been gone. I'm tired of life now—nothing holds any interest. Before, when I worked, I liked my job. When I retired I became useless. I go to the teahouse every day to see my old coworkers and try to get back a little of the feeling of when I was working. But I'm disappointed. Staying home is even worse. Your mom doesn't understand me at all, and I don't want to complain to her. For a long time it's just been keeping up appearances, even though we still live together. She brought up the possibility of separating not too long ago. Do you think I should agree?"

"Dad, I don't know enough about the situation. I'll ask Mom about it."

"Since I retired I don't know how to spend the days. My mind is empty. We argue so often that we've grown incompatible. She and I both have bad tempers. Would it be better to part ways? I'm not sure. For the past two years I've been so tired of life. Is this a disease?"

"Dad, aren't you still interested in your profession?"

"I retired early, years ago. I lost all interest and can't get it back again. Besides, my memory is deteriorating. Even when I read the newspaper I can't grasp the essentials. Your mom used to be a devoted wife and mother, but now she has a frightening temper, and she's less able to tolerate me . . . I've thought many times about moving out to rent a room by myself."

Looking at her morose father, Xiao Sang had an inward sensation of pressure until she couldn't breathe. Her dad had been a simple soul, a good father who had always given Xiao Sang whatever she'd asked for. Now all of a sudden he'd changed. Something bad might easily happen to him, if her parents really separated.

That night, in bed at her parents' home, Xiao Sang struggled to sleep until it was almost dawn.

The next morning Xiao Sang woke up late. She heard her mother making noise in the kitchen and jumped out of bed, ran to the bathroom to freshen up, then dressed and went to the kitchen to help.

"Dad?" Xiao Sang asked her mom.

"Of course he's gone to the teahouse again. He can't stay put at home."

Xiao Sang's mother had bought a roast duck, and now she was making a large pot of soup.

"Mom, do you still love Dad?"

"What talk of love is there for people our age? I thank heaven and earth if he doesn't make me angry."

"Does he often make you angry?"

"I get angry just looking at him, and he doesn't like looking at me either. He's changed so much—he isn't your dad like he was before, he's turned into some cold-blooded animal. So I've brought up living separately. It turned out he's thought about moving out, too."

"Yesterday I talked with Dad and could tell there was something wrong with his spirits. If you separate, something might happen to him."

"He, oh, he has plenty of spirit for starting a fight. A few times I've been so angry with him it made me ill. I figure that if I get sick again I'll be done for, so I brought up separating."

"Mom, I haven't seen you for a few years. What happened between you and Dad to make you hate each other so much?"

"I don't know. For him it could be because he's bored. For me, I've gotten more and more impatient with him and even feel the urge to swear . . ." Xiao Sang's mother lowered her voice at this point, moved closer to her, and asked:

"Are we abnormal?"

Xiao Sang saw that her mom's face was full of gloom. Her thoughts were spinning at the speed of flight.

"Mom, isn't there anything Dad still likes?"

"I don't think so. He doesn't like anything now—that's why I call him cold-blooded. Oh, separating would be better, but like you say, I'm afraid something will happen to him. If something does happen, won't everyone blame me? It's hopeless, we'll both come to the same end."

"Mom, let me ask you a question: why don't you read novels any more? Where did those two bookshelves go?"

"What use is reading? There's too much of a difference between real life and fiction—there's no link between them. I sold the books for recycling."

Watching her mother say this with a wooden, expressionless face, Xiao Sang felt her heart ache for her.

That afternoon her younger brother's family came over. They all seemed to be doing well and looked healthy. When Yangyang came in she went right to the bookshelves and picked out her picture books. She demanded that Xiao Sang read her *The Story of the Lion King*. When Xiao

Sang reached the sad part of the story, Yangyang's mouth pursed and she started to cry loudly. Xiao Sang realized that the little girl was being brought up to read. She lamented to herself: Mom, oh, Mom. Chun brought her daughter into their parents' bedroom. Now there was only Xiao Sang and her brother sitting in the living room.

"Qingqing, what do you think about Dad and Mom's relationship?" Xiao Sang asked.

"I don't see any hope for their relationship. The future is dim. I had to take Mom to the hospital twice this year."

Xiao Sang was silent.

"Mom says they should separate, but separating would be deadly for Dad. He's always said so little, and if he moved out on his own, wouldn't his mind deteriorate? I tried to help him find something to do, but he's older and has no skills. Where can he find work?"

Xiao Sang thought: my brother takes such pains for the family!

"Ah, as heaven wills." Qingqing heaved a sigh, his eyes becoming dull.

"Qingqing, that tea you sent me—my friends love to drink it." Xiao Sang hastily changed the topic.

"Haha, that's the best green tea company!" Qingqing grew livelier. "The owner is my friend now. Sangsang, what solution can you think of for this family issue? You read so many books."

"Let me think about it. Heaven doesn't close off to us all the ways out."

"For the past few days I've been looking forward to you coming back. I knew *you* would come up with a plan for what to do," Qingqing said admiringly.

"Your big sister is getting old."

"Sangsang, have you met someone suitable in the past few years?"

"How can I put it—maybe there'll be someone soon."

"Congratulations, Sangsang! Bring him back here soon."

"But I'm not sure yet." A smile floated across Xiao Sang's face.

"My sense is that this time isn't like in the past."

"Maybe. But our family having this problem now is a major blow."

At that moment there was a sound at the door. It was their dad back from shopping. He put down the shopping basket, and Qingqing promptly ran over to put away the items he'd bought.

"Dad, are you tired?" Xiao Sang asked.

"No. My health is still fine, only my spirits aren't too good."

Xiao Sang thought of her father's hardworking, straightforward life, and her eyes stung again.

The third afternoon since Xiao Sang had returned home, she and her father came back from the park and saw her mother waiting in the entryway as they entered the courtyard. She held a letter in her hand. Xiao Sang's heart started pounding.

"Sangsang, a letter for you! It's from Meng," her mom said excitedly.

Xiao Sang took the letter and placed it in her handbag. As she went upstairs with her parents, she wondered: "Why is Mom so excited? She probably thinks it's a letter from my boyfriend. I can tell she's been worried about me still being single."

Sitting in her bedroom she tore open the letter Heishi had sent her. Heishi's words were just as affable as himself: grown-up and poised.

We had just parted when I remembered about writing you a letter. You must be having a very pleasant time with your family now? But I hope this letter will embellish your happy days.

Yesterday I went to the Pigeon Book Club. Everyone mentioned you as if by arrangement, because you weren't there. Fei was uniquely complimentary: he called you the "queen" of Meng's reading world. Haha! He also said that only Han Ma's writing can compare in beauty with your reading. You two are the bravest people in literature. Fei has the keenest vision among us, so he could tell at just one glance what your worth is. I completely endorse my good friend's opinion.

In reality, I was informed by Uncle Yi about your literary views and your appreciation of literature. Before I invited you to the book club, there were many occasions when the idea to go see you took root in my mind, but I worried that you would think I was boring. I waited and waited, until one day I drummed up the courage to follow you . . . You know what happened next. Wasn't it a poor performance?

I wanted to tell you that when everyone at the book club praised you, I was surprised to feel as happy as if they were praising me! In my heart I thanked everyone on your behalf.

Regarding the plan for us to travel to the ocean together, for now I am closely observing my soul. I want my thoughts to develop, and then, after I am completely sure, I can put these thoughts into practice. See how pedantic I am. Re-

gardless, you are my lifelong friend. I remember every little thing that happened when we were together and also all of the help that you rendered me. I feel myself greatly elevated, changed for the good, since meeting you.

Now it's late at night, and I am in my room writing you a letter. The letter will go quickly from Meng to the capital, where you will receive it after a little more than a day has passed. I am imagining what you look like reading this letter and feel especially happy.—Heishi

Xiao Sang read Heishi's letter three times through and also inspected the back.

"My classmate Heishi's writing is flawless," she sighed.

Her emotions were awakened: it was a letter Heishi had written for her. And it also let her know what she wanted to know the most. How intimate! Xiao Sang cheerfully stood and went into the kitchen to help her mother.

"A letter from a good friend?" her mom asked.

"Yes, from my best friend, a man."

"Will he become my son-in-law?"

"I don't know yet, Mom, and your eagerness makes no difference. I'd already decided to stay single. But if I meet someone who I'm very, very partial to, I could also change my mind."

"This young man—you just got home, and his letter hurried after you. He seems to really like you."

"There are many kinds of liking; liking someone isn't the same as loving them."

"Oh, our generation didn't make so many distinctions. If you liked, then you loved, and you spent your lives together."

"Did you love Dad?"

"I must have loved him. I liked his honesty, his hard work. I only disliked one thing, which was that he saw money as all-important. But we had you two children, and there weren't major conflicts. Since he retired, though, he's had no sense of security and keeps worrying that we'll fall ill and have to spend money on treatment. So he considers every cent crucial and is afraid I'll spend money carelessly. You've seen how he's managing the money and makes our purchases himself every day. If I buy something he thinks we shouldn't buy, or the price is too high, he berates me and even loses his temper. So, Sangsang, when you find a husband, whatever else, don't pick a miser. You need to find a man who doesn't see money as important."

"Dad isn't a complete miser. Didn't you say he has no sense of security?"

"Hmm, what he has is some mental problems. Maybe it's because of retiring and then feeling lonely. Sangsang, you're the one he likes the most in our family. Why not wait until you're married and have him move in with you?"

"That would require planning. Besides, I still don't have a boyfriend. Just a moment ago you said that Dad sees money as all-important. Doesn't that mean he'd be interested in making money? He had a good salary when he was on the prospecting team. Let me think this over carefully."

"You were always a problem-solver—that's why your dad is so fond of you. Your coming back home gives me and your brother hope. Otherwise these days would really be difficult."

"I'll make inquiries first on my end. Also, I want to understand Dad's wishes."

"It seems as though reading novels is still really useful, Sangsang. You're so clearheaded and adaptable—this must be because of reading fiction."

"Mom, you should pick up books again. That way you won't just fight with Dad."

"Maybe. I go to extremes, and I threw all the books away on a whim."

Mother and daughter talked up to this point and stopped because Xiao Sang's father came up from downstairs.

He had brought the newspaper back from the mailbox. He sat on the sofa and started to read, but he hadn't read for long before he became drowsy, his head tilted, and he fell asleep on the sofa, the newspaper falling from his hand to the floor.

"You see your dad? He's always like this," Xiao Sang's mom quietly said to her.

Xiao Sang went into the living room and picked up a blanket to cover her father, not thinking that he would immediately wake up.

"How comfortable. I can fall asleep any time—I nap lightly," he explained.

"Dad, do you sleep well at night?"

"I can't say that I sleep well, but it's not too bad either. I always wake up a few times during the night. Once I'm up I can't go back to sleep for a while, and there's nothing to think about, so I get pessimistic. I've been sleeping a little better for a few nights since you came back."

"Then you should come with me to Meng. You'll sleep well with me there and won't be pessimistic."

"Is that a possibility?" Xiao Sang's father asked, looking wide-eyed at her.

"I'll give it a try, and let's see. I hope to find a long-term solution. We can always give it a try."

Xiao Sang saw her dad's eyes shine briefly before they became gloomy again. She knew he wasn't holding out any hope for his life. After a while he added dryly:

"Of course, it would be good to have a solution."

For the moment Xiao Sang didn't want to give her dad hope, because she knew that for someone like him stirring up hope and then extinguishing it would be dangerous.

That evening she dialed the department store manager's phone. Unfortunately she was away on business, and her husband answered. He told Xiao Sang that she would be back in five days. Putting down the phone, Xiao Sang sighed and opened the book she had brought. Uncle Yi's face seemed to suffuse the book. Xiao Sang missed Uncle Yi particularly on a night like this. If he had encountered a problem like hers, what would he do? Entranced, Xiao Sang thought of a few possibilities.

Xiao Sang didn't answer Heishi's letter right away, because her family was in turmoil, and she didn't want to tell him about the situation. Just let him think she was enjoying family cheer. Xiao Sang laughed bitterly. Then she told herself to brace her spirit to solve the problem and keep calm like Uncle Yi. She finished reading a chapter. Everything she read in the book was about how Uncle Yi would have approached things. How strange!

Xiao Sang slept until the middle of the night and then woke up when she heard the sound of movement in the living room.

She put on her clothes and felt her way in the dark to the living room, where she saw her father sitting on the sofa.

"Dad," she called, sitting down close to him.

"Sangsang," her dad quietly answered.

"What are you thinking about?"

"I'm not thinking about anything. I'm just happy."

Xiao Sang took hold of her father's hand, asking him again:

"Dad, you really don't blame me?"

"I don't blame you at all. It's my own problem."

"Then tell me, are you willing to change your life?"

"Of course I'm willing. But how can it change? I don't want to be a burden to you."

"Let's think of ways together."

"Sangsang is so filial, I'm pleased. All right, it's already three. Let's both go to sleep."

Because Xiao Sang hadn't written back, Heishi wrote another letter and mailed it to her.

Xiao Sang, I know you must be busy since returning to your parents' home, so I didn't expect you to write me back a letter right away. And I'm not at all busy right now, so I will just write some more to you.

My mother and her boyfriend Zhong (he lets me call him that) want to climb Mount Huang. They're in good spirits, and Zhong is an attentive man who will take good care of my mom. Maybe it's the opposite, and my mom will take care of him. Ha! My mother's said she will just continue living with Zhong and not marry him. She asked me what I thought about this. I said it was fine, or that it was also fine if someday she wanted to remarry. You see, my elderly mother is much more interesting than someone old-fashioned like me! Now the two of them are as close as body and shadow, always together, and when they're together they never run out of intimate things to talk about. At last I've experienced what "agreeable companionship" is like. One time the three of us went out for coffee and Zhong asked me when would I get married. I told him I don't even have a formal girlfriend. He said he'd already seen my girlfriend and that "no walls are impervious to secrets." Then he and my mom started laughing. I felt baffled. After a while my mom said: "Don't pressure young Hei. Water will find its course, and then he will tell us."

My mom is fairly optimistic, a side of her nature that was revealed once she and Zhong got together. I really feel glad for her. I know you've been concerned about my mother, too, which is why I'm telling you this. I think life is quietly transforming in a positive direction. I'm also much more optimistic than before.

As for the future, we can't necessarily see into it, but at least life is meaningful for now. Do you feel this way?

Now it's afternoon. The place where your family lives isn't far from my father's family. There are many scholartrees in those streets and parks. I imagine you walking under the trees with your parents, imagine you together in that atmosphere of warmth. This image relates to my image of your family from our classmate days. Isn't this a little strange?—Heishi

Xiao Sang thought: Heishi's letter is like himself, plain and succinct, and memorable. Did he write a letter to tell me indirectly that he still doesn't have a girlfriend, or to tell me that our relationship still isn't settled? Oh, Heishi, Heishi. Maybe there is a third possibility! She started to laugh.

Xiao Sang went into the living room and saw that Qingqing and Yangyang had arrived. Yangyang sat to one side, concentrating on a picture book. Qingqing smiled at Xiao Sang:

"Mom said you've had a letter from a good friend. She said that it's that same friend again."

"It's the same friend, but he hasn't reached the point of being our parents' son-in-law."

"I think that whoever falls in love with my sister won't give up so easily."

"It's too bad other people don't think like my brother."

"My sense is that this man knows who he's after. You're too cold. When looking for a spouse, good enough is enough."

"The less I worry, the better the outcome. Once I start worrying, things will go wrong."

"Hmm, my sister is deep and calculating. Do you plan to write him back?"

"Let him wait. My mind is entirely on the problem of Dad and Mom. I'm not in the mood for romance. Our parents have nothing to depend on—their only hope is you and me. You've done well, but I've been disappointing, and now I'm trying to make up for that. I'll give the store manager a call this evening. Don't let Dad know ahead of time."

"Maybe Dad's rescuer has arrived. He hasn't cared for you for nothing."

Xiao Sang showered, said she would go to bed a little early, and closed the door to her room. On the phone she exchanged greetings with her manager, asked about how things were, then rushed directly into her main topic. It went even better than she expected—her manager immediately agreed. She said there was a job as a night shift warehouse guard. The salary was relatively high, because it required being up at night to make inspections. The store had offered the position to many people, none of whom stayed for long. First, the job was dull, and second, they weren't willing to get up in the middle of the night. If Xiao Sang's father were sure that he could manage the job long-term, he could start right away. Xiao Sang told her manager that she would ask her father and answer in just a short while, if she waited.

"Dad! Dad!" Xiao Sang shouted with excitement and ran to the living room.

Her father was watching TV, but turned if off at seeing his daughter.

"There's a job—it's guarding the warehouse for my department store. You'd be on the night shift. Will you take it?"

"That's great! I will!"

"Will your health be up to it? You'll have to get up once during the night to make an inspection—"

"That's not a problem! I get up in the night now, even though I'm not on night shift. My health is very good!"

Xiao Sang's mother came over and asked her where he would live.

"Of course there'll be somewhere to stay. Wait until Dad is earning money, then let's buy a house in Meng!"

Xiao Sang returned to her bedroom, picked up the phone, and told the department store manager that her father had accepted the job and would soon head to Meng with her. Her manager said not to rush—you're still on vacation. Xiao Sang said she wouldn't finish her vacation—let's resolve my father's situation first. He's been almost sick with boredom because of not having a job.

When Xiao Sang finished her call and went back to the living room, her parents looked at her eagerly.

"It's settled, it's settled! Get ready right away. In two days I'm going back to Meng with Dad!"

"What about the housing for him?" her mom asked, still worrying.

"I know the building—the conditions aren't bad at all. But we'll need to buy an apartment. In the future I'll have you both living next door to me. Right, Dad?"

"Mm-hmm, right." Her dad nodded, embarrassed.

"Tomorrow I'm going to buy two new sets of clothing and shoes for your dad," her mom announced. "You can't look shabby when you get there. Our Sangsang needs to save face."

Oh, the excitement! Oh, what a sigh of relief! In the bedroom Xiao Sang took several deep breaths, then thought of Heishi. She immediately sat down to write him a letter. She told Heishi that she hadn't written him back because of some misfortunes in her family. Now the family's major problem was resolved, and she'd booked plane tickets for herself and her father to go back to Meng. When she returned she would give him a detailed account about what had happened with her family. Xiao Sang expressed deep gratitude to Heishi for the two letters he'd sent. She told him that his letters had brought her valuable information and given her more courage in life. That she could successfully solve her family's problems was a benefit of Heishi's assistance and influence on her. This trip had allowed her to understand many things. *I'm rushing into the nets of life, Heishi!* She ended with this statement.

Xiao Sang tossed back and forth in bed and couldn't sleep. Whether her dad would adapt to the location, the issue of how he would get along with people, the problem of nutrition for the elderly, and so on, went round and round in her brain. Her thoughts also turned to Heishi from time to time. Every time her thoughts turned toward him, a hint of warmth reached her face. Wasn't his being her best friend, after all, giving her the greatest support? On this trip she'd become more like Heishi without knowing it. This made her pleased with herself.

When Xiao Sang got up in the middle of the night, she heard her parents still talking quietly in their room. They must be so excited. This sudden transition could let them escape from a nightmare and anticipate a new life. She secretly resolved: in the future, after her mother moved to Meng, she must try to restore her habit of reading novels.

The next day the elderly couple finished breakfast and then went shopping. Xiao Sang cleaned up her room and exclaimed: the week had passed so busily, just like in a dream! During the years when she'd been alone and carefree and happy in Meng, her parents' household had met with disaster, while she had hardly known . . . If it weren't for her taking a vacation and visiting them, the family might have experienced a major disruption. Thinking of it now was frightening. She was almost thirty-six and had read so many books. How could she still behave like a naive young girl? It was disappointing! Xiao Sang bit her lip. She reflected, too, that as a result of this incident she'd recognized some of

Heishi's better qualities. It was because of these qualities that Uncle Yi had said people like Heishi were rare.

After a while Qingqing arrived with a chicken he'd brought as a gift. Xiao Sang told him what had happened the previous night, and hearing the news made him so happy he grinned open-mouthed. Sister and brother raised their voices, chatting as they cooked, their emotions running higher than ever before.

"This is a good omen. It seems like the greatest event in my sister's life will be settled soon, too," Qingqing abruptly changed the topic.

"Nonsense, superstition! There's no connection," Xiao Sang said.

"Only a fool would give up my sister, and that man isn't a fool!"

"He's no fool—I suspect he's too smart. People who are too intelligent find it hard to get along with other people."

"But not too intelligent and also not a fool—you're too hard to please!"

"Let nature take its course. Maybe something will happen soon, or it could be nothing after all."

"Sis, you're so pessimistic. Two letters in one week. How could it be nothing after all?"

"He's hard to understand. I'm not always sure of myself when I'm with him."

"You're thinking too much. I don't think so much. After you and Dad go, I'll just focus on waiting for your good news."

"I'll do my best."

Their parents didn't come back until that afternoon, carrying several large shopping bags. They said that they'd eaten snacks out, so the lunch Xiao Sang and Qingqing were preparing became dinner. Qingqing said in Xiao Sang's ear: "They haven't gone shopping together in years."

Shortly before dinner Chun and Yangyang also came over. Qingqing said to Yangyang:

"Grandpa and your aunt are going south. Will you miss them?"

Yangyang ran over and leaped into her grandfather's arms, shouting: "I won't let Grandpa go!" and then starting to cry.

Chun had to drag her into the kitchen.

Qingqing shook his head and said:

"She isn't used to saying goodbye."

Their father's eyes were red, and he kept repeating: "This child, this child . . ."

At the dining table the family didn't say much, just urged one another to eat. The strain from their days of distress wasn't entirely gone, even though they could heave a sigh of relief now. Xiao Sang was relaxed in comparison. She was more sure of things, because she was bringing her father back to the familiar city Meng. Her close friends were there, and no problems that couldn't be resolved.

"Mom, wait until Dad settles in, then come as soon as possible," Xiao Sang said.

Their mom nodded firmly. She couldn't speak for excitement.

"I'll be waiting for you to join our store's reading group. Dad, I've asked my coworkers, and you can go to the sailors' club to play croquet. Many elderly people buy annual memberships," Xiao Sang continued.

"My family will hurry over to Meng when we have vacation!" Qingqing held back tears as he spoke these words.

After they ate, Xiao Sang's mom made her dad try on his new clothes and shoes for everyone to see.

"I never imagined that Dad could still be so handsome! Look at this figure. The store manager will be so happy!" Xiao Sang said.

She started to applaud. Her father, full of composure, walked in a circle around the room. He was stately, like a model.

"If a couple of thieves come, Dad will scare them away!" Qingqing exaggerated. He sighed and added, "I wish I could go along to see you start your new job."

"Don't be sad. You'll have plenty of chances later on," Xiao Sang consoled her brother.

Then Yangyang came over and hugged Xiao Sang and kissed her. She said with hesitation:

"Aunt . . ."

"Yangyang wants to whisper to her aunt." Xiao Sang put her ear close to the little girl.

"Wait until we're on vacation. We'll go to the south to see you and Grandpa," she said in a very small voice.

"Good! It's agreed, let's shake hands!"

At last Xiao Sang was bringing her father back to Meng. For this week and more, the family's moods had been like riding a rollercoaster. Now things would gradually quiet down a little, although her mother and brother's agitation wasn't gone. They would be calm only once Xiao Sang's father gave his report of arriving safe and sound, without incident.

The night before they set out, Xiao Sang lay in the dark saying many things to Heishi into the air. She was grateful many times over for his invisible help, because it was his influence that had prevented her nature from moving in a bad direction. She could still remember the conversation they'd had beneath the large tree in her courtyard, when he told her about his family's misfortunes. Why had he wanted to tell her about that? It might have been caused by extreme loneliness pouring from his soul. Uncle Yi understood Heishi, but Uncle Yi was a man, after all, so Heishi would be embarrassed to share everything he felt in front of him. That evening Heishi had felt like he needed someone of the opposite sex to hear this outpouring, and so he'd thought of Xiao Sang . . . but maybe it wasn't by accident. Could there have been some other factors? He had shared his feelings for a while and then, when he finished, just stood and said goodbye. How strange, when at the time they had only recently become reacquainted. Heishi had said she'd always been on his mind. Actually, hadn't it been the same for her with him? If Heishi hadn't come looking for her, she and he would have drifted like two lonely little boats in the large city of Meng, each in their own sphere. Uncle Yi had led to them meeting again. Heishi had learned incidentally about his former classmate from Uncle Yi, then let his thoughts run wild. But there must have been something that prevented him from coming to find her. He'd hesitated repeatedly, until at last he'd drummed up the courage to follow her. This had been the overall process, which he had told her in part, but far from the whole. Heishi ought to have good intuition, considering the lessons learned from his special experience of the world. So his opinion of her had most likely never altered. Then what kind of opinion of her did he have? Was there a subtext beneath those enchanting words that he said to her? Were there certain subtexts that led to his being neither here nor there with her? At this thought, Xiao Sang immediately stopped and accused herself in her soul: here I go again. This kind of guessing is meaningless, and it's also unnecessary. Heishi was a true friend who at any time would be there to help and support her. Wasn't this enough? His mindset was attractive to her—she was attracted by him. So just let nature find its course. Why keep speculating? He had attracted Qiaozi before, and didn't she still praise him constantly? Xiao Sang should treat Heishi like Qiaozi did. She made up her mind that from now on she wouldn't be short-tempered with him; she would be candid as far as possible and not be calculating. With someone like Heishi that would be shameless, and she should believe that Heishi wouldn't be calculating with her. Everything he did came from his principles, which must be good principles. After all, if Heishi were unprincipled, could he be so attractive to Xiao Sang?

"Very good," Xiao Sang continued, "I have two close friends who are the protecting spirits of my life. I know a lot of people envy me: Xiao Ma, and Han Ma, and Qiaozi . . ." She steeped again in the warmth Uncle Yi and Heishi stirred up in her heart.

Xiao Sang was fairly sure about her dad, because she knew he loved her deeply. For him the most difficult moment had already passed.

She kept tossing and turning for a while about Heishi, and for a while about Uncle Yi, and for a while about her father, until dawn when she finally went to sleep. But she was soon woken up by her mother. She got up in a single bound, not feeling a bit tired, and instead sensing that her spirits were invigorated.

At the airport entrance Qingqing held on to his father and said over and over:

"Dad, when you go out at night you must be sure that you can see the way clearly. You should carry a big flashlight. Call the police right away if you encounter anything . . . Also, don't walk too quickly. Don't go onto roads where the streetlights are out . . ."

Their father nodded along. His thoughts were on the flight, because this was his first time taking a plane, and he was incredibly excited. Their mother watched her husband and seemed to be recognizing him anew.

Xiao Sang and her father were eventually seated in the cabin.

"Dad, you look like a different person, full of spirit, dressed like this."

"Your mom picked it out: clothes, shoes, scarf, hat. She has refined taste."

"Yes, Mom has a strong aesthetic sense. I'm so far behind her."

"You're not behind her, because she taught you."

Xiao Sang sat beside her dad contentedly, holding one of his large hands like when she was little, pressing her cheek against his palm.

"My princess, you will have to marry a good man," he suddenly said. "You deserve the best."

"I don't even have a boyfriend."

"You can't start to compromise because of getting older. He has to be the best," her father stressed again.

"Don't worry, Dad. If I can't find someone suitable, then I won't get married and can keep you company for the rest of my life."

"That's no good, you have to keep looking. My sense is that someone has his eye on you."

"Ha, my dad and my brother are both making predictions. Wait and see: it will soon be confirmed one way or the other."

The flight attendant brought them fruit juice. Xiao Sang watched her dad sip the juice like a child, smacking his lips, and couldn't help but enjoy the sight. "My life is interwoven with life in books," she told herself.

Father and daughter disembarked, picked up their luggage, and went to board the airport bus, each pushing a suitcase.

"Xiao Sang!" a familiar voice rang out.

It was Heishi waving at the exit. Xiao Sang felt the blood rush to her face.

He ran over, dressed in work clothes.

"This is my friend Heishi, this is my father," Xiao Sang introduced them.

Smiling, her dad looked at Heishi.

"Mr. Shu, hello! I came to help you with the luggage." Heishi took her father's pushcart.

"I never imagined that you would come to meet us," Xiao Sang said, her heart welling with gratitude to Heishi.

"You told me the flight number in your letter, so I came."

"Good, good! The young man's healthy, and he's handsome . . . ," Xiao Sang's father nodded and said.

"Dad—" Xiao Sang complained, interrupting him.

The three of them got off the bus. They went to the Crown Department Store first to put down their luggage.

The store manager came over and, pretending to be amazed, said in a loud voice:

"Xiao Sang's father is so good-looking!"

Her surrounding coworkers started to boom with laughter, but Xiao Sang's father stayed calm.

Then one of her coworkers brought them to the housing that had been arranged.

The apartment had two rooms and a kitchen in the back. From now on her father would live here and also be on duty here. He looked at the new items on the bed with satisfaction. Xiao Sang told him to try to rest, then in a while she and Heishi would take him out to eat.

Heishi helped Xiao Sang carry her suitcase as they walked together through the department store doors. Xiao Ma unexpectedly followed them out.

"Xiao Sang, Heishi, we should have a gathering this week," she said.

"All right," Xiao Sang nodded in agreement. "I'll contact all of you about which day."

As they rode the bus, Xiao Sang said to Heishi:

"Xiao Ma has changed—she's become steadier. She's growing up quickly."

"I think so, too. She's a very kind-hearted young woman. Xiao Sang, did something change with your family?"

Xiao Sang told Heishi simply about what had happened with her family. Her narration was calm, but after hearing her out he seemed moved. When she'd finished, he just said:

"Xiao Sang, I very much admire your way of handling things. You and I are both willing to take action, like it says in the book—you went from Meng to the capital, and entered another of life's nets."

"We live in an era that is advancing by leaps and bounds," Xiao Sang said. Then her expression looked a little dazed.

She unconsciously glanced at the windows of Uncle Yi's home on returning to her courtyard.

Heishi picked up her suitcase, and they went upstairs one in front, one behind. Reaching Uncle Yi's doorway Xiao Sang pointed it out to Heishi, and he smiled.

She pulled open the curtains as they entered the apartment, illuminating the small living room.

"Your home is so clean, there's no dust on the table or chairs." Heishi sat down.

"That's because I've only been gone for a little over a week."

Heishi stood up to leave, but Xiao Sang held him back. She wanted to make tea for him.

“It’s good tea that my brother sent. My dad will still be sleeping anyway, no need to hurry.”

So Heishi sat back down. He looked uneasy. Xiao Sang thought: “Here we go again.”

Sipping her tea, she said:

“Heishi, don’t mind about what my father said. Older people love to make a big deal out of nothing.”

“Just the opposite, I liked listening to Mr. Shu praise me. I was even a bit pleased with myself.”

“Really? Really?” Xiao Sang looked at him teasingly.

“Of course, really.”

“Then I’ll ask my dad to flatter you more later on.”

They both started to laugh. Xiao Sang pointed to the floor, and Heishi smiled. He asked her whether they should invite Uncle Yi out to eat. She signaled no with a movement of her hand.

“I’m worried that my dad might feel awkward, when he’s only just getting used to you. There’ve been so many new things for him to experience today.”

“I’m honored. Today I should treat, the host’s privilege.”

“All right. From now on I’ll keep letting you treat, until you’re poor.”

When they arrived back at the duty room apartment, Xiao Sang’s father was already up and had folded the new blankets neatly.

“I went for a shower. The water is so hot, it’s delightful! Your store manager is a very fine woman. I was planning to be on duty tonight, but she insisted that I rest for a couple of days first. She told me I need to become familiar with the surroundings and get household supplies,” he said.

Grinning, Xiao Sang took his arm and walked out to the street. Heishi brought father and daughter to his favorite restaurant.

After they took their seats at the table, Xiao Sang noticed her father mumbling something.

“Dad, what are you saying?”

“I was saying: better if I had come sooner. If I’d come a few years ago, so many things would be different.”

“It’s not too late now. Many things will be different because you’ve come to live near me.”

“That’s exactly what I mean. Oh, I’m so stupid, oh.”

Xiao Sang suddenly realized the meaning hidden in her father's words, and she blushed.

Heishi was listening off to the side, smiling.

"You two are keeping me guessing—I don't understand," he hastily declared.

"Once I met you I felt that I knew you so well," Xiao Sang's father said, turning toward him.

"Dad, you should flatter him more. He just said what he likes most is hearing you flatter him." Xiao Sang made a silly face.

"We should plan on seeing each other often. Whenever I see him, I'll flatter him. He deserves my praise."

They ate the meal with delight. It was homestyle food, but cooked exquisitely. Xiao Sang's father flattered Heishi some more, including praising him for being capable and thoughtful.

When they had just finished eating, Heishi said that he needed to leave for his work shift.

"He's a good match for you, Sangsang. Have you known each other long? Two years? Three years? It would have been better if I'd come here sooner—maybe you would already be married," her father said, watching him go.

Xiao Sang smiled without speaking. She was pleased her father was so talkative, and she was enjoying his doting affection.

They went to the supermarket to buy some household supplies, then went back to the duty room. On the way they ran into several of Xiao Sang's coworkers, who all greeted her father enthusiastically. Arm in arm with her dad, she noticed his expression of contentment and pride in her. Xiao Sang rested for a little while before telling him:

"I should go back to my apartment to give Mom a detailed report on the situation. In the evening you should eat at the store's cafeteria. The food's quite good. If you run into any problems just give me a call."

"I won't run into any problems. It's very convenient here. A time-tested establishment with solid finances. Everyone has been kind to me. I've looked over the warehouse, and there's a lot of merchandise. I have a significant responsibility."

Xiao Sang chuckled and said: "You're really proactive—you've made a complete survey of our store this quickly."

She returned to her courtyard, went up to the third floor, and knocked on Uncle Yi's door.

"You're a little thinner. You must have had a fun time at your parents' home," Uncle Yi said, beaming.

Xiao Sang turned to the armchair and sat down, suddenly tired.

"It's hard to tell you everything at once, Uncle Yi." Unexpectedly, she wanted to pour out her feelings.

"Come on, first drink some tea. These snacks are really good, have something to eat. I heard from Xiao Ma that you and your father came back together. She said he's found a security job at your department store. This is a very good thing."

"It is a very good thing. But the reason for it isn't so good."

"You don't need to worry about the reason. It's good now, everything will be fine. You're like the heroines from ancient times. You young people are much stronger than our generation. It's gratifying!"

At Uncle Yi's words Xiao Sang abandoned the idea of sharing her feelings and overcame her weariness. She straightened up and cheerfully said to him:

"If I've made any progress in life, it's all because of your influence. Today I've finally found my way, and learned how to read books and how to take action."

"Speaking of reading, recently I discovered another good book. Look, it's this book, *XXX* . . . I've already read it once. You take it to read, I've bought another copy."

"Thank you, Uncle Yi. In the capital I thought of you often. I kept asking myself: if Uncle Yi were to encounter this situation, how would he handle it? I brought you with me, never losing you."

Her eyes twinkled as she spoke.

Smiling, he watched her and gently nodded.

Xiao Sang went back home, took a shower, drank a glass of milk, and sat at the table to give her mother a call.

"Mom, everything's fine. Dad's already settled in—he's really able to adapt. He likes the store and is also talking more."

"Oh, that's great, Sangsang. I'll tell you something, but don't tell your dad. After you left, I went back to the empty house and couldn't stop crying. I hated myself for being so useless, still needing to burden you at this age, and waste your time and energy . . . Ah, I just cried for a while."

"Mom, you sound so serious. Isn't everything fine now? How is this wasting time? Shouldn't I do something for you and Dad? I can't even say how much I regret not taking care of you or asking how you were doing sooner. Mom, Dad likes it so much here. You and he will be reunited soon. He said he should have come here earlier, so he could play matchmaker for me, so I wouldn't be single. Dad's acting young again."

"Does that mean the man who sent you letters . . . ?" her mother asked excitedly.

"Yes. His name is Heishi. Dad flattered him to his face and tries to praise him to the skies."

"Oh—wonderful! Wonderful! Your dad's back to normal—he used to be warm-hearted. You've found the solution. Wait until he's worked for a few days and gotten used to things, then I'll arrange for somewhere to live and move there. I'll tell Qingqing the news right away. It seems like your greatest event in life is also on its way. We will be doubly blessed in this household."

"It seems like there's been a little progress, but I can't be sure."

"I won't rush you. Qingqing said we need to let nature take its course."

After the call, Xiao Sang felt weary at last.

She slept tranquilly until waking up at nine the next morning.

Heishi had said goodbye to Xiao Sang and her father, then came again the next day. He gave her father a raincoat, one he said was issued by his work unit every year, so that there was no end of wearing them. It rained a lot in the south. Xiao Sang's father could wear it while he patrolled outside.

Her dad, smiling, stared at Heishi until he was embarrassed, then finally asked him:

"What does your mother call you?"

"She's called me young Hei ever since I was little."

"Then from now on I'll call you young Hei."

"All right."

Once Heishi left, Xiao Sang said:

"Young Hei is what his mother calls him. Wouldn't it be better for you to call him Heishi?"

"But he likes me calling him young Hei. Young Hei, Sangsang, what a match," he laughed.

"Oh, Dad, Dad, you leave me helpless."

After a while one of Xiao Sang's coworkers came to bring her a message from the store manager, who wanted to invite father and daughter out to lunch that day.

"I haven't even done any work yet and just like that she honors me. Honestly, it's too much," her father said.

"Dad, your coming to work at the department store solves a major problem for the manager."

"Really, Sangsang? I'll be happy to make an effort for a good manager like her."

Xiao Sang passed along to him the news from their family in the capital. After hearing it, he said nothing for a long while.

Then he told Xiao Sang that for the past two days he'd been regretting what had happened before. It was like waking up from a dream—he couldn't sleep when he remembered how he had hurt her mother. When she moved to Meng, he would treat her well and make her happy.

"Your mother makes the greater contribution to the family," he said. "Later on, if I lose my temper again, just kick me a few times to remind me. Now that I have work to do, I'll be busy and cheerful and won't lose my temper."

"You'll be earning a good salary. We can buy a house in the city," Xiao Sang encouraged him.

"I was thinking that, too. When the time comes, we'll be one big family. The three of us, and also that, that, haha, I won't say. I just look forward to someday."

That day Xiao Ma had told Uncle Yi about Xiao Sang and her father coming to the department store together. But she didn't mention that Heishi had been with them. She wasn't concealing this intentionally, just overlooking it. Afterward she felt she had done well. She was no longer the little girl who loved to make a big deal out of nothing—a grown woman would act this way. Look at Uncle Yi, who didn't show surprise and hadn't asked about Xiao Sang's father coming to work at their store. This was how to behave. She needed to learn, eventually becoming cultured and considerate of other people.

Xiao Ma's relationship with Uncle Yi had progressed over these days of exerting herself to read and delving into the study of literature. When they were together they were on closer and closer terms. They talked about literature, life, and their experiences. The topics grew more varied. Uncle Yi hadn't met a young woman like Xiao Ma before. He thought that she was unbelievably perceptive, in an emotional sense, even though she hadn't read many books. Her halting accounts were like the sounds of nature, able to pierce the human soul. As for Xiao Ma, she was enchanted beyond compare by these exchanges with Uncle Yi. She wasn't trying to like everything he liked, but instead believed from the bottom of her heart that Uncle Yi's state was also her own ideal. She had been pursuing this state, first discovering a few traces of it through Xiao Sang, whom she eventually followed to Uncle Yi. Xiao Ma had fallen deeply in love with Uncle Yi without Xiao Sang realizing it. She'd made up her mind from the first day to never, ever surrender. This young woman, who hadn't known a father's love, didn't need to be taught her plan for how to pursue Uncle Yi, because she felt that he was destined for her, and that her life would only be good and she would only gain the happiness she desired through being with him. Xiao Ma had been with quite a few young men before, but she'd felt dissatisfied with them and thought that wasn't the kind of love she wanted. She hadn't been aware yet of what she actually wanted. Until sitting in Uncle Yi's study, listening closely to him discuss literature with Xiao Sang, when a window in the depths of her soul finally opened. That was what she wanted! She wanted to have long talks with Uncle Yi like Xiao Sang did, to enter into such a joyous and happy state. She saw how far away it was—she knew that she must make an extraordinary effort to approach that state. It wasn't too hard for her, because what she sought was what she wanted most. Didn't even Uncle Yi think she had a natural talent? Now she had no other choice but to desperately demonstrate her gift.

A turning point came unexpectedly, during the period when Xiao Sang went to the capital.

Xiao Ma and Uncle Yi had been discussing parts of *XXXX* in his study for three hours until they were both lightheaded. But they weren't out of ideas yet.

"Let's go to the bar and have a glass of wine," Uncle Yi proposed, "then come back for dinner. We can make steamed carp."

"Wonderful! What a heavenly life!"

As Uncle Yi and Xiao Ma walked into the bar, she saw Heishi sitting at the counter. She moved close to Uncle Yi's ear and quietly said: "Look, Heishi . . ."

They slowly walked over to him. Uncle Yi patted Heishi on the shoulder.

"You've come here to relax, too," Uncle Yi said.

"Mm-hmm. You and Xiao Ma are here, too. What a coincidence!" His eyes shone.

But his face seemed tired, which was unusual for him.

"Here, a glass of wine for each of us," Uncle Yi said to the server. "Heishi, have another drink."

"I can't drink any more," Heishi waved to him. "Just two glasses. Any more and I'll be drunk."

Heishi said he had to go now because his mom was waiting for him at home. He added something about having a drink with them next time. Then he went to pay his bill.

After Heishi left, Uncle Yi and Xiao Ma stared at each other uncertainly. Actually, Xiao Ma understood, but she didn't want to tell Uncle Yi. She'd vowed not to gossip any more about her friends' private business. She knew that Xiao Sang wasn't back from visiting her family, and that Heishi's behavior probably had something to do with Xiao Sang. "Things must be difficult for him," she told herself.

Uncle Yi and Xiao Ma drank slowly while they continued their discussion. Under the stimulation of the good wine, Xiao Ma became a fountain of literary ideas, her brilliant remarks arriving in waves. Even Uncle Yi was astonished at her hidden potential.

"You should write this down. It could be lecture notes for a literature class," he said.

"But, Uncle Yi, my writing style isn't good enough." Xiao Ma was bewildered.

"Style can be learned through practice. The more you write the better," Uncle Yi encouraged her.

"Now I feel like I'm soaring. Thank you, Uncle Yi."

He looked appreciatively at red-cheeked Xiao Ma, his expression almost like he was in a trance.

They hadn't sat there for long when he proposed going home to cook. Xiao Ma agreed with pleasure.

While they were busy in the kitchen, Uncle Yi suddenly asked her:

"Xiao Ma, you are always coming over to my place. Doesn't your family mind?"

"My family is just my mother and two younger sisters. My sisters have their own problems. As for my mom, she's been through hardships, and now she's hopeful that I will achieve happiness. I'm almost thirty, so she trusts me," Xiao Ma answered frankly. She paused for a moment, then added:

"Uncle Yi, I won't hurry you, but I want to make you fall in love with me."

When she said this, he actually got red in the face. She felt so happy, since she hadn't seen him blush before. Xiao Ma controlled herself and helped Uncle Yi prepare the food in an orderly way. After a long while he finally said:

"Xiao Ma, I don't dare speak to you."

"No need to think it over, just say whatever is in your heart."

"All right."

Uncle Yi saw Xiao Ma out on her way home. As they walked along the river, she told him:

"My mom's heard rumors, but she doesn't criticize me. She just wants me to be careful, to keep an eye out, and to think things over."

"Your mother's marvelous," Uncle Yi said, "but our relationship hasn't reached that stage, has it? You need more time. No matter what happens in the future, I will always be your most dependable friend."

"You're right. But I'm not the one who needs more time, you are. Never mind, it's all the same. I'm willing to wait. I'm busy studying now—it's been the most fulfilling time of my life."

She hopped onto the bus and waved to Uncle Yi standing under the streetlight.

When Xiao Ma was back at her small apartment, her emotions still rose and fell like a tide. Suddenly she thought of Heishi and Xiao Sang's affair. "Dear Xiao Sang, could you have broken my dear Heishi's heart?" Intuitively she knew that Xiao Sang must have stayed in contact with Heishi after she left . . . Xiao Ma felt agitated for Xiao Sang. She even had a strange dream in which Xiao Sang wanted to break off her friendship with Heishi, and Xiao Ma desperately defended him. "You cannot surrender him!" she shouted aloud, waking herself up. "How strange," she told herself, "maybe I'm saying that I cannot surrender Uncle Yi? I won't surrender him, of course." She started to laugh, "Today was my happiest day ever. I've matured, gained Uncle Yi's approval, and am nearing my goal one step at a time. Because I'm happy, I'm wishing for

Xiao Sang to be happy. Heishi loves her so much!" Xiao Ma tossed and turned until the middle of the night before falling asleep.

Three days later Xiao Sang brought her father and also Heishi to the department store. Xiao Ma blossomed with joy when she saw this scene! But afterward she couldn't ever find time to meet with them, because she was busy reading, taking notes, then seeking instruction from Uncle Yi . . . She was simply mad with busyness!

"Xiao Ma, you haven't been back for a long time. Your sisters are never home either. You're all in relationships. I'm the only one left over, an old woman with no one to love." Xiao Ma's mom was a little reproachful.

"I'm not dating, Mom—I'm pushing myself to read. My goal is to give lectures on literature at the Youth Literary Research Institute," Xiao Ma said.

"Good, I'm in support of your reading. I regret reading so little when I was young, and now every day I read what you're reading . . . Let me ask: is he highly educated? Do you think you will be able to keep up with him? Isn't there a generation gap between you?"

"Uncle Yi is highly learned. When I read the commentaries he's written for literary magazines, the blood rushes to my head. Of course, I don't understand it all yet. It's not a generation gap, it's because I began late. I'll be able to keep up with him in the future. I'm determined to reach Xiao Sang's level . . ."

"Then, he loves you very much?"

"Loves me? No, he hasn't fallen in love with me yet. But I can tell that he likes me very much."

"He doesn't love you?" Xiao Ma's mom said with disappointment. "Who wouldn't love you? What is he thinking?"

"Oh, Mom, it isn't like that. Uncle Yi is a learned man. He's not like the boys I went out with before, who were so wrapped up with me right after we met. Uncle Yi said he's giving me time to consider. Everything will come with time. We could be partners body and soul, don't you understand?"

"So that's how it is. I was just frightened, thinking you were the only one in love."

Xiao Ma started to laugh, her charming face glowing pink.

"Every day is like a holiday for me now, and at the same time I'm trying extremely hard to study. I'll become educated like Xiao Sang someday. I've been so busy I haven't been able to come see you very often."

"Never mind, Xiao Ma. I'm also trying hard to read. If not for anything else, then for when you live with Uncle Yi in the future, so I can have some slight conversation with him."

"Thank you, Mom. But Uncle Yi, oh, he can have a conversation with you even if you don't read books. He's so understanding, so . . . In the future when you meet him you'll know. Mom, let me ask, do you think I've changed a lot in five months?"

"I think you've transformed. You were always the most intelligent one in our family, and now when you start talking even I can't understand right away. But I'm happy, it's wonderful that my daughter is making daily progress! You should also guide your sisters to do better. Don't let them marry just anyone like I did."

"All right, I'll bring some books for them to read."

At noon mother and daughter shared a large bowl of sparerib and lotus soup, eating until they were full.

"Do you still remember what happened to you in first grade?" her mother asked her.

"What happened? Can you remind me?"

"When I went to pick you up, I had to stand waiting for a long time outside the school entrance. Suddenly I saw you running out desperately with a large group of boys chasing you. Your face was covered in sweat. You told me that they'd been trying to hit you. I led you away, my heart bleeding for you! When you were little you were terribly skinny and always getting sick."

"Mom, you should find a partner again. You still look so young."

"I don't want to, I just want to be by myself in peace and quiet. Besides, I'm planning to read more books, and this takes time and energy. I want to live next door to one of my three daughters."

"Mom, if I succeed with Uncle Yi, you can move into his building. That way we can discuss literature together."

"Good, I'll look forward to that day."

"There's something I forgot to tell you: Uncle Yi said you're a marvelous mother."

"Me, marvelous? What?" Xiao Ma's mom seemed stunned and started to weep.

"Mom, why are you crying? He was flattering you."

"I know, I know. Thank him for me."

Even more tears flowed from her eyes, until she'd used up half a pack of tissues.

"Xiao Ma . . . you've gotten onto the right path. As your mother, I'm so happy . . . ," she sobbed.

"Don't cry, Mom. I love you, you're the best mom on Earth."

They heard footsteps coming from the hallway. It was the older of Xiao Ma's younger sisters coming home.

Their mom hastily ran to the bathroom to wash her face.

"Yanzhi, where are you coming back from? Did you enjoy yourself?" Xiao Ma asked her sister.

Yanzhi tumbled onto the sofa, complaining in a loud voice:

"I'm so bored, I don't know how to enjoy myself."

"Don't you have a job? When your work is done, you can have as much fun as you want. And you're still not happy?"

"What kind of job is that—looking after a group of children. I've been thinking of quitting. Every day I look forward to getting off work, but then after work I have nothing to do. I just date randomly. Sis, I heard that you're with an old teacher now, congratulations! I don't understand, though: why did you want someone so old? You're very pretty, and young."

"Let's not talk about my affairs. What do you plan to do once you quit? Get married?"

"I haven't thought about that yet. I don't want to get married, just to have fun."

"Then you're not allowed to quit! Mom's getting older and can't keep taking care of you. You have to take care of yourself," Xiao Ma berated her loudly.

"All right, all right. Don't get angry, sis, I'm scared. I won't quit, I'll keep the job at the preschool. It's not like I can do anything else . . ."

"I already spoke with Mom. You and Xiao Hong need to start taking care of yourselves. Don't think you can always rely on Mom. If either of you want to quit your jobs, then move out of the house," Xiao Ma announced decisively.

"My god, you've become bold! 'Knowledge is power'—the saying is true. I want knowledge, too. Ah, but who's going to teach me?"

"The next time I come back I'll bring a big pile of books for you and Xiao Hong to read. You could both also join my department store's reading group. It's full of knowledgeable young people."

"OK, I'll listen to you, and Xiao Hong will, too. I know I've been behaving badly. This is all because my life has no purpose. Xiao Hong and I have a poor foundation."

"No one is born with a good foundation. It will come with time."

"Sis, it seems like your boyfriend is pretty fascinating. You're behaving differently. Is it because of him?"

"I said don't talk about my affairs. I will do the best I can to help you both." Xiao Ma kept a straight face.

At this moment their mother came out. She'd heard the sisters' conversation.

"You and Xiao Hong need to listen to what your big sister says. Don't behave so badly," she told Yanzhi. "I worked hard to raise you, and now I want to retire. You won't be able to rely on me even if you want to. I'm going to study in my retirement and fulfill myself."

"I understand, Mom. I promise I won't quit, and with Xiao Ma's help I'll try hard to study," Yanzhi said.

The sisters sat down one on each side close to their mom, just like when they were little. Their mother had been a mountain of support. Now they were healthy grown women, while their mom was getting older by the day, thinner and smaller than before. Xiao Ma and Yanzhi both realized this.

A couple of weeks passed busily for Xiao Sang. She kept worrying that her father wouldn't adjust to his new life. Reality proved that her apprehensions were usually excessive. He not only adjusted to life in Meng, he also showed himself to be resilient and became familiar right away with the people around him, like they were old friends. At two in the morning he got up to patrol for an hour, then returned to his room to sleep. This wasn't difficult for him. He said that when he came back from his inspection he could get back to sleep once he lay down, all the way through until he got up at eight-thirty in the morning. "This job is made for me," he said. What he liked most was taking the opportunity to shower when there was no one else in the shower room. He talked about how the hot water was so good, making showering delightful. He also enjoyed standing by the cash register to watch Xiao Sang work, although he only went to watch her a few times because he was afraid of what the people in the store would think. "Meng is so much better than the capital," he said again and again to Xiao Sang.

Xiao Sang felt relieved, so then she thought of Heishi again.

Recently, as if by arrangement, she and Heishi would meet at her father's room every couple of days. Xiao Sang secretly thought that her father had become Heishi's excuse. One moment he'd come to give her dad rainboots, the next moment he'd come back to bring him something to eat. Before this he'd rarely gone to where she lived. Was he afraid that if he met her alone, their relationship would become an item? But it didn't seem like that, because now her father was obviously treating Heishi like a member of the family and before long might urge them to get married. Xiao Sang didn't know how this transition had come about and didn't try to guess. She even whispered in private: let's get married, just get married. Hadn't she had her eye on Heishi for a long time? It was just that before she hadn't wanted to admit it. Of course, it had been Heishi first of all who wasn't willing to admit it. She couldn't figure it out then, just like she couldn't figure out the cause of his transformation now. Thinking this, Xiao Sang again felt that her father was her lucky star. Heishi's manner had transformed once her dad arrived. Now all of her coworkers at the store considered Heishi her fiancé and sometimes made jokes, and, when they did, Heishi looked like he was enjoying it. Naturally Xiao Sang enjoyed it, too. After experiencing the changes in her family, she felt profoundly that Heishi was the man she wanted to marry. There was no one who was a better fit for her. The fog enveloping him had vanished, and now she finally knew that she and he were "engraved on each other's hearts."

Finally the day for the gathering of the Pigeon Book Club arrived. Heishi called Xiao Sang and said: "Meet at the old place." The old place meant the bus stop. Heishi's voice on the phone didn't sound in any way different.

Yet, riding the bus, Xiao Sang suddenly began to feel excited and a little nervous. Why? She'd only missed one book club meeting; she'd come back to Meng right away. Everyone ought to be happy. Was she nervous, then, not because of her book friends, but because of Heishi? Heishi was the same Heishi, only his relationship with her was a little more intimate than before. What was there to be nervous about? He wasn't going to devour her. Nonetheless, Xiao Sang couldn't relax.

Her bus reached the stop. Heishi was waving to her. He walked over and casually put his arm around her waist.

"I'll take you along a new road," he said in her ear.

Xiao Sang held close to his body. She whispered to herself: "It's Heishi."

After a while he turned with her into an alleyway with no streetlights. There was a high wall on one side of the alley, and on the other side stood a long row of dark brick, tile-roofed houses. Scholartrees had been planted out in front of all the buildings. The sky wasn't dark yet. Feeble lamplight shone from the windows of the slightly antiquated houses, so that, without looking carefully, she would have thought the lights weren't on. Xiao Sang heard Heishi saying that it was all sailors' families living in these houses.

"Oh." This surprised Xiao Sang.

They slowed their steps in unison. They heard the cooing of pigeons coming from inside the buildings, as if every household raised pigeons. The pigeon coos were gentle and a little suggestive.

"Aunt Fang's home is up ahead," Heishi said quietly.

Suddenly he let go of Xiao Sang, held her face in both hands, and they kissed under the scholartrees.

It was a long kiss. Xiao Sang felt like she was about to faint. She clutched Heishi close as if they were drowning. The sky had grown dark, and that house under the tree wasn't lamplit, so maybe the sailor hadn't come home yet. Their bodies trembled slightly in the darkness.

Xiao Sang slowly came to and felt Heishi kissing her neck. He was gasping, calling every once in a while: "Xiao Sang . . ." They both trembled violently.

Xiao Sang thought: "I want to kiss him, too, for a long time I've just wanted to kiss him."

Then she undid the buttons of Heishi's jacket and kissed him from his neck down to his chest . . .

Eventually, they heard a noise at the entrance to the alleyway. They sobered up at the same time.

"Let's go to Aunt Fang's, OK?" Heishi was saying.

"OK."

They walked forward a few steps and reached her doorway. The door was half-open, so Heishi lightly knocked and said:

"Aunt Fang, it's me, Heishi."

A light in the room immediately turned on. Aunt Fang cheerfully let them into the building.

"Will Heishi and Xiao Sang get married soon?" she asked.

"How did you know?" Heishi asked.

"I can tell. Also, Uncle Lan told me yesterday."

The elderly woman brought out snacks and wanted them to sit down to have some tea.

"We won't stay, Aunt Fang. Our friends are waiting for us at the book club. Next time we'll come for a visit."

Heishi walked out embracing Xiao Sang. Before going very far, with one turn, they reached the street of used bookstores. He told her that the quiet alleyway they'd just been in was called Sailors' Home.

"Such an unforgettable place! Those pigeons are reporting that all is well," Xiao Sang gently said.

"Yes. The sailors are back home. You and I have also returned home," Heishi said in a soft voice.

"Heishi, are you saying that we've returned from a sea voyage?" Xiao Sang called Heishi the informal *you*.

"Yes, we've returned home. I love you so much, more than anyone. The voyage was long, but it has turned out well. Those sleepless nights at sea . . ."

Xiao Sang grew silent. She held Heishi even tighter. She thought: "Heishi and I are rewriting history."

When they were almost at the entrance to the book club, they let go of each other and entered one in front, one behind.

They'd arrived late. Everyone else had already gotten into discussion. Xiao Sang discovered that there was a new face. It was a young man, the marketing department manager from the large bookstore opposite her department store. She'd met him a number of times, his name was Xiaoyue. He had been helping her organize the reading group at the store. Xiao Sang cheerfully nodded to him in greeting.

"We are discussing chapter 29. Everyone has brought up questions about an emotional outlet." Fei turned to Heishi and said, "Everyone's tired of cutting their way out, like in classical literature. Is this aesthetic fatigue? Or has civilization developed today? Next we continued to discuss the topic you put forward last time."

"Has there been a conclusion to the discussion?" Heishi asked, his expression unchanging.

"Everyone agrees there's been a development," Fei said.

"I think," Han Ma spoke up, "that problems can always be solved as long as one dares to face one's own problems, isn't afraid of suffering, and is willing to follow, venturing deeper. Of course, some solutions themselves mean immense suffering . . . Provided you don't transgress, there must be progress. The most difficult part is to judge how not to transgress."

As Han Ma spoke, Xiao Sang watched her appreciatively, nodding.

"Chapter 29 doesn't provide an obvious answer. However, based on the characters' untimely actions, we can approach the core . . ." Fei suddenly halted and stopped talking with a deflated expression. Some worry seemed to overwhelm him.

Han Ma drew a chair close to Fei and embraced him.

"I'm so pleased, we've made progress," Heishi said. "A few months ago, we were at a loss when faced with this extraordinary novel, and now we seem to be having a collective breakthrough. Xiao Sang, Fei, and I were the earliest to experience confusion and suffering while reading this novel, but in the end we harvested its fruits—no matter what these are. We have devoted ourselves, just like people in love devote themselves to their feelings."

"In this sense, reading is as magnificent as fiction itself," Xiao Sang continued Heishi's point. "Maybe, for now, we haven't achieved happiness, but we have all elevated ourselves."

"Writing like this can also strengthen our endurance for suffering," Han Ma said in a quiet voice.

As she spoke, Fei took one of her hands and pressed it to his chest. Xiao Sang noticed his movement and thought: how has Fei become so fragile?

"You can see that it is hard to gain long-term, lasting satisfaction by rushing regardless toward desire," Fei sat up straight and continued. "People have ideas and also have passions. These two functions are often expressed at the same time by taking action, which also means that there's an emotional mechanism that moves back and forth and is constructed of both. Modern people can no longer be partial to one or the other, but must harmonize them to advance toward their goal. This scenario is what Heishi called the 'nets of life.'"

"Everyone present is in at least two nets," Li Hai said unexpectedly.

"I think you can't go a step further," Qiaozi clapped him on the back.

"You ought to say: this is how we prophets become most powerful." Li Hai rolled his eyes.

They both stood up, because it was time to go home.

Xiao Sang approached Han Ma and asked her quietly: "Is everything all right?"

Han Ma answered with confidence: "Yes, I'm always all right."

Once Heishi and Xiao Sang left through the front entrance of the bookstore, he pulled her into a narrow lane. He said this alleyway was close to the backyards of Sailors' Home. Because there were no streetlights, Xiao Sang couldn't see its real appearance. She told herself: "Ah well, chickens marry, so do dogs—for better or worse." Then she held close to Heishi, as if he were pushing her along as they went.

"It's only a ten-minute walk from here to my company's living quarters," he said, pressed to her ear.

"You mean that we'll go to your place this evening?" she asked.

"Mm-hmm. Do you want something to eat?"

"No. It seems like you've planned this for a long time."

Heishi started to laugh, then emphatically kissed Xiao Sang's neck.

Her body started to tremble again.

"You've made it so I won't be able to go to work on Monday," she said.

Heishi's apartment was on the third floor, and the lights were on. They went in and fell onto the roomy bed. Xiao Sang smelled the faint fragrance of newly washed sheets. "You've planned so well." She thought, distractedly, "He's kissing me in earnest, and I enjoy it . . . I want to kiss him, too . . ."

Then she turned over to kiss Heishi. She heard him moan . . .

That night was the most passionate of their lives.

Xiao Sang sat on the bus on her way to work, watching the not yet familiar street scene outside the window, and saying to herself: "I am already a married woman." This feeling made her proud—she was smiling.

"Dad, Heishi and I are getting married," she said.

"Mm-hmm, good. It's not too late, because you only waited so long to find the best."

"You understand me."

"Wait until I've earned the money, we'll buy a house for everyone."

"We don't need to wait. Heishi has money, he's a high-level electrical engineer."

"What, how come I haven't heard you say so?"

"I only found out yesterday," Xiao Sang said. "I met him again six months ago, and we've only just confirmed our relationship. I'd never thought of asking him what his job was."

"Right, I don't care how much money he makes either. I care more for my son-in-law the more I see of him. I can't imagine how overjoyed your mom will be when she finds out! Our Sangsang is captivating."

Xiao Sang thought back to when she was in the capital and her mother had said that her father was a miser, and she couldn't help laughing. She sighed to herself: "Environment and state of mind can transform people. My dad is becoming more and more loveable."

She entered the courtyard where her small home was and saw Uncle Yi downstairs reading the newspaper.

"Uncle Yi, Heishi and I are getting married."

"Are you? Wonderful. Are you going to have a wedding ceremony?"

"No. I'm living at Heishi's for now. Time is tight for both of us."

"Hmm, a good decision. You two will be happy—I've always believed this."

"Uncle Yi, I can't stand to leave you, and Heishi can't either. But we won't leave, we'll see each other often, won't we? My love for you is even deeper than for my parents . . ."

"I feel the same way. You're like my daughter, and Heishi is like my son. I've looked forward to such a day for a long time. I can't even say how happy I am!"

Then Xiao Sang suggested that they go out for a drink to celebrate the beginning of her new life.

They sat down at the bar, and the server brought their wine.

"In chapter 19 of *XXXX*," Uncle Yi sipped his wine and said, "the two travelers climb to the mountaintop and toll a giant bell, so that the mountains resound from top to bottom, in a chain reaction."

Deeply intoxicated by his emotions, he continued:

"Today is my happiest day. It's like I'm the one getting married."

They silently toasted. Xiao Sang was so moved she couldn't find the right words.

After a while Uncle Yi continued:

"You, and Heishi, and Xiao Ma, you've conquered the mountain range. Your energy amazes me. For the past few years I've hardly stepped foot out of the house, but I've seen the world renewed, the new sun and changing moon. Thank you, Xiao Sang, and thank Heishi for me—you've given me such a pleasant surprise."

"Uncle Yi, if you keep on talking like this, I'll start crying. I really can't bear moving away from you. The courtyard, the trees, the cat, and the windows of your home, your table lamp: those are my home forever. Without you, how would there be me and Heishi today?"

Xiao Sang took out a tissue to wipe her eyes.

"Have you and Xiao Ma made any progress?" she asked, with tears in her eyes.

Uncle Yi nodded, smiling.

Then she smiled in spite of her tears and said:

"That Xiao Ma, I love her so much! But for the past few days I haven't even seen her shadow. Once she gets off work she just disappears. I didn't know if she was trying to avoid suspicion."

"Xiao Ma is a woman of many intrigues," Uncle Yi said.

"She isn't like most young women."

As they left the bar, Xiao Sang proposed:

"Let's arrange a day for the four of us to go to the park outside the city."

"Very good, Xiao Sang, I'd wanted to suggest that, too. All of you are making me young again. My heart fills daily with gratitude. But I won't sob like you."

Xiao Sang ruefully said goodbye to Uncle Yi and left for Heishi's place.

On the bus she thought: it's only been a few days. Why did she want to run to Heishi as soon as she got off work? This was so different than her former loves. It seemed unimaginable.

"Heishi, Xiao Ma and Uncle Yi are together!" Xiao Sang burst out as she entered the apartment.

"I'd noticed, too," Heishi answered her.

"So you've seen the two of them!" Xiao Sang was surprised.

Then he told her about what had happened that day at the bar.

"I was feeling depressed because you hadn't answered my letters, so I went out for a drink. I never thought I'd run into them."

"Oh, Heishi, Heishi, so it's—no, I won't say. Now I love you even more, classmate."

"Love, love, Xiao Sang's love, I don't mind much."

They kissed again. Kissing over and over and removing each other's clothing.

Later, Xiao Sang also told Heishi that Uncle Yi had thanked the both of them for making him young again. Heishi said that meeting Uncle Yi had been the greatest good fortune in his life. Uncle Yi helped him to pursue the happiness he had today. Xiao Sang went on to tell Heishi that she couldn't keep from crying when she'd shared the same feeling with Uncle Yi. Twelve years were many days and nights.

"Heishi, I remembered something. Last time at the book club, could you tell there was something going on with Fei?"

"There's a situation, I'd guess. The nets of life are entangling him. Fei's great, though—he shows a certain integrity," Heishi said, sinking into thought.

"He and Han Ma will find a way out. Even suffering will always pass. Heishi, let me tell you something else. The past few days I've been anxious to rush over here when I get off work, so I haven't touched a book for a week. I'm terrified. What do you think: am I going to regress? I'm not young any more."

"You are still very young, in every way," Heishi said, caressing Xiao Sang. "I think maybe it's because you have both a pursuit and a passion. For now we're reading a different, invisible book, but soon we'll return to our original books. Maybe we'll have new impetus. I miss my books, too. Tomorrow we'll begin to read. I have two large bedrooms here, so we'll each take one room, each read on our own, then discuss our reading together afterward. What do you think?"

"Good idea! Starting tomorrow," Xiao Sang said.

The next evening Xiao Sang sat at the desk, opening the book Uncle Yi had recently given her. She swiftly found herself confronting a familiar challenge. Yet she persisted for over half an hour, before she couldn't help but call out:

"Heishi! Heishi . . ."

Heishi ran over to ask what was the matter.

"When you're not beside me, I feel empty. I just can't."

"It's all right, then we'll share a desk."

"Then there's no way to read," Xiao Sang said, dejected. "You go back to your room. Wait, hold me first. All right, go."

Xiao Sang calmed down and got back into her book. She said to herself: "I've said before: if a book can't enter my life, and melt into my life, then it isn't the book I am seeking. Ha, today I finally know what these words mean!"

She finished speaking and raised her eyes. She saw Heishi standing at the door smiling at her.

"What were you saying, Xiao Sang?"

"I was reading lines from the book aloud."

In the chapter Xiao Sang had just reached, thick fog inundated the capital city. An old-fashioned train stopped at a platform, and some elderly people got down from the train car. They walked and talked . . . "How familiar, how nostalgic. I love this type of opening. I'm adjusting, preparing to devote myself," Xiao Sang thought. Next the protagonist appeared, another elderly person who disembarked last by himself. Carrying a suitcase and walking slowly, he looked around in all directions, not as if he were waiting for someone, but rather as if he were reacquainting himself with his hometown. The elderly man wore a long coat and a cap, and had a curving mustache. Xiao Sang whispered: "He's something like a prophet." Next he vanished into the thick fog. Seemingly the author's interest shifted away from him. But Xiao Sang knew this was because real life was beginning. Xiao Sang adored real life; she'd grown attached to fiction because of it. The year she'd met Uncle Yi—from then on the sky over Meng sparkled with light most of the time . . . Yes, it must be Xiao Sang herself taking that train to Meng, the same train as Uncle Yi, but they didn't know each other then . . . Ah, what a wonderful description! Xiao Sang was relieved; she felt that the beautiful scenery hadn't deserted her. It wouldn't desert her, because Uncle Yi was in that landscape. She eventually entered its bounds, and read on, kept reading, until Heishi came calling her.

"Oh, how satisfying!" she sighed.

"For me, too. When I think of you just next door reading the same book, my perceptions are enhanced. Let's take a shower together."

"Yes."

The pale curtains weren't completely drawn. Xiao Sang opened her eyes and saw the sparkling night sky. She remembered Uncle Yi, who had brought Heishi to her. Now she felt glad beyond compare, because Xiao Ma had entered Uncle Yi's life. Heishi was murmuring something, as if everything in his dreams were exciting.

Part Two

HAN MA AND FEI, UNCLE YI AND XIAO MA, HAN MA AND XIAOYUE

Xiaoyue hadn't made a speech when he first joined the Pigeon Book Club. For one thing, he felt a little uncomfortable as a newcomer; for another, he wanted mostly to hear these book friends' appraisals of the novel. He had himself been reading this novel for a period of time. He paid rapt attention, not letting any statement each of them made slip away. He quickly realized that every single person here read on a high level, the highest level he'd been able to classify among various reading groups. Xiaoyue was just thirty but already an experienced reader of fiction. He read widely and seemed to spend the better part of the day with books, but he loved fiction the best. Since he had such a strong memory, he gained a rough knowledge of every book friend's preferences by listening closely at the Pigeon Book Club discussion. Xiaoyue participated in a number of reading groups around Meng because his job was to survey the actual situation of Meng's readers: in one sense establishing the level of each in order to analyze their different needs, and in another applying new ideas and information to guide them and enlighten them. The members of the reading group that Xiao Sang led at the Crown Department Store were his grassroots literary readers. He'd met Han Ma at this reading group and, with one look, been toppled over by the way she carried herself. He knew many young women and had been in two romantic relationships before, but a young woman like her was honestly too special. When Han Ma gave her speech, Xiaoyue sensed that she was a free and easy spirit. He only learned afterward that she was newly married and that her husband was someone he'd known by reputation for a long time: Fei.

Even though Xiaoyue now knew that Han Ma had a husband, and that her husband was someone he greatly admired, he was still deeply attracted to her. The day of the typhoon, Xiaoyue found an excuse to approach Han Ma. At the outset he worried that he was being too abrupt, or that she would evade his proposal. When they'd just chatted back and forth, though, he discovered that she was as enthusiastic as he was. She not only cheerfully accepted his proposal right away, she also advanced it a step further by inviting him to attend Fei's and her reading circle. She even turned out to appreciate him so much that she said he represented "a new influence." After that, Xiaoyue became a bit muddled and said things to Han Ma that he thought were too much. He even felt a little scared after he finished speaking, so he had said goodbye to her immediately. Yet Han Ma didn't take offense at his excesses. A few days later she enthusiastically called him to invite him to a gathering of the Pigeon Book Club.

Coming out of the Pigeon Book Club that day, Xiaoyue felt himself falling into the abyss of unrequited love. Confusedly, he walked the alleyways recalling the words Han Ma had said at the meeting, her image filling his mind. He had also formed a good impression of Fei, recognizing that he had a heart full of sincerity toward literature and was his senior, someone who deserved respect. This meant that Xiaoyue would hide his passion for Han Ma for a long time, only interacting with her in the capacity of a good friend. He thought it must be her natural literary gifts and her obsession with fiction which gave her a kind of magic. He felt deeply that he was a similar type of person and attracted to her for this reason. To him this woman was the embodiment of beauty. Luckily the department store where she worked was near his bookstore, and he could often catch sight of her. He was willing to watch her from afar, because he would become too excited once he got close to her.

Xiaoyue kept busy with his work in the bookstore during the day, while every evening he cultivated the universe of fiction he had chosen. His aim was the highest level of literary appreciation. He read as if drunk, pondering what he'd read again and again, and had written out several volumes of notes over many years. He'd also published some essays, but he was uniformly dissatisfied with them and believed himself to be a late bloomer in the literary sense, despite being experienced in everyday personal relationships. He awaited an overall turning point in perspective. He vaguely felt that attending the Pigeon Book Club and his one-sided love for Han Ma were seemingly related to this turning point. "I must catch up, otherwise I will be too late. This might be the direction life is taking," he told himself.

In everyday life Xiaoyue had many personal connections. Men and women, young and old, were happy to associate with him, since everyone thought that he understood the general feeling and deserved their trust. Yet with Han Ma this life skill of his was basically useless. Her straightforward nature and enthusiasm and sincerity made his sort of habitual circumspection unnecessary. In fact, at the bottom of his heart what he liked the most was her attitude toward human existence. Fondness and affection brought about unrequited love naturally. No matter whether it were Han Ma's looks, the way she expressed herself, her talent, her passion for literature and experiencing its depths, or her habits of speech: Xiaoyue was endlessly excited whenever thoughts of her occurred to him. He still couldn't follow his heart to approach her. The twice-monthly gatherings became his holidays: one at the Pigeon Book Club, one at the Crown Department Store's upstairs reading group. Almost every morning he would arrive a little early at his office to watch the entrance to the department store across the street through the window, waiting for Han Ma to appear there.

There were many women employed at the bookstore who were fond of Xiaoyue, and a few of the older ones showed frequent concern about his getting married. There was one woman who had introduced him to three potential girlfriends, pretty younger women, but he ultimately said that they weren't the right match for him. Because people were always making introductions, later on he just openly declared that he was a confirmed bachelor and asked them not to take the trouble for him any more. Even if they didn't really believe what he said, there were eventually fewer introductions. Xiaoyue had abundant energy and a self-disciplined lifestyle. These days he read and wrote wildly every day, while his yearning for Han Ma grew stronger by the day. In the moments when he missed her, he felt as though he existed in an unreal world. That was usually at night, or when he'd finished a piece of work and was taking a break. Many times, in order to forget Han Ma, Xiaoyue redoubled his efforts at his job. His coworkers from the bookstore noticed and thought he worked too hard.

"Xiaoyue, what's wrong with my friend's daughter?" Button Woman asked him.

"It's not her, it's me. I'm not the marrying type," Xiaoyue said sincerely.

Of course he knew that there was only one Han Ma in the world, and that Han Ma already had a husband, but he couldn't shake his longing for her. When he entered the profound world of fiction, he always thought about how he could only talk about these scenes with Han Ma—only Han Ma could best understand what affected him, because very few people had as broad a field of vision as she did. His book friends at the Pigeon Book Club had high standards, but only Han Ma's approached his own. The expression in her eyes when she spoke, her particular gestures, rippled through his heart. Once he learned that she was writing fiction, he even believed himself capable of entering the world of her stories as simply as he could enter the state of his customers' psychology in real life. The perception was powerful and vivid, so that while taking notes on his reading Xiaoyue continuously imagined that he was in discussion with Han Ma. Recently, every evening when he finished reading he would say: "Han Ma, today's conversation is over. Good night."

Now Xiaoyue intended to write fiction, too, not for publication (he thought his writing style didn't suit fictional expression), but just to go deeper into Han Ma's future stories. He was always guessing at the form and content of her fiction and believed without knowing why that her stories would be about some everyday happenings and also bizarre events. That kind of fiction is not so easily understood, but, for Xiaoyue, it was accessible. Just like Han Ma saying a few quiet words into his ear. Han Ma didn't plan to publish her writing yet (he had asked her), so he could only imagine. All kinds of assumptions crowded his existence. Of course, Han Ma had Fei, a connoisseur with high standards, for her to discuss fiction with and sharpen her skills, so she would progress quickly. Yet maybe, sometimes, she would need another response of a different kind? Xiaoyue sensed himself preparing for this every day. He thought of himself as reading books for his beloved, which was itself a major impetus. Since he'd known Han Ma, his reading had made a qualitative leap that embodied his ability to more easily enter a kind of "other place." He'd perceived before how all first-rate fiction contained that "other place," but readers didn't succeed at entering it every time.

He thought that if he could now, communally, like the book friends from the Pigeon Book Club, build an extraordinary place with Han Ma, a place that extended to all of the fiction they read, surely he could stake a flag on this land, its scenery, together with her. This preparatory work stimulated him and sometimes gave him confidence.

The day arrived for the Crown Department Store reading group. Xiaoyue had prepared a theme for their discussion. He invented a young reader, G, and introduced his reading process. Xiaoyue realized that among the listeners present only Xiao Sang and Han Ma would know that what he was describing was his own experience. The two women's appreciative glances encouraged him to free his emotions and thoughts, so that his speech became eloquent and moving.

"Reading isn't a piece of handiwork that you can grasp. Instead it's a trek to an unseen end. As the evening's wind blew against G's face, the state he was longing for quietly drew near him. G evaluated: 'Have my struggles over the past few days had any effect?' Not yet—getting nearer was actually distancing him from the state he sought. To capture it was impossible: he could only stay in place working intensely, constructing his own plot. I have been acquainted with the reader G for a long time. He's clumsy but always tirelessly, tenaciously clambering upward. What is there above him? This isn't the kind of question he considers. He believes that his job is to differentiate among things intensely. Every time he sees a contour emerge, he stops where he is, because he knows that the function of his hands is to build. Many years have passed, but G still cannot distinguish among the things he has constructed, even though, before comparing them, his ability to differentiate had grown stronger. Along the way he leaves behind more and more of these where he has paused. They don't reveal any obvious trend, and are merely irrelevant relics marking where he has paused. They don't stay in his memory; he remembers only a precipice and the evening wind, and an unending trek since daybreak. At this high altitude, there are often piercing winds, but G doesn't cower and instead climbs more boldly. Past experience tells him: harshness conceals happiness. He can remember stopping on a certain evening—the sudden arrival of happiness. He had sensed that he and the enormous rock where he'd sat down were momentarily joined into one body. The mountain made a rumbling noise, although it only lasted an instant. 'Everything has happened before,' G said. 'Like those relics—one night they will finally make a sound.'

"How many years have passed? He doesn't know, because there are no points of reference in his surroundings. His sole points of reference are the relics he's left behind, but they don't reveal a trend or point toward any specific thing. Only after countless years of the Earth's shifts do they now and then show themselves, towering before G's eyes."

This was the prologue to Xiaoyue's introduction of G's reading process to the young readers. The twenty-plus book friends fell silent. They hadn't been able to understand all of what they'd heard, but they were fascinated. At this moment Han Ma started to speak.

"The kernel of literature is like a seed planted in every person's heart. Its growth relies on people's inner sight. Then how does inner sight emerge? I think it comes from the gift of our everyday lives. I would guess that this friend of Xiaoyue's, this journeyer who tirelessly climbs literature's peak, is a superior person capable of discerning the beauty of our daily lives. I long to know him and even more to enter this extraordinary place. I also long to shed tears with him, laugh aloud together, savor delicious food together, work together as colleagues, talk together about literature, all on ordinary days. I think that seekers absorb enormous energy and sublime conviction from these beautiful things, so that they are able to subsist day after day at high altitude and build in that state. I also believe myself to be a member of the seekers. What Xiaoyue is describing coincides with my experience."

Heart pounding, Xiaoyue glanced toward Han Ma. Extreme appreciation, gratefulness, and love. That was how the book friends saw through Xiaoyue's image to his everyday life. They whispered among themselves, signaling to one another, nodded, and said in low voices: "Yes, yes . . ." In their mind's eye he was a sincere, enthusiastic friend who recommended literature as hard as he could, and had high literary achievements. He had been helpful to the majority of them. He wasn't just a bookstore manager, though, or friend to the book friends: now everyone believed he had a burning heart, too.

Next Xiao Sang made a speech. She was newly married, and happiness was written all over her face. She'd always regarded Xiaoyue as a true friend and someone on the same path as her. He'd never disappointed her. She integrated her knowledge of reading to speak about the yin and yang that make up the reader's soul. She took Xiaoyue's friend Mr. G's experience to be reading's yin, and her own part to be the experience of reading's yang. Her yang part of reading merged with worldly existence to extract the element of beauty from all of the trivialities of life. She said that the best readers, as summed up by Han Ma, ought to be outstanding in aspects of both yin and yang. Xiaoyue's characterization had fully demonstrated literature's uniqueness by using such imagistic words to outline an ideal; Han Ma then connected the source of the power of this ideal to our daily embodied existence. This was literature's truth—she seems too distant to reach, but breathes every breath of our lives with us because of her universality. Xiao Sang also reminisced about what a young person named Yan had said at a Pigeon Book Club meeting. Everyone had been discussing the relationship between ideal and action. Xiao Sang asked Yan what taking action meant for him, and Yan replied that he took action when he did housework. She had felt his answer pluck at her heartstrings. Through Xiao Sang's analysis, everyone present thought they'd partly understood Xiaoyue's and Han Ma's speeches, and they all started twittering and commenting afterward.

That evening's discussion was especially lively, but the other book friends were reluctant to make public speeches. They felt that their reading wasn't yet mature enough, so they preferred to discuss in private. Xiao Sang and Xiaoyue thought that this format would also prove inspiring, because they both sensed everyone's eagerness to elevate their status and better understand the small number of readers who had led the way, while striving for the day when they could keep up with their forerunners' pace.

"Xiaoyue, your speech was brilliant!" Han Ma came over and shook hands with him. "Once you finished, I wanted to go right on speaking where you left off . . . What is happening? We didn't discuss this beforehand, but we seem to be like the 'seamless garments of the heavens.' Then there was Xiao Sang's summation tied so tightly to your and my descriptions. We didn't think of these questions in the moment, did we? It just seems like, seems like we decided together on something a long time ago, and now there is only putting it into action."

As Han Ma spoke, she kept hold of Xiaoyue's hand, not letting go until she'd finished. She didn't notice that his face had grown pale.

"Han Ma's right," Xiao Sang added, "but it isn't 'seems like'—it's that we have truly decided together to seek literature. Do you still remember when you'd just started working at the department store, and I said I hoped you'd learn to write?"

"Of course I remember. I'll never forget it. Xiao Sang, you are a magnet attracting us literature lovers."

After the meeting broke up, Xiaoyue didn't return directly to his apartment complex, but instead took the long way around and went to a park on the outskirts of the city. At this time of day, there was no one to be seen in the park as he walked along the lake. He knew it had been completely inadvertent, but this was the first time he'd had physical contact with Han Ma! The sky was dark now, much like his state of mind. He didn't know which direction the way out was, or if there was no way out. Could this be another of the nets of life? Han Ma's hands were powerful: this was the sole perception he could name; his other perceptions he couldn't articulate. In that moment he'd lost the ability to feel, with a blank space in his mind. The strange thing was that he could remember every sentence that Han Ma had said. Her way of expressing herself was so enchanting. So she must be a novelist, and he wasn't. This was no illusion, but instead something that had really happened . . . The deep level of communication between them was easy to take up, in the way that two people sometimes combine into one. Of course, a similar type of exchange might also take place between Han Ma and Fei. Han Ma had had practice. Thinking of Fei's existence and his influence on Han Ma, Xiaoyue felt his frenetic passion gradually calm down. There was a shadow like a large animal on the path ahead. Xiaoyue stopped in his tracks.

"Young man, are you unlucky in love?" The man straightened up.

Xiaoyue couldn't see him clearly, but felt that the man could see him.

"Being unlucky in love is a good thing—it can rouse you. Believe an old man's experience."

Then they walked back shoulder-to-shoulder. Xiaoyue asked him:

"Uncle, did you lose hope then?"

"There are no rivers that cannot be crossed. Believe me." He patted Xiaoyue on the shoulder.

At the instant when Xiaoyue exited the garden, he suddenly understood that the reader G must be a combination of himself and Han Ma.

That was why Han Ma had so quickly continued his thoughts. Thinking this over, Xiaoyue's mood brightened: wasn't this where the happiness of his present life lay, in being able to create with Han Ma, as one combined person (even by peculiar means)? Maybe they were destined not to be able to watch over each other day and night, but he could continue his pursuit. What the older man had said a moment ago was right: being unlucky in love pushed people to rouse themselves. One-sided love was the same. Provided he explored onward along the path of literature, he would have frequent opportunities like this later on. When Xiaoyue was almost to the apartment complex, his desperation finally subsided, and his mind was filled with Han Ma's way of speaking, which was so distinctive. He recalled Han Ma's attitude toward her work at the department store. Wasn't that similar to his attitude? Might they be like twins who resembled each other in every way? It was so exciting, and probably a very rare coincidence. Yes, through tireless study he would become a companion Han Ma couldn't do without in her literary career.

Xiaoyue quieted down. He was essentially someone who could keep his composure.

Han Ma's writing progressed quite successfully. She belonged to the category of writers who find their way fairly quickly. But she didn't want to publish right away, because she thought that she could write even better. She would make attempts in many ways. Of course, she didn't know as yet what the concrete sense of attempts in many ways was, so for now she could only define it like this: the more writing, the more experience. Han Ma wouldn't let herself be idle: she would just write, just read, whenever she had time. When she did so, some of life's worries were pushed to the back of her mind.

She still loved Fei deeply. But like she'd anticipated, there were more days than before that he vanished from their home. Han Ma thought that, as long as Fei still loved her, she ought to treasure every single day together with him. No human is perfect, and the affairs of the world can't be perfectly beautiful either. Since there'd been ardent love between them, her attitude now was both loyal to her choice and also faithful to Fei. Xiao Sang, who'd attained satisfying love, for example, understood Han Ma's choice on a deep level and enthusiastically supported her all along. Han Ma said to herself: "I'm fortunate, and I can write, and I have love." Even though Fei sometimes disappeared from home, she was slowly getting used to it. She no longer felt alarmed. She believed that a mature woman should behave this way, like her. It could even be said that among the trio of Han Ma, Xiaoyue, and Fei, she was the calmest one, because the two men's emotions fluctuated. Han Ma thought that if one day Fei chose Yue rather than her, she would be sure to quietly withdraw. There would be immense pain if that took place. Even so, she was ready to endure it. For now, though, it was Fei who suffered the most. Han Ma thought that he hadn't shown any sign yet that he would forsake her. She sighed: "This is that kind of love 'carved into bones and inscribed on the heart.' In the end, whose bones are carved deeper, which heart more inscribed?" She didn't know. An answer hadn't emerged; people are tormented by going back and forth.

Han Ma did notice that ever since coming back from the recent Pigeon Book Club gathering Fei often had a distracted look. She guessed that there was probably some situation with Yue. She wouldn't ask him. Sometimes she detested herself, feeling that she shouldn't pretend as if nothing were wrong and should have an honest and open talk with Fei. Yet she knew that if she brought up this issue, Fei would be hurt. He'd already caused himself enough injury. How could Han Ma add salt to a wound? The difficulty of keeping up their relationship surpassed what she'd imagined initially. She often asked herself: is Fei exhausted now, physically and spiritually? If so, what was the sense in maintaining this kind of relationship? People in this world ought to have their pursuits and live assured of the rightness of what they do. It could be called an "unprincipled life" if both of these aspects weren't within reach. Of course Fei wasn't unprincipled, and he still hadn't abandoned literary research—his own or Han Ma's—only he smiled less and less. Han Ma's thoughts, in the time she had left over from writing, were always pulled in this direction; she considered the many possibilities of Fei and Yue's relationship . . . She'd eventually learned from Fei that Yue wasn't a forceful woman. Yue must be fairly gentle by nature, but her emotions were very determined. This meant that she had never loved anyone besides Fei. When Han Ma thought of this once late at night, she couldn't help but gasp, her hands and feet turning to ice. Was it that she, Han Ma, should be the one to withdraw from this game? If Yue were a little more assertive, Han Ma might have been more carefree. It was Yue's passivity and indecisiveness (think of her first marriage) that instead caused Fei's endless worry and sympathy for her, and naturally also his love. Han Ma had to consider the situation constantly now.

Finally the day came when Han Ma walked into Fei's study, sat down with a smile on her face, and said:

"Fei, I think you should make a choice. I wanted to tell you that I can endure it, no matter who you choose. With your help I've become quite strong. Why should I get all of the benefits, while the other one gets nothing? Without meaning to, have I deprived her of what she needs to live?"

Fei looked at her, watching her for a while, then sighed and said:

"Han Ma, your words just a moment ago overlooked one person, which is me. This issue isn't only between you and her—there's also me. I love you, and if I abandon you I may have no interest left in life. Have you thought this over carefully? I'm not a strong person like you—this is why I love you so much. When we first got married, my choice was you, and today it still is. I'm not so determined, I'm easily moved—this is my weakness. But when it comes to choices, I have never changed mine."

"I love you, too. I have never loved anyone like I love you, Fei. But there's suffering here, I feel this pain, and it's hard not to take it to heart. Do you have any way to resolve this?"

"I don't know yet, Han Ma."

Fei went over to Han Ma and held her. They embraced silently for a long, long time, able to hear each other's heartbeats.

Even though Han Ma was dissatisfied with Fei's "getting along" behavior, she couldn't think of any better way either. What she'd thought at first was: if she didn't withdraw, Yue would always suffer. However, the situation now was that if she withdrew, Fei would suffer a fatal blow. She knew he wasn't exaggerating. Then the sole choice was to endure for a while. Perhaps time would bring about a turn for the better. Han Ma sympathized with Fei and understood Yue, but she knew the problem couldn't be decided by her on her own. "Now it's a deadlock," she said to herself. Despite meeting with such great difficulties in her personal life, Han Ma had smooth sailing in her literary pursuits. New turning points appeared continuously before her, with inspiration coming in flashes so often that she couldn't keep pace. She hadn't expected these new circumstances when Fei had first helped her push open the window. Her experience of this undertaking became one of daily increasing confidence. Han Ma thought that she suffered much less than Fei or Yue, because she had the support of literature, and literature gave her greater independence. Yet Han Ma felt incapable of helping Fei when it came to the issue with Yue. Now she was mainly suffering on their account, and so she had told Xiao Sang: "I'm always fine." In contrast to Fei and Yue, she really was always fine, which was verified by her being able to write fiction every day.

"Han Ma, you'll change into a hawk soon," Fei joked.

"What does that mean?"

"It means you will fly higher and higher, further and further away, and not need anyone."

Han Ma heard Fei's anxiety. In her mind she rebutted him: "No, I need Fei. For him I can make any choice, never fear if it's the most agonizing decision." She couldn't foresee for now, and didn't want to foresee, whether she would reach a state of not needing anyone. But she really was different than before: for example, she no longer had the impulse to communicate with Xiao Sang about this problem. Wasn't that an even more independent stance? From now on it might be possible for her to trust her own judgment in all matters; it could also be harder and harder for her to be defeated. These were the benefits of literature, and Fei had given them to her.

She'd noticed that at home Fei was burying himself in his work to suppress the agony of his soul. He'd published a number of new and incisive literary critiques, when before he hadn't attached any importance to publishing his writing in journals. The thing he set the most store by was managing the book club's meetings, because his passion for literature was only released at these gatherings. It was universally acknowledged that no one held the same fascination as Fei did in this regard. Han Ma encouraged Fei to publish even more. She said, "Prophets must work." Fei said he wasn't satisfied with the pieces he'd published, but couldn't write better ones either.

Lately Han Ma had been immersed in writing a short story collection. She felt her inspiration to be focusing in a more apparent direction. She thought: maybe the crucial moment for the final sprint is here?

Then Fei was gone for three days in a row right at this decisive juncture. This had never happened before.

When Fei came back it was the weekend, as Han Ma sat in the living room drinking tea.

He looked a number of years older; his cheeks were sunken. He accepted the cup Han Ma passed to him and stood there sipping the tea, his appearance making her apprehensive. When he finished his tea, he went to shower without saying a single word.

They went together to eat at the bamboo restaurant. She asked him:

"Fei, can I help you?"

"No, no need. I'll handle it. Probably it's only a question of time."

The two of them sat down and ordered Lanzhou pulled noodles and shaobing.

"Young Han, young Fei, a joyous occasion has arrived: our bamboo restaurant is expanding!" Lao Yao said.

"Congratulations, congratulations! There is something new happening every day and night!" Han Ma responded.

"I think Fei seems to have a weight on his mind today?" Lao Yao added, "Finish eating this large bowl of noodles and let out some sweat. It will push any worries to the back of your mind. In life, the simpler the better!"

"Lao Yao has spoken the truth," Fei nodded with heartfelt approval.

He was thinking secretly: why hadn't he ever learned how to live a simple life? Not only hadn't he learned how, his life was also becoming more and more complex—that net tangling him so tight that he seemed to be suffocating . . .

Back home Fei gave a long sigh and said to Han Ma:

"Han Ma, I'm so unfair to you. I'm worthless!"

He pounded his head, his face full of despair.

"Fei, don't talk this way. From the beginning you didn't deceive me, and I'm a grown-up. It was my own choice to be with you. Since I've chosen, of course there's this problem now. Don't keep blaming yourself. Let's face it bravely, consider soberly, and find the best plan . . . Maybe it's like you said, there isn't a best solution at the moment—everything should be allowed time. Let's be more patient. 'When the cart reaches a mountain, there is always a road.'"

After Han Ma spoke these words, her mind was also in chaos, but she had a faint premonition of something. She knew that it foreboded what she wanted to happen the least. Then, seeing Fei's reaction, she realized for the first time that their relationship probably didn't have a future. She relied on that voice inside her heart to decide that she would accompany him unwavering to the end.

"You're right, Han Ma, you understand everything. Blaming myself is useless, and it seems like making excuses. Believe me, this difficulty will soon be over."

"Even though I don't believe this difficulty will soon be over, I believe you. I've believed you all along, Fei."

The two of them embraced, then they each returned to their studies.

Later Han Ma discovered that this evening Fei hadn't written anything, or read anything. She knew the situation was becoming complicated. She resolved to treasure every day with him.

Over this stretch of time Xiaoyue read books actively and used all of his time outside of work to do battle with literature.

One weekend afternoon he got tired of reading and went for a walk by the artificial lake. There were usually not many visitors there, so it was Xiaoyue's first choice of location to sort out his feelings. This was where he had met the old man who had transformed his mood after he'd left Xiao Sang's reading group at the department store the last time.

As Xiaoyue slowly walked along the lake, he suddenly heard, coming from below him, the sound of a woman crying. There was a slope from the road to the surface of the lake, and Xiaoyue looked down to see a man and a woman sitting there embracing each other. The man's silhouette seemed familiar, so Xiaoyue unconsciously went another few steps forward. Then he immediately turned around and walked back toward the road he'd come from. He'd seen that the man was Fei, but the woman wasn't Han Ma. Xiaoyue's face reddened and his heart pounded as he went all at one go to the exit and quickly left the park. He felt his back soaked through with sweat. He felt so many mixed feelings. Oh, Han Ma, what was happening? Xiaoyue's mind had cleared by the time he was nearly home. What he had seen was a forbidden zone. As an outsider, he didn't have the standing to pass judgment on this incident. Han Ma was a mature and highly ethical woman, who had her own point of view even more so than Xiaoyue. The affair he'd accidentally discovered therefore had nothing to do with him.

The event still affected Xiaoyue's view of Han Ma, even though he believed it had nothing to do with him. Was Fei deceiving her? Xiaoyue felt that there was only a small possibility of this. For one thing, Fei had a good reputation in Meng's reading world as a mentor who'd devoted his youth to literature; for another, Han Ma wasn't any naive young woman who could easily be fooled. Xiaoyue thought back and forth without ever being able to break away from what he'd seen that afternoon. The woman had cried with extreme, brokenhearted despair, as if her soul were calling for help. Meanwhile, Han Ma was somewhere else. An idea suddenly flashed through Xiaoyue's mind: could Han Ma and Fei have some kind of agreement? "God, how frightening," he muttered. He sensed an insoluble problem binding these three people, one that might end in tragedy. If that were to happen, wouldn't it flout the new literary aims they'd all been discussing? Considering Han Ma's independence, decisiveness, and human understanding, Xiaoyue felt that there was only a small possibility of something happening. Then how could Han Ma, who was so good at understanding people, allow a scene like this to take place in her marriage? Xiaoyue thought this over many times without understanding it. The moment the curtain of night fell, Han Ma's vivid image transformed in his mind. He couldn't say for sure in which way, only that he felt she had become a woman with an intricate soul, while he seemed to be simple and unworldly next to her. Xiaoyue came into contact with numerous women through his work connections, and more than a few of them formed deep relationships with him, but someone like Han Ma was beyond his experience. Her inner cultivation was without a doubt more profound than his. Could this be the main reason she attracted him? No matter what, Xiaoyue couldn't understand how this kind of love triangle was maintained. Hadn't Han Ma brought up "endurance for suffering" at that evening's gathering of the Pigeon Book Club? She must have meant this affair. Ah, Han Ma, Han Ma, your personality must be so powerful. How did she regard suffering, now that it was someone else's? Where, too, was her way out?

Xiaoyue paced in his room until late at night, still thinking about the problem of Han Ma. The strange thing was that the afternoon's discovery hadn't altered his trust in her. Instead her difficult position became his own predicament. It was like he was plotting out a novel, trying to envision a way for her to escape her difficulty. Of course, in the end his plans didn't mature and couldn't possibly have the desired effect. Han Ma was nearly the same age as him, but the world of her soul didn't exist on the same plane as his. Xiaoyue felt that he must expend his greatest effort to enter that world.

For many days in a row at the office Xiaoyue observed Han Ma from across the street with extra care. He saw her entrance through the department store's doors, so light on her feet, then her disappearing inside. She was full of youthful energy, and so steady, not like someone entangled in suffering. Xiaoyue suspected that Han Ma might know the art of compartmentalizing herself and could set aside her pain, only entering the state that she wanted to enter. It was probably her engagement with writing that resisted the corrosion of pain to her soul. This was the net they'd talked about at the book club discussion. How had she transformed agony into impetus? This showed amazing courage! Xiaoyue preferred powerful women in his life. Han Ma's strength was the strength of the soul's depths, almost invisible from the surface. He felt that Han Ma must be sure of all aspects of herself. She would rarely be sorrowful, and instead brimmed with enthusiasm, with life force.

"Xiaoyue, my niece really likes you," Button Woman said.

She had interrupted Xiaoyue, who was sunk in thought.

"She's so pretty. And she's sure to have good luck—you won't need to worry about her."

"Maybe, maybe."

Button Woman walked away, embarrassed.

Xiaoyue briefly recalled having met this young woman and discovered that he could no longer remember what she looked like. His mind probably only had the space for one lovely figure.

He didn't think that Han Ma being involved in a love triangle gave him an opportunity. He'd been fairly pessimistic from the start, believing there was little possibility of her falling for him. She was dazzling, so even if she didn't have Fei, there would be other people pursuing her. The kinder she was toward him, the more it proved that he wasn't in her heart. Yet Xiaoyue would love her—this was unalterable. The secret he'd discovered by the lake only deepened his hopeless love.

After Xiaoyue experienced the scene by the lake, he found that his comprehension of the novel *XXXX* went to a deeper level. He sensed how the human heart was a bottomless abyss; the excavating of it was without limit. “It’s no wonder she would speak this way,” Xiaoyue told himself, staring at the book. The choice of words used by the protagonist “her” in the book was very unusual. Sometimes one sentence had three meanings. Xiaoyue squeezed his brain as he pondered, and the more he pondered the more attracted he was, just as if that “her” were Han Ma. Later on he even thought that maybe his love for Han Ma would have stayed on a superficial level, if the incident by the lake hadn’t taken place. His thirty years of existence hadn’t given him this kind of knowledge. He wrote down some of his impressions, intending to express these reflections in a twisting, turning way when he went to the Pigeon Book Club. When he thought of the phrase “twisting, turning way,” he began to laugh at himself. He said good night to Han Ma, then got ready to sleep.

When Xiaoyue switched off the lamp and lay down, Han Ma appeared in his mind. She sat all alone beside the artificial lake wearing a long black skirt. Xiaoyue sensed that the woman’s thoughts had already flown far, far away, such that he could never catch up with them. Was she coming up with plots for her stories? More likely she wasn’t thinking of anything: the kind of fiction she was going to write wasn’t thought up—instead the words poured themselves out. Xiaoyue couldn’t write that kind of fiction, but he could ponder what it was like. He wanted to call out to her, but was also afraid to disturb her, so he would only watch her from afar. When he gazed at her this way in his imagination, he felt that it would be impossible to love other women again. Han Ma wasn’t a young woman any more; she was a wife experiencing an emotional prison. If she spoke, perhaps one sentence would have three meanings, even more. Xiaoyue loved her, loved her alone.

One weekend Han Ma decided to go stay for two nights in a hotel on the summit of Meng Mountain to finish revising a short story. Fei supported her decision. The story already seemed perfect, but Han Ma didn’t think so. She said she could still write better. Maybe the story needed her to take a knife to it and abridge it. Maybe she needed to rewrite. Fei trusted her intuition, having faith in her, and said that a miracle would happen.

Toward evening Han Ma said goodbye to Fei, then the bus she took drove toward the far outskirts of the city. She sat by the window watching the scenery, thinking back on how just recently she and Fei had set up their little household with hearts full of confidence. Without knowing why, she felt as though those circumstances had been long ago. In such a short time, her view of many aspects of life had transformed. Of course, there might have been no change and instead her opinions hadn't been completely formed before. There was less and less of the city scene along the road. The countryside's pure landscape under the curtain of night alarmed her in an unfathomable way. "It was always going to be this way—everything will happen this way because the other one is also a living being," she said to herself. She had a foreboding that from now into the future everything that took place would be unfathomable.

Meng Mountain wasn't tall, with an elevation a thousand or so meters above sea level. There were streetlights along the looping mountain road. The ten-odd passengers on the bus were all going to the hotel on vacation. The road narrowed, and sometimes the bus passed swaying by steep drop-offs. The alarm in Han Ma's heart thickened. She shut her eyes, persevering in one thought: I want to write fiction.

"Not even the fear of death can keep my daughter from her goal!" a woman in the back row suddenly said.

"Then, does the other one just concede?" the man sitting beside her asked.

"Concede? Impossible. But the ride can't stop now."

Han Ma opened her eyes and saw black objects violently careening toward her from outside the bus window. She covered her head with both arms to avoid them. At this moment the speeding bus screeched, and she was knocked out of her seat, tumbling into the aisle. She leaned against the seat to stand up, her face full of embarrassment. The other passengers all disembarked ahead of her.

"Ms., your bag rolled into the cab over here." The driver handed the small bag to her.

The entrance to the hotel was a stretch of darkness, but looking carefully Han Ma could just see a small orange light.

She went to the front desk, intending to check in, but a kindly old man came over and told her that she didn't need to. Her room was on the second floor, number 203. The old man's voice was hoarse. Han Ma memorized his appearance.

She entered the room and only then discovered her clothes were soaking wet—from such an alarming, dangerous journey in the nighttime.

She hurried to the shower, finished showering and blow-dried her hair, and then sat down to drink tea. She finished a cup of tea and felt herself gradually calming down. Did the scene on the bus signify the roughness of life? This question appeared in her mind. She turned on the electric heater even though the weather wasn't chilly. It was because her body would get cold while she wrote. When she was about to sit down at the desk, someone lightly knocked on the door.

It was the old fellow from the front desk.

"Girl, have you come here looking for someone? Everyone who visits this mountaintop is looking for someone."

"Hmm. But I haven't decided who I should be looking for," Han Ma said.

"Have you forgotten? You'll remember when you and I go somewhere together," the old man affirmed.

Han Ma followed him out of the hotel and along a path that wound around the mountain. The moonlight was lovely, and the landscape before her eyes beautiful. Han Ma thought: maybe I am about to go inside a story. Before long, a white two-story building appeared before her eyes. The old man said she would find the person she was looking for inside the building.

"What is this place?" Han Ma asked.

"This is the 'death building.' A wealthy businessperson donated it. The patients in there all have incurable illnesses. They are cared for here. To the outside world it's known as the White Building. The White Building is famous, so there's an endless flow of volunteers who come here to help out. Do you want to go inside to have a look around?"

"Of course, thank you."

"Let's go to the second floor. There's an older woman who has only a week to live."

The lights weren't on in the second-floor room. The patient reclined peacefully on a bed covered with a white blanket.

The old man's flashlight sliced through the room twice as he called out "Mrs. Qi!" and the light at the head of the bed quickly switched on.

"Welcome, welcome," Mrs. Qi said. "Please sit over here on the sofa."

Mrs. Qi was a widow in her sixties, clean and with her hair neatly brushed.

"The nurses just gave me morphine, so I'm comfortable. This woman must have come up from below, I heard the sound of the bus driving up the mountain. You can hear anything coming from that direction around here."

"My name is Han Ma. It's so good to meet you. I like the atmosphere here."

"Han Ma, it means 'a strong horse in winter.' Are you a writer?"

"Mrs. Qi, how did you guess?"

"I wasn't guessing. I thought: a pretty maiden coming to see me on such a beautiful evening, she is someone who writes—writes stories. This was the path my thoughts took. These days, I often think of things this way."

"Mrs. Qi tells parables. I'm not the only one who thinks so—the young nurse Yan does, too," the old fellow said. "Han Ma, I forgot to tell you, my last name is Gao."

"Han Ma writes fiction, look at her forehead!" Mrs. Qi said cheerfully. "I've read so many novels since I became ill. I feel like the novelists are my friends. They give me courage, so I haven't been afraid for a long time. Look, this cabinet is full of books, and I have a long-term reading plan. Han Ma, this evening I am meeting an author for the first time. Tell me whether I should have a long-term plan for reading fiction."

"You're right! I'm the same way, I read books following a long-term program . . . Oh, Mrs. Qi, I think you shouldn't only be able to read: you can also try to write. Reading and writing are always connected. But it's late already, tomorrow I will come visit again."

Han Ma and Uncle Gao went outside.

"Such a beautiful soul! I was afraid she was getting too worked up. That's why I left in a hurry," Han Ma said. "Uncle Gao, I feel that the White Building is a Daoist paradise where immortals live."

"I'm so glad that you said so, because I think the same. The patients here, as long as they can still move, are always helping other people. This Mrs. Qi goes to read to an old man every afternoon, because he can't see. Sometimes she passes out from pain while she's reading."

Han Ma glanced at the moon and quietly wiped away the tears from her eyes.

"Since I met you, I've felt like you're my granddaughter. What kind of stories do you write?" Uncle Gao asked.

“I write stories about the search for happiness,” Han Ma answered with deep emotion.

“Then you’ve come to the right place.”

Han Ma went upstairs. Uncle Gao, watching her go, whispered: “Such a loveable young woman!”

Han Ma went into her room and saw that there was a piece of paper beside her notebook, and written on it: *Young woman, let’s work together and encourage each other.—Your fellow travelers.* She said to herself: so it turns out these guests were all coming to the White Building to visit patients! Maybe the patients in the White Building are used to people from the outside and open up their souls, like Mrs. Qi did. The White Building truly was a tranquil dream. People from the city might visit to experience the romance of life here.

Late in the night there were owls hooting outside. Their calls weren’t distressing, but instead like a summoning of deep emotion. Han Ma sighed, “Truly a piece of paradise.” She decided to visit even more patients tomorrow.

Because she hadn’t pulled the curtains, through the window she saw some glittering flying insects moving around in the air and forming a few designs. Han Ma fell into a daze. “Who is this one? And that one? Oh god!” she said involuntarily. She regretted not coming here sooner. The insects’ performance lasted for a while, as the owls hooted once in a while. By the time stillness was restored all around, Han Ma couldn’t keep her eyes open.

The next day when she went downstairs for breakfast, she saw that the guests seated in the dining room were all her fellow travelers from the bus. She nodded to them in greeting one by one. She wondered: who was it who’d left her that note? Maybe it was all of them collectively? No one brought up the subject while she ate. When she’d finished, she discovered they’d all gone, with only one woman remaining. The woman looked like the one who’d sat in the row behind her on the bus. She seemed to be waiting for Han Ma.

“Are you going to the White Building, too?” Han Ma asked her.

“Yes. My daughter is there. She’s not a patient—her beloved has an incurable illness. He’s an elderly physician, and when my daughter was young, he treated her severe asthma. Now the doctor’s life will be at the end soon, and my daughter wants to see him on his way. I heard you’re called Han Ma—it’s a good name.”

"Aunt Wan, I'd like to ask you: does your daughter feel happy?" Han Ma asked.

"Of course, of course, this is the happiest moment in her life. Seeing a loved one on their way—does this need saying? Wait a while and you'll see. The doctor has strong self-control. They make an enviable couple."

The doctor's room was on the first floor. When the two of them pushed the door open and entered, the daughter was giving the aged doctor juice to drink, just like she was feeding an infant. Afterward she turned around, to Han Ma's surprise: this girl was as beautiful as someone in a painting.

"Hello," the daughter said with natural poise, "this is my husband, Doctor Yu."

The old doctor looked at Han Ma and rakishly winked an eye.

"Are you the future major writer?" he asked.

"I'm only a future minor writer," Han Ma answered.

"It's all the same. I have the greatest respect for writers. Before I became ill I often read novels until late at night."

Doctor Yu said he wanted to shake Han Ma's hand. The daughter covered a laugh off to one side.

The doctor's hand was jutting with bones, but Han Ma immediately felt his buoyant life force.

"I have the greatest respect for you," she said irrepressibly.

"See, everyone is fond of you," the daughter said, and kissed him on the face.

The doctor smiled with satisfaction. Aunt Wan brought out her gift for him, again to Han Ma's surprise. The gift was a book, and the title of the book was *XXXX*! Han Ma recognized the cover at a glance.

Doctor Yu received the book gratefully and then said to Han Ma:

"I have four hours of the day without pain. I plan to use these hours to read this novel and strive to finish it. I've heard of your Pigeon Book Club. Perhaps in the future I can discuss this book with you. I will look forward to that day."

"That day will definitely come," the daughter hastily added. Han Ma also nodded repeatedly.

After saying goodbye to the beauty and the doctor, Aunt Wan and Han Ma went downstairs to the building's lobby.

"On the east side of the second floor," Aunt Wan told her, "there's a twenty-nine-year-old boy with leukemia. He only has two or so hours of relief daily, and he uses this time to study philosophy."

Han Ma promptly declined to visit him. She thought that taking up his time would be a crime.

She didn't go to see Mrs. Qi again, either. She told Aunt Wan that she needed to go back to the hotel right away to write.

"It must be an outpouring of inspiration. There's inspiration everywhere in this kind of place," Aunt Wan said cheerfully.

The stimulation of the image of the doctor was too much for Han Ma. She was overwrought and also had a dizzy sensation. So she walked back to the hotel with quick steps, sat at the desk, picked up her notebook, and recorded her wonderful encounter with the White Building.

"I'm still not trying hard enough . . . ," she said to herself. "The White Building is both a paradise and a battleground."

"It's hard to tell you about it all at once," Han Ma said to Fei. "Those patients were more like literary workers than we are. It was deeply provocative—something is turning over inside of me."

"Han Ma, your account amazes me. I cannot regress—if I do I will be unworthy of you and my life would lose all meaning. I will resist," Fei said, looking up at the ceiling.

"Good, Fei."

They each read their own book and did their own writing. Han Ma was thinking secretly that Fei was now trying to struggle, and that she would also exert herself, would also resist, and never be senselessly sentimental again.

She realized that her writing had reached another level after returning from the White Building visits. She was even more capable of pressing out some kind of object from inside her. The products of this pressing out were unexpected language and strange plots. She silently cheered herself on: "This is what I wanted, this is right! To live forever like Mrs. Qi and Doctor Yu and also that boy I didn't meet . . . They are the real vanguard."

After a few days Han Ma gave her cleaned-up draft to Fei to read.

After Fei finished reading he said to her:

"Han Ma, I have nothing to say. My love for you has already reached as far as possible, accompanied by deep, deep fear. While you are pressing on yourself, you are also pressing on me. And for me, as someone who has always drifted with the waves, not to resist means death, doesn't it? My true self will be revealed, showing what I am after all."

Han Ma was silent. Fei's explanation of himself gave her a sense that whatever was gathering around the top of their heads would finally fall away. Everything that they needed to do must be done with haste, not only for herself, but also for Fei. She must make him stronger. This was her responsibility.

"Han Ma is a hawk. Now I've seen clearly," Fei said as he kissed her hair.

At noon on a Saturday, after lunch, Fei told Han Ma that he was getting together with his close friend of more than ten years, Heishi. Fei hadn't had an opportunity to speak with Heishi on his own since he got married.

Watching Fei walk away, Han Ma reflected that at this crucial juncture Heishi was the best conversation partner for him. Just like Xiao Sang had been her best conversation partner before.

Fei rode the bus to the park in the suburbs. Heishi arrived at almost the same time.

Fei brought Heishi to the edge of the large artificial lake. Not long ago he'd had an agonizing talk with Yue at this lakeside.

"I'm trying to make things clearer. I want to find a solution that involves the least harm. Now that seems nearly impossible."

Heishi noticed the incredible desperation on Fei's face. He was silent.

"I misjudged her. Originally I believed that since I had chosen Han Ma and established a home with her, Yue would be able to leave me and seek her own happiness. Heishi, let me ask you: do you think I've also misjudged myself in this matter?"

Fei's words seemed like they were said to Heishi, but also like he was debating with himself. Heishi deeply understood his close friend, so he answered:

"It's not that you're wrong. Sometimes, a long time needs to pass before people's innate qualities finally appear, whether to themselves or to others. When we make judgments, everything is still unclear. This is my experience. I wanted to ask you, Fei: do you have any regrets?"

"No, not regrets. Although there's a kind of despair, and many kinds of hurt."

"You don't need other people's advice—that's a good thing. Taking this walk by the lake with you today, I've been thinking that my good friend is in the process of maturing. There's hope, even though the journey ahead seems unfathomable."

The haze in Heishi's mind had dispersed. He believed Fei—believed Fei could endure. So long as he held out, things would reach a resolution. There'd been a few times before when his friend had sunk into a hopeless condition, but Heishi realized that this time Fei had begun a transformation. This was probably the benefit of Han Ma's influence on Fei. Naturally, their recent reading would also exert a subtle influence on him.

"Heishi, I am always talking about my own problems. I haven't even congratulated you yet. Speaking of Xiao Sang, we all love her so much . . . Heishi, you've caught hold of happiness. Even I was in a sweat for you and anxious that you'd fumble things. Of course you didn't. You and she are a perfect match. Afterward all of our book friends gave a sigh of relief."

"Thank you, Fei. Han Ma, and our book friends—you give my life meaning. Yesterday Xiao Sang said to me: Fei's difficulty is only temporary. Her intuitions have consistently been right. I think she means that there will be a resolution in the not-too-distant future. Seeing you now, I think you're bolder than in the past. On the inside, Fei, I'm cheering you on!"

The two friends talked and talked this way, wound a circuit around the large lake, and then walked another loop.

Fei took the bus again on the way home. He sat thinking back on his meet-up with Heishi and sighed: "This really came just in time!" Heishi had given him encouragement, and at the critical moment. Fei felt that he'd overcome his panic, even if the future ahead was still dim. Heishi had suggested to him that in this love triangle he needed first of all to understand what he wanted. If he couldn't even be sure of himself, how could he understand the situation the others were in? This meant that from now on he would try his utmost to change this habit of drifting with the waves. He could only possibly help the others in this difficult predicament if he were able to get his footing.

When Fei got back home he was terribly hungry. Han Ma had brought home the Yangzhou fried rice he loved to eat.

"It is my great fortune to have a close friend, Han Ma," Fei talked while he ate. "Now, through you and Heishi guiding me, I am sure of myself for the first time in my life. This also proves that our marriage is a success, doesn't it?"

"Of course it's a success, whether for you or for me." Han Ma nodded her affirmation.

The subtext that they hadn't said was: regardless of how things turned out from now on.

"Did you read this afternoon?" Fei asked.

"I was writing. I need to speed up," Han Ma said.

"I need to speed up, too. Just now on the bus I kept repeating: you must be strong, and don't disappoint Han Ma."

They had both already made up their minds to face steadfastly whatever the situation was. Fei was still suffering, but he was much steadier than in the past. Something had been clarified in his mind: that he shouldn't spend his entire life on personal emotional entanglements, which was selfish and would make him loathe himself. He was only pleased with himself when he studied literature. As for personal affairs, just allow them to develop naturally, wait for issues to appear, and then pass judgment. This was what Heishi expected of him.

The next evening Fei and Han Ma went out to eat together at the bamboo restaurant. The building had been expanded so that there was now a bright, spacious main dining room and much more variety on the menu. Xiao Fei and her husband had hired two helpers. Han Ma noticed that there were more than twice as many customers ordering food.

She had just stepped through the door of the main dining room when Xiao Fei pulled her aside and quietly said:

"Young Han, I noticed that your and Fei's spirits aren't in a good place. Maybe you've run into some problems. Don't ever be discouraged. Everyone encounters difficulties, but all will pass. Look at me and Lao Yao . . ."

"Thank you, Xiao Fei," Han Ma said gratefully. "There really are some problems, but we'll persevere. We need to stand tall like you and Lao Yao. You are both always encouraging to us. It's so good to be your neighbors."

Han Ma returned to Fei's side and sat down. Fei asked her what she and Xiao Fei had been talking about.

"She said we don't look like we're doing well and wants us to brace our spirits to persevere through this difficult period," Han Ma said.

"This couple is my lifelong model," Fei said. "I was just thinking: I have such good fortune to always encounter good people. But with people always helping me out, I've formed the habit of inertia and don't make enough effort."

"But you also help other people. For example, me; for example, our friends at the Pigeon Book Club."

"I haven't done much good. Because I'm selfish, I've wasted so much precious time. You are far better than me, and living beside you I feel surrounded by healthy energy. I used to be the type of person who accomplishes nothing."

"But that's not what I feel. Without your guidance, I couldn't have set out on a literary path so soon. It's just that now we've both realized that time is short. This is a very good thing. Fei, promise me, not under any circumstances to abandon literature," Han Ma said, looking him in the eyes.

"I vow: I won't abandon literature, under any circumstances," Fei said, one word at a time.

They'd been eating while they talked, so the meal took a fairly long time. When they eventually stood, the other customers had almost all gone. They had just left the restaurant when Lao Yao caught up to them.

"Young Fei, young Han, I'll see you a few steps along the way. I just heard from Xiao Fei that you've encountered some difficulties. I won't ask you what the problem is, I only want to tell you as someone who has been through bitter experiences: don't lose trust in the human heart. Life isn't entirely what it looks like on its surface. Life can transform, and you will mature along with its changes. OK, I need to go back to work."

"Thank you, dear Lao Yao!" Fei and Han Ma said in unison.

They came to that path through the middle of the scrub where not long ago Fei had lost his way, so that now every time they passed there Han Ma felt a little anxious. But today Fei took the initiative to bring up the time he'd gotten lost.

"That exposed how the true condition of my soul was chaos. I hadn't accepted responsibility and was acting like I didn't know how to behave, making it so that there was no way forward for me. I think that from now on I will transform."

"Fei, that you can talk about it in such a moderate way shows how you are already changing. I'm so glad to hear this."

"Mm-hmm, that makes sense."

Han Ma was thinking secretly about how Fei was making such an effort now. He also had such good neighbors and friends around him that there was no need to worry too much. He would struggle to break away from difficulty. Although she would hate to give him up, no matter what happened, she would support him.

For many days in succession the lights stayed on in their studies until late in the night. They were overextending their physical stamina in exchange for the soul's equilibrium.

"It's like I'm in a race with Death," Han Ma said, "and you are, too, Fei."

"My research has finally made progress. I want to set up a special mechanism to communicate aesthetic appreciation, to help our book friends perfect themselves in many ways. I've learned that I really am in a race with Death. The former me doesn't exist, while the present me has a future that's unfathomable, because not trying equals death. Han Ma, you've helped me to understand myself. You are the most precious gift heaven has given me."

"So are you, Fei. We're grateful for each other and also to heaven."

Xiaoyue wrote the outline of a speech, read it through, then tore it up. He wanted to talk about his impressions of chapter 31 of the book *XXXX*, but he could never find the right point of entry. Later the night deepened, and he lay in the dark continuing to think of his speech. Dissatisfied with himself, he seemed to be walking the main streets obliviously until he arrived at the lakeside and saw Han Ma sitting there wearing a black skirt and shirt.

"How should my speech begin, Han Ma?" he went over and asked her.

Han Ma stood up to meet him, her face a little indistinct in the moonlight. She stretched both hands toward him.

Xiaoyue took hold of her hands, and neither spoke. Then her figure gradually melted away and soon disappeared.

A few sentences came into Xiaoyue's mind, but he didn't know what they meant. Still, they brought him a sense of fullness as he neared the artistic conceit of what he wanted words to say.

The next day at dusk, when he arrived at the Pigeon Book Club, only Qiaozi was earlier than him. She was boiling water on an electric hotplate. Xiaoyue promptly helped with rinsing the teacups. In a while everyone had arrived, all in pairs. Xiaoyue tried to sit in the corner furthest from the lamplight, but Qiaozi pulled him to sit in the middle of the room without letting him object.

"Xiaoyue, today you must make a speech. We all want to hear you speak," she said.

Across from Xiaoyue, Han Ma and Fei were both looking at him. Once he met their eyes his face flushed red. To cover up he started to speak, his words coming out rapidly, although he didn't know why.

"Chapter 31 is about love. But what I discern from what is depicted in the book is the yearning and passion for writing. Yes, all of it seems like my own impulse to write, even though I'm not any good at writing real stories. I read this chapter a few months ago, and now every time I read it there's this impulse again. I think of the person I love, or let's say it's my fictional lover, and in my mind I keep constructing story plots around her, imagining love scenes. That kind of yearning is hard to calm in any way other than writing. This is the magic of fiction. The mechanism is a circle: I want to love this person either hypothetically or in reality, I read about her in a book, then in order to pursue her I start to write, and writing makes my love for her grow . . . This life of passion, I think, ought to belong to every person who is willing to write—whether writing on paper, or writing in the mind. I've heard from my book friends that Fei regards this novel as his lover, and my feeling is the same as his. I'm especially interested in those descriptions of romance: the longing which is like writing, which is also the author's longing, should be a relationship between lovers. Therefore I think everyone ought to write, especially people who care about literature. Love isn't fictional—instead there is a high degree of consistency between the two aspects of flesh and spirit, as writers transfer into their books the love that happens in real life or an affection similar to love, while we readers then use the text as the basis for doing the same thing. Therefore I think that every reader is actually also a writer, even though some people never take up the pen or publish their whole lives. So long as the reader enters from their own love into the love of an author, the reader is writing through the author. Furthermore, the best stories are both writing the soul and writing the body, because readers need both aspects to be satisfied."

Once Xiaoyue finished speaking he tried to leave, but Qiaozi wouldn't let him go. "You can't go when these questions are as big as the heavens!" she said.

"Xiaoyue's brilliant speech has deepened what I said on the topic of taking the novel as a lover," Fei said. "It's true, as he said, that it is hard to enter into the best of contemporary fiction if a reader lacks the ability to love, or cannot activate the organic function. I feel ashamed in comparison to Xiaoyue. I always stop at acquiring a smattering of knowledge. Maybe I've also gotten used to being like this in life. His analysis makes me wonder."

Xiaoyue sat there nervously, his knees trembling. He didn't dare to look toward the couple opposite him. He heard Han Ma gently saying to Fei: "You'll do better in the future."

"Love as portrayed in this chapter is truly enchanting," Xiao Sang said. "The whole body and mind are engrossed in love to the extreme, love to the point of dizziness. Reading fiction and writing fiction should both be like this: what Xiaoyue said is right. And he has emphasized bodily longing, which is what I appreciate the most, too. If love that is analogous to the love in fiction hasn't happened in real life, it's hard for a reader to experience so deeply, or to experience at all. The organic function sustains the spiritual function—neither can be missing. Fiction like this requires its readers to have the potential to create. It is creation and not merely understanding. This is fiction that transforms the human worldview. There should be no shortcuts to reading this type of novel, other than, like Xiaoyue, to bring the entire self into it, and even further into it."

Li Hai and Qiaozi whispered as if she were prompting him to make a speech, but he hesitated. He coughed dryly twice, swept his eyes in a circle around the interior of the space, and asked everyone in a lowered voice:

"Do you hear someone in the room weeping?"

Everyone looked at him, not knowing what he meant.

"There is a thick kind of love," Li Hai raised his voice, "to the extent that when you speak you just want to cry. I'm an outsider to literature, and my experience doesn't run very deep. But a moment ago I heard the sound of suppressed weeping. Oh, I wish I had an instrument to measure the intensity of this sound! What's fascinating about this book is that if you dare to enter into it in your own way, you'll unconsciously find yourself on the author's stage for the performance of freedom. Who was weeping tonight?"

Xiaoyue responded to Li Hai in his mind: "It was me, because of too much love, so I wept. Thank you, Li Hai."

"What a fine evening! It makes me remember previous evenings at the book club," Heishi said. "We arrive with the idea of devoting ourselves to our love, then we harvest love."

"Yes—yes!" Li Hai and Qiaozi, and also Yan and Yang, chimed in with an exaggerated response.

Heishi wasn't embarrassed by their teasing. He continued:

"In life people always weep because of love; because of yearning for and not attaining it; because of its loss; because of its disappearance . . . All of this, everything, is so beautiful. Let us bravely devote ourselves to our emotions, like Xiaoyue. Only through devoting ourselves will we not have regrets. Even happiness is hidden in weeping."

"Heishi, thank you!" Xiaoyue said sincerely.

"I also want to thank you—many of the members of Xiao Sang's reading group at the department store—people who are enchanted by books—follow in your footsteps, counting on their fingers how many days there are until they will meet with you again," Heishi said.

That evening, taking advantage of the animated conversation, Xiaoyue pretended to be going to the bathroom and slipped out. He knew they were all paired off and that he was the only person in the group who was single, so the best thing was to leave early. This was his second time attending the Pigeon Book Club. He walked along a darkened street of used bookstores, his heart brimming with passion and happiness. Yes, this was the kind of happiness Heishi had meant.

Xiaoyue had just left the alleyway when someone called to him. It was his former girlfriend Hong. They had broken up almost two years before.

"I saw that you looked like Xiaoyue, and it really is you. You look like you're doing well," she said.

"Things are all right. Keeping busy every day. When I'm not, in the evenings I go to reading groups. And you?"

"Me? I'm not busy. I read a little outside of work, too, all on the professional side."

Xiaoyue thought about how he and Hong lived in the same city, but hadn't run into each other once since breaking up!

“Are you married now?” Hong asked.

“No, I don’t even have a girlfriend. It seems like there’s something preventing me,” he said jokingly.

“Then let me ask you, Xiaoyue, could we possibly get back together?” Hong asked in earnest.

“It wouldn’t be possible. I’ve changed too much in the two years since we broke up. You can’t even imagine.”

“I understand, Xiaoyue. Wishing you good luck!”

She crossed the street and walked down another road. Watching her lithe figure, Xiaoyue noted that she was still as pretty as before, even prettier. So why was he hardly aroused by the sight of her?

Xiaoyue wanted to relax a bit, so he went to a bar for a drink, but then he felt his heart tense up again and couldn’t relax. He increased his pace back to his apartment complex.

After cleaning up the apartment and taking a shower, he sat down and opened the book to chapter 31 again. While he read he thought back on the evening’s discussion and took down his reflections in a notebook. He felt that his own speech hadn’t turned out too badly. He’d basically communicated his state of mind, and the reaction was better than he had expected. This book club was a miracle, and the first ones to create the miracle had been Fei and Heishi, and Li Hai. What had the scene been like then? It seemed that the questions he had raised were familiar old topics for the book club friends; however, these were the kind of topics that one could go infinitely deep into, so everyone was affected by them. He wanted very much to hear Han Ma’s perspective, but unfortunately she hadn’t made a speech. Most likely as an author she wasn’t willing to share her thoughts in advance.

He read chapter 31 again trying to use Han Ma’s eyes and then sighed: “This description is marvelous!” It was as if he sensed Han Ma’s heartbeat within the words and in between the lines. Feeling contented, he lay down.

At daybreak he asked over and over in a dream: “What is the way to the Pigeon Book Club?” Then he woke up.

After Han Ma and Fei had left the street of used bookstores, they walked along the familiar road toward the river, making their way to the riverside to take the night bus. On the walk they talked about Xiaoyue.

"This young man has so much energy," Fei said excitedly. "I don't just mean how he absorbs knowledge, but also his astonishing persistence, it's a kind of ethos. He's exceptional. You always have unique insight. It's fortunate that you introduced him to the book club."

"Xiaoyue stands out from the crowd," Han Ma said cheerfully. "I've only interacted with him a few times, but once we talk about literature we sense that the other is 'in the know.' He really does pursue literature as if it were a lover. He's profound—people who talk with him come away enlightened."

"I've noticed that he's also very disciplined."

"He must be. People say that he's honest and reliable, and always happy to help out. His bookstore is right across from our store. One day he came to find me to talk about the department store reading group, and his enthusiasm for literature made a deep impression on me. Later there was his speech at the reading group, an extraordinary statement . . . I feel it's a love for literature with no factor of material gain." Han Ma was immersed in recollection.

"We gather the finest friends around us—even someone like me cannot regress . . . ," Fei said.

He was also sunk in thought.

Soon their bus arrived. Something strange happened after they took their seats.

As the bus was going through a riverbed tunnel, Fei and Han Ma were both thinking silently. All of a sudden their surroundings turned pitch black, while the bus kept going. Fei reached out a hand to feel to the side. Han Ma wasn't next to him.

"Han Ma! Han Ma!" he stood and called frantically.

No one answered him, and he sensed that he was alone. He shouted again for the driver, but still no one answered.

The bus seemed to be going so fast that he had to clutch the handrail on the back of the seat. He spread his arms across the seats and swept them back and forth without touching a single person.

"Han Ma! Han Ma . . ." He felt sweat like rain running down his face.

Precisely at this moment the bus braked violently to a stop and Fei was thrown back into the seat.

The lights inside the bus turned on. Fei saw Han Ma beside him.

"When I took the bus to the hotel on Meng Mountain," Han Ma said, "I experienced something like you just did."

Fei felt a little weak when they got off the bus, so Han Ma held him by the arm as they walked ahead.

"That scene a moment ago was like a drill," he said.

"We will get used to this kind of drill, Fei. I have a premonition that you will grow stronger and stronger. Recently you've been going through a slow transformation," Han Ma said calmly.

They arrived back at their familiar home. Fei sat on the sofa in the living room, measuring every piece of furniture and each appliance with his eyes, looking back and forth until tears flowed.

"Fei! Fei . . . ," Han Ma cried out.

She hugged him, suddenly understanding the depth of his sadness. She got up and brought a towel to wipe the tears for him. Then she turned her face away, because she also felt a heartbreaking despair, but suppressed her tears. A long while passed before she finally heard him say:

"Han Ma, I'm a little scared."

Han Ma knew what Fei was afraid of. To console him, she said:

"This is also something you can get used to. I have faith in you."

They held each other all through that night. Han Ma woke up midway and heard Fei say to her: "Don't let go, Han Ma, once you let go it will all be over."

Xiao Sang and Heishi had just turned into the darkened alleyway when she burst out urgently with the question:

"How likely do you think it is that Fei and Han Ma will break up?"

"It seems more and more likely. Ah, the world is inconstant. I know you're fond of Han Ma, and so am I. The problem is that Yue has only loved Fei her entire life. Now she's thirty-eight and has no children and no husband. She even brought up wanting to have a child with Fei. She doesn't care about appearances . . . poor woman."

"What kind of woman is Yue? Is she pretty?" Xiao Sang tried her hardest to imagine.

"She's very pretty. Though she's a little weak by nature. I think she would be a good mother. But a child born without a father, that's always a little tragic." Heishi carefully put his arm around Xiao Sang as he spoke, having her walk in the center of the pathway.

"Yes. If they have a child, Fei won't let the little one not have a father. We'll have a child soon, too. We're so lucky, maybe it will be a boy like you . . . How can we possibly help Fei and Han Ma? When Han Ma told me that she'd decided to get married, she was so hopeful about their future!"

"Han Ma doesn't need help—she's brave and decisive. Fei is the one to worry about. He loves Han Ma more, but he also won't hurt Yue. After so many years he can understand Yue's sadness very well. He's an empathetic person."

"Then do you think he'll let Yue have a child?"

"It's possible. Fei is soft-hearted and sympathizes with the weak . . . Xiao Sang, do you think Fei is worthy of love?"

"Yes, he is. Though he and you aren't the same type. He probably belongs to the late-blooming category."

"You really have keen insights."

"Having children should be a wonderful thing. I hope our child will be a boy like you."

"In my imagination it's a girl like you."

"See, we're starting to flatter each other again."

"Last time I talked with Fei, I felt that he was changing. He's struggling in an attempt to analyze himself. He was never like that before. Han Ma's transformed him."

"Han Ma, Han Ma . . ." Xiao Sang was immersed in memories. Her heart trembled for her dear friend.

When they were almost to the company housing, a comet drew a large arc across the sky up ahead, then vanished.

"Often, to love is to seek out pain," Heishi said.

"But we're still drawn into love with all our hearts, just like we long to read and write. The difference lies in how love's outcome cannot be predicted, while reading and writing are sure to bring about happiness. That is why humankind invented literature," Xiao Sang said.

One day Xiaoyue returned to his office for a break after he'd eaten at the bookstore cafeteria.

As he pushed open the office door, he was surprised by Han Ma sitting in the chair where he usually sat himself. She smiled and nodded at him.

"Xiaoyue, I traded shifts this afternoon and wanted to take advantage of your lunch break to come have a chat with you. Do you have any business to handle at the moment?" She stood.

"No, Han Ma, I don't . . . Sit down, I'll make tea for you," Xiaoyue said, flustered.

He poured tea for her and pulled over a chair and sat opposite her. Then he calmed down.

"You have so many books here. I admire you: you're a complete talent, with an amazing memory and sensitivity. Someone like me who's only able to write stories needs your help."

"There are many people who have my kind of talent, Han Ma. You're the one who's rare. To tell the truth, if you hadn't come to find me, I would have gone looking for you. There are so many questions I want to ask you, but at the moment I've completely forgotten them. I'll ask them later on."

"Xiaoyue, your speech at the book club gave me the sense that you were helping me to write. It was so relevant, so apt. I didn't make a speech that day, but I said to myself: I must find an opportunity alone to tell you. I don't know why, both of your speeches—I mean that when you talk I feel as though I'm writing fiction with you. It's a wonderful sensation: someone taking those things that I am always trying to say about writing but cannot say, and stating them clearly. Wait, I know you're going to tell me that Fei frequently says these kinds of things, too. True, Fei is sharp like you, but he's not the same as you. You have drive and also tenacity, so you can go deeper, without stopping. You go deeper into a primeval region, where few people reach now. You're the kind of person who doesn't show emotion, but has the ability to appeal to people. Fei commends me for introducing you to the book club. Your two speeches were the utmost encouragement to me! I wanted to say that you 'march right in,' yes, you are on the march."

As Han Ma spoke Xiaoyue had to work hard to keep himself from trembling.

"Han Ma, drink your tea. These are tea leaves I brought back from Fujian. Today is worth celebrating."

"These tea leaves are special. They can make you drunk, can't they?"

Xiaoyue nodded, smiling. He was so excited that he couldn't speak.

Han Ma continued praising the tea, then added:

"From now on when I don't have anything to do I'll just come here to drink tea. Get some extra tea leaves ready. You make me clearheaded and give me courage—it's like fate arranging you to be near me."

Han Ma finished her tea and stood to go, saying she was worried she would affect Xiaoyue's work.

He saw her to the bus stop. After the bus had driven off, he stayed standing there, not moving.

"Xiaoyue, was that your girlfriend?" Button Woman suddenly appeared.

"No, it's a friend from the reading group."

"She has a really good air about her. Now I know what type you like."

"She has a husband," Xiaoyue said resentfully.

"Excuse me, I won't keep talking."

The entire afternoon and all through to the evening Xiaoyue's mind was in tumult, like scenes flashing by in a movie: Han Ma smiling; Han Ma speaking; Han Ma drinking tea; Han Ma standing and looking at him . . . The two or three sentences he had said lingered in his memory. He wondered: had he said anything inane in his confusion? It seemed like he hadn't.

He felt that this turn in his life was unexpected. He should thank literature, because this communication with each other could only take place through literature. He was almost manic with happiness. He was so excited he couldn't read, so he decided to give himself the evening off. He knew he hadn't attracted Han Ma as someone of the opposite sex. She'd been moved by his speeches both times because of literary communication. "Oh, literature is truly good," he thought. Her temperament and his were complementary, as if they were close friends excavating the depths of literature's mineshaft. Thinking and thinking this way, Xiaoyue went to the bar cherishing an excited state of mind.

He sat there drinking slowly and watched a young woman sing. He hadn't been here in a while, and this singer was a new face, with a gentle voice, and she looked a little like his ex-girlfriend Hong. At first Xiaoyue, steeped in his imaginings about Han Ma, didn't pay attention to what she was singing. Later he suddenly realized that she was singing "Song of the Cliffs," a folk song he'd heard in Tibet a long time ago. The song told of the confrontation between youth and Death. Xiaoyue hadn't thought that it could be sung so mellifluously, so close to a whisper. Listening and listening, he almost shed tears. He felt that he shouldn't indulge in such sensuality and had to put on the brakes. He stood, paid the check, and left the bar.

The night sky over the city was very beautiful. Meng didn't have many tall structures, and the houses and buildings formed a decorative border against the clear night sky. Living on such a beautiful Earth, how could people not do something for this world? This must be the subtext of what Han Ma had said. She'd said she would come looking for him frequently, which implied that she would frequently try to understand what he was redoubling his efforts to accomplish. He looked forward to even more contact between them. He'd make a tireless attempt not to disappoint her. What was Death in the young woman's song? Xiaoyue felt that for the first time he understood the emotion of the song.

He went back to his apartment complex and then read for an hour and took notes for ten or twenty minutes. It was already past midnight. He went to sleep right away, in a satisfied mood.

When Xiaoyue arrived at his office, sunlight spread across the floor. Another day filled with hope began. He dusted the desk and chair while he gazed at Han Ma going into the department store opposite with joy rising in his chest.

Xiao Ma went to Uncle Yi's home every other day. The residents of the courtyard all recognized her. The elderly people greeted her kindly. The young people didn't say hello to her, though, because they worried she would be embarrassed. Xiao Ma found this amusing, telling herself: "I can't be embarrassed." She felt that her romance with Uncle Yi couldn't be more natural. This was why in the past she could believe that Uncle Yi and Xiao Sang were romantically involved. On the weekends and holidays Xiao Ma would spend an entire day at Uncle Yi's home and return to her own apartment building only in the evening.

Thanks to her intensive studies, her sensitivity to fiction grew stronger and stronger. She and Uncle Yi could discuss back and forth in his study for a long time without the least sense of fatigue. Xiao Ma aspired to finish reading all of the best fiction in the world within a few years and to take detailed notes. Uncle Yi fully supported her, of course. He not only discussed fiction with her, but also read her notes attentively, helping her to expand her thoughts and express her astonishing ideas.

There was one day, when the two of them were together in the kitchen preparing food, that Xiao Ma couldn't bear it and just said:

"Uncle Yi, my running back and forth like this wastes time. Don't you think I could simply move in here and be done with it? That would be both economical and efficient. Your place is large enough that we'll each have our own bedroom."

Even though Xiao Ma used a joking tone of voice, Uncle Yi listened and then didn't utter a word for a very long time.

Xiao Ma grew a little nervous, not knowing whether she had said something wrong.

The food was ready, and the two of them ate while continuing their discussion.

She glanced at Uncle Yi occasionally, not daring to repeat her proposal.

When Uncle Yi was seeing Xiao Ma back home and they walked out of the courtyard, he finally said to her that he hoped she would test things out for another six months, and then they could talk about it again.

"Or else you could be my girlfriend?" he asked, sounding her out. "Next year I'll be sixty. It would be unfair if you and I married."

"If I were just your girlfriend, my mother would be furious with me. I won't do that! My mother's generation isn't the same as ours, and I need to be considerate of her. I've never asked you before, so now I will: 'Do you love me or not?'"

"Love you or not? Do you even need to ask? Of course I love you and have loved you for a very long time. All of the plans I've made for my life in the future include you. I think of you every day."

"Then let's get married. If you insist, I will wait another six months."

"Yes, six months. Take advantage of this time to try to achieve your goals more quickly."

"Oh, Uncle Yi, Uncle Yi, how can you only think of me in all things? You are a living person yourself."

"Myself? I'm not important, and I'm old . . ."

"Then let's kiss," she said and embraced him.

Uncle Yi leaned his face away, saying they shouldn't kiss, they needed to wait for half a year. Xiao Ma got onto the bus indignantly.

She went back to her apartment, thought back on the scene that had just taken place, and couldn't help but laugh aloud. She laughed until tears flowed.

She loved Uncle Yi even more, loved him in her bones. She knew that if she lost him then life would lose all meaning. Now that she loved him this way, what did it matter having to wait another six months? Uncle

Yi always had his reasons. She didn't think she needed any trial period, but it wouldn't be so bad to focus on her reading. After all, she'd gotten a late start, and there was still a large gap in comparison to Xiao Sang and the others. Thinking of this, Xiao Ma started to cheer up. Once she felt cheerful she called Uncle Yi.

"Uncle Yi, don't be angry with me. I love you."

"I'm not angry. I love you, too, Xiao Ma."

"You won't let me kiss you, so I'll just kiss this book that has your signature in it."

"Hmm. You are progressing fast in your studies, so happy things will happen to you every day. New discoveries, new experiences . . . Six months will pass in the blink of an eye."

"I really want to hurry over to your study now. But I'll just take notes here. Goodbye."

She sat down and went into a new round of sprints.

When Xiao Ma was off on the weekend, she bought a large pile of heavy groceries and carried them to Uncle Yi's home.

"It's too much, Xiao Ma. How did you manage to carry it all?" he said while he put the food into the refrigerator.

"Of course I could carry it, I'm no delicate flower."

Xiao Ma pulled out her notebook and sat down. The two of them looked at each other and smiled.

After their discussion ended, Xiao Ma said:

"I feel proud all the time, now that I've become your student."

"You will surpass me soon. Besides, I'm also learning from you, and I'm trying to improve. All of you—you, Xiao Sang, Heishi, Fei—you are spurring on my progress."

"Don't worry any more about whether I'm at a disadvantage. The reality is, I can't be without you. I wouldn't want to live and would regress instead."

"Didn't we already get past the crisis? So waiting for a while longer won't matter."

"I'll do what you say. I've been guiding my mom and my two sisters, and I gain energy from you. You're so fascinating!"

"I'm not the only one who holds so much fascination for you. Xiao Sang and Heishi are an influence, too, and most significant is your own pursuit of an ideal. You have also guided me."

Xiao Ma didn't stay to eat, since she had to go visit her mother.

As she went outside she noticed that the city of Meng was glistening and glittering everywhere.

"Mom, Uncle Yi and I have basically decided to get married in six months," Xiao Ma announced as soon as she came through the door.

"Why do you want to wait, when you're no longer young?" her mom asked.

"He's afraid I will have regrets. He keeps thinking he's too old and says that I'll be put at a disadvantage by marrying him. Uncle Yi doesn't consider himself, he only thinks about my interests."

"He is such a good person. With some people it's exactly the opposite. As for this waiting half a year, you should listen to him. If you listened to me, I'd be eager for you get married right away."

"Are Yanzhi and Xiao Hong still doing well?"

"Yes, yes! They went to your store's reading group, and when they came back they were all excited. Now they read books and take notes every day after getting off work. It's completely different than before. Xiao Ma, do you think they'll be able to learn?"

"Of course they'll be able to learn. They're both smart."

"We've all had a change of fortune. I can be free from this lifetime of worry, after enduring so much. Uncle Yi is dependable and in good health, even though he's older. You'll learn so much by being with him . . ."

"Mom, I wasn't thinking of that. I just fell in love with him as soon as I met him. I like the kind of person he is."

"Your judgment can't be wrong. You've been intelligent ever since you were little. I used to worry you wouldn't find a good partner and couldn't sleep out of anxiety. Normally a child without a father's love has some deficiencies, but you don't have a single one by nature. You belong to the type of person who accomplishes things. Now I can retire to the rear guard and read books all day, aside from making a bit of food. No need to say how relieved I feel now."

"Mom, I've been making secret inquiries about Uncle Yi's building. Once we get married, you can move there. Don't keep making meals for my sisters, let them learn to cook for themselves. Make food for yourself, live a life of ease, and then you can discuss literature with us."

"You understand how best to love your mother, Xiao Ma."

Xiao Ma finished eating at her mom's home, then immediately returned to her apartment to read. She was afraid of wasting time. She didn't even go to see Xiao Sang and Heishi. She told Xiao Sang that she was crazily busy and couldn't manage it. On the phone Xiao Sang laughed aloud, expressing her understanding.

Fei was at his work shift waiting for the phone to ring. There hadn't been a call for repairs the entire morning. When it was almost noon, a call came in, but it turned out to be Yue.

"I'm scared, Fei," she said in a small voice. "Can't you come over for lunch?"

"What happened?" Fei asked anxiously.

"Nothing, I'm just scared and don't know why."

"Wait, I'm coming over right away."

He rode his bike in a rush to the teachers' dormitory where she lived.

Yue didn't have class, and she'd made a number of dishes—all the foods Fei loved to eat. Her expression was wooden.

Fei thought: there's something very wrong. A sadness welled up in his heart.

"Let's eat," Yue said, feigning a smile.

Fei sat there slowly eating, though it tasted like wax. Afterward he straightforwardly put down the chopsticks, draped an arm over Yue's shoulders, and said, looking into her eyes:

"Yue, tell me what you're thinking about."

"Our school has a quota of people to send to support the frontier region, and I want to apply. I'll live there, I won't have children, and won't plan to marry again. Life seems to have no meaning for me."

She looked at Fei with dry eyes. Her tears must have already been shed.

"I want to help the Tibetan children."

"Don't go," Fei said, "You're not in a good place. I can tell that it will be very unlucky for you to go. The state of your spirits isn't right for going to Tibet."

"Then what do you think I should do? I can't stay on here any more."

She lowered her head, waiting for judgment to be pronounced.

"Wait for me one week. I'll think of something. All right?" Fei said.

Yue's hollow eyes stared ahead.

"Promise me," Fei said then.

"All right, I promise you not to apply now," she answered mechanically.

Fei knew Yue didn't believe him any more. He felt a twinge in his heart and wanted to cry. But he was a man, and here was a woman in danger—how could he not rescue her?

"Be patient and wait for me to decide. Don't do anything before I call, all right?"

"All right."

"Don't be afraid. Believe me, I will come to you at any hour."

"Yes."

In the evening Fei went home. Han Ma came down the stairs. They kissed. She said:

"You have a weight on your mind today."

In reality, when Yue said that she intended to move away, Fei, who could see the peril of her future ahead, had already decided in the depths of his heart. It was just that he didn't know it yet.

That night Fei couldn't sleep. Han Ma couldn't sleep either.

By the morning, he still hadn't told her about the problem with Yue.

Seeing his bloodshot eyes, Han Ma said to him:

"Fei, I've sensed that there's something wrong with Yue. Go to her right away and stay for a while. I will wait here for you to make a decision. Rescuing her is the most important thing now—believe me. The past few months, with your help and encouragement, I'm already very strong. I won't have any problems here."

Fei looked at Han Ma dully, watching her for a long time, then finally nodded gently and said:

"Han Ma, I love you. You've helped me become a real man. Without you, I don't know what an awful person I'd be. I'm the one who's hurting you."

"Not at all, Fei. I don't regret things, and I still feel lucky. We've had such beautiful times together. You've led me into the world of fiction and given me enormous support and a whole body and mind full of love. How could you say that this is hurting me? I cannot agree with you thinking this! We both overlooked Yue and harmed her without meaning to, and now there's still time to fix it. Go. Take whatever steps you need to take. Don't worry about me, it really doesn't matter. I feel that she's desperate now, and something could go wrong."

Han Ma helped Fei pack clean clothes and his books, then he left hurriedly.

This event took place in the early morning. Han Ma sat paralyzed on the living room sofa for over half an hour, then stood up energetically, picked up the small bag she carried, locked the door, and went to catch the bus. She had to go to work.

When Fei rushed to the teachers' apartments it was still early—Yue was just cooking breakfast. She invited him to eat with her.

"I can't not worry about you, so I decided to come stay here for a while," Fei said.

"Did she let you come? She's so good."

Fei saw that Yue's eyes were bloodshot like his.

"Fei, now you can see, someone like me who doesn't know how to behave only deserves to be alone. It doesn't matter who I live with, it will destroy the other person. You actually had a premonition about this before. You and Han Ma both have kind hearts, and I'm endlessly ashamed. I asked for today off already. I need to visit my parents' graves. I'll tell them that from now on I'll live well and do my duty. Living alone is still living."

"Yue, when you visit your mother's grave, could you bring her a message for me? Tell her that from now on Fei will surely take care of Yue with all his heart and strength. I need to go to work, I'll be back in the evening."

After Fei left, Yue saw the changes of clothes and the books he'd placed on the sofa and wondered: why had he done this? Before her eyes scenes from their childhood appeared—when their belongings were always placed side by side.

As Fei rode his bike to the office he thought carefully about Yue's words. He judged that her saying that she would exert herself from now on was only a fleeting thought. In the future she would become even more downcast and hopeless, and, if he didn't help her, bad things were almost doomed to happen. Han Ma's intuition was right: he must spend some time with Yue—maybe a lifetime. Hadn't he loved her for a long time before? Hadn't she once brought him so much joy? Even though he wasn't very pleased with Yue's temperament, he wasn't satisfied with his own, either. No human is perfect. He couldn't erase his past, only improve on it as best he could. And now, it already held many responsibilities . . . He couldn't only consider himself.

When he got off work he went back to Yue's home.

Now the two of them were relatively calm. Yue cooked while she asked Fei about how things were with the Pigeon Book Club. It seemed like she admired Fei's book friends. She said she wanted to expand her views through reading, so that he wouldn't always have to take care of her. "I gave up the idea of moving to Tibet. I can't destroy your life," she said.

Fei watched her, not really believing that she was saying what lay in her heart. But he could also see how, because of his coming to stay with her, Yue had recovered her lively nature. She talked with him about some amusing goings-on at the school, examples of a few of the musically gifted students, and also her reflections on visiting her parents' graves, and what she had said to her mother.

"I told my mother that my heart will forever be joined to you, even though I haven't been able to become your wife. My mother answered me: she said she will bless and protect me and you. She wants me to become stronger. I also told her what you wanted me to say for you."

As Fei helped to wash the vegetables he thought: "She's trying to make it seem like nothing has happened, just like right after I'd gotten married, when she sometimes called me to stay overnight . . ." Yet he sensed a subtle change in Yue's psychology, although what that actually meant couldn't be said for the moment.

The whole night Yue held Fei without letting go, apparently afraid he would disappear. Fei woke up midway, affected by her childlike clinging to him, and involuntarily thought: "She and I are a natural pair. We should have always supported each other, forgiven each other, but instead I avoided responsibility and let her struggle on alone."

On the third morning Yue packed up Fei's things and demanded that he go back home. She said that if Fei didn't go, she would go—to Tibet.

"This is the last time. Don't come back," she said.

"Then promise me, don't go anywhere, all right? I'll still come to visit you, because you are the person dearest to me and are also family."

"All right, I promise," she said, without expression on her face.

Heavy-hearted, Fei returned to his and Han Ma's home.

"Yue said she's thought it through and told me not to go back over to her place. But I think she's lying."

"Hmm, it's possible. She's trying to help us have what we want," Han Ma said.

"Now there's only waiting again. I'm really sorry, Han Ma."

"Don't think like that, Fei. You did what you should have done. I will always support you."

Another ten or so days had passed when Fei received a call from Yue as he was about to get off work.

"Fei, I want to get an abortion, but I'm scared. When you came here last time, I already knew I was pregnant. I want to have an abortion, and after the abortion I'll move to Tibet. Will you go with me to the hospital? I promise that after this I won't entangle you."

"Wait for me, I'll come over right away."

Fei flew along on his bike, dashing to Yue's home.

Yue sat on the sofa without the slightest expression. Fei walked into the room, sat down close to her, and embraced her.

"I'm going to be a father—it's wonderful," he said.

Yue gazed at him uncertainly, not speaking.

"I'll be a father, it's decided. I'll move in here with you and not go back there any more. My marriage to Han Ma—I can make arrangements," he added.

"And her?" Yue asked.

"She'll agree. Because she let me come to you."

Yue lowered her face, and her tears fell like rain.

"Don't cry, don't cry." Fei used a tissue to help her wipe her tears while saying, "Crying is bad for your health. Yue, once I heard the news, I felt everything transform. I can't be who I was before. I will make an effort, will make a good family, will make our child happy. I feel this is also what your mother expects of me. When I was little, she gave me so much love, so that I became a sensitive person who threw myself into literature. I'll give our child that much love."

"Fei, I'll study in earnest, too, and fight to understand you and myself better. I've just gotten by before and been such, such a disappointment. I know you're not, not satisfied with me," Yue stammered.

"These things no longer exist now, because you're the child's mother. There's only one thing: you must be careful, a thousand million times over. You're an older mother—you can't let there be any accidents while you're pregnant."

"But Han Ma, she'll be so bitter . . . ," Yue said in a low voice.

"She's a brave and strong woman. She'll struggle her way out eventually," Fei said.

Then he said he wanted to wrap wontons, to celebrate, and to forget the unhappy things temporarily. Yue agreed, saying she happened to have made wonton filling. So the two of them started in immediately. Fei remembered that before it had always been Yue's mother who had wrapped wontons for them. He'd hovered around the pot, and her mother had laughed at him for being a "greedy cat."

"You'll have to think of carefree, joyful things. This will benefit the baby," Fei said.

"Starting from today, I'll begin to love this child. I definitely won't do anything to harm him or her," Yue answered.

After they'd finished eating, Fei gave Han Ma a call and said he was at Yue's. Tomorrow evening he would come back home and tell her the specifics then.

"How is she?" Yue asked, agitated.

"She still sounds calm. She had a premonition about this," Fei said.

"It's all me hurting Han Ma." Yue started to cry again.

"Don't blame yourself. There isn't an absolute right or wrong in this situation. Han Ma can withstand the blow."

"All right, I won't blame myself. Blaming myself won't fix anything. I'll eventually transform myself, the same as you."

After dinner the two of them took a walk around the residential area. Yue held Fei's arm, feeling that everything that had happened was like a dream. She breathed a sigh of relief, while also harboring deep guilt toward Han Ma. This child's arrival was unexpected, and she'd been almost at the point of collapse. She wasn't going to analyze this, either, because she felt that what she had done wasn't right.

To cheer Yue up, Fei talked about some amusing incidents from when they were children. He started out each one with, "Yue, do you still remember . . . ," while Yue waited until he'd finished to say, "Of course I remember . . . ," and then filled in the details with flavor and color. Talking about these events from the past, Yue's mood slowly shifted. Fei noticed and felt gratified. He thought that he ought to assume responsibility for the problem with Han Ma. He couldn't let Yue carry this burden. Yue was a relatively plain and simple woman, unable to bear such a heavy, complex emotional burden.

When Fei rushed into the house, Han Ma wasn't there. He agitatedly checked over every article in their home without finding anything different. After a while the phone rang. Over the phone Han Ma told Fei not to worry about her. She said she was fine. That evening she would stay at a hotel, since she felt that letting Fei be alone at home to sort through his things would be better. She also said that she was making successful progress on her stories. Fei asked her how she knew that things had changed, and Han Ma said she had guessed. "Now, finally, each person can make the right choice," she said.

"Don't worry about me, a thousand million times over. Everything is fine with me. Concentrate on what you need to do."

These were her final words.

Fei forced back tears and kept telling himself: "I can't be sentimental, a thousand million times over—don't disappoint Han Ma more."

At last he packed up his things and went upstairs to sit in Han Ma's study for a while.

On the large desk were arranged two books they had recently read together along with two of Han Ma's notebooks. Fei sat down and immediately sensed Han Ma's powerful aura. He picked up a piece of notepaper and wrote on it:

Han Ma, I am going to be a father and won't come back again.
I will wish you well to the end of my life, my young hawk.—Fei

He went back downstairs, yet couldn't stop looking left and right around the house, saying farewell in his mind to the appliances and the furniture.

Later he finally got into bed and fell asleep. He felt his entire self tired almost to prostration.

Unexpectedly, once he was asleep he slept until the sun was rising. "The sky hasn't fallen," he said.

Fei made a call to the office, to say he would be a little late to work. Next he called a moving company to come to take away his books, his manuscripts, and other clothes and things.

That day he left work a little early and returned to his home with Yue.

"Fei, Fei . . ."

Yue hugged him and began to sob.

"You must have so much sadness in your heart," she raised her face and said.

"Stop crying, quickly, Yue. We will begin new lives and forget about our old lives. OK?"

"OK," Yue said through misted tears, "but I've deprived you of happiness."

"People can't only care about themselves. I've chosen to return to be a father—this is my choice."

"Hmm. I will make an effort to help you, too, and won't let your choice become a failure."

At the hotel, Han Ma endured a difficult night, and the next day only returned home after work.

She went upstairs and saw the note Fei had written to her. She sat at the desk, feeling the strain that had left her unable to breathe suddenly slacken. Her and Fei's choice was over, and now what was left for her was deep, deep sorrow. Outside the window was a black and misty sky where her youth had already slipped away. "I've done what an adult should do; I've lost my husband; I still have my career," she said to herself. She thought that as long as another day passed, she could eventually recover, eventually adjust to life without Fei.

Thinking back over the entire course of the relationship between her and Fei, she still felt there were few things worth regretting. Therefore, though there was sorrow, it was the aftermath of love. Hadn't she envisioned this outcome early on? It didn't matter. This was also good for Fei, who seemed to have matured all at once, to have his own views. His relationship with Yue could only become more harmonious, because soon they would have a child . . . As for herself, so long as she could endure this period of time, the pain would decrease little by little. She needed to have patience, needed to use literature to fill the gap Fei's disappearance had left. She inwardly resolved to do so.

She decided to keep living temporarily in this house full of memories. As to how long she would live here, she would look to circumstances to decide. She imagined herself to be a silkworm that would slowly molt dead love. Although the process was agony, the result was always good. Han Ma rested for a while and then went to the bamboo restaurant.

"Young Han, why hasn't Fei come with you?" Xiao Fei asked her.

"He won't be coming—he's gone back to his lover's home."

"Oh? It is complicated?" Xiao Fei's eyes widened.

"It isn't complicated at all. It's like this: Fei used to have a lover, but he married me. Later it turned out that his lover was pregnant, so he went back to her," Han Ma said.

"So that's how it's turned out. Han Ma, you have a kind heart. You will definitely find someone else who's to your liking in the future."

"I think so, too."

When Han Ma had finished eating and was heading home, Lao Yao and Xiao Fei ran out as a pair to see her off.

Xiao Fei put an arm around her, Lao Yao walked at her side, and none of the three of them spoke. They walked quietly this way past that stretch of bushes, and only then did the two of them finally say to her: "Goodbye, Han Ma."

Han Ma returned to the still house, finished drinking her tea, showered, and lay down in her and Fei's bedroom. The pillows and blankets on the bed all had Fei's smell from that morning when he'd gotten out of bed and left. She lay there for a while, found it hard to bear, then got up and changed her clothes and switched out all the covers, sheets, and pillowcases. After that she went back to bed.

This time she felt things were a little better. When she was almost asleep, she heard the phone ring, so she picked up the receiver. But there was no voice. She seemed to be having hallucinations. It was hard for her to fall back asleep after waking up.

Han Ma changed her clothes again and went upstairs, sat down at her desk, and thoughtfully opened the book *XXXX* . . . that Xiao Sang had given her. She turned to the chapter she was most enchanted with and began to read it again. She and Fei met again in the book, because she and Fei had read this chapter together, when he was helping her to expand her outlook. Its descriptions were startling to the heart and moving to the spirit, its layers so delicate! Now she was writing this type of fiction, too, and once she thought of that she felt inspired and ready to try, try again. Yes, she couldn't waste her best years over this. Fei had been saying a few days ago that her fiction would make readers open up their psyches, which was something most authors couldn't accomplish. Han Ma read the chapter through twice, sensing the restless movements of her heart gradually settle. "Tomorrow evening I'll be able to write again. Fei was protecting my talent," she told herself.

She returned to the bedroom, turned off the lights, and in a while just fell asleep.

She'd made it through the two most difficult days to withstand.

On the third day, in the same study, she felt herself approaching what was officially, entirely, new writing.

The weather was cooling, and the dry fall scenery of the city outskirts stimulated the inspiration inside of Han Ma. Now she constantly felt the impulse her book friend Xiaoyue had talked about at the Pigeon Book Club—obscure, coming in wave upon wave. Han Ma called this "the impulse of Fei's disappearance." Could that thing inside of her be making a counterattack on fate? "That thing" was difficult to articulate. It suggestively entwined her, tempting her into even darker depths without her knowing or sensing it. It was a bit clammy, but also a familiar affection. Its movements made Han Ma feel that she couldn't resist its lead. She thought: it's my new lover, the kind of lover Xiaoyue spoke of. It has appeared to me at the most dismal time. Some sentences whose meaning was indefinite but full of composure started to appear under her pen. She felt a bit apprehensive, but even more excited.

"Come out, come out, the way is clear," she said to herself.

"A new lover to replace Fei," an unfathomable but infinitely alluring prospect, appeared. It seemed like it was nothing; its tail pulled behind it a ray of light. Han Ma couldn't catch hold of it, but she wasn't impatient. She slowly, sentence by sentence, focused on it. She taught herself the ancient maxim that haste never arrives. After writing several lines she felt that she should pause, so she stopped and walked around the room. She even went downstairs and brewed a cup of tea for herself and carried it back upstairs. She wanted through this process to renew the sensitivity of what was inside of her. When she went back to read those several lines, the sentences had become vivid, and they signaled to her as if indicating a sense of direction. Then she wrote out several more sentences. "This is a good mindset," she thought. "I am independent and free: I can write however I want to write. This is engaging work, and through writing I discover that I'm an engaging person." What gratified Han Ma most was that this new lover was always there, where she could meet with it whenever she wanted. Its appearance was indistinct. It wafted the smell of seaweed, it evidently brimmed with sensual appeal—she even felt that it had a bellyful of ruses, although it was also incomparably caring.

Han Ma existed within this atmosphere for three days in a row. She stole a laugh in her heart: is it possible that it won't leave me? How fortunate this is. Every day she wrote little, anxious that writing too much would ruin her inner sense of novelty. Yet this writing of even very few words brought her immense joy and satisfaction—she felt that the sentences were a gift that Fei had left her. Her suffering was greatly reduced. Even though she didn't give anyone what she was writing to read, she had confidence in it. By the fifth day Han Ma felt that she had a tacit understanding with this new lover.

She sat down, lightly greeted it, and began to wait. After a minute or two, she would hear its arriving footsteps, then she would write down a sentence. Next another sentence would follow from her pen, then after that came the third, the fourth . . . The success simply surprised her. Just then Fei called.

"Are you all right, Han Ma?"

"Everything is fine, Fei. I was writing, I've made great progress. This is the gift you left me."

"Wonderful, Han Ma! I'm so relieved. Tonight I'll be able to sleep well. Good night, Han Ma."

"Good night, Fei."

Han Ma smiled in the direction of the distant Fei and continued, returning to her desk to write. She discovered that the phone call hadn't interrupted her writing, which showed how the lover inside her was very patient. She wrote again for a while, then paused. Her heart filled with gratitude to Fei for his call to her. Fei was always like this, placing her first in life . . . but now he had weighty responsibilities, he would be a father. Han Ma hoped he would bury his love for her as soon as possible. Oh, Fei. Han Ma didn't need to try to think about him—he was, like that other one in her heart, always there. The two of them—one was interior, one was exterior. Han Ma thought about how she was still happy. Someday she would adjust to this kind of happiness, and her pain would vanish. She believed this.

Han Ma hadn't told Xiao Sang about the problems between her and Fei yet. She wanted to wait a while longer, wait until she'd calmed down enough and finished her collection of short stories, and then see. She wanted Xiao Sang and Heishi to be the earliest readers of her stories. Once Han Ma thought about this, the tide of her emotions rose and fell. It would be so beautiful! Naturally she would also give the stories to Fei to read before publication. That could wait until he was calmer. It turned out that the happiness of writing was not only in the writing itself, but also in letting other people read what she wrote. Every time it was read it brought about even more happiness . . . Then wasn't that just like the writing of a book shared with all of its readers? So Han Ma imagined the scene of Xiao Sang reading her work, and she read what she'd written again, in imitation of Xiao Sang. She had fallen in love with her own new writing, which had never happened before. Once discovered, this made her confidence surge higher than ever.

"I can write fiction—I can just sit down and write! My new lover is always there and won't abandon or leave me! I'm so lucky!" Han Ma cheered herself on.

The thirteenth day after breaking up with Fei, Han Ma took advantage of some extra time from getting off work early to go visit Xiaoyue.

"Xiaoyue, has your research progressed?"

"I've been thinking of collaborating with Fei to set up a kind of advanced literary appreciation model. This requires us first to establish our own aesthetics of appreciation, to synthesize some of the junctures in communication . . ."

Xiaoyue poured tea for Han Ma as he talked in a torrent. He no longer held back and was no longer nervous. While he spoke he kept receiving a response from her bright eyes, and the doors of his heart opened little by little under those eyes. Han Ma said that Xiaoyue's plans made her feel elated! For literature to be promoted, especially her kind of literature that was for a limited audience—this link between Xiaoyue and Fei was the most crucial. The spirit of Xiaoyue's chipping away at his studies both touched her deeply and let hope rise in her heart, because she was its future beneficiary. Next they discussed some details on the professional side.

"Xiaoyue, this is a different kind of tea leaves than last time. They have a nice aftertaste!"

"These leaves were picked from Xishuangbanna's ancient tea trees. I entrusted someone to bring them back. I'll give you some, I still have a lot left," he said cheerfully.

He picked up a packet of tea leaves and placed it in Han Ma's crossbody bag personally.

"He's just like sunlight in winter," Han Ma said to herself as she sat on the bus. "I have such a close, enthusiastic friend and am making successful progress in my literary undertaking. I should be content."

At this moment in Xiaoyue's office a young man who had just started a job at the bookstore asked him:

"What is it like to be enchanted by someone? Is it like my love for model airplanes?"

"Hmm, it's somewhat the same and not the same, too. The difference lies in the object of your enchantment being able to fluctuate unpredictably—so you can't predict either the sense of happiness that can be communicated or the sense of hopelessness that can't be. Jing, you've asked a profound question."

Jing left, laughing. Xiaoyue was immersed in thinking back on Han Ma. He remembered how the previous night he'd dreamed about her. The two of them sat beside the lake, where Fei and his girlfriend had been. They were having an ardent conversation. As if guided by some spirit he'd abruptly stopped and said to her:

"Han Ma, I like you so much."

"I like you, too, Xiaoyue!"

The "like" that they both used had two kinds of meaning. Xiaoyue felt very worried because of this.

"Then may I kiss you?" he asked, his voice trembling.

"Kiss me, kiss me." Han Ma unaffectedly stretched out a hand toward him.

So he imprinted his kisses on her hand. Then he woke up.

Just a moment ago in Xiaoyue's office Han Ma's manner had been hesitating when he brought up the Pigeon Book Club meeting in two days. She'd said the gathering might be postponed because Fei had some personal matters to attend to. It was pending her having precise information, so she'd tell him more tomorrow. Now Xiaoyue thought of this problem and whispered to himself: "What kind of personal matters?" But then he held back from thinking about it any more. He shouldn't speculate, and he wouldn't be mean. He was an outsider, no matter what had happened between the two of them. He loved Han Ma, but could only love her in secret. Only he still felt it was a pity, because he had made some preparations for this meeting. But hadn't Han Ma come by today? This temporarily made up for the regret that the book club wouldn't meet. He shouldn't be as greedy as the snake trying to swallow an elephant. He'd also given Han Ma the delicacy of the tea leaves, perceiving that she already thought of him as one of her best friends. With developments like this between them, they would probably talk about anything and everything. Thinking this over, Xiaoyue felt inspired. Han Ma's appearances always brought him inspiration.

Once Han Ma had returned home she called Xiao Sang.

"Xiao Sang, Fei and I have been broken up for almost two weeks now. I'm doing fine, and so is he. I'm carrying on writing and making substantial progress. Before too long I'll let you and Heishi read my work. I called to tell you that the meeting of the Pigeon Book Club in two days will need to be postponed. Fei and I have already decided to wait until the two of us are psychologically prepared and can face each other, then we'll go back to the book club."

"Han Ma, I admire you from the bottom of my heart! Heishi and I are both here, we'll support you! I said to him such a long time ago: I won't worry about Han Ma, she can't be down and out. Your writing will be published—such news to celebrate! I think it must be a honed product now. I want to read it as soon as possible! For the sake of us readers, I must ask you to take care of your health, to sustain your creation."

"Xiao Sang, I've already come up with a plan to stay fit."

"Good! Han Ma, you're the star of hope for the Pigeon Book Club."

After the phone call Han Ma remembered her exercise plan. She intended to get off the bus one stop early every day after work and jog back home. After this she would have more energy for the evening's writing.

Now she opened the packet of tea leaves that Xiaoyue had given her and immediately smelled a strong, unusual fragrance. Oh, Xiaoyue—he was on par with Fei when it came to living well! She felt glad once again, and once again moved. It seemed everyday daily life hadn't come to a standstill, but instead was ceaselessly dividing, developing, while behind it hid immeasurably deep enigmas. Although she'd been dealt a heavy blow, she knew that from now on she would be like Heishi and Xiao Sang, righteously devoted to the nets of life and never turning back. She drank the fragrant tea her good friend Xiaoyue had given her, imagining the ancient tea trees of Xishuangbanna on Nannuo Mountain, at times hidden and at times visible in coiling clouds and mists, rejoicing in their ties to humankind.

When Han Ma sat down, sentences came to her mind as if unbidden. She continued in the previous day's state and wrote them down, in phrases like a string of pearls, one after another, surprising herself. What was happening? She didn't need to construct meticulously: words and phrases and sentences lined up waiting in her mind. If only the pen in her hand led them along, they emerged in a continuous stream, so certain, so experienced. The work of it was completely different than before! What kind of content was this? She wasn't too sure; she only felt that it was interesting and wrote it down. These sentences were somewhat strange. Yet they had such wisdom, in downy line on line, each line appearing so full and independent, like clusters of herbs in the fertile earth, assured of their rightness, forming themselves into a whole, taking shape in all sorts of patterns.

Immersed in writing, Han Ma sensed her life quietly transforming. She still enjoyed her job as a saleswoman. Welcoming the customers always excited her, and she worked with vigor. But a longing arose from the depths of her heart every day once she got off work and took the bus. She thought: "I'm going to meet him, this lover who is different than Fei. The passion between us is restrained and continuous. It could also be described as an untroubled surface, despite invisible and frightful waves raised in the abyss beneath. He is always there and will accompany me until the end." She longed to return to her desk. Now she'd had an apt experience of what Xiaoyue had described the last time at the book club. It was because of wanting to love that she wrote and read. This was the source of her life of passion. In real life, her love had been impeded, therefore love shifted to her soul and was expressed through writing. "This is my good fortune," she thought proudly. "My passion hasn't been wasted, now everything is expressed through literature." She wanted to take advantage of the times when she had more energy to write and read even more, both to fully enjoy the freedom of creation and also to do some good for humanity.

Sometimes, when Han Ma was at rest, she would still think of Fei. Those glorious moments often came to her memory. She yearned for his body, his caresses, his particular stare . . . but eventually the acute pain at losing everything lessened. Through a period of exercise (running and dumbbells), Han Ma's body also gained strength and endurance. She was pleasantly surprised, because she knew intuitively that her health guaranteed that her inspiration would last. She hoped that she could always write, always create until the end. In her heart she believed that the first work she was writing would be dedicated to Fei. However, this would become an eternal secret that only she knew.

After Xiao Sang received Han Ma's call, finished speaking with her, and put down the receiver, she sat at the table in a daze. Heishi was in the room with her. Recalling events from the past, she felt a burst of sadness.

"Han Ma's resourcefulness and courage leave me in the dust. I realized that a long time ago. So she will become the kind of author I admire. She gathers life and writing into one, besides having a rare gift for language," Xiao Sang said.

"We really are fortunate to be so close to a future author who's someone we care for," Heishi chimed in. "I feel glad for Fei, too, because he's finally resolved to take responsibility. He and Yue will have a harmonious family in the future, all in all. As for Han Ma, the grief will pass, and her creativity will become even more lavish."

"You're right. Through sincerity they both break through the net and achieve new impetus, elevating their lives to a higher level. These are the circumstances you were talking about. Everything is depicted in books, but only the keenest people have the appropriate understanding."

Xiao Sang said these words, then excitedly stood to embrace Heishi. The two of them returned to that time. How their souls had raged that evening at the book club! It was just like it had happened yesterday! Literature surely was the most like love, Xiao Sang thought. Uncle Yi had discovered this before her, so he'd brought Heishi into her life. "There is a powerful law," she said thoughtfully, caressing Heishi. "This is the law of love. It's invisible, but people obey it. It's also the spirit that protects humankind. Han Ma and Fei are living examples before our eyes . . ."

"The next time we go to the book club, our baby may be four months along," Heishi said, kissing Xiao Sang's ear. "I can never love you enough. At the office, whenever I finish working on something and sit down to rest, I think of you."

"Probably because we are both literary types. Han Ma will find a new lover soon—she's so outstanding, many people must have their eyes on her."

“That’s for sure. Everyone in our literary circle, whether young women or young men, has an exceptional charm. So, haha, people inside the circle always find people inside the circle,” Heishi laughed enthusiastically.

“No wonder you pulled me into the circle first, trying to let me appreciate your charm.”

“It was also to appreciate your charm.”

“Now that Han Ma and Fei have broken up, I wonder what other changes might happen to the couples in the circle,” Xiao Sang continued, musing.

“There will be unforeseen coincidences, like in Borges’s stories.”

Fei finally passed through the most difficult period and began eventually to be able to sleep. His missing Han Ma abated day by day as his everyday life and literary research gradually got onto the right track. Now he was carefully attentive to Yue and the child in her belly, looking after each of them, large and small. He felt this kind of caring was the best way to ease his suffering. When he had time free, he forced his thoughts to turn toward the baby, immersing himself in imagination. He would think and think, while a smile floated across his face. At such times Yue would often stroke her stomach and say to the future baby:

“Darling, Daddy is thinking of you. When you come out you should listen to what he tells you.”

Fei thought that Yue was most charming at such times. She was a born mother.

He gave Han Ma a call and asked her what to do about the Pigeon Book Club gathering, and she said to call it off for now. He thought it over and felt this was the only thing to do. He didn’t have the courage to face Han Ma, but there would come a day when he would drum up the nerve. The Pigeon Book Club was the literary home he’d built with his good friends, where the meaning of his life lay, so naturally, later on, he would have to return there. Otherwise, where could he go? The setback in his life required time to repair, but a turn for the better would surely come.

Yesterday Yue had told Fei that she was making an effort to read books now, too. Not only reading about music, but also reading what he was reading. Recently the school had reduced her classes as a consideration, so she had even more time to read. She'd added that she aspired to join the Pigeon Book Club as an auditor and elevate herself. Fei had heard Yue's words and whispered in his mind: "But Han Ma hasn't found a new lover yet." He imagined Han Ma keeping watch over their former home and felt a stab of pain in his heart. To divert his emotions, he talked to Yue about other topics. When Fei had quieted down, he found himself hoping that Han Ma could find a new lover as soon as possible. He felt there would be plenty of opportunities in a major literary city like Meng, much more for someone like her who stood out from the crowd. Though Fei cherished this expectation, time and again he imagined involuntarily what Han Ma was doing.

Han Ma was fiercely independent and gifted at arranging her life. But she wasn't skilled at handling life's trivial matters. Before, when she and Fei had lived together, he had taken care of all their concrete routines. Now that she'd lost his helping hand there would be busyness and muddle. Fei hoped that Han Ma's new lover would be an attentive and considerate man, someone able to understand her. These anxieties were among the reasons he was losing sleep. He wished so much that he could help Han Ma himself, but that could only be a fantasy. He also wished that Han Ma would move out of their small house soon. Fei felt endless, grave remorse when he thought of her living there all alone. He knew, too, that she hadn't moved because their home was a memento, but this attachment would be a disadvantage for her future life. Each day she didn't move out, the hurt couldn't be removed from Fei's heart—this hurt that was the transformation of love. It was likely the same for Han Ma. She stayed where she was because her love for him remained there. A turn for better required time. Oh, oh. Afraid she would misunderstand, he didn't dare call her and urge her to move. He could only secretly worry.

Another few days passed, and Fei's agitation grew more severe, so he called her.

"Han Ma, move out, move to an apartment in the city. Begin a new life as soon as possible. My heart aches when I think of you living there alone. You living there alone isn't as convenient as living in the city, either."

"Hmm, Fei, I'll listen to you and move as soon as possible. Don't worry about me. Actually, my whole body is full of energy, and I'm busy with elevating my writing. I often think of Yue and wish her well—you two will have a healthy little baby."

When the call ended Fei felt more carefree. Eventually, motivated by the news that Han Ma's writing was going well, he went back to his literary research and pressed ahead, because he also bore heavy responsibility to literature. In fact, it didn't need Han Ma's hint: Fei had always treated her maiden work as his own, other child. He would never forget those moments that excited the heart, instants shared by two people together. Ah, how fortunate to have literature! Without it, he and Han Ma would have parted and eventually become strangers. Only the effect of literature was both beneficial and harmless to anyone. He must elevate himself more and more through literature. It was the only way he could catch up to that soaring hawk.

Fei's life now was fulfilling, and Yue noticed and was also glad. She sensed him treating her with even more patience than before, and he was also gentler. She thought: good days are still to follow, wait until the little baby is born . . . She could already imagine Fei as a father.

"Fei, could you take me to the Pigeon Book Club?"

"Yes. But we have to wait until Han Ma finds a lover."

"She'll find one soon. So many people could love her. Think about it, even you loved her so much."

"You think too highly of me. You and she are both wonderful, while I'm just the dregs."

"You'll be an excellent father."

"I hope so."

When a month had passed since the breakup with Fei, Han Ma was still thinking over the problem of moving out. She didn't want to move somewhere near her parents' home, because she was afraid that they would worry over her too much. She didn't want to move somewhere near the Crown Department Store either, because her coworkers and friends would all try to introduce potential partners, or become concerned about her. She thought back and forth, then all of a sudden remembered that Xiaoyue had told her he'd bought an apartment at the other end of the city far from both the Crown Department Store and her parents' home. She thought that it would be pretty great to rent a place where Xiaoyue lived. It was a good location, and if she ran into any difficulty she could ask him for help.

So Han Ma called Xiaoyue to tell him that she wanted to rent a place at his apartment complex.

"A rental for two people?" Xiaoyue asked calmly.

"I'll be renting by myself. Later on I'll tell you why," Han Ma said.

"I can help you with the rental. Do you prefer to be on a high floor or a low floor?"

"I'd prefer a unit that's a bit higher."

"No problem. There are a lot of vacant apartments here, and the rent isn't high."

A few days later an apartment was rented, then on the weekend Xiaoyue came over to help Han Ma move.

The previous night she'd already moved all of her things into the living room, pile upon pile.

"I've broken up with Fei," Han Ma said as she poured tea for him. "It's like this: before he married me he had a girlfriend. I knew about her. He was still in contact with this girlfriend after he married me, then she got pregnant. I had to break up with him. Xiaoyue, can you understand?"

"I can understand." Xiaoyue nodded seriously. "I have respect for both of you."

He immediately went to work. He had Han Ma find all of the old boxes in the house, put her clothes, shoes, books, and other things into the boxes, then used rope he had brought to tie them shut. His movements were quick and agile.

Han Ma said: "Xiaoyue, you're like someone from a professional moving company."

"I often move books around at the bookstore," he answered.

After her things were sorted, the people from the moving company arrived. Xiaoyue watched them transfer the boxes and things onto the truck, then carefully counted up the quantity. After the truck drove off, he promptly called a taxi. They locked the door, got in the taxi, and sped toward the small apartment complex where Xiaoyue lived.

She said to him:

"I hadn't imagined you were so well-trained. You're the most competent member of the Pigeon Book Club."

Xiaoyue's face reddened when he heard Han Ma's praise, and he smiled happily.

"You've also lightened my sorrow. I'm so grateful to you," she added.

"I feel energized when I'm doing things for you. Call on me if you have any problems that need help later on."

As they entered the apartment, Han Ma discovered that the rooms were especially clean, and the lights were scrubbed until they shone, with every lamp functional and in a good location. Xiaoyue said he had asked the electricians to repair the three lights in the living room and the bedrooms. It was a two-bedroom apartment, neither too large nor too small.

"I figured that you'd have a lot of books, so the one-room apartments here would all be too small. Besides, if your family comes to visit, or a friend stays the night, a one-room apartment would be too tight. So you needed a two-room place. The extra room could usually be the study," Xiaoyue said.

"Oh, you really are a dear. This apartment is perfect. How large is your apartment?"

"My apartment is larger, a three-bedroom. I planned it for when I got married, then my girlfriend and I broke up. I haven't been dating again, so I live there on my own."

"Haha, Xiaoyue, why not hurry up and find a girlfriend? You're so handsome, overflowing with talent, competent—simply the best! Keep looking, keep looking," Han Ma said warmly.

Xiaoyue didn't answer and only looked at her. He felt he wouldn't grow weary of the woman before him even after seeing her hundreds of times.

Just at this moment the moving company knocked on the door.

Once Han Ma's things were arranged, she went to heat up water. Xiaoyue busied himself back and forth in the apartment helping to organize her belongings.

"Xiaoyue, these are still the tea leaves that you gave me. When I thought about moving, I thought of you right away. I wanted to live in your apartment complex and bask in your light. To me, you're like the sun in winter—so bright, so comforting."

Xiaoyue finished busying himself and sat down to drink the tea. He restrained himself, keeping his eyes away from Han Ma's body.

"I want to give you a pair of flower vases—I've already bought them. You can put them in your study with roses. This neighborhood has the largest flower shops," he said.

Han Ma remembered the red roses Fei had planted. She was distracted for a few seconds, then recalled herself right away. Luckily Xiaoyue wasn't looking at her. She let slip:

"Do you like red roses, too?"

"Yes, I like them, too," Xiaoyue said earnestly, "but I'll get going when I finish this cup of tea, and you can call me if you need anything. Look, my apartment is just across the way, diagonally on the fifteenth floor."

After Xiaoyue left, Han Ma sat down in the study. She was very pleased to see that her new study faced a flower garden, with several large weeping willows in the view. She also discovered that Xiaoyue had already helped arrange the study for her much faster than she could have done it. "He's so good," Han Ma thought. She felt as though her writing would flow while she sat at this desk. She immediately connected her thoughts to the previous evening's, and to her surprise she wrote several more brilliant paragraphs.

"Xiaoyue, this study is wonderful. It inspires me—I've started to write again. I was a little anxious about whether inspiration would follow me after the move. Now it seems like there's no effect on it at all. I don't know how to thank you. What help do you need? For example, certain things that women are good at?" she said on the phone.

"I'm just willing to help you, Han Ma. The more I help the happier I am. Do you want to help me? Let me think—your store sometimes sells that top-grade muskmelon, but it doesn't stock enough. Every time I get there too late and they're sold out. It's my favorite fruit. Could you buy some and bring them home, then give me a call to tell me, and we can eat them together?"

"It's too easy to help you this way! You're too kind."

"I'll bring over the vases to celebrate you starting to write in your new home."

Xiaoyue arrived after a while. He placed a pair of milk-white jade vases on the side table in the study, then put red roses in them. He asked Han Ma whether she liked them. She nodded with tears in her eyes.

"Let's go to a restaurant to eat. You must be hungry. There's a Guangdong restaurant next to the apartment complex. It's quite good, the best quality for the price," Xiaoyue suggested.

They took the elevator downstairs together. He took her to look over the apartments' flower garden. Because her writing was going well, her mood had changed for the better. The previous night's grief over her departure had been suppressed. Her state of mind was already stimulated by the time they sat down in the restaurant.

"Is this your girlfriend? Are you getting married?" the restaurant's owner asked Xiaoyue.

"Han Ma is a friend from the world of books. She's just moved into our apartment complex," he answered.

"It's all the same, all the same," the owner said cheerfully, smiling.

The restaurant's food was Guangdong style, fairly light, and the soup was delicious. Han Ma enjoyed it. Xiaoyue ate little, his thoughts completely on Han Ma. He kept urging her to eat a bit more, saying that "writing is heavy physical labor," and besides she lifted weights and needed to eat better. Han Ma said to herself: "I am so relaxed around him, he's just like a brother. In this world, if someone is occupied with the cause of literature, people appear all around who protect him or her."

After they'd finished eating, as they paid the check, the owner came over again.

"Xiaoyue's qualifications are outstanding, he's perfect marriage material. Go ahead and get married," he said.

"All right, all right," Xiaoyue said.

On their return to the apartment complex Han Ma said to Xiaoyue:

"You see, everyone urges you to get married, but you don't even bother about it."

"I already have a literary lover, I think she's enough for me to cope with."

"Nonsense, nonsense," Han Ma shook her head disapprovingly. "Literature encourages romance."

Xiaoyue said to himself: "She has sustained such a heavy blow, without it changing her mindset." His heart quaked. He felt that her enthusiasm toward him was sisterly affection, but this was all for the good. She'd just broken up with Fei—how could she forget about him? Moving apartments might not ease her longing for Fei either. Xiaoyue missed the Pigeon Book Club, but he didn't dare to bring it up with Han Ma—it was a significant taboo. What he could do was help her in life, let her feel warmth. He was touched by the thought of how Han Ma had said he was like the sun in winter. Literature was the center of his life, while Han Ma was the symbol of this center.

"Goodbye, Han Ma."

"See you soon, Xiaoyue. Shall we go for a walk around the neighborhood side streets this evening?"

"Sure, I'll call for you at seven-thirty."

They each returned to their homes to be industrious.

Han Ma continued to read the novel Xiao Sang had given her. She didn't know whether it was because of the fragrance of the roses inundating the room, but today her reading brought out a thick sexual innuendo in the book. She didn't return to the nights she and Fei had enjoyed together, but instead from within the words and between the lines saw the figure of an unknown man. Could the desire that had slept deeply and for so long in her body have revived? In her daytime consciousness, her sexual partner was still Fei. Yet she knew Fei would never again return to her. Could there truly be a stranger who would appear in her life in the future, the same as depicted in the book, who would take an old-style train always letting people on and off, then disembark at her city, and then afterward disappear without a trace? Whose image was he? There was no one like him. Perhaps he was lust itself.

Han Ma looked for an answer, immersing herself in the diversion of these sexual aesthetics, reading aloud while she pondered. She read to the point of enchantment, not even noticing the sky growing dark. Later on she was finally tired and went to the kitchen to cook some noodles and eggs. She recalled as she ate that Xiaoyue had brought these over. He resembled Fei in such ways, but was steadier than Fei.

Xiaoyue arrived just when she had finished eating and was cleaning the kitchen.

"It's so good that I've moved here, it's like being in a family with you. It warms my heart to think of it. You're also better at life than I am," Han Ma said in the elevator.

"It's like that for me, too. For a very long time I've been alone when I come home. Now, though, you'll be keeping me company," Xiaoyue said.

"But you should still hurry up and find a wife. I can't substitute for your girlfriend."

Xiaoyue didn't respond to her. They silently walked into the curtain of night. The voice in his heart sounded again: "I love her so much, I love her alone."

"This is the longest street in Meng," he said, "and along both sides of the street there are flower shops and bonsai shops. Most of the stores are closed now, but they'll be full of people if you come here during the day. If we keep walking we'll reach the suburbs."

"These parasol trees along the street are so distinctive. It's a good city. Do you like Meng, Xiaoyue? Or would you prefer to go to the capital?" Han Ma asked him.

"Meng is better—it suits reading and doing research. The capital is too noisy. Besides, the people I love are here, along with all different types of readers."

"Speaking of readers, oh, the problem between me and Fei has affected all of you at the Pigeon Book Club. Fei said he needs to wait until I find a new boyfriend before he dares to face me there. But right now I'm busy with writing. How could I think of dating?"

"Han Ma, I've thought of something: who will you give your stories to read first? Or will you submit them directly to the publisher?"

"I won't submit them directly to the publisher. I've promised Xiao Sang and Heishi that they can read the stories first. Then I'll ask Fei and you to help me read them. I'll be finished soon. It's a series of stories."

"Let me read them first, please, Han Ma. I'll help you print a few copies to have everyone read together. I can't wait. I can also come over to your apartment to read them out loud for you to hear. That way you can understand the fascination of your writing even more."

A smile floated across Han Ma's face.

"All right, I'll let you read them first. Afterward you have to tell me your honest opinion."

"I definitely will. I'm so happy, because it's your writing! Han Ma, every day I will hope for your stories to come out soon."

They'd walked to the entrance of the largest flower shop. Xiaoyue said that he was friends with the florist owner. The employees welcomed him to come in and sit down. He led Han Ma to the inner room, where the two of them sat down on a sofa. Han Ma discovered they were surrounded by red roses. So fragrant. She had experienced this before in the study, as if everything were becoming suggestive. "But this isn't some unknown man, it's Xiaoyue!" Han Ma cautioned herself. She rose slightly, as if about to stand, but sat back down. Beside her Xiaoyue was speaking with the florist. She heard a roaring in her ears and couldn't understand what they were saying. All of a sudden she embraced Xiaoyue's shoulder beside her. She distinctly felt his breathing grow rapid. He seemed about to kiss her face. She jumped up and said to him in a loud voice:

"It's late, let's go."

The florist insisted on giving Han Ma a large armful of red roses. Since she couldn't decline, Xiaoyue helped her carry them.

They silently walked a stretch of road.

"I'm sorry, Xiaoyue." Han Ma broke the silence.

"It doesn't matter, Han Ma. I know you were taking me for Fei. At the book club I saw how you and he were such, such a loving couple. Only you shouldn't think about it, Han Ma."

"Xiaoyue, you're just like, just like a brother to me. No, you understand me even more than a brother."

Her voice was choked with tears. Today she had been through great waves of emotion.

Han Ma accepted the roses and took them upstairs.

Xiaoyue's heart tightened in bursts as he alternated between an extreme degree of pity and an extreme degree of love. He took a cold shower to cool down his wild thoughts. Yet he kept thinking about Han Ma. He didn't know what to do, so he went downstairs. He walked out of the apartment complex, going quickly down the street, and finally arrived back at the park in the suburbs. He went into the park, following the road along the side of the large lake. The wind blew against his face as he looped around the lake and then ran another loop. He looked at his watch. It was already midnight. He'd finally quieted down. At the main entrance to the park he came across the man from the previous time.

"I said before that being unlucky in love would be good for you. See how much you've roused yourself!" he said.

"Thank you, you were right."

Xiao Yue ran back home, took a hot shower, and then lay down.

He went to sleep in an ardent state of mind.

The next day he woke up on time. He jumped up to get ready because he wanted to hurry to catch the bus before Han Ma. He'd decided to leave for work early and not take the same bus as her.

When Han Ma had returned home she was still somewhat distracted. What was happening? Her indescribable behavior a moment ago in the flower shop, amid the overwhelming fragrance of the red roses, seemed unimaginable. At that instant, the contact of her body with Xiaoyue's had resulted in a response she hadn't expected, and she'd felt Xiaoyue's impulse directly. Of course, the impulse wasn't his originally—she had provoked it. Sex often caused lustful fantasies that could wreck a relationship between good friends. The more Han Ma carefully recalled the details of what had happened, the more unsure she was of herself. She had just left Fei and was drowning in longing for him, and the sex she imagined was with Fei. Yet her body had inclined toward another man's body. That man had appeared at first in the novel, as a stranger, then suddenly he'd been embodied by her good friend Xiaoyue. Also, Xiaoyue's body had responded to her . . . She thought: we're like a healthy, lonely man and a widow shut in a dark room. The memory of the incident wasn't lewd, of course. Han Ma still blamed herself a little though. After all, Xiaoyue was there to help her, not to find sexual comfort with her. Also, he knew how devastating the blow of the breakup with Fei was for her. It seemed that it was easy for young men and women living alone to cross boundaries, especially for people like her and him. So, had Xiaoyue's impulse toward her been anything more than a physical reaction? She wasn't sure. The whole evening Han Ma felt alarmed and flustered by this event. It appeared that life from now on wouldn't be merely writing fiction, there would be other content . . . She'd persistently believed that life and fiction were connected. However, when something new happened to her, she couldn't understand its significance all at once. Comprehension always lagged behind. Tomorrow morning when she took the bus it might be the same bus as Xiaoyue, so she had to talk with him pretending like nothing had happened. If they became estranged, she would hate herself for being unworthy of his kindness. After all, she liked Xiaoyue, and Xiaoyue liked her, so they should always be able to get along, without distancing themselves out of fear of so-called "crossing boundaries." Acting that way would be doctrinaire. What's more, Xiaoyue didn't have a girlfriend yet, so there was no talk of her being in the way. Wait until he found a girlfriend, then there would be time enough to distance herself.

Han Ma stood in front of the living room window, glanced toward the fifteenth-floor window opposite, and saw it was dark. Xiaoyue must already be asleep. What had happened in the flower shop was only a minor interlude for him. Han Ma found that she liked this intimate kind of relationship with Xiaoyue. Even without sexual love, a close friend of the opposite sex would surely elevate her interest in everyday life, even more so if it were a man like Xiaoyue, who was congenial by nature. Han Ma felt encouraged, too, that she could still attract someone like him. She remembered Fei saying that reading and writing could improve your sex appeal. So, was she sexy in Xiaoyue's eyes? She recalled each of their interactions, but the answer seemed equivocal, because until today she'd always been Fei's wife. Besides, she was the one who'd asked Xiaoyue to help her rent the apartment, while his actions had been moderate and conventional. He had managed to restrain himself, even though she'd acted so brazenly. For now she admired his restraint, noticing how he was much steadier than her in handling things.

Sleeping in her new home, she tossed back and forth, sometimes asleep, sometimes awake. In her dreams that man kissed her over and over. He was a little bit like Fei, but it wasn't him—he was more like that man in the book. It kept up until after midnight when she eventually went to sleep. She still woke up on time.

Once she reached the bus stop Han Ma discovered Xiaoyue wasn't there. She felt a little disappointed but also breathed a little sigh of relief.

On her lunch break she gave Fei a call from the department store. Afraid that he would be jealous, she didn't tell him that she was living in the same apartment complex as Xiaoyue.

"That's great, Han Ma. You'll start a new life and completely forget the unhappiness from the past. I think you'll find a lover soon who's much better than me. I'm fine now, too. I'm wholeheartedly getting ready to be a father."

With that, Han Ma's new life began in a home full of red roses. The residential complex was actually named Red Roses—what a strange coincidence! She sighed with myriad emotions. When she talked about it with Xiaoyue, he said:

"This name matches your personality perfectly."

Now her relationship with Xiaoyue had become quite natural. She thought: this is all credit to him, since he is someone who brings people comfort. They would meet each other quite often during the week, whenever they wanted to, because it was so convenient. Meanwhile this close association eased the pain in her heart. Sometimes a thought like this one would occur to her: "Should I, possibly, start anew with Xiaoyue?" Yet Han Ma gave up the idea immediately. First, she believed Xiaoyue hadn't fallen in love with her. He loved literature possessively, and so by extension was fond of her, and that meant they could communicate without any barriers when they were together. Second, Han Ma herself wasn't ready to start a new romance, because Fei hadn't disappeared from her life.

Finally the day came when Han Ma's short story collection was finished. She called Xiaoyue to come pick it up.

"Han Ma, I'm as excited as if I wrote it myself!"

He carefully placed the manuscript in his bag as if it were his child.

"Tomorrow it's the weekend, so I was going to ask you out for a drink, but now I can't wait to read your work."

After Xiaoyue left, Han Ma's entire body grew tense. She was a little scared. What if her writing couldn't move him? She walked back and forth across the room, groaning. She tried reading an essay by Fei, but couldn't get into it at all. Later she felt hungry, so she boiled the free-range eggs and red jujubes Xiaoyue had brought her and ate.

She kept having bursts of nervousness even when she lay down in bed. Half-asleep, she heard the phone ring, looked at her watch, and saw that it was already two in the morning. Could it be a hallucination? The phone started to ring again and was no illusion. It was Xiaoyue—what a faithful friend!

"Han Ma, were you asleep?"

"No. I was waiting for your report."

"I believe there is no other author in the world who is like you. You have countless possibilities ahead of you."

"Oh, oh . . ."

"Han Ma?"

"I'm out of breath. I want to kiss you through the phone. You won't be angry?"

"Of course I won't be angry. I'll even feel happy," Xiaoyue said.

"You really are crazy about literature. Good night."

"Good night, Han Ma, sleep well."

Han Ma made a sound on the phone as if she were kissing Xiaoyue on the face, then imagined what he would look like. "Does he not love me at all, aside from my writing?" Thinking over this question, she happily entered dreamland.

The following day Xiaoyue had printed several copies of Han Ma's stories. She mailed a copy to Xiao Sang and another copy to Fei. Now she was steeped in happiness, because she trusted Xiaoyue's appraisal. He'd read so much more fiction than she had and was discerning about literature. She would continue to make an effort—she started writing a new work.

She sat in the new study, inhaling the thick fragrance of the roses, and seemed to become a little drowsy. She knew this wasn't dozing, but rather a kind of sensual state, a primordial chaos. She arrived "there"; she started to create. Ah, wonderful! As soon as she wrote down the first sentence, the chain of life would start. She found herself no longer using draft materials—she could write directly on lined paper! When she finishing writing each passage, she would sigh: "I'm so fortunate! I will share the scenes I see with Fei, with Xiaoyue, with Xiao Sang and Heishi, with everyone in the book club and the reading group . . ."

After resting for a few minutes, she would start a new passage. It hardly took effort since the sentences leaped out spontaneously. Yet she knew by some instinct that it was best not to write for too long, to maintain the freshness and acuity of her perceptions.

Fei soon gave her a call. He was incredibly excited, and his voice kept trembling slightly. Han Ma's love for him was stirred up once again, but she tried to restrain herself. Next Xiao Sang called and outlined in detail her and Heishi's encouraging views, while congratulating Han Ma again and again.

"Han Ma, Han Ma! I called the editor in chief of the capital's best literary magazine, *The Future*. They are looking forward to your manuscript."

As soon as Xiaoyue came in he told Han Ma this piece of good news. She hugged him, kissing him once emphatically on the face. Xiaoyue felt his whole body go limp, his face paled, and he sat down on the sofa, dazedly staring at the woman in front of him.

"Xiaoyue, are you angry?"

"Not at all, not at all," he said only after a while. "I'm overwhelmed. Good news has arrived so quickly, Han Ma, and I'm still getting used to it."

"So that's what it is. I'm so fond of you."

Han Ma sat down next to him, rested her head against his shoulder, closed her eyes, and said:

"You are a priceless treasure."

Then she opened her eyes, stood, and proposed:

"Let's go have a drink. I should treat."

At the bar the young woman was still singing "Song of the Cliffs." Xiaoyue noticed Han Ma leaning in to listen. She moved nearer to him and said in a low voice: "Xiaoyue, you've helped me fly across the chasm . . ."

They each ordered a drink. Han Ma's tolerance for alcohol was pretty good, so she'd never gotten drunk before. She didn't plan to drink too much anyway.

The singing was so alluring—both of them felt their emotions rising and falling. Han Ma ordered another drink for herself and for Xiaoyue.

Then she ordered a third drink. He tried but couldn't stop her.

After Han Ma finished it her eyes filled with tears.

"Xiaoyue, Xiaoyue, you're so good. Could you possibly love me?"

She stood up, grasping Xiaoyue's shoulders with both hands, and looked fixedly into his eyes.

With an effort he took hold of both of her hands, pressing her back onto her chair.

"Don't be silly, Han Ma, you're missing someone else. Don't cry, Han Ma, let's go back."

Xiaoyue drew Han Ma by the arm out to the street. A cold wind blew and the neon lights were garish. He had perceived another side of Han Ma's nature, and he loved this side of her as well.

"Han Ma, you've changed my life so much," Xiaoyue said, then sighed.

"You've been even busier on my account, I'm so sorry," Han Ma said in a low voice.

"There's nothing wrong with being busy. I like who I am even better now. Imagine what it will be like if we still live in the Red Roses Apartments thirty years from now."

"That would be beautiful. A setting sun, white hair, two literary elders.

"Xiaoyue," she added, "will you promise me one thing?"

"Tell me."

"To take the bus to work together with me every morning."

She felt Xiaoyue shiver as if he were cold, but he calmed back down right away.

"All right. Tomorrow morning I'll call for you."

"I don't mind what other people say behind my back," Han Ma said.

"I will definitely call for you."

The next day Han Ma had just gotten her things ready when Xiaoyue called. He was downstairs waiting for her.

She went downstairs cheerfully, then the two of them went to the bus stop together.

On the bus, they talked in low voices about literature as if there was no one around them, all along until they got off at their stop.

They said goodbye to one another, each going into their own store.

At lunchtime Han Ma tried to find Xiao Sang, but the store manager told her that Xiao Sang had taken off work to go look at condos, because she was planning to purchase one. Han Ma felt glad for Xiao Sang when she heard. Then she crossed the road again to go find Xiaoyue.

Xiaoyue's office door was open, and the new employee and Xiaoyue were sitting there facing each other, chatting—but once the young man saw Han Ma he quickly came up with an excuse to slip away.

Smiling, Han Ma sat in the chair where the new employee had been sitting. Xiaoyue helped brew tea for her.

"We're so close by, it's very convenient," Han Ma said.

"It is, this is like heaven-sent."

"Xiao Sang and Heishi are looking for a home. I know that place, it's near the park. Her parents have both moved here now, so I've heard they're going to buy two units and live in the same building as them."

"I really envy them," Xiaoyue said.

"You should make the time to find a girlfriend."

"My plan is to accompany you, to pursue literary causes together with you. You see, even though we're busy all day, I feel the present is the most passionate, the happiest time of my life. I intend to go on like this."

"How could that be, Xiaoyue? You're so stubborn . . . but if you insist, I won't be angry, and I'll even be secretly happy. When I originally came looking for your help it was a decision to bask in your light."

Han Ma laughed cheerfully. Xiaoyue was also cheerful, and he said:

"Pursuing literature together can be much happier than romance."

"Even though I don't agree with your point of view, I don't intend to pry into your situation."

Once Han Ma left, the new employee Jing came back in.

"That woman is so enchanting!" Jing sighed.

"Enchanting in which way?" Xiaoyue asked, laughing.

"I can't say exactly—it must be her whole demeanor. She's your literary colleague?"

"Yes."

"I want to study literature, too."

Xiaoyue truly felt that his life was permeated with passion and joy. Just as depicted in fiction, when a person persevered about one thing, it would be a dream come true. He couldn't stand to be apart from Han Ma. Slowly, he also felt confidence in the developing relationship between them. *I seem by nature to be a better fit for Han Ma than Fei was. Maybe she doesn't see it yet, but as time passes, she will eventually realize,* Xiaoyue wrote in his journal. *I am filled body and soul with longing for her, but for now I must suppress my physical desire. This is a trial for me.* After he finished writing these sentences his entire self felt incredibly encouraged. He resolved to treat Han Ma with superhuman patience, because his relationship with her was his relationship with literature. Novelists should have a changeable side; this was where her enchantment lay.

Xiaoyue was even more determined to study literature. He thought: wait until the day Han Ma falls in love with me. The book club gatherings would be reinstated then, so his preparations needed to be intensified. Recently he'd attended several other reading groups, where he roused the book friends with his newly achieved inspiration. There'd been an impact, which was also something that brought him joy. All things work out together, "all roads lead to Rome," and Rome was literature. Xiaoyue kept pondering a collaboration with Fei someday in the future, to establish communication mechanisms for literary appreciation among the best readers, and this work also enchanted him. Xiaoyue wasn't just familiar with literary theory, he was also a pragmatist and an organizer. Han Ma admired precisely this side of him, because he could realize the state where "the heart succeeds in what it wants," then perfect it step by step. For example, when it came to Han Ma renting an apartment, she'd had a profound experience of his uncommon charm. It was Xiaoyue who was quietly easing her pain, and encouraging her to write even better. Han Ma felt happy whenever she thought of this entire process.

A month flew past, and Han Ma grew more and more used to not wanting to be apart from Xiaoyue. As for Xiaoyue, he gradually got used to his repressed desire not to be apart from her as well as her emotional shifts and sudden attacks. He believed himself capable of forgiving her anything, so long as he could slowly train himself in a kind of stamina. He had to give Han Ma time to allow her to slowly leave the shadows. His days now passed so richly, because of her arrival! Even though human emotions are the most difficult thing to predict, in his relationship with Han Ma, their shared love of literature ought to be the firmest basis. Han Ma made concrete his pursuit of ideals. Before he'd met her, his life had not had such surety as now, nor such active investment. This intensely enthusiastic life left him fulfilled like never before.

"Xiaoyue, do you think we'll fall out someday?" Han Ma asked him.

"Impossible."

"Then will you fall in love with me?" she asked next.

"What do you think about this question?" Xiaoyue asked her back.

"I don't know. I'm confused—I'm not as naive as before. But it doesn't matter, either way you still haven't . . . We get along well as we are, don't we?"

"Yes, Han Ma. But I am always thinking about you, as a literary memento."

"Since you take me to be literature, then you can never fall out with me, but also never fall in love with me."

"Which one do you want from me?"

"I want—no, I don't know."

"Then just let it be 'unknown.' It's not necessary to keep thinking about it."

"You're cunning, Xiaoyue, an expert in personal relationships."

"What I want most is to do what you want. That always makes me happy."

"You understand me so well. In the future I'll probably be captivated. Then I'll pursue you."

"I'm waiting for that day."

They sounded each other out this way, half-joking, half-serious. Han Ma's creative passion ran high under the provocation of this ambiguity. That was when good news arrived from the capital. The day the news came, Han Ma couldn't resist kissing Xiaoyue again. This time he kissed her in return. It was only a kiss on the forehead. He gently hugged her, staying close to her, like he would breathe her into his body. His actions moved her incredibly.

Later Han Ma asked herself: "Is this partnership or dating after all? Could I have misjudged him?"

She couldn't answer her own questions. She decided not to mind these questions, following what Xiaoyue had said. "I 'thrive on chaos,' which is fine," she added, laughing. She knew Xiaoyue was able to control himself and was sure about the goals he pursued. So, if she proceeded based on what he'd said, then all would be well. Xiaoyue wouldn't make a mistake—at least he was much more clear-headed than her. If there hadn't been Fei first, if Xiaoyue had been the one she'd met, maybe she would have fallen in love with him all the same. Yet there had been Fei, that love had been deeply carved into her bones, and Han Ma didn't know whether she could get over it.

Han Ma's short story collection *Expedition* was published by the literary magazine *The Future* in the capital. Everyone in the Pigeon Book Club read it. Even though they weren't able to gather for the moment, they were all exhilarated and had conversations with each other over the phone. They all said it was truly inspirational, that an extraordinary author had emerged, like a miracle, in their midst. They believed Han Ma to have countless possibilities ahead of her and called profusely to congratulate her.

Han Ma was thus even more roused to make an effort. She wrote every day, and she felt that she could write even better. Thanks to Xiaoyue, the purview of her reading was also widened. He brought her a large number of novels that he thought were highly important, until the books almost no longer fit in piles on her shelves. On the weekends Han Ma often wrote until late, then afterward sometimes couldn't help calling up Xiaoyue. He would come over to her place and carry on animated discussions with her. Sometimes they'd talk until almost dawn, when he finally went back to his place. They were young, healthy, and both lifted weights, so they could work hard.

One day Xiao Sang invited Han Ma to see the condo she and Heishi had bought. Han Ma said that she wanted to bring a guest along. Xiao Sang asked her who, and Han Ma said it was Xiaoyue. Xiao Sang applauded, saying: "That's great!"

"But it's not that kind of relationship," Han Ma said.

"Who cares what kind of relationship it is! Xiaoyue's our friend, too. Come over, bring him along. Han Ma, you can relax a little," Xiao Sang said.

Xiao Sang told Heishi about Han Ma and Xiaoyue coming over, and he was as excited as she was.

"It seems that there's hope. I'm anxious, though: we should help Han Ma out, as her friends," he said.

"She isn't able to let go of Fei. But I think Xiaoyue and Han Ma are a born match! Xiaoyue also helped me recently to organize a large-scale reading group and invited many readers to it. We should play matchmakers, in secret."

"Just like the Pigeon Book Club did with the two of us," Heishi laughed.

Cherishing hope, they got ready for the arrival of Han Ma and Xiaoyue.

When Han Ma told Xiaoyue about Xiao Sang's invitation, his heart pounded, and he said:

"I've always admired their relationship as a model, to a great extent. But our model isn't bad either. What do you think, Han Ma?"

She thought earnestly for a while about what he had said, then answered him a little confusedly:

"I don't know, Xiaoyue. What model are we? It seems like you know. For me, I only know to do what comes naturally. I'll do so, whether or not there's a good outcome."

"Doing what's natural is our model. You and I are very much in agreement."

On the weekend Han Ma and Xiaoyue took the bus to the Joy and Peace Apartments to visit Xiao Sang and Heishi's home. Once on their way they were both in a slightly excited mood. The Joy and Peace Apartments were near the city suburbs, but the transportation to get there was convenient and it was next to one of Meng's largest parks. Xiao Sang and Heishi's unit stood beside a forest. The gray buildings were all five stories high, with elevators, and they lived on the fourth floor.

Getting off the bus, Han Ma saw Xiao Sang and Heishi walking right toward Xiaoyue and her.

"Xiao Sang, your color's really good. Maybe it's a boy," Han Ma jokingly said.

"A boy or a girl are both welcome," Xiao Sang said. "Xiaoyue, why are you carrying such a large package?"

"To be ready when the time comes. This kind of stroller is really useful," Xiaoyue said.

As they entered the home, Han Ma sensed the large square footage and many rooms.

"This is a four-bedroom condo, because Heishi and I each need a study, so there's a lot of space," Xiao Sang said by way of introduction. "In the future when Han Ma gets married she should also buy a four-bedroom apartment, to settle in."

"The condition is that the man I marry is also a bookworm," Han Ma said.

Han Ma toured the two large studies in an admiring way, carefully looking around for a long time. She heard Xiaoyue saying beside her: "These bookcases and shelves are a good design. There are the open rattan bookshelves and also large bookcases for collectible books. You need a lot of space to arrange a study this well." Han Ma said: "You're starting to learn from experience."

Afterward they toured the bedrooms and kitchen, and agreed that the design was both reasonable and useful.

When the two of them sat down, Heishi and Xiao Sang jubilantly brewed tea and brought out snacks for them. Then Heishi said he needed to go to the kitchen and make lunch. Xiao Sang kept their guests company in the living room.

"Han Ma, are you sprinting ahead again? I feel like you're in a good state."

"I need to write a new work—I write every day. And I exercise every day, I have to, however busy I am. He is the same, we're competing," she said, pointing to Xiaoyue.

"I really miss the book club gatherings. That was the first place Heishi ever took me."

As Xiao Sang said this she had a rapt expression.

"The Pigeon Book Club brings me the greatest enlightenment," Xiaoyue said. "Right now I'm getting ready for when the gatherings start up again. Afterward, I plan to work with Fei on the communication of literary appreciation. My work progresses more and more now that there's Han Ma's writing functioning as a living example."

“You two are literature’s match made in heaven,” Xiao Sang nodded appreciatively.

Han Ma hadn’t spoken. She wanted to change the topic, so she asked Xiao Sang about the condo’s price. Xiao Sang told her.

“Not much more expensive than your place,” she turned toward Xiaoyue and said.

“Hmm, I’ve thought of buying one with this kind of design, but I don’t have anyone to marry,” Xiaoyue said.

“Then what are you waiting for?” Xiao Sang said, laughing.

“I haven’t found someone, and being in a rush won’t help, either. The one I like doesn’t love me.” He made a sullen face.

“That proves that you haven’t tried hard enough. You should learn from Heishi’s experience,” Xiao Sang said.

“Really? I’ll wait to ask Heishi. The man who can make you fall in love with him must have superb ingenuity. I need to study him.”

While Xiaoyue was speaking, he went to the kitchen to help.

Xiao Sang made a face toward his back, moved closer to Han Ma, and said:

“He’s really loveable.”

“Hmm, he’s OK. The apartment I’m renting is in his apartment complex. He made all the arrangements.”

“I thought at first that Heishi didn’t love me. For the most part these good men don’t reveal themselves,” Xiao Sang said.

“Xiaoyue’s determined to dawdle with me and not let the relationship grow deeper. I also think this is a good thing.”

“Han Ma, he probably suffers in ways that he can’t tell you about. The initiative is in your hands. I could tell this as soon as you arrived.”

“I’m still not sure of myself.”

“Then just wait. But don’t drag things out too long, Han Ma. We all miss the Pigeon Book Club.”

Han Ma gazed into space confusedly, as if there were chaos in her heart.

The door of the kitchen was open, so that the two people outside heard the two people inside talking nonstop, *weng weng weng, weng weng weng*.

Xiao Sang pointed to the kitchen with a laugh and said to Han Ma:

“Heishi has many wicked qualities, and he used to always be secretive. I’m worried he’ll lead Xiaoyue astray.”

"How bad could the two of them be?" Han Ma finally laughed, too.

At noon they ate pork chops stewed with meng bean noodles and baicai, and there was a made-to-order Peking duck. Xiao Sang had also readied champagne for their guests. Han Ma saw that Xiaoyue looked overwrought.

The food was delicious, but Han Ma and Xiaoyue both drank one glass and weren't willing to drink more. Only Heishi drank two glasses. Xiao Sang didn't drink.

When they'd finished the meal Han Ma and Xiaoyue left. Heishi and Xiao Sang saw their good friends to the bus stop.

On the bus, Han Ma asked Xiaoyue what he had learned from Heishi about romance.

"We were talking about the literary appreciation mechanism," Xiaoyue said. "I thought you were feeling awkward when I was sitting with you and Xiao Sang, so I found an excuse to go to the kitchen."

"Xiaoyue, you're too good."

The bus drove steadily. Han Ma was a bit drowsy and wanted to sleep, so she quite naturally rested her head on Xiaoyue's shoulder. He thought to himself: she's exhausted.

She slept until it was time to get off the bus and only then woke up.

"Xiaoyue, was I snoring?" she asked uneasily.

"A little, but it was nice to listen to."

"You never bring up my flaws."

"You have none. Those so-called flaws are all good qualities."

"Just like literature. I know that's how you think. Oh, oh . . ."

"Why are you sighing?"

"I can't say exactly. Nothing can be said exactly." There was melancholy in Han Ma's eyes.

"We can just not think about what can't be said, and act according to our intentions."

Once Han Ma and Xiaoyue left, Xiao Sang asked Heishi right away what he and Xiaoyue had talked about.

"We discussed setting up the literary appreciation mechanism. Xiaoyue is exceptional, he's highly talented."

"So that's it. He fooled me and said he was going to get the *Lover's Bible* from you."

"What *Lover's Bible* do I have? I'm just clumsy and stupid." Heishi laughed aloud.

"I feel even more like he and Han Ma are compatible. He probably took aim at her from the start. Actually, Han Ma is attracted to him now, too, but she's in a state of contradiction, because of Fei," Xiao Sang said.

"Hmm, 'water will find its course' for them. I'm so stupid, but you haven't forsaken me yet. I don't know how many times more clever Xiaoyue is than me, so how could Han Ma cast him aside? Wait and see."

"I'm so relieved to hear you say that. Han Ma should have good fortune."

When Han Ma returned home, she was still thinking of what Xiao Sang had said. She reflected: people see most clearly as bystanders. So Xiao Sang's judgments ought to make sense. Before, with her whole heart on Fei alone, she might have overlooked some things. The more Han Ma reminisced, the more she thought about how Xiaoyue possessed some excellent qualities that most people rarely did.

"But do I really love him?" she said out loud.

The answer was still: I don't know.

During the day the sexual partner she imagined was still Fei; the sexual partner in her dreams was the unknown man in the novel. She had never once seen Xiaoyue in her dreams. Naturally, when she had physical contact with him, she desired his body. Thinking back and forth, she decided to set aside the issue, in the way he and she had decided together: to do what came naturally.

Han Ma started to read again. Now when she read fiction she always felt that the descriptions were both sensual and beautiful. Was it because of some change in her physically that she could learn things she was unable to experience before? She glanced at the red roses in the vases and thought that the roses were the greatest cause for her transformation. Were these Fei's roses, or Xiaoyue's roses? Look at this paragraph: it's about a young woman running through a graveyard carrying a large bouquet of wild roses. The color of the sky is gradually dimming, while she's still waiting for the train . . . Later there was someone who disembarked at the small station beside the cemetery. Yet he was like a shadow, and the young woman's yearning for him could only be fulfilled through dialogue. This was a good thing, though—she'd gotten part of what it was she wanted. Although she was left unsatisfied, her life gained meaning. "But I also want to have a real life!" she shouted toward that unknown man's back. The title of the book was *XXXXX5*, a full-length novel that Xiaoyue had recently given Han Ma. He'd said that he had a copy, too. Han Ma knew about this author, had read her short stories, and was filled with intense love for her. She thought that, perhaps, someday, this novel would give her the answer to her feelings for Xiaoyue. Why was there only assurance about things written down, whereas taking action in reality was like being half-blind and at every step seeming only able to move around tentatively? These were the nets Heishi had spoken of. Then was love inherent to the nets? Had people invented nets because they must take action? In Han Ma's relationship with Xiaoyue, it seemed she was always the one to rush ahead to take action; Xiaoyue, though, was the one who mastered the general direction. This was why she felt safe and gratified in the midst of this linked form of expression. Could Xiaoyue be the stranger in the book, that stranger who belonged to her? Had she failed to recognize him because of his appearing in her everyday life? The woman in the book couldn't see the man's body, but instead she could hear his enchanting voice. Would there be a transformation in her perceptions? Han Ma thought: from now on she would continue to function in her own way. She didn't want to be someone who couldn't live in reality. She should "relax" like Xiao Sang had advised her.

In fact, in life, she'd become better able to do what she wanted, with Xiaoyue's guidance. He was a practical genius, even though he was about the same age as she was. Han Ma felt intuitively that, if she followed Xiaoyue, she would as soon as possible move beyond her suffering while also respecting her former love. Xiaoyue's nature was attractive to her, and this attraction wasn't without basis, as it seemed from the surface. Just like the young woman in the book and the shadowy man: that man would eventually reveal himself, while the woman would discover that there was a secure connection between them. People are all in the know after the fact, but those who can act beforehand in obscurity—for example, herself, for example, Xiao Sang, Heishi, and also Xiaoyue—belong to the wise. Thinking all of this over, Han Ma grew cheerful. Oh, it was dusk outside!

"Xiaoyue, I've fallen in love with the novel you gave me!" she said on the phone.

"Then I'll take you out somewhere for vegetable noodles. I'll be right down."

Xiaoyue looked invigorated and said he'd just exercised. As they walked he told Han Ma that Xiao Sang and Heishi's condo was in the best location for them, but he still thought the Red Roses Apartments were the best for her and for himself. Because the Red Roses Apartments were closer to the city center, convenient for shopping, and had all kinds of delicious food nearby. Xiao Sang's family included elderly parents, and they didn't need to always eat out, while he and Han Ma were single, without elderly parents at home, so they could rely on the restaurants all over the place. Talking this way, the two of them turned into a circuitous alley. Xiaoyue said that it was called Chicken Guts Lane, because it was shaped like chicken intestines. The restaurants lining both sides of the road had thatched roofs and were dimly lit.

Han Ma followed Xiaoyue into a thatch-roofed building, which was a restaurant run by a husband and wife.

After a while the meal was brought out: vegetable noodles mixed with small pieces of fried tofu and bok choy, and a "three fresh ingredients" soup. Han Ma tasted a bit with her chopsticks, and her appetite was stimulated. She said to Xiaoyue:

"Between my exercising every day and eating the food you arrange for me, my figure will improve."

"You'd be good-looking whether you were a little fatter or thinner."

"Because Han Ma is literature," she said mockingly.

"No, it's not like that."

"Then how is it?"

"You think a person is good-looking because you like them."

"I'd forgotten this piece of common sense."

When they'd finished eating, Xiaoyue asked Han Ma whether she wanted to keep walking, saying that the alleyway's aromas of food would help to give rise to inspiration.

"The smell of cooking also has a sexual component," Han Ma said. "If I'm not careful I'll lose my composure."

"It doesn't matter, I'll be right beside you."

"Now you're making sense."

So the two of them walked to the end of Chicken Guts Lane, then turned and walked back.

"Even though she wanted to, the young woman picking wild roses couldn't meet the shadowy man who was on the train of freedom. She could only wait, so she made her home at that small train station. I've just read up to there," Han Ma said.

"She was also forging a life of freedom. I'm willing to be the one who waits."

"I would never be content to be a shadow. Do you remember the speeches from when we were at the Crown Department Store reading group? It predicted what would happen afterward."

"Thank you, Han Ma, your words are like warmth through my heart."

"Goodbye, Xiaoyue, I'm going back to be diligent. I'll be hardworking until the middle of the night. If I can't help it, I'll give you a call again."

"Call me, go ahead and call me, Han Ma. I wait for your calls all day."

"Why can I not stand being lonely?" Han Ma was troubled.

"It's unnecessary to wait things out. Your personal style is to do what you want to do."

Han Ma finished reading the chapter. She daydreamed for a while, then sat down at her desk to continue writing fiction.

Now she could write more than when she had just started, but it wasn't very much yet, since she was still willing to abide by the ancient wisdom that "haste never arrives"—slowly exploring, slowly going deeper. She sensed herself achieving a calm demeanor, and the silent lover at the end of language guarded her the whole time. "I love you." Han Ma wrote a few sentences, then read them aloud. When she'd finished writing two long passages, she felt she had already exceeded the set amount, so she stopped. Now she was content, as she should be; after writing, no matter what she was doing was bestowed with meaning. She didn't want to mess around, which was the habit of many classical authors, who would relax and think that their writing was superior. Han Ma wasn't this way: she subsumed writing into everyday life. She and the book friends around her were in agreement on this point, and they all enjoyed their lives.

It was late at night now. What did she want to do? She wanted to talk with Fei, tell him about her joy in creation, but she couldn't. She had known for a long time now that this would be impossible. She wanted to find Xiaoyue, rest her head on his shoulder, talk with him about literature. Thinking back, though, she felt that this would be taking advantage of him. Because he was tired, too, and had sexual desires with no release. She shouldn't tease him again.

So Han Ma showered, picked up the book *XXXXX5*, and got in bed. Eventually she couldn't keep her eyes quite open, although she kept reading: a wilderness, walking along in the dark of night, whispers of love . . . She turned off the light. Later the unknown man arrived and lay beside her, caressing the sensitive places of her body . . . He said, "It doesn't matter, I'll be right beside you." So it was Xiaoyue! Han Ma woke up in surprise. Then after a while she went back to sleep.

She said in her dream: "I've been young for so long. One lover after another."

At eight the next morning she was woken up by noise, which turned out to be Xiaoyue. He was saying that yesterday they'd agreed to go running together at the apartment complex's flower garden and asked if she was ready. When had they agreed? Had he really been there in the middle of the night?

She got dressed and saw him standing there glowing with health.

"You didn't give me a call last night?" she asked as they ran.

"No, I was writing an essay."

Han Ma felt a little disappointed. She didn't ask him about the essay he'd been writing.

"Maybe she's started to think about me at night," Xiaoyue wondered. "I'm so happy."

"Originally I thought of calling you, but then I remembered that you fell asleep on the bus yesterday, so I held back."

"You really do have willpower. I thought of calling you, too, but I feel like I've been taking advantage of you."

"But I was looking forward to your call the whole time. Is that 'taking advantage'?" Xiaoyue said.

"It seems like our literary cause is advancing successfully, but our feelings aren't making any progress."

"I don't agree. Haven't we made progress? Day and night, hung up on each other, longing."

Han Ma thought: I'm teasing him again, it's inappropriate. Fortunately the run was over.

That morning Han Ma wrote in a sexy mood. She wrote easily and soon finished the quantity of writing she had set for herself. Next she read the novel that Xiaoyue had given her. The following chapter was about the man on the train of freedom. He took off his hat and sunglasses and turned into an ordinary person. He was wondering what sort of city he'd visited when he got off the train, and whether he would plan to spend his life in this city. Han Ma read up to here and started laughing, perceiving that the fragrance of the roses was even thicker in the room. "That wasn't deliberate at all—instead it's an attraction of natural instinct." Without realizing it she spoke these words aloud. In a while the phone rang again.

"I'm making mala chicken to bring over there to eat," Xiaoyue said.

He'd placed all of the food he'd prepared inside a rattan basket.

"Xiaoyue, you could be a chef. You can do anything, and you do everything well. Most people couldn't manage it. Me, for example, I'm only able to knock out a few words, and I'm bad at everything else. This shows that I don't love life as intensely as you do."

"Your talent is focused on one thing, while my talents are scattered. So only you can write fiction."

"Look, I'm the only one eating, I'll finish all of this chicken on my own. Eat up."

"All right. My heart hasn't known such happiness before, if you're enjoying this food. I am dedicating my abilities to literature."

"Again it's with literature," Han Ma dragged out the words.

"What I mean is, you and literature are one whole, and are also two, and I like both."

"You can really talk. But I also enjoy your genius at expressing what you mean."

Between the two of them, they ate the dishes clean. As Han Ma washed the dishes, she said:

"Isn't this becoming what they call 'friends only when there's food and drink'?"

"I like eating, and am leading you astray.

"Besides eating, my research has progressed and been successful recently," he added. "Sometimes I write during the night and really hate not to read the sentences I've written down aloud to you immediately."

"I benefit infinitely from your essays. If you see me as literature, you are the father of literature. Am I right?" Han Ma said thoughtfully.

"No. I'm a technician helping literary communication spread. I've always seen it like this and take pride in it."

"Xiaoyue, I want to kiss you again. Quick, take your basket and go, otherwise something will happen."

Xiaoyue went out, laughing.

Once the door was shut, Han Ma sat down on the sofa in a daze. Something will happen? What will happen? Had she fallen in love with him? Of course not. Yet he'd enlightened her so much, really, as though through personal practice he made literature into reality. He was also so optimistic, so unhurried . . . One could say that he'd enhanced her creativity without her knowing it. "How couldn't I love him?" Han Ma asked herself. "But I still love Fei. Only Xiaoyue, he's made me love life even more intensely than before. Also, I'm physically attracted to him. Maybe the man at night is him?" Han Ma thought up to here and halted. She hurriedly washed her face in cold water, then continued her reading. The book became more and more engaging, and what was written in it seemed to be the same as her life now. Every time a plot appeared in the book, she could find correspondences in her life. Though when seen from the surface, those plots were prosaic.

Another three months had passed since the time Xiao Ma had tried to move into Uncle Yi's home and been rebuffed. She thought a lot about marriage, in addition to her efforts to study literature. She knew that Xiao Sang was already pregnant and came up with the idea of discussing this aspect of things with her close friend. So on Wednesday, when the two of them got off work early, she invited Xiao Sang to a teahouse to drink a variety of fruit tea. After cleaning up the department store a bit, they went out gladly.

"This tea has a very good flavor. I haven't tried it before," Xiao Sang said.

"It seems like you aren't as indulgent about enjoying things as I am. Uncle Yi made me fruit tea once, and I learned to like it. Of course, the tea I make isn't as much of a specialty as this teahouse's."

"Will things be happening soon?" Xiao Sang asked with a smile.

"I need to wait another two or three months. It's Uncle Yi's rule—there's nothing I can do."

"Do you plan to have a baby?" Xiao Sang asked.

"That's exactly what I wanted to talk about with you. Seeing that you're pregnant, I'm incredibly jealous. I want to have my own child, too. But I care so much about literature—I don't want to give it up. If I get married and have a child right away, and I still need to go to work, both will need my attention, so I won't have any time to study literature. This will last at least two or three years. Won't I be illiterate after that? But I can't make myself not want to have a child. I love Uncle Yi so much that I have to have a baby that's mine and his. I've thought it over, without finding a way to have both. It makes me depressed."

"Have you and Uncle Yi discussed having a child together?"

"No. I'm a coward—I'm afraid if we don't agree that he'll get angry and then not want to get married."

"Xiao Ma, I think you're worrying too much. The way Uncle Yi loves you, how could he be angry?"

"Do you mean that I can talk about this with him directly? That he'll know what to do?"

"Of course you can talk directly. Maybe he's already thought it through. You're too much of a modern woman to be so traditional. Uncle Yi is deliberate in whatever he does."

"You're so highly accomplished and must understand Uncle Yi deeply. I still desperately need to catch up."

Xiao Ma became cheerful. She stroked Xiao Sang's pregnant belly and asked the long and short of things, trying to learn from her experience. Xiao Sang was especially happy, too, for Uncle Yi, and also for Xiao Ma. She thought: "They're so well-matched!"

On Friday evening, after Xiao Ma finished discussing literature with Uncle Yi, she decided to put her cards on the table.

"Uncle Yi, our wedding day is approaching. Have you thought about having a baby?" was how she asked.

"I've thought it over. This depends on what you want," Uncle Yi said, watching her.

Xiao Ma thought: he really has thought about it. Xiao Sang understands him.

"I want to have a baby with you, but—," she was too nervous to keep on speaking.

"But you're afraid that afterward you won't have any time to study literature, is that it?" Uncle Yi helped to finish the words that she was going to say.

Xiao Ma nodded hard.

"Let me ask you first: do you really want to have a child?" Uncle Yi said next.

"Yes, very much so. Because it would be having a child with you. You're the man I want to have a child with. I saw Xiao Sang was pregnant and felt incredibly jealous."

"Then there's no problem. You can take off from work and stay at home for a few years. I'll help out, too. You will have time to study."

"What about money?"

"There's enough. If you didn't work from now on we would still have enough money. Of course, if you like going to work, then you can keep working in the future. I've been writing essays for so many years that I have some savings, so if you don't have expensive tastes, there should be enough for us."

When Uncle Yi finished speaking, Xiao Ma jumped up and embraced him, kissing him once firmly on the face.

"Ha, today I finally kissed you!" she said in a loud voice.

He looked at her happily.

"Let's get married right away," she said.

"No, we still need to wait a while. Let's not casually change our plans."

"No wonder you said that the plans you've made for your life in the future include me. It turns out you were planning in advance!" Xiao Ma said.

"In advance? No, I hadn't thought of a child then. I'm only starting to think about it now. I'm also worried I won't be able to have children. I'm older, and if you weren't so determined to have a child, then I wouldn't insist."

"Why not? We love each other—we must have a child. I hope the baby will be like you."

"All right, all right, we'll give it a try. I've kept in shape, so it should still be possible."

"We'll definitely have a baby!" Xiao Ma said confidently. "When the time comes, you will become father to two people. I've always seen you as my father, haha! I'm so happy today."

Xiao Ma returned to her apartment complex humming a song on the way. She made a call as soon as she reached her apartment.

"Xiao Sang, I've talked it over with Uncle Yi. There's no problem at all. He'd already made plans!"

"That's what I thought. You see how deeply he loves you—just as deeply as Heishi loves me. We're both very lucky."

"Xiao Sang, I wouldn't be who I am today if it weren't for you. You brought me to Uncle Yi's home, and you helped me pursue him—I could cry."

"If you want to be a mom, you can't just cry at anything. Good people get what they deserve. You and Uncle Yi are my dearest family, and now you'll be married to each other. The things I dreamed about wake me up laughing."

"OK, I won't cry! Kiss the baby and Heishi for me."

Xiao Ma sat up straight at the table and looked at the notes Uncle Yi had helped her to revise. She read a section, then, sighing endlessly, thought about him. At this moment the phone rang. It was her mother.

"Xiao Ma, I was thinking about the move. I've spoken with Yanzhi and Xiao Hong. Do you think I should wait until a few months after you've married?"

"Why should you wait? It'll be better if you and I move in at the same time!"

"You think it's better to move at the same time? I'll consider it. I also think that when you have a baby I'll come help out so you have time to study."

"Mom, you don't need to worry, I've already discussed this with Uncle Yi. When I have a baby I'll take off work, so he and I can take care of the baby ourselves. Uncle Yi is financially stable. I can stay at home to care for the child and study, too."

Xiao Ma's mother was surprised to hear this from her.

"You two haven't even lived together yet, but you've already decided about this? It really is a different era!"

"Of course it's different. I'm a modern woman. Thank you, Mom, we'll also need your help."

"You'll definitely need some of your mom's help. You're my dear oldest daughter. I have experience in caring for children. You can just focus on bravely giving birth."

When the call ended, Xiao Ma felt surrounded by happiness. She would have a child with Uncle Yi! It was so new, this future that inspired her! Now she would try even harder, striving to work someday at the Youth Literary Research Institute and do what she enjoyed the most.

Uncle Yi always amazed Xiao Ma. The better she knew him, the more she felt that his nature and affections were abundant treasures, enough for her to study for a lifetime. Had those lofty novels cultivated Uncle Yi as an individual, or were people like Uncle Yi the prototype for fiction?

This was a profound question, one that Xiao Ma needed to continue exploring before she could eventually feel for the threads. When she and Uncle Yi had gotten together what attracted her most was how he was never boring and always a pleasant surprise. She saw him every other day now, but this wasn't enough, and she thought constantly about getting married right away. Xiao Ma believed that the days after they married, although busy, would be their happiest. With every day that passed, she tore off another day from her calendar with excitement.

A few days later Xiao Ma's mother came to talk with her about buying a wedding dress.

"Mom, Uncle Yi and I didn't discuss that. I want to be like Xiao Sang: two people move in together and that's the end."

"How could this be? The greatest event of once in a lifetime . . . I couldn't give you a happy childhood, now it's time to look forward to your wedding, and you want to finish it off in a rush." Her mother started to wipe away tears.

"Oh, oh, Mom, don't cry, don't cry. I promise you I'll wear a wedding dress. I don't have much time free, so you can go help buy it for me—buy the best one. You and I are about the same size. You can try it on for me."

"Xiao Ma will be the prettiest bride on Earth."

"It doesn't matter if I'm pretty. Everything's fine so long as Uncle Yi likes me."

"Wearing a wedding dress will make Uncle Yi like you even more. I've figured everything out: your sisters will carry the train of the dress from the taxi as you slowly walk into Uncle Yi's home. We won't set firecrackers or have a formal ceremony, but you have to wear a wedding dress. Do you promise?"

"OK, fine, I'll wear a dress!"

Xiao Ma's mom was finally satisfied at this.

"Also, have Uncle Yi wear a suit. He must be handsome in a suit."

"OK, fine, I'll tell him to wear a suit!"

"Also, you have to invite all of your friends, and everyone will sit down to a meal together."

"OK, fine, I'll invite them!"

"Uncle Yi, my mom insists that I wear a wedding dress and wants you to wear a suit, too. I had to promise."

"Hmm, we should do what she asks. For her this is such an important event."

"Thank you, Uncle Yi. You understand my mom better than I do. I was planning to do things casually, like Xiao Sang."

"But your mom has this image that's been stored up in her heart for years. We can't only care about ourselves!"

"You understand everything. I'm so disappointing. Can you forgive me?"

"Didn't you say I was your father? Are there any dads who can't forgive their daughters? You'll need to forgive me, too."

"Let me kiss you again! Good, but there are still two months and twenty days. It's so slow!"

"What do you think I should call your mom?"

"Just call her 'Xiao Ma's mom,' this will be most natural. She worships you."

"That's because she doesn't know my shortcomings yet."

Uncle Yi wanted to make some renovations to the apartment. Originally he'd thought of exchanging it at this point for an even larger four-bedroom unit, but Xiao Ma said there wasn't enough time: they should improvise and stay here, waiting until afterward when there would be time for them to move. For now it would be good enough, provided the unit was fixed up a bit. Uncle Yi didn't need to tire himself out. "I don't have any opinions about the renovations. Your old apartment is very comfortable, and life here is convenient. Let's use a bedroom for my study," Xiao Ma said.

After that, she finally understood why Uncle Yi wanted to wait six months before getting married. It turned out there were so many things he considered in his plans. Of course, in all things he took Xiao Ma's wishes into account. They agreed after much discussion that, after they were married, they would wait a few months until Xiao Ma was pregnant and then think about switching to a larger apartment. "Having a baby will be the greatest event for me," she said. Uncle Yi had to agree with her. She remained carefree about a wedding, and not traveling for a honeymoon or having a ceremony and formal invitations. Instead it would be the same as usual—she'd do whatever needed doing.

"Following your heart is truly romantic, isn't it?" she said.

"You're right," Uncle Yi chimed in.

Later on Xiao Ma's sisters came to Uncle Yi's home to meet him. Xiao Ma remembered Yanzhi's opinion of Uncle Yi and couldn't help but feel a little nervous about whether her sisters would be agreeable.

Yet, to her great surprise, they not only behaved properly but also called Uncle Yi "brother-in-law," asked him about this and that, and were on familiar terms with him right away. They said that from now on they would visit their older sister's home frequently to ask for advice, and in this way improve quickly so that the book friends in their reading group would look at them with new eyes. Uncle Yi gave Yanzhi and Xiao Hong each a novel when they left. They were delighted to the skies. "Look, there's an inscription from our brother-in-law on the title page! Everyone knows that our brother-in-law is a literary figure."

The three sisters went outside, where the younger sisters said that they'd never imagined their brother-in-law would be so handsome and energetic.

"Didn't Yanzhi say he was too old?" Xiao Ma asked in return.

"Because I hadn't met him yet," Yanzhi explained.

"I like Uncle Yi. It doesn't matter that he's a little older," Xiao Ma said.

"He's not old at all!" her sisters said in unison.

When Xiao Ma returned to Uncle Yi's home, she asked him what his impression of her sisters was.

"They are our successors, so we need to train them well. Their development is your work and my work."

"They said you don't seem advanced in years and are full of energy."

"That is because I bask in your light. I don't look so old, as long as I stand beside you."

"Since that's the case, why don't we get married right away? Hmm? What do you still have to arrange?"

"Then let's get married a month early. Xiao Ma, you have more courage than I do. You have a pragmatic spirit."

"There's good news, spread the word! I'm getting married soon!" Xiao Ma clapped her hands.

Xiao Ma's mother finally bought the wedding dress for her.

Xiao Ma did her hair and tried it on.

"My heavens!" her mom said, "like a goddess descended to Earth!"

She wiped away tears again. Xiao Ma was resplendent.

"My sister is more beautiful than anyone else!" Yanzhi said.

"Xiao Ma, I don't dare to look at you, I feel so inferior," Xiao Hong said, covering her eyes.

"You two will also have a day like this," Xiao Ma told her sisters. "The more you mature, the more beautiful you will be. Uncle Yi wants me to train you both well."

"Did he say so? Our brother-in-law's terrific!" Yanzhi said. "When we met him it was just like seeing someone from our own family. He has a kind of affinity about him. When you talk with him you feel a warmth."

"It looks like Yanzhi has learned many things from the reading group," Xiao Ma said.

"They're both improving quickly. Now they've learned how to cook," her mother said.

"Keep it up, you two! I'm getting more and more fond of you."

After Xiao Ma finished trying on the wedding dress, she went back to her apartment. Then she gave Uncle Yi a call.

"Uncle Yi, my mom bought the wedding dress, and I've tried it on."

"How is it? Extremely beautiful?"

"It's all right. I'm tired of all these rehearsals. Why can't I come over to your place right now? I've read all day, now I want to come over. Would that be OK?"

"Then—you can come over."

"Wonderful, Uncle Yi!"

Xiao Ma pushed open the door and Uncle Yi came over to embrace her, pulling her onto the bed.

"Uncle Yi, you're so strong!" Xiao Ma heard her voice trembling slightly.

Busy helping Xiao Ma take off her clothes, Uncle Yi didn't say anything. There was central heating in the bedroom, so it was very warm. The two of them were completely naked. They didn't kiss for very long before they began to touch each other. Xiao Ma dizzily thought: "His body is still so young. Now we can finally let go, I'm so turned on." Then Uncle Yi entered her, in wave upon wave. She made a moan like a low roar . . .

Xiao Ma slowly came back from a world of bliss. She thought: Uncle Yi is still powerful.

"Uncle Yi, you gave me—" After a while she finally spoke. "I'll be pregnant with your baby."

Uncle Yi didn't speak, sensing that Xiao Ma's youthful body was stimulated again. He began caressing her body with his mouth and hands. He kept stroking, sucking.

"Uncle Yi, Uncle Yi, I love you, I love you in my bones!"

His caresses became focused.

"Ah . . . ah . . . I'm dying!" Xiao Ma shouted.

After this another while passed, and she heard him say in her ear:

"Xiao Ma, I'm old, I can't satisfy you fully. But if you like, I can always touch you."

"I like your mouth and hands as much," Xiao Ma said. "But it's late now, we're both exhausted. Let's sleep."

Xiao Ma went to sleep in Uncle Yi's arms. Then he went to sleep, too.

In the morning he woke up first. He gazed at Xiao Ma's nakedness, his heart full of joy and remorse. He shouldn't have made her wait so long—this senseless waiting had nearly consumed her. It was all because he didn't understand her well enough yet. Her single-mindedness toward him left him incredibly moved.

"Uncle Yi, I'll stay here and won't leave you," Xiao Ma said once she opened her eyes.

"Xiao Ma, maybe you should still wait a bit. Your mother won't be happy if we live together before we're married. She'll suspect I don't have good intentions. This is our wedding, why make your mom anxious? It wouldn't be fair, don't you think? Come back again next weekend, all right?"

"All right. We'll be underground lovers first. I'll have breakfast and wait a while, then slip secretly away."

They ate breakfast together, both gazing at each other, as if lost in their thoughts.

"I used to believe that someone with my temperament was destined to live alone," Uncle Yi said. "You broke through the barriers in my nature, and now it's like I'm reborn."

"I think," Xiao Ma said, "that in this world there are lonely men and women who fumble around in the dark. Then some of them feel their way to the turning point of love, are drawn to it, and start on a new course, and are finished with being alone. You and I both used to be this kind of lonely person, but I wasn't resigned to it. I wanted to find the other half who belonged to me. I sniffed everywhere like a hunting dog."

"Xiao Ma, you are also rushing ahead of me when it comes to literature. I'm so happy."

"I'm grateful, thankful to Xiao Sang, thankful to you for accepting me, and also thankful to my mother for supporting me."

"I want to catch up to you, Xiao Ma. You stimulate me in every way. You make me feel like I'm reversing time and returning to childhood. Our lives are so closely associated with literature, which fills my old age with passion. I am grateful, too, every day. Literature is truly magnificent."

After Xiao Ma had returned to her apartment, she wrote in her diary: *Last night I finally became a complete woman, becoming one with the person I love the most. Only he can intoxicate me, satisfying me in ways I've never been satisfied before!* She started to read, to take notes. She felt that her experience of literature was now a layer deeper, so she whispered: "It seems like sex can spur the imagination."

She studied until the afternoon, went to a noodle house to eat, then came back to continue reading.

Toward evening her mom called again.

"Xiao Ma, a bride should wear a garland of flowers. We'll need to buy one the day before the wedding. What kind of flowers do you like? That slightly smaller white flower is the best."

"A white rose garland would be good."

"I'll go order it right away. I just bought a platinum necklace, too. It wouldn't be right without a necklace."

"Thank you, Mom. I love you. Our wedding date has been moved up a month."

"Wonderful! I've always thought that it wasn't necessary for Uncle Yi to wait so long. You're not demanding, and you don't need him to renovate the apartment. Why wait so many months? There's only a month left, I'm so excited."

When the call ended an impulse stirred in Xiao Ma again. She longed for Uncle Yi's body. Then she went outside for a run and came back to continue studying.

Late in the night, before sleeping, Xiao Ma couldn't resist calling him.

"Uncle Yi, I've been writing and just put down my pen. I miss you."

"I miss you, too, Xiao Ma. Let's have good dreams," Uncle Yi said.

"Now I'm in bed, touch me for a while."

"Good . . . how is it? Thrilled?"

"Very! I'm also touching you, using my mouth . . . good. Good night."

"Good night, Xiao Ma."

Xiao Ma at first had many dreams about sex, then she finally entered a deep level of sleep.

The next day when Xiao Ma was having lunch at the department store she told Xiao Sang that her and Uncle Yi's wedding date had been moved up, so there was only a month left. Xiao Sang was glad to hear this. She told Xiao Ma that on the day of the wedding she would attend with Heishi to witness the bride's graceful bearing. She wanted to bring two other guests, one who Xiao Ma knew, which was Han Ma from the store, and the other someone she didn't know too well.

"You're marrying my and Heishi's idol. This way we'll be even closer," Xiao Sang said.

Xiao Ma put a few questions to Xiao Sang about pregnancy, too, asking attentively.

"Is Xiao Ma also—"

"Not yet. It should be soon," Xiao Ma said.

"You'll be out ahead. You were always the smartest in our group," Xiao Sang exclaimed.

They started to talk then about events from a few months ago, both women immersed in sweet recollection, in a state of knowing laughter.

The day that Xiao Ma didn't come over, Uncle Yi brought in a renovation company to paint the rooms thoroughly. Then he called Xiao Ma and told her not to come back for a few more days, because even the best painting materials have a little contamination. He would open up the windows to let the air dry the walls.

"Let me think—today is Monday, you can come back on Saturday."

Xiao Ma assumed that Uncle Yi was starting to prepare for pregnancy. He truly was showing a husband's concern for her. She felt warm all over her body. Then she asked him where he would sleep for the next few days, and Uncle Yi said that he'd book a hotel room. He also told Xiao Ma that she was right about not doing a full overhaul, because then the rooms would be occupied for even longer. Arranging things this way, they could just wait until she was pregnant and then move. There were quite a few well-renovated four-bedroom units vacant in the building. Xiao Ma's mind turned quickly, and she understood at once. After this he would consult with her more often about their plans.

Xiao Ma was pleased with what Uncle Yi had told her. She said again and again that he shouldn't tire himself out and to take things slowly. She added that she wasn't particular about such things and wouldn't be picky. She already knew, though, that even if she emphasized this, he'd still insist on having the apartment cleaned and prettied up and seen in a new light. Ah, Uncle Yi was Uncle Yi. Now she loved him even more and was afraid he would get tired, afraid he would fall ill. When Xiao Ma thought about him being so good to her in bed, she was moved almost to tears. She bought two pregnancy manuals to read, determined to have a healthy baby to comfort Uncle Yi in his old age. For the past few days she'd been energetically reading a new book that he had given her. She had a vague feeling that the elderly prophets in the book (there were three all together) were based on Uncle Yi. The more she thought about it the more she felt this was so. Of course, Uncle Yi wouldn't accept this idea; he claimed he was just an ordinary old man who enjoyed literature. If he had any good qualities, that was the benefit of literature. He loved Xiao Ma in large part because of her intense love of literature. He'd had two girlfriends before, neither of whom loved literature like she did, and so they didn't make it all the way with him. Xiao Ma was the one he loved the most; she was the gift literature had given him. Now he had more confidence about life in the future. "I am the one he loves the most, because I love literature," Xiao Ma whispered as she read.

She read until late at night, reading and rereading two chapters and taking notes to record her impressions.

Xiaoyue was going to the capital to select books for purchase by the bookstore. Han Ma wouldn't see him for a few days.

When she got back to her apartment she sat in her study roused to writing and reading. Xiaoyue called to tell her about the response to her debut fiction in the reading world of the capital. There wasn't enough of a reaction currently, but in private there had been some comments. Han Ma's writing was so advanced that most people in the world of literary criticism and in reading circles couldn't appreciate the style yet. Xiaoyue added the good news that several enlightened experts in the literary world who had high standards were very appreciative of Han Ma's work. With their lavish recommendations, sooner or later Han Ma's work would win over readers. Even though Han Ma felt excited about the news from the capital, at the same time she noticed that once Xiaoyue left the Red Roses Apartments, the greater part of his attraction for her and that feeling of repression disappeared. She didn't have the impulse to call him, because she knew he was in a distant city. It was as if she'd temporarily forgotten him.

Han Ma worked until midnight, because she was off the next day. All of a sudden she wanted to go outside for a breath of air and to take a walk. She went downstairs, left the residential area, and strolled along a street nearly emptied of people. She knew it was hard to get lost in Meng. She didn't know how much time had passed when she unexpectedly found herself at the sailors' club.

The entrance to the club wasn't completely shut, so Han Ma squeezed inside. There were ground lights on the lawn, and she followed their path, circling the large building where the auditorium was located until she came to that unevenly shaped rock. This was where Fei had made his confession of love to her after they had first met. Han Ma once again remembered that day's enthusiastic sunshine and the blue sky. "This is an era when literature is changing. I feel an impulse to devote myself . . . Han Ma, you possess a rare natural gift." His words were distinct in her ears even now. Afterward they'd kissed ardently. That passion, that longing not to be separated—Han Ma felt that she hadn't loved Fei enough. He was a poet in his bones, writing poems with his body, always, and never changed his intentions. Han Ma stroked the icy stone, as if feeling for the remnants of sunshine on the rock. Suddenly she felt a powerful yearning for Fei's body, and her tears flowed. Someone was calling to her.

It was a grown woman.

"Miss, is something wrong? Do you want to come sit with me for a while in the night duty room?"

Han Ma followed her.

"The nighttime is so lonesome," the woman added, "but this kind of loneliness has its advantages. You can return by yourself to beautiful scenes. This was the benefit I had in mind when I applied to be on night shift."

"To live in memory, Ma'am?"

"Yes, and I haven't left after three years."

Han Ma sat on a chair in the night duty room, drinking tea that the woman had brewed for her. She smelled an unusual fragrance.

"That smells good," she said.

"It's angelica. He and I both like to carry it on us."

"Is it very difficult to transfer your love, if you've loved someone deeply?"

"I still don't know. I am trying, without much effect . . . Maybe it's that I haven't come across someone yet who can divert my love?"

"Thank you, Ma'am. I'm much better now. I need to go back home, goodbye."

Han Ma came out onto the main street again. Late at night Meng seemingly hid many secrets. Were those alternating deep and shallow shadows of the buildings in conversation with what was inside of her? Oh, how was this street never at an end? She remembered there being a side road that could take her to her residential area. Fei's home was that way, her home was this way. Would Fei be asleep now? He'd had such severe insomnia . . . When they were just married, Han Ma always went to sleep in his arms at night. Now he had become a poem in the darkest depths of her soul. She walked on again for a long time and later discovered that she'd arrived in the suburbs. Then she walked back again. Walking, walking, her tears flowing again.

Afterward the sky finally started to grow light, and Han Ma found that she had missed the side road. Probably because it was too dark all around, so she hadn't been able to see it. This side road was the other end of Chicken Guts Lane, where Xiaoyue had brought her.

Once Han Ma walked into the alleyway she was surprised at its liveliness. All of the eateries had already opened, and the early risers came and went, some here to eat breakfast, and even more buying breakfast for their families. Long lines had started to form at the entrances to some of the restaurants. Every kind of smell permeated the air. "Life!" Han Ma exclaimed to herself. She seemed to see Xiaoyue's figure amid these people. "Last night I shed too many tears," she thought, a little embarrassed, "but I've never regretted my choices."

Han Ma ate several jianbing at Chicken Guts Lane, then went back to the apartment complex.

She saw that there was a message on the phone—it had been Xiaoyue calling her that morning. She tidied the apartment, then sat down to write. Even though she hadn't slept all night, her inspiration wasn't affected. She took only half an hour to finish the quantity of writing she had set herself. The substance of what she wrote was brilliant and also unexpected.

Han Ma put down her pen, took a shower, and lay down to sleep. She slept through until dusk.

When she got up she looked at the telephone. No one had called her. She thought: Xiaoyue is telepathic, to have most likely realized the change in her mood. She went downstairs, walked back to Chicken Guts Lane, found the vegetable noodle shop, and ordered the same kind of noodles she had eaten with Xiaoyue the previous time.

"Your husband hasn't come today," the woman owner said.

"He's on a business trip to the capital."

Han Ma abruptly remembered that Xiaoyue had probably come here to eat noodles with his former girlfriend. What was she like? She must have been pretty, because Xiaoyue himself was handsome . . . Han Ma stopped her wild thoughts. Sitting in a peaceful thatched building, eating delicious food. This wasn't a bad life.

When she'd finished eating and went back home, she read an essay by Xiaoyue. It was about his response after reading Musil's novel *The Man without Qualities*. The essay gave Han Ma tidal surges of emotion, and for a long, long time she sank into reverie. She'd always thought that Xiaoyue was made of special stuff, and now she was firm in this belief. Only this time she didn't make that kind of sexual association. Could Fei's image have been renewed because of the events of last night? For example, at this moment Han Ma felt a powerful longing for Fei's body. His mouth, his eyes, his sexual habits, his hands, all appeared like shots in a movie. Fei came back out of the darkness where he had been. Han Ma's whole body was dry and hot and restless. She went downstairs for a run in the flower garden of the apartment complex.

She felt much better after she came back from her run. For dinner she ate a sandwich and drank a glass of milk. Then she read fiction again, reading until late at night before going to bed.

In the morning, when Han Ma was getting ready to go to work, she remembered that Xiaoyue hadn't called her.

For the entire day he didn't call.

At night she slept peacefully.

The next morning she walked out of the elevator and saw Xiaoyue standing in front of her. She mused: "He really is handsome and talented, but that has little to do with me."

"Han Ma, I came back late yesterday evening and was afraid of disturbing you, so I didn't call."

After they took their seats on the bus, he asked lightly:

"What has changed?"

"Nothing. I'm making good progress with my writing," Han Ma answered.

"There's progress in the capital, too. The magazine *The Future* will continue to publish your fiction. There's another magazine that also wants your stories."

"Thank you, Xiaoyue. You've helped me make so many connections . . ."

Han Ma didn't continue—she was a bit absent-minded. Xiaoyue noticed. He told himself that he needed to give her time. She'd shared so many memories with Fei.

The next several days the two of them only met in the morning on the bus. They each went out on their own to eat.

On the morning when Xiaoyue called Han Ma from the capital and she didn't answer, he knew that there'd been a setback. He carefully thought back over the entirety of their relationship and felt that this kind of setback was inevitable. He needed to redouble his patience with regard to her. She and Fei had been forced to break up, so how could she easily forget Fei in such a short time? Xiaoyue could only adjust himself to her rhythms. He resolved to do so.

One day Xiaoyue saw Xiao Sang at the Crown Department Store reading group, and she asked him:

"Are you making progress with Han Ma?"

"Far from it. She had a deep foundation with Fei," he answered.

"You're right. But I believe you're the one who suits her better. You should wait patiently for an opportunity. Oh, the Pigeon Book Club! I miss it so much."

"Xiao Sang, believe me, I will not give up on her. She is the ideal of my life."

"Good, Xiaoyue! You're a true hero."

Though Han Ma didn't come looking for him, Xiaoyue didn't think that he'd been unlucky in love. He still saw her as his beloved. If she made any sign, he would rush to her side. For the present phase, he needed to calm down and not neglect his literary research on account of all this. Life is so brief—being sentimental is a waste of time. Wasn't she still taking the bus with him daily? This at least proved that she hadn't found someone else. She had her creation of stories and also the memories of her former husband, so for now she naturally didn't need Xiaoyue. There would eventually come a day when she would see the enormous hole in her life—there must be.

Xiaoyue noticed that when Han Ma went outside for runs in the residential area she always took pains to avoid him. Actually, she'd resumed her habit of getting off the bus one stop early after work to run back home. She and Xiaoyue left work at different times. Ever since he had stopped sending her red roses, he'd seen her from a distance buying flowers herself and bringing them back to the apartment complex.

Over these days Xiaoyue wrote an appreciation of Han Ma's short story collection *Expedition*. He was fairly satisfied with the essay, but hadn't sent it out to magazines yet, because Han Ma didn't have enough of a reputation. He also hadn't given it to Han Ma to read, because he wanted to wait for an opportunity. Otherwise, his plan about establishing a literary appreciation mechanism with Fei was becoming clearer and more concrete. He had even mentally chosen several readers who he believed showed the most potential.

In the long nights of winter Xiaoyue still yearned for Han Ma's body, but he knew he couldn't trouble her at this time. The sole thing he could do was wait. "It doesn't matter. This can't last longer than half a year or so," he encouraged himself. "When the time comes, she will see me still here and think of all of the things that have happened between us. What's more, she's still buying red roses like we did before. She hasn't completely left me aside." He remembered what it was like living here with his former girlfriend, as well as why they had peacefully broken up. "The major issue was difficulty in communication—there was nothing to say. It's the opposite with Han Ma." He also sensed that Fei must not be able to forget Han Ma. Who could forget her? Xiao Sang was afraid Xiaoyue lacked the patience to wait, and Heishi must think the same. Heishi was Fei's oldest friend . . . The two of them, Xiao Sang and Heishi, were the most aware of the entire situation. They supported him in pursuing Han Ma, and had said that he and Han Ma were a better match for each other. Xiaoyue wouldn't get discouraged, even though the journey ahead wasn't certain.

One day Han Ma returned to her father's home and stayed for the entire afternoon. Her mother had passed away young, of cancer. At only fifteen years old Han Ma had taken responsibility for the family. She had four little brothers coming after her. Their father taught at a distance education college and was terribly busy, so Han Ma handled all of the housework. That was why she'd only gone to middle school and then taken odd jobs outside the home, working part-time while doing double duty with chores. Her father felt that he owed his daughter, so he hadn't gotten remarried. After her brothers were independent, and she had a stable job, he finally married a colleague who he'd met at the college. He loved his older daughter dearly and in private thought she was the most intelligent and talented of his children. So he wasn't at all worried that she wouldn't become cultured, even though she'd left school early. He believed Han Ma had the capacity to gain knowledge by studying on her own.

"Dad, I'm back. Mother Lin?"

"She went to a calligraphy and painting class for the elderly. Hanhan, I read your stories. You're really remarkable now."

"Hmm. I'm still trying."

"It seems it was right for you to break up with Fei. Now you've recovered, so I'm relieved. Fei was all right, and he's gifted, but when you got married he wasn't very mature yet. This way is better, now that he's honored his responsibility to be a father. You can find someone else to marry."

"Dad, right now I'm terribly busy with writing. There's no time to find a boyfriend."

"Why not look? You have to look. You've had such a bitter experience, and you've taught yourself to be an author, plus you have a strong nature and ideas of your own. The young men will all like you. Besides, you can have a life and write without neglecting either."

Han Ma was silent.

"I don't think dating or marrying will affect your writing," her father added. "It might even encourage your creativity. If you don't look for a husband, you will regret it afterward when you're older. Because you'll have missed such a wonderful part of life."

"Dad, that makes sense. Don't worry, I'll eventually start looking."

"That's right. Yesterday I dreamed that you'd gotten married. In my dream I told the groom that my daughter Hanhan is a shining pearl in my hand. Our family considered you the most promising. Is anyone pursuing you now?"

"There is one man. But I haven't made up my mind yet whether to let the relationship develop."

"Is it a friend from the Pigeon Book Club?"

"Exactly. How did you know?"

"After you broke up with Fei, I thought that you would still find someone who loves literature and can understand you. Does this man love you? That's really the most crucial."

"Maybe. There hasn't been enough time, I can't come to any conclusions."

"You're right. Keep observing him. What is he like?"

"He's talented and handsome, too, much better-looking than me."

"Handsome . . . Would he be committed in love?" Her father seemed apprehensive.

"I don't know. I don't care about that too much. No one can guarantee love lasting as long as heaven and earth. My problem now is that I'm always thinking about Fei. Dad, we were a loving husband and wife . . ."

"I can understand how it is for you. But when something ends, life must continue, right? Will this man get impatient if you won't decide about the relationship?"

"He hasn't been impatient. He understands my psychology so well. He always treats me right . . . Now I feel almost guilty. I want to tell him not to wait for me."

Seemingly, during the conversation with her father, Han Ma for the first time faced up to the complication that had come between her and

Xiaoyue recently. She thought: maybe I should make a decision? Yet Xiaoyue hadn't plainly indicated his intentions to her. He'd said before that he and she were a different model. Then was her indifference now a continuation of their model? Could the outgoing tide of past love prevent the incoming waves of new love? Was she being evasive?

"Hanhan, I don't know the specifics of your situation, but I feel like you're in a transitional state."

He didn't say anything more. Father and daughter both sank into thought.

Han Ma got off the bus to run back to the apartment complex. She thought over what her father had said. "Transitional state"—transition to where? Could it only be to Xiaoyue? He'd returned from the capital so many days ago. He was always there, without appearing hurried, constantly ready to help when she allowed it . . . This man was made of something special. But Han Ma was still unwilling for him to substitute for Fei. Though she also couldn't make herself tell him not to wait for her. Because he hadn't said that he was waiting for her, as a lover. Ah, Xiaoyue, Xiaoyue, no one can understand my heart better than you.

Han Ma took a shower, then started to write. This was a longer work, because some passageways appeared out of the darkness that required expansion. Her creative state was steadier than in the past. She knew that if she turned to the desk and sat down, the plot and characters would start to develop spontaneously, so that control of the ideas on the surface was hardly meaningful, and on the contrary restricted something's free expansion. She lowered her head, quickly wrote another few passages, then lifted her pen. She thought: could there be a mysterious cohesion between her writing and her relationship with Xiaoyue?

Han Ma went to the window, looking toward the windows of Xiaoyue's home opposite. The lights there were on: he was also battling as hard as he could. Han Ma sensed that she was being unfair to him, but she couldn't do anything about herself. She could only, like Xiaoyue had said, allow everything to be "unknown." After all, her writing was doing some good for people; she couldn't regress. That sentence again: Literature is truly good. Persevering at literature would never err. The reason that Xiaoyue staked everything on a single toss of the dice and still seemed like he was sure of himself was because of literature. "Fei and I were truly in love, but I've lost Fei," she said in her mind again and again, at the same time thinking of what her father had said about a "transitional state."

The book that Xiaoyue had given Han Ma, *XXXXX5,* described a city of fog. People groped along in the mist carrying on with everyday life, without feeling that there was anything inconvenient about it. After they had adapted to this way of life, they felt instead that a cloudless sky would be insufferable. Gardeners determined wind strength, temperature, and humidity according to the rustling sounds that chrysanthemums made. People's thoughts could control the opening and shutting of doors and windows. Han Ma recalled that she and Xiaoyue had discussed this chapter. Xiaoyue had said: "Perhaps this is the ancient custom of 'spontaneity.'" The dialogue in this chapter was especially brilliant. The protagonist went out looking for someone, and everyone's response had two or three meanings, with the natural result that this someone was hard to find. Yet every single person that he asked was the person he was looking for. They all liked to say: "As long as the fog hasn't dispersed by nightfall, this beautiful little city won't disappoint you." Afterward a train that was always running late arrived unexpectedly, and the protagonist didn't even board the train, because he hadn't made up his mind.

He remained in the beautiful little city. Han Ma thought: this person is just like me. People should stay like this, in literature. The novel had greatly calmed the panic she felt from time to time.

Fei had been the mentor who'd enlightened her about literature, and at the same time was also the person she had loved most deeply. These two things in combination destined Han Ma to her trouble with forgetting him. She felt that the atmosphere in which she now existed, like the "city of fog," did not lack for aesthetics, even though it agitated her soul. Could it be that as long as she didn't stop writing, she would always more or less be in a "transitional state"? Was suppressing her physical desires abnormal—when she was still so young? Ever since Han Ma had come back from her father's home she'd been stirred by the elderly man's words. Besides, her affairs weren't entirely hers alone, because this involved harm to two people. The fog was like the nets Heishi referred to: nets that didn't allow people to settle down and instead made them yearn for life . . .

Han Ma read up to here, stood, and then walked over to the window that faced the flower garden of the apartment complex. Oh, Xiaoyue was exercising on the parallel bars. His flexible, well-proportioned body was so handsome! She stared. This was the first time she'd appreciated the dynamic beauty of his body. "He's like an athlete!" she exclaimed in surprise. What was happening with this man? He transformed art into life as if this were his vocation. He wasn't even arrogant, just as though these things were trivial and ordinary, things that anyone could do . . . Later, tired from exercising, he went home.

Time flew by in busyness. One day at the department store, Xiao Sang invited Han Ma to attend Xiao Ma's wedding. She told her that the wedding would take place within a month, and that she hoped Han Ma would bring Xiaoyue, adding that it was a small-scale family gathering. Han Ma started to show reluctance, so Xiao Sang urged her:

"Han Ma, overcoming emotional barriers from the past is also a kind of growth!"

On the road home Han Ma counted on her fingers. She and Fei would have broken up more than four months ago by the date of Xiao Ma's wedding. Such a long time had passed since she and Fei had agreed over the phone to temporarily halt the Pigeon Book Club gatherings, during which time there'd only been the once when he had called to congratulate her on her debut publication. In her imagination Fei was still her sexual partner, and his image was so distinct . . . Could it be, as Xiao Sang had hinted, that going on like this Han Ma would lose the capacity for new love? She didn't want to have two separate lovers: one in her mind and one in reality. That would be hurtful to Xiaoyue. But if she stayed in this current transitional state, continually, wasn't that itself settling down? How could she, someone occupied with literary work, be so sure about her body, be capable of using her mind to analyze her body? Didn't this violate the principles of creation—the principles she followed every day? This was the first time Han Ma thought of these new questions. She suddenly felt that she shouldn't use her mind to anticipate things. Hadn't there been so many times when Xiaoyue had excited her physical desires? Why conceal this? She realized instantaneously: this was a net of life. Now there was Xiao Sang—her guide prompting her to throw herself into the net. What she meant was: no matter what the result might be, she should make the attempt and devote herself.

"Xiao Sang, I promise that I'll bring Xiaoyue," Han Ma said over the phone. "Promise me not to tell him yet, OK? To avoid him holding out hope."

"Terrific. Even I can't figure out whether Xiaoyue is holding out hope. He's too clever. I promise you not to tell him. It's up to you to."

Han Ma reminded herself that the day of the wedding was still far off, and she could decide then. She also thought of Xiao Ma from the department store who had found the person she loved best just as she'd wanted to, which probably had something to do with Xiao Sang. Another literary couple. Han Ma was curious to see what Uncle Yi was like after all. Would Fei attend? He was Uncle Yi's student, too. She felt a little anxious and asked Xiao Sang, who said that Fei wasn't going. Han Ma only then set her mind at rest.

"Xiaoyue, one of our coworkers is going to marry a famous literary figure. They're both close friends of Xiao Sang. She hopes you and I will go to the wedding to liven things up. Are you interested?"

One day Han Ma asked Xiaoyue on the bus.

"It must be Uncle Yi. I've already heard of the romance of Uncle Yi and Xiao Ma—my book friends told me. It's an extremely beautiful story. Of course I'm interested. Especially in going with you."

Han Ma thought: this is Xiaoyue. He doesn't blame me, no matter how frivolous I am.

"It's more than ten days away. You can help buy a gift for us to bring. You're much more of the expert."

"All right. I'll buy cloisonné tea caddies."

After saying these things, they didn't speak. For Han Ma, it was because she was a bit embarrassed. For Xiaoyue, it was because he was pondering, and going deeper in understanding Han Ma's state of mind.

The next day on the bus, she also asked him:

"What have you been writing recently?"

"I wrote a review of *Expedition*."

"Oh? Would you let me read it?" A familiar warmth flowed through her heart.

"I'll bring it to you after work."

Xiaoyue called at seven in the evening. "Finally," Han Ma said to herself.

He came in, placed the manuscript on the desk in her study, and was just about to leave.

"Wait!" Han Ma said. "Have a seat on the living room sofa and wait for me to finish reading it."

She read the essay quickly, twice through. A blush rose on her face as she stood to leave the study.

She sat down close to Xiaoyue on the living room sofa, resting her head on his shoulder. She didn't speak.

He didn't speak either, carefully letting his face nestle Han Ma's hair.

They just sat there like this.

Later Xiaoyue discovered that Han Ma's face was covered in tears. He found tissues on the table and helped her wipe the tears away.

"Xiaoyue, I think I can fall in love with you eventually."

"Love me then, Han Ma. I won't ever change. Let's go take a walk to the street with flower shops, OK?"

"OK."

Holding Xiaoyue, Han Ma went down the stairs and outside. She was still somewhat misty-eyed and couldn't make out her surroundings.

They arrived back at the entrance of that flower shop.

"Let's buy some red roses. You have none left at home."

The two of them entered, bought roses, and came back out. As they left, Han Ma held on to Xiaoyue again.

"Let's go for a walk," Xiaoyue said gently.

It was a long street, and they went all the way to the end before turning back. As they walked back Xiaoyue started to tell Han Ma in detail about the response to her work in the capital's literary world. Who were her reliable supporters; how there were some readers who were confused, and how her supporters were understanding; also about the complaints of readers who were confused. The opportune time to engage her writing wasn't ripe yet, so they needed to wait.

"I feel that knowing about these circumstances is important. A work is published. It becomes everyone's. Its fate is associated with the significance of the writing. Those of us who work in communications should keep track, no matter what misfortune a work meets with readers. Classical literature wasn't as concerned with these activities, because exchanges among people then were far, far from what they are today."

"I agree with your viewpoint. For every work I write there are readers in my imagination, and I am also eager to give my writing to friends to read and interested in their responses. Even though I write without being influenced by others. As for the literary works I've read that have elements of contemporary style, their greatest characteristic is to interact with readers. If this weren't so, one couldn't enter into the work," Han Ma said thoughtfully.

"That's why I think the links within communication are also so important," Xiaoyue said. "I keep thinking about how to establish this kind of literary appreciation mechanism with Fei. The book club has real power in this regard."

Since this involved Fei, Han Ma didn't respond to him. However, Xiaoyue sensed that the crisis had passed. She was silent for a while, then finally said:

"I'm so lucky, Xiaoyue. First Xiao Sang pointed out my talent and encouraged me to write; then I met Fei and with his help started to make attempts and gain confidence; now I've also met you, who constantly bring me inspiration, compelling me to take literature to a higher level . . . I think of those lonely ancients, many of them writing without an audience who knew them, without anyone to appreciate them, and without anyone to enlighten them. It must have been very difficult for them to write under such circumstances, but they still left so many works to be passed down. Of course there were some that were neglected. Now I feel it's urgent . . ."

They were about to arrive at the apartment complex. Han Ma asked Xiaoyue to kiss her.

One arm holding the roses, his other arm pulling Han Ma in, he kissed her on the cheek.

Standing in the elevator she said to herself: "Very good."

She sat down at her desk and threw herself immediately into her writing. She was still astonishingly successful.

After returning home Xiaoyue was still excited by the turn things had taken just a moment ago. Passion rose in waves in his heart, along with sexual impulses. He sat in his apartment for a long time without being able to quiet down. "No, I can't be lazy," he told himself. He went back downstairs to run a lap and returned. Taking advantage of the impulse not yet rising he hastily sat down to continue writing his essay. This method proved truly effective. So long as he was absorbed with literature he forgot the worldly things that were happening. He wrote, wrote, wrote until he was tired and only then stopped. He was pleased with himself.

He lay in the dark thinking that with the stimulation of Han Ma's body and spirit his writing might gradually achieve a standard that would satisfy him. When Xiao Sang had said that he and Han Ma were a born match, it meant this, the way they could provoke each other, derive impetus from one another. Han Ma would be the perpetual wellspring of his inspiration, so long as his madness for literature didn't vanish. Fei's influence on her, in comparison, would eventually, gradually weaken. Han Ma would someday turn toward him with her whole body and mind. Even if she weren't conscious of it, hadn't she been turning toward him little by little since moving here? It seemed like he was the one who understood Han Ma best. He would persevere. Thinking this, Xiaoyue tossed back and forth for a good long time, then finally went to sleep in an ardent mood. Even having sex with Han Ma in his dreams couldn't calm down his excitement.

The next day at noon, while Xiaoyue was in his office sorting through books, Jing, the new employee, came in again.

"Jing, have a seat. I'll brew tea for you."

"Xiaoyue, sir, I've come to tell you that I'm going to make an effort to study literature."

"Really? That's great! What gave you this idea?"

"I met Ms. Han Ma at your office, and the way she carries herself enchanted me . . . I used to be in the science department at college. Even though I liked literature, too, I didn't keep going. I've also had two girlfriends and broken up with both of them. When I remember now what my girlfriends were like, I feel like they couldn't be compared with Ms. Han Ma. Of course, there's nothing special about me, I'm someone people don't remember at all. That's how it was until now. You see, I'm determined to attack reading literature, to become someone like you, to find a girlfriend like Han Ma. Is this so naive?"

Xiaoyue heard Jing out and started laughing. Then he controlled his smile and said to him seriously:

"Not at all, Jing. This shows how you are maturing. But you should learn from Ms. Han Ma, not from me. I'm just plain and ordinary. I'm happy about your improvement: the literary world of the city of Meng has another successor. I've always believed that the science department and the literature department are two sides of the same reality, that only in combination become global reality. I studied science, too, and then switched to literature. Jing, you're very intelligent, so I have hope in you. There will come a day in the future when you will find a girlfriend like Ms. Han Ma."

"Thank you, Xiaoyue, sir."

Jing cheerfully left.

Once he was gone Xiaoyue was in a daze again, and the hand picking up a book started to shake. "Han Ma, Han Ma," he repeated in his heart. He remembered his dreams the previous night and a smile floated across his face. "Who wouldn't love Han Ma?" he said in a low voice. "Even a young man like Jing . . ." He thought how the world was truly different, where an author's personal life would finally, gradually combine with her (or his) writing. While the classical viewpoint had always preferred to keep them apart. Perhaps his vocation was this work of merging them. The activity of the human spirit would always be mirrored in its flesh. There was no means whatsoever to hide this. So Jing had actually learned at a glance from the way Han Ma carried herself. Hadn't it been like this for him, too? At the time, what he had been seeking for so long had appeared: one could say it was a demeanor, or an aura—it was Han Ma's body. From then on Han Ma had been entangled with his soul and dreams and had never left him. He loved her body as much as he loved her spiritual being. He knew that Han Ma's physical being had been tempered by a difficult life. Hard and difficult early years hadn't crushed her, but instead made her more courageous the more she struggled. She'd never stopped casting her own model of character. Xiaoyue wasn't impatient yet to declare his feelings to her, because he could still do even better and go even deeper in understanding her. In speaking of a new type of person, there were more elements of this new person in Han Ma than in himself, so he had to be infatuated with her. Her body had more "spontaneity" and could never tolerate falseness, which is what had stirred Xiaoyue's empathy. This profound empathy also permeated his love for her. Xiaoyue thought back and forth like this, the model of their coming together in the future growing clearer.

Ever since Han Ma had moved in, the model Xiaoyue had in mind had been "keeping her company." His sense of what "keeping her company" meant had been murky. After going through these days of their setback, his experience finally made this more explicit. To keep her company was to be in rhythm with her, driven by her primeval momentum, to marry the strength of his own body with her strength to constitute a combined strength and sprint toward the same goal. Before she and Fei had been taking action together, and now he was replacing Fei. Fei was a literary talent he had worshipped. Xiaoyue needed to make an all-out effort, often blazing a new trail on his own, to keep pace with Han Ma. Overall he still had confidence. He could admit that he wasn't the most outstanding when it came to natural ability, but he was young, with good energy and physical vigor, in addition to his rigorously disciplined life. He ought to be able to approach Han Ma's state.

While Xiaoyue was thinking this over, someone came into the bookstore looking for him to talk about work, so he rushed to the main office.

It was already late evening when he finished the meeting and returned to the apartment complex. He glanced at his watch—it was eleven. His phone displayed a message, which had been Han Ma calling at ten. He picked up the phone.

"I just got home, Han Ma. Is everything OK?"

"Yes. When I finished writing I just thought we might go exercise together in the garden, so I gave you a call. Afterward I went to exercise by myself. I'm so happy, there's lovely moonlight tonight. I was also just reading the book you gave me. Such a beautiful story. Xiaoyue, I've started to have a sense of your body. I've seen you exercising on the parallel bars in the garden, so gracefully. Xiaoyue? . . . Are you angry?"

"No, no, just the opposite. I've looked forward to this day . . ."

"When I brought up bodies, it wasn't in a purely physical sense. Do you understand?"

"Of course I understand. This type of question is what I've been experiencing. It shows that we are in sync. My coworkers at the bookstore love you, and other people, too—an older woman, and a new employee, for example, a young man. They're all attracted by your body."

"Was it that young man who saw me coming and slipped away?"

"Yes. He's named Jing. He was enchanted by the way you carry yourself and said he was going to attack reading literature."

"Wow, I'm so glad! Do I have that much charm?"

"My opinion is the same as his. He believes you are the embodiment of beauty."

"I can't imagine. I'm not pretty at all."

"But I think his response is more natural than anything."

"Then, Xiaoyue, have you thought of spending the night with me?"

"Of course I've thought about it, only now isn't the right moment. I'll keep waiting."

"You're so well-behaved, and deserve my love."

Xiaoyue's heart pounded after he hung up the phone. Han Ma's extraordinary frankness in conversation had always surprised him, but this was also what he liked so much about her. She'd approved of his loving her, so it was only a question of time. Xiaoyue was honestly so tired he couldn't keep his eyes open, so he lay down to sleep, planning to read and write again tomorrow when he was off work. He slept until early dawn and dreamed of Han Ma's body again, and having sex with her, but it couldn't extinguish his burning desire. He heard himself say in his dream: "Han Ma, Han Ma, where did you come from . . ."

When he woke up it was already eight in the morning, and he realized that Han Ma had gone to work. He ate a sandwich and drank some milk, then went to run a few laps in the flower garden. After that he returned home to be diligent.

Reading Han Ma's writing produced in Xiaoyue's mind a kind of primeval scenery. He thought: Han Ma hasn't read many literary works, and even less literary theory, yet when she started to write it was like unusual music that no one could imitate. Did this belong to an ancient, nearly endangered artistry? The question lingered at the bottom of his heart. He planned to continue to observe and make an effort to study this aspect of things. At the same time, he thought that the question was connected to an idea that he agreed with: "the writing is like the writer." This could be the germination phase of a new kind of literary theory. Of course, this "writing is like the writer" wasn't in the classical sense, and instead meant whether a writer had an expressive mechanism and what level this expression could reach. The more perfect the mechanism, the freer the person making use of it, the more the writing could charge into this primeval zone—and the work's universality would be greater. Yet how did this mechanism take shape within human existence? This question was too complex. In Xiaoyue's early-dawn sex dream, hadn't he asked Han Ma where she had come from?

By the evening Xiaoyue was tired from reading, and Han Ma also returned around this time. He knew when she got home she would write first, so he arranged to go for a walk with her at night, because the next day was a day off. He decided not to go out to the bar with Han Ma, to avoid overstimulating her.

Han Ma finished the call she'd made to Xiaoyue and sat down to write. When she finished writing and looked at her watch, it was only eight-thirty. Then she reread Xiaoyue's essay about her story collection *Expedition*, reading for a while, thinking deeply for a while, nodding constantly. She imagined what he'd looked like when he was writing these words. By ten at night she finally couldn't keep from picking up her phone.

"I'll come right down," Xiaoyue said.

They went back outside, arm in arm again. Xiaoyue said he wanted to take Han Ma to the municipal park because she hadn't been there since she'd moved in. Xiaoyue had the instinct as in the past to talk about literature once he and Han Ma were on the way, as though he were sorting through his thoughts. Han Ma interjected a sentence or two from time to time and seemed to be provoking him to continue talking.

Without realizing it, they reached the entrance to the park, where the gate was only open on one side because it was already late at night. They followed the wide road lined with French wutong trees. Xiaoyue kept talking in a torrent of words and couldn't have stopped if he'd tried. Han Ma thought secretly: this is probably a sexual impulse? Still, she liked listening to him talk, because it enlightened her.

There was a wooden bench under the large trees where they sat down to rest for a while. Han Ma asked Xiaoyue whether he wanted to kiss. He asked in reply: "You're not afraid things will get messy?" She said he was right to worry, she wasn't ready for this. He said, "Then just wait some more." Then Han Ma kissed Xiaoyue on the cheek and buried her face in his overcoat, raising her head only after a while.

"Xiaoyue, you're so handsome. I feel inferior just looking at you," she said.

A very light northern wind started to gust when they turned back. Even though it was winter, their bodies were burning like fire. When they were almost home, Han Ma said to Xiaoyue:

"My trick for keeping up my impulse to write is continuing a relationship with you."

After Han Ma got back home, at first she wanted to go right to bed, but for some reason it was hard to sleep. So she picked back up the book Xiaoyue had given her. She followed the character in the book, a reader, who kept walking and walking and finally reached another book. In this other book, all of the settings fluctuated, and the plot was unfamiliar and completely unique, but Han Ma felt dim with drowsiness and couldn't guess at the meaning of this new book. She saw that there was a reader character standing with his back to people, so she went forward to ask the bystanders: "Who is he? Who is he . . ." Someone answered her, but in a voice so low she couldn't hear. Han Ma's reading was thwarted by obscurity. She told herself: "I'm still not strong enough. Tomorrow I'll make another sprint." With this thought she finally went to sleep.

As long as there was time in the day, Han Ma's writing was the task she finished first. It was because she always had a secret worry at the bottom of her heart: what if someday she couldn't write. She had a premonition that if she couldn't write on a given day, the day wouldn't go well. The fortunate thing was that ever since she'd started creating, no day had arrived that wasn't successful. In the morning she woke up and swept the apartment, changed out the water for the roses, made a simple breakfast, and ate. Then she sat down to write. In a while she finished writing. After she finished writing she picked up the book and began to read from the place where yesterday she'd been baffled. Han Ma carefully read the chapter twice and finally discovered a passageway through the words! She was so happy she immediately drew the pattern that had appeared in her brain in her notes. All of the words lined up forming ranks, coalescing toward this pattern. She thought of Li Hai from the Pigeon Book Club and remembered his reading method that was like a hunting dog following a scent. "I should use my sense of smell, and not use logical thought so much. In the end, though, this will set in motion a more powerful way of thinking," she said to herself.

She put aside the book and went downstairs for a run with joy welling up from the bottom of her heart.

"Xiaoyue, let's go out to eat for lunch."

"OK, I'll be right down. I'll take you to Yun Restaurant, where they have Meng's best Wuchang bream."

They both went downstairs and outside. Han Ma sighed:

"Today is such a fresh, new, hopeful day!"

Xiaoyue told her about how he'd felt such a sense of loss when he'd gone to the capital and hadn't seen her for three days. Once he returned to Meng, he felt more peace of mind than in the capital, even though things between them weren't intimate yet. "You can tell that 'the locale produces a local resident.' Meng is the magic weapon calming our turbulent souls," was the conclusion he reached.

"Xiaoyue, do you think the way I create can continue for long?"

"I just happened to be thinking about this question recently. Whether any author's creation can last depends on their foundation and also on their powers of expression. It isn't flattery that, judging by your debut work, I think you possess both. Your foundation goes deep into primeval scenes; you have abundant strength, so you have expressive freedom. There are some writers with deep foundations who can write first-rate works—but if they aren't strong enough, the quantity of their writing will be less. One's strength is determined by many factors. I personally believe that curiosity about everyday life may be a crucial factor. I was honored to learn that your standpoint on this topic is the same as mine. Do you agree?"

"Yes, you're right, Xiaoyue! For example, in my relationship with you, I've kept being curious about you, so I cannot deny myself. My body doesn't agree with some of my opinions."

Since it was the weekend there were a lot people at the restaurant. Because Xiaoyue was a frequent customer, the owner invited the two of them to sit in a private upstairs booth. Han Ma said, looking into Xiaoyue's eyes:

"It's so good that we're eating together again. This is just like the everyday life depicted in *The Story of the Stone*. Only we are modern, and more amusing than people from the past."

Han Ma always had a good appetite. Xiaoyue, feeling very cheerful, kept giving her more food with his chopsticks.

"Look how greedy I am!" she said uneasily.

"Eat up, eat up, you can only work if you eat," Xiaoyue said. "Next week I'll cook this kind of fish and you can come eat at my place. How about it?"

"You've startled me—you've never invited me to your home." Han Ma blushed across her face.

"I haven't invited you because I was worried things would get messy. Now we've both calmed down, there shouldn't be any danger."

Han Ma laughed.

"All right, all right, now I'm a virtuous maiden. You don't need to take precautions against me."

Xiaoyue was embarrassed by this, too, but still cheerful. Although he was coming to know Han Ma better and better, he wasn't sure what went on in the dark depths of her interior. No matter what happened there, it couldn't be a fatal threat to him, of course. Meng's sky and earth sheltered them. In fact, Xiaoyue had been thinking that perhaps his relationship with Han Ma would reach a turning point after Uncle Yi and Xiao Ma's wedding . . .

"Xiaoyue, I'm taking advantage of you again. I'm vicious." She was a little upset.

"I actually wish you would take advantage of me more. We are breaking through a barrier—but this takes time."

"I really admire Xiao Ma." Han Ma had a rapt expression.

"I've heard that at first things between her and Uncle Yi weren't so smooth either," Xiaoyue said.

"It was probably a trick of the nets of life at work," Han Ma said.

"Now we can tell that it was both a match made in heaven and also the result of human effort."

"Xiaoyue, I appreciate your willpower. You and me are so much alike in this way."

They finished eating, then each went home to work diligently. Han Ma felt that her reading was gradually more skillful since she'd moved to the Red Roses Apartments. She thought: this owes a great deal to Xiaoyue. Naturally she must also credit her writing—once she'd brought out a piece of writing, other people discussing it had the effect on her of "comprehension from a hint." Understanding one's own literary works is more difficult than understanding other people's literary works, especially when it came to her type of writing. Yet Xiaoyue was constantly enlightening her, elevating the state she was in . . .

Han Ma recalled the past week: her longing for Fei had decreased, while Xiaoyue's influence on her had grown. Also, the physical desire that was part of this influence was increasing. There'd already been two instances when the one who came into her dreams was no longer the unknown man from the book, but instead a man whose features and figure were much like Xiaoyue's. "You've finally come, Xiaoyue. I was waiting for you." That man didn't speak—he embraced her, kissed her, stroked her breasts. She woke up at the height of excitement. Was that man him? She seemed familiar with his movements, but she and Xiaoyue hadn't had sex before.

When Han Ma next saw Xiaoyue, she felt nervous and carefully observed his mouth and hands, her attention distracted as she remembered what had happened in her dream. So maybe it was him, maybe it wasn't, but at the time it had been so stimulating. It had been dark all around, with a ray of light illuminating their foreplay.

"Han Ma, what are you thinking about?"

"I was thinking about when I'd just moved in and you brought up what it would be like after we'd lived here for thirty years. Did you have a premonition then?"

"A vague one. I'm not very self-aware."

"Before, when Fei and I were still together, did you have feelings for me?"

Xiaoyue didn't answer Han Ma's question. He thought he would probably never answer.

They walked along the street of flower shops all the way to the suburbs, where they sat down on a bale of hay beside the road. The slanting afternoon sun shone on both their faces—they both looked full of energy.

"Xiaoyue, let me look at your hand."

He reached out a hand to her.

Han Ma moved nearer to his hand and carefully looked at it for a while. She still couldn't be sure.

"At first I didn't notice how handsome you are."

"I'm ordinary," Xiaoyue calmly said.

"Ordinary, but also extraordinary. We're both like this, aren't we?"

"No, only you, not me."

"Am I literature?"

"And also a woman. The kind I desire the most."

Xiaoyue changed the topic to talk about the wedding gift. He'd already bought the prettiest cloisonné tea caddies, and he also planned to give Uncle Yi and Xiao Ma a large packet of tea leaves from ancient tea trees.

Han Ma, however, was thinking that Xiaoyue had just expressed most explicitly—that she was his one and only.

"Have my hands appeared in your dreams?" he suddenly asked.

"Similar ones. Similar."

"But the desire is real," Xiaoyue sighed. "These past few months have lasted so long, yet they've passed richly! I'm happy, thanks to you. Although not very satisfied. But why do people need to constantly satisfy themselves? When continuing to long is most vital. Before, when I used to live alone, I didn't have intense longing or satisfaction. I was far, far less contented with myself then than I am now."

When they stood to walk back, Xiaoyue started to talk torrentially again about the literary appreciation mechanism. Han Ma listened attentively, trying her best to follow the path of his thoughts.

As they walked through the main entrance to the apartment complex, Xiaoyue abruptly proposed:

"Come up to my place to look around?"

"OK. I've always been curious about what it's like."

Han Ma apprehensively followed Xiaoyue into his home.

The apartment was a bigger three-bedroom unit: clean, modest, bright. Of the three bedrooms, one was a bedroom, one was a study, and there was also a room with several kinds of exercise equipment in it. The living room and kitchen were both large. The study was Xiaoyue's focal point, with a few Beijing opera masks hung on the walls, books stacked in the bookcases and on the shelves, and several thick books and dictionaries placed on the generous desk. The chair at the desk didn't look very comfortable. Han Ma tried sitting in it—it was a hard seat. She asked Xiaoyue why he didn't use a soft chair.

"I don't want to get too comfortable when I read books and write my essays," he explained.

"It seems like you lead a pretty spartan life."

"It's always like that when it's one person. There's nothing to be energized about—you just think of saving time, so the aesthetics of life are lacking. I prefer living with a woman."

"Didn't you used to have a girlfriend?"

“I did. We didn’t communicate well, so it was painful. I also wasn’t who I am now.”

Han Ma pulled open the pale curtains and saw flower vases on the large windowsill, the same as the vases in her study, with red roses in them.

“You’re much more disciplined than me,” she said, pretending to be calm. “I’m a glutton for pleasure.”

Her heart pounding, she said that she needed to go read for a while. Xiaoyue said he would see her downstairs. In the elevator, he suddenly embraced her and kissed her on the lips. Then he let her go. Han Ma thought: he didn’t kiss me deeply.

After she got back home she kept remembering Xiaoyue’s mouth. Had his lips appeared in her dreams? That man like Xiaoyue had also sucked on her breasts. She sat there swooning in a daze. Later on she suddenly jumped up to take a cold shower. “Visions of sex again,” she said, making fun of herself.

Xiao Ma went to Uncle Yi’s home on Thursday. She hurried there as soon as she got off work. She’d worried that he would have worn himself out working too hard. The door was half-open, but she didn’t see him.

The rooms were already fresh and shining, with most of the furniture changed for new, high-quality pieces. The appliances in the kitchen were also switched out for new ones. One of the two bedrooms had already become Xiao Ma’s study, with two photographs of her when she was twenty-two or twenty-three, which Uncle Yi had asked her to provide, arranged on the desk. Everything in the study was brand-new, comfortable, and high-end. Uncle Yi had bought her a number of books that were placed in the bookcases and on the shelves. A very pretty white jade flower vase was set on the tea table with blooming narcissi inside. A wool rug was spread across the floor of the study.

“It’s simply too luxurious!” Xiao Ma said aloud.

Then she went to look at the bedroom, which had a new bed and an attractive wardrobe. An enlarged photo of Xiao Ma smiling against the backdrop of a bamboo grove hung on the wall. Xiao Ma thought that her expression was a little silly, but Uncle Yi liked it. She thought: how could there not be a picture of Uncle Yi hung in their marriage room? She decided to wait until the wedding and ask Heishi to help take a few pictures of her and Uncle Yi together, then she'd select the best one to enlarge and hang on the wall above the head of the bed. Looking further inside the wardrobe, Xiao Ma noticed that Uncle Yi had only three coats, including one that was his newly bought formal suit jacket. The wardrobe was otherwise empty, ready for Xiao Ma to hang and store clothing in the future. Uncle Yi really wasn't particular or demanding! She thought of how he had a special aura about him, even though he wore old clothes every day. Xiao Sang had sensed this, all of his students had sensed this, even Xiao Ma's younger sisters had a sense of it. It was a quality that demanded respect. As she was thinking about this, Uncle Yi returned.

"I went to buy the guotie you like. Quick, let's eat," he said.

"Uncle Yi, you must be exhausted."

"No. These were all some easy, minor things. I enjoy doing work around the house. How could it be exhausting? I'm not a bit tired," he said.

They sat down to eat the dumplings. Uncle Yi told Xiao Ma that even though he could stay the night now, he'd let her come back again on Saturday, to be absolutely safe. They needed to make sure of "zero contamination."

Xiao Ma said that she would just come over next week, instead of on Saturday, so that Uncle Yi could get some sleep. She couldn't stand making him more tired when he needed to rest.

"Nonsense, nonsense, Xiao Ma. I know what you want, you don't have to hold back. I'm not tired at all! What does this little bit of housework count for? I've been happy every day, no need to say how joyful! You should come over on Saturday. I don't need any rest and will look forward to you coming."

"OK, OK, don't be angry, Uncle Yi! I will be sure to come over. I miss you every night."

"That's as it should be."

When they'd finished eating and cleared up, Xiao Ma remembered something.

"Uncle Yi, I've heard people say Heishi's mother used to be your girlfriend. She's a great beauty."

"Hmm, yes. That is a thing of the past."

"But she's more beautiful than me."

"It's not like that, Xiao Ma. She was just what ordinary people think of as pretty. Your beauty is the beauty of wisdom, which has more lasting appeal."

"Then do you prefer my kind of beauty?"

"Of course. I've already said that you are who I love the most."

"Then touch me now, on this sofa . . ."

Xiao Ma took off her clothes and lay down on the sofa, and Uncle Yi caressed her with his mouth and hands.

Soon Xiao Ma climaxed. Lightly biting her earlobe, Uncle Yi said:

"You've been holding back for too long."

She put on her clothes and told him:

"I'll come back the day after tomorrow, Uncle Yi. I have a feeling that we'll have a baby soon. I'm almost thirty and need to hurry up. Haha, I can't neglect studying or pregnancy! Xiao Sang told me so."

Uncle Yi saw Xiao Ma to the bus stop, where she said in his ear:

"Today there's not enough time—on Saturday I'll come back and touch you."

"Now I'm starting to look forward to Saturday," Uncle Yi said.

On Saturday afternoon Xiao Ma brought a notebook to Uncle Yi's home.

Uncle Yi marked up her notes and discussed them with her. He was discovering that Xiao Ma not only had preternatural sensitivity and excelled at melding her personality into her reading, but also was gradually forming her own method of profound literary exploration. Her reading personality also involved all kinds of strange and wonderful ideas.

"Xiao Ma, I suppose that eventually you won't need my guidance. Someday you will even guide me. Today's young people are remarkable. Your generation has the ability to remold the classics and create your own, new type of classics.

"I'm considered a rebel within my generation, but in comparison to yours it is not enough," he added. "I must study your generation. Your union with me has made this easy. Last night I thought a lot about the trials we will face in our future lives, about the trend of my studies . . ."

"Uncle Yi, the union of two people is stronger, isn't it?" Xiao Ma said.

"Exactly so—the old shines anew, the young become wise. We will face the struggle daily from now on. This is the kind of life that we've longed for."

"When I sought you out at first, I didn't have as clear a view as now about my goals. I just wasn't satisfied with my life, with living haphazardly for thirty years, and I wanted wholeheartedly to transform myself. I had the good fortune to meet such a good friend in Xiao Sang. I've felt an earthshaking change take place in my life over these past several months. But I know that I'm not on solid ground, and that I must try hard for a few years to be genuinely on the way. Uncle Yi, isn't it so easy for people like me to fall in love with literature? I usually see literature as you—my loving this man is loving literature. From the beginning I haven't left this atmosphere for a moment. Meanwhile, reading literature returns me to you. I often think about my mother growing older without finding anyone to love, and I've found my love before I'm even thirty. I'm so fortunate, how could I not hold on tight? But what I found isn't just a living person—it's also an ideal. For this happiness to continue, I need to persevere with literature, I must strive. Before, when I didn't have literature, my life was full of emptiness and pain—it's unbearable to look back. If I go back to that kind of life, it would equal death."

Hearing Xiao Ma explain this, Uncle Yi fell silent. He embraced her, stroking her hair, and saying to himself: "My understanding of her has been superficial."

"Uncle Yi, I won't be diverted from my goals. My strength is multiplied now that I have your support. I feel that literature is the most wonderful cause. I've not only been transforming myself, but also guiding my family to transform. This is literature's power of subtle influence."

"You are also literature for me," Uncle Yi finally spoke. "Coming to understand you more deeply is the same as my cause. Most people believe that we get more rigid as we get older, but, with this cause, even the elderly can remold themselves. Your appearing in my life was a great shock, the only time in my entire life that I have been so shaken. Thank you, Xiao Ma, you've made my life become brilliant in old age. You were right: the power of one person can't compare to the union of two."

Then they talked about many things, about writing, about the relationship between authors and texts, about the significance of human life, about how their lives would be arranged in the future: topics which wholly revolved around literature as the center. Now that they both saw the other as being literature, it gave them immense confidence, not only with regard to their ideas, but even physically. Uncle Yi had never imagined a marriage like this. He felt that, without literature, his union with Xiao Ma would have been impossible. Now the impossible befell him. Thinking back on the entire process, wasn't the reason he could communicate with Xiao Ma that her thriving life force had found a chance to express itself through literature? If a woman like this wasn't literature, what was literature?

"You've brought me to a new world; you are the joy of molten lava," Uncle Yi said at last.

"I love you and will offer my all to you," he added.

"I love you in my marrow. I want to be one with you, one literary person," Xiao Ma said.

They made dinner together. Xiao Ma couldn't help but kiss Uncle Yi once in a while. Every time she kissed him, he sighed.

"Are you becoming sentimental?" she asked him.

"I was thinking back on my decades of searching. At last I have found what I wanted the most—though my body has lost the vigor of youth, so my strength isn't what I wish it was."

"Uncle Yi, that is a traditional viewpoint. Can't older people pursue happiness in their unique ways? There are issues with your perspective on happiness."

"My god, you've become invincible. You are advancing far ahead of me. I will learn from you how to overcome this meaningless sorrow—I will focus my eyes on the goal ahead and advance courageously."

Uncle Yi thought about how in his entire life he'd never experienced the kind of harmony and joy that there was between them, which was full of novelty to explore. This joy was also to some extent a return to primeval scenes. "Xiao Ma is a rarity," he told himself.

Together they cooked a lot of dishes. Xiao Ma had an appetite—she ate until her face was flooded with pink, sending warmth surging through Uncle Yi's heart. She said, joking:

"I'm eating so much, I'll have excess energy at night. From now on I'll eat a bit less."

"What do you mean eat less? You need nourishment," he said.

"Yes, there may be two people inside me who need to eat."

Uncle Yi started to laugh, saying Xiao Ma always had that same topic in mind. He added that he didn't care whether it were for one or for two; he was in love with Xiao Ma and would always love her.

"I care, though," Xiao Ma said. "I get so excited when I think about having a baby who'll be just like you."

"The baby might not be like me, or not like you. There's an equal probability."

"I'll like the baby just as much either way. After all, it will be like literature, in a completely different form."

"I can't put it better than you have."

When they'd finished eating and clearing up, Xiao Ma went to admire again the study Uncle Yi had furnished for her.

"Uncle Yi, you spoil me too much. Look at this study—such luxury! I am the daughter of commoners and never had my own study before."

"It's even more important exactly because you haven't. Besides, it's not luxury, just a bit more comfortable. Researching literature is hard labor."

"I'm willing to work at it. I don't think it's too hard, and from time to time there are even pleasant surprises and a sense of happiness. I didn't have any of this before. Oh, to live like this . . ."

"There's still more than three weeks left until you'll come live here," Uncle Yi said.

Next they went to admire the wardrobe. Xiao Ma suggested that they should pick a day to go shopping for clothes together. They both needed some attractive and practical outerwear, not much at all—just enough to wear would be all right. She also told him that he had a handsome figure, so it was a pity if he didn't dress up a bit. Uncle Yi agreed with pleasure.

"Before this I didn't care about my appearance, but now there'll naturally be some differences, because of you. Help me pick out clothing—I'm sure I'll like what you like."

"Your aesthetics with furnishing are very much the same as mine—simple and also grand, just like you as a person."

"I will continue to make an effort," Uncle Yi said in all seriousness.

Xiao Ma laughed out loud. She walked back and forth through the rooms, praising every new appliance and piece of furniture in the home. She said that they should keep a few pieces of the original furniture instead of throwing them away: these were heirlooms and also held memories of their romance. Uncle Yi praised Xiao Ma for being able to live so well. The suggestions she made were always fitting.

At this moment Xiao Ma glanced at the clock on the wall and said:

"Seven o'clock, we need to go to bed. Tomorrow morning I have to get up at seven to go to work."

Uncle Yi remembered that the last time he hadn't kissed Xiao Ma properly, so he embraced her and kissed her. After a long, long time, Xiao Ma finally said: "Oh, Uncle Yi . . ."

Taking off their clothes and getting into bed, they enjoyed much longer foreplay than before. They took turns stroking each other, caressing with their tongues, sucking on each other. Xiao Ma felt like she was going to melt. Uncle Yi sensed that he could enter Xiao Ma more easily, probably because the previous time he wasn't familiar with her body yet, and had been a bit nervous, anxious he wouldn't do well. He felt even greater arousal this time. He heard Xiao Ma moan like a sound made by an animal he couldn't name. He finally released. She held him, and he lay in her arms for a little while.

He wasn't sure how much time had passed when she said gently:

"Uncle Yi, let's go to sleep."

"Xiao Ma, you're so thoughtful about me, but you're still swelling, and I'm not a bit sleepy."

So Uncle Yi started again. He called this "a game." Xiao Ma said this was what she enjoyed the most, too. After a burst of caresses, her nipples hardened again, pressing against his chest. Xiao Ma gasped, saying she was almost there. Uncle Yi, sucking on her and stroking her, was incredibly excited. Then he suddenly stopped. He talked with Xiao Ma about some domestic matters, talked about their future plans together. He waited until Xiao Ma calmed down slightly, then he began to stroke and kiss her again.

Afterward he kept stroking her faster, stimulating the same place, until Xiao Ma screamed, and he only stopped then. Both of them were covered in sweat.

"Uncle Yi, Uncle Yi, I will never forget how good you are to me," Xiao Ma said, crying. "You're not just my daddy—you also let me enjoy the love between husband and wife that I wanted the most."

Uncle Yi wiped away Xiao Ma's tears for her and coaxed her:

"Xiao Ma, be good, don't cry. From now on you should just enjoy yourself. We still have many years of good days ahead of us. I enjoy this, too—and Xiao Ma's pleasure is my pleasure. Just think, to have such good fortune at my age."

“We are truly joined into one body and soul, aren’t we?”

“Of course we are. You’re cleverer than me, always educating me.”

“In the blink of an eye hours have passed—‘pleasant nights are bitterly short’!” Xiao Ma said exaggeratedly. “I never imagined you would have such a profound effect on me, as if two people are becoming one person.”

Xiao Ma was young, after all, and soon went to sleep. Uncle Yi, though, couldn’t fall sleep right away. He thought about many things. The more deeply he loved the young woman in his arms, the more extraordinary he discovered her to be, but at the same time, she was also from an ordinary family. Was this characteristic of literature of the present era? All these hopeful young people were mostly the children of ordinary families, and they were building a secure foundation for literature of the highest level. They had a burgeoning life force and the willpower to pursue their ideals. This kind of literature that put the grassroots first was unlike any previous literature. In comparison, these young people’s vision was broader, with deeper knowledge of the inner workings of things. The world’s increasing interconnectedness would give rise to a new, unimaginable model from among them.

Uncle Yi helped cover Xiao Ma with a blanket, then, after counting to two hundred breaths, he finally entered the jungle. There were cries of apes and monkeys, galaxies of stars and the Earth about to kiss . . .

“Uncle Yi, I have to go to work. You should get some more sleep.”

“I’ve slept enough. I’ll come make a sandwich for you.”

When they finished their sandwiches, Xiao Ma kissed him goodbye.

Sitting on the bus, she thought: how strange, that Uncle Yi could always bring her to climax. Once he began to stroke her, kiss her, she became so excited, when before with her young, strong boyfriends, whose organs were readier than Uncle Yi’s, she had only really reached climax infrequently, despite having slept with them for a long time. Also, it hadn’t left any impression on her afterward. One reason was that there’d been so little foreplay, always rushing directly into sex. A more important reason must have been the lack of a sense of beauty and love and literary imagination. Xiao Ma remembered a former boyfriend who’d had a great figure and was full of vigorous energy but always fucked her until it was painful, without her getting what she wanted. After she broke up with him definitively, he still couldn’t understand why and kept pining for her. "Everyone said we were compatible," he repeated, following her around. In her mind she rebutted him: "Compatible my ass, I'd rather have sex with a tiger—it would be more interesting than sex with you." Thinking of these incidents from her past, Xiao Ma smiled knowingly. Sex with Uncle Yi made her understand the connection between literature and sex. She had many ideas about this that she planned to write down one by one in her notes.

When Xiao Ma thought about how she would soon move into the home that Uncle Yi had arranged so well, the blood rushed up from her heart so that her face burned feverishly. Her plan was to read through the world's best literary works over the next several years and also raise a child. Thinking about how she would have Uncle Yi's help in doing all of this, she was full of confidence. She remembered her mother, feeling deeply that her mom had remarkable intuition. She hadn't had a good feeling about Xiao Ma's former boyfriends; Uncle Yi was the only exception who had gained her approval. Her intuitions had probably been taught by hardship, which was why Uncle Yi said she was a marvelous mother.

"Xiao Ma's blissful, because she's getting married," her coworkers all teased her.

Han Ma had only been home for a short while when Xiaoyue called asking her to come over to eat Wuchang bream.

She combed her hair a bit and went downstairs. She decided she would eat and then come back to write.

The door was half-open, and Xiaoyue sat at the table quietly waiting. Han Ma recalled the kiss in the elevator and was slightly reserved.

"This fish is really delicious. You'll get me used to being a glutton."

"Let's have a drink," Xiaoyue said.

"No, I don't want a drink. Just you sitting beside me makes me feel giddy. If I drink, too, I'll topple over."

"That's OK if you do, there's a separate room for each of us to sleep in."

"But I planned to go back to write."

"Well, that *is* a serious reason. I support you."

They were silent for a while and only heard the sound of their chopsticks on bowls.

Then Xiaoyue brought up again his constant topic—forming a literary appreciation organization through the Pigeon Book Club. Han Ma seemed to hear him mention several different methods, several familiar names. But she was so very distracted that she couldn't grasp the sense of what he was saying. She suddenly realized that it was the fragrance of the roses disrupting her thinking. She left the dining table to look into Xiaoyue's study and found the desk piled full with red roses.

"Xiaoyue, you're wicked," she said jokingly.

"Do you mean the roses? I bought some extra, ready for you to take back."

Han Ma sat down and continued to eat.

"The key is that the book club needs to reopen. Han Ma, it may be a long wait?" Xiaoyue asked, sounding her out.

"I don't know—why aren't you eating? You've hardly eaten anything."

"All right, I won't ask you. Let's keep eating. Having you sitting next to me is already a high-quality pleasure. This part is the best, eat this piece."

"I know I've hurt everyone, and I feel guilty. But I also have a self-protective side. I don't dare confront my own body. Xiaoyue, Xiaoyue, you're unhappy with me. Why have you never said so? Hmm?" Han Ma's voice had a tone as if she were crying.

"Han Ma, that's wrong. You shouldn't feel guilty. Everyone understands you."

Xiaoyue stood up and bent over to hug Han Ma, and lightly kissed her on the lips.

"It won't be long, I think," she said at last.

"Don't worry about it, Han Ma. I'm too selfish and shouldn't have asked that kind of question. Let's have a drink, to ease the pain. This is at my home, where it doesn't matter."

So Han Ma had a drink. Her mood really did improve.

"Xiaoyue, how long until we go to Xiao Ma's wedding?"

"Twenty days. I get excited when I think about it."

"Their union is perfect," Han Ma sighed.

"I agree. The same perfection as Xiao Sang and Heishi."

"Xiaoyue, I'm not a good person, but you are. You'll get your reward."

"Now I don't know about that. Because I only recognize one kind of reward . . ."

"You just need to wait a bit more and it will be OK."

"Can I kiss you again? A bit deeper . . ."

Han Ma raised her face, and Xiaoyue embraced her again.

He kissed her more deeply. Then he abruptly pulled back. He pushed her away.

"I need to go back to write," Han Ma said.

"Let me see you home. I'm worried you're dizzy."

He held Han Ma close as they went downstairs, walked across the courtyard, then got in the elevator in her building, seeing her all the way to her door. He said goodbye, and Han Ma responded mechanically.

After a while Xiaoyue knocked on the door again, saying that he'd forgotten about the roses. He changed the water for her, then left after arranging the flowers. Han Ma looked out the study window, where there were two kids playing on the parallel bars. She felt that what had happened was like a dream.

"It seems like I can't be without him," she said.

She sat down to work on her writing and soon finished.

After Han Ma finished her writing, she continued to read the novel *XXXXX5*. She'd already followed the protagonist through several wonderlands. Now the character came to a mountain named Stone Forest. Not everyone could enter this mountain, because there were stones that sprang up densely like bamboo shoots everywhere and no roads. These meaningless stones made scalps tingle and people lose confidence at the sight of them. But he arrived beneath the mountain and pressed his face to the stones, perceiving the vibration, *weng weng*, inside of them. He made a bed on the ground and kept watch beneath the mountain, waiting for things to turn for the better. What turning point could there be? He envisioned a few possibilities. Days passed one by one, while none of those possibilities was realized—the forest of stones was still a forest of stones. The protagonist reluctantly left Stone Forest Mountain to travel "the five lakes and four seas" that make up the world, carrying with him from beginning to end his memories of the mountain. Those stones like bamboo shoots; their standing facing each other, meaninglessly; the cold wind on the mountain; the somber arc of the moon, constantly telling him something at the bottom of his heart. These were precious memories: inside those stones was a conspiracy of sunshine, were the ocean's rising tides, were the racket of a hundred species of birds. There were no roads, but roads were everywhere, and no use in looking for them. Han Ma liked the syntax in this chapter: succinct and transparent, decisive and powerful. She thought about how she had her own Stone Forest Mountain, a place that both opened up and was resistant. Xiaoyue knew this mountain's laws, so he wouldn't be knocked around until he was broken and bleeding—instead, he would interact with it. When had he started to become so knowing? Had he always been? Or since she moved to this apartment complex? He wasn't willing to reveal this; might never disclose it. Han Ma sensed that Xiaoyue must understand her much more than she did him. In reality, she didn't know him at all, and was familiar only with his literary standpoints. She was often moved by his love for her, but as to his past, his family, his history growing up, and so on, she only knew a few superficial details that did not form a complete chain of recognition. However, didn't this *not* being knowing increase his fascination in her eyes? Han Ma liked direct incisions, just like in her relationship with Fei. Emotion itself was the most important thing; she wasn't too much concerned with the rest. Her marriage to Fei had probably been a failure from the perspective of bystanders, but she herself didn't believe it was at all. Even if time could be turned back, and she could try again, she would still seek out Fei. Oh, Xiaoyue, Xiaoyue, I keep tormenting you—I am truly ashamed. When things had developed to this point, how could she go back now? But did she really want to go back? Why not try? Try, and if it didn't work out, then go back—this was the attitude she ought to have.

Han Ma remembered Xiaoyue's mouth. His way of kissing was familiar to her. Was he telling her with his lips that he was that man? Even if Han Ma didn't want to confirm whether it was him, she couldn't help her body trying to conform to his. Exactly when she had this thought, Xiao Sang called her.

"Han Ma, are you sure you'll come?"

"Xiao Sang, yes, definitely. Xiaoyue already bought gifts. He's looking forward to the wedding as if he's the one getting married. Xiaoyue, he—"

"What about him? Are things good between you? Han Ma?"

"He's helped me to make connections everywhere in the capital and gathers news about responses to my writing."

"You're so fortunate—I should say, literature is fortunate. Your responsibility is to sit down and write, and you've done extremely well at that. But I feel that, aside from writing, you should also relax."

"I understand, Xiao Sang. I am slowly freeing myself. After all, Fei can't come back."

"I know all about what's happened with you, so I can see things very clearly. Devote yourself to life, Han Ma!"

Han Ma felt much more peace of mind after she'd shared with Xiao Sang.

She went downstairs to run a few laps in the flower garden, then took a shower. She slept well.

The next morning she woke up a little late. She looked out the window, where the sun was already up.

She wrote in an incredibly inspired frame of mind. She saw the plot gradually unfold under her pen, its meaning emerging progressively. After she'd finished her writing, she reread the chapter she had read yesterday.

Han Ma thought: traveling "the five lakes and four seas," memory will only then present its meaning. If the protagonist had stayed where he sat at the bottom of the mountain, then Stone Forest Mountain wouldn't have revealed the magnificent billows of its landscape to him. "Xiao Sang can see so clearly. She witnessed the emotional complications between me and Fei, and she knows how deep my love for Fei runs." At this moment, when Han Ma imagined Fei once again, his image seemed to be covered by a layer of membrane. "He is slowly going far away. Stone Forest Mountain will continue to erupt."

"Xiaoyue, shall we go out to eat together?"

"I was about to tell you that I'm cooking a shrimp dish. Come right on over."

As they sat down to eat, Xiaoyue looked carefully at Han Ma and said:

"Writing is good for you. Writing helps you maintain stable emotions. I think you'll be able to write until you are very, very old. If we still live here then, it will be such a beautiful scene."

Han Ma praised Xiaoyue's culinary skill endlessly.

"Xiao Sang said I was fortunate, meaning my writing. She doesn't know that I also have good luck with tasty food."

"Xiao Sang is a woman of rare sympathies—Heishi is really fortunate," Xiaoyue sighed.

"I'm not sympathetic at all, though. Can you make allowances?"

"You are also extremely sympathetic. If not, how could we have reached the point we're at today?"

"Like it says in the book you gave me, to travel 'the five lakes and four seas' . . ."

"I've read that chapter over and over again. If it weren't for literature, my relationship with you would be hard to imagine. But with literature, everything follows logically, as if written in an essay."

"What does that mean: 'logically, as if written in an essay'?"

"It's like our relationship is now. Every day I feel a sense of happiness."

They finished eating an entire large plate of shrimp, Han Ma doing most of the eating.

"Recently I've gotten a bit fatter. I think I should diet," she said.

"Don't diet, your appearance is just right. You exercise every day, and write every day, so you expend more energy than other people and should eat more."

"If I'm too fat, I worry I won't have an air about me."

"You couldn't be too fat. Even if you're a little fatter, it won't affect your aura."

"Your talking this way puts me at ease. But I'll still be on my guard."

"How about a drink?"

They each drank one glass. Han Ma's face became completely alluring.

"I want to kiss you. May I?" Xiaoyue said, looking at her.

"Yes."

He embraced her tight, his tongue deep inside her mouth. Han Ma sensed a violent reaction in his body and couldn't help but hesitate. It was this little hesitation that made him immediately pull back. Han Ma thought: he's very sensitive to me. They were both gasping.

After a while, Han Ma lightly said:

"Xiaoyue, I'll wash the dishes. After I'm finished I'll just go back to read your new essay."

"OK."

He lowered his head and sat there without moving.

For the rest of the day afterward, Han Ma thought back on that kiss while she read Xiaoyue's essay. She felt herself long for his body like never before. That was him—it wasn't just anyone! She started to worry about whether this kind of ruthless restraint would harm his health. She sank into deep self-reproach.

Han Ma walked over to the window in a trance and saw Xiaoyue exercising on the parallel bars again. He was so handsome! Her heart tightened in bursts, until she was about to cry aloud. Later he finished and went back, lowering his head.

Darkness fell, and Han Ma carelessly ate a bit of something, finding it hard to carry on with her reading.

She washed her hair and showered, busying herself for a long time in the attempt to cool her temperature. She looked in the mirror at her slender, even skinny, body. She felt that this body already showed a tendency toward being an old maid. "I'm awful."

She slowly combed her hair and trimmed her fingernails. She wondered: why hasn't he called?

She walked back and forth across the room, continually watching the clock on the wall.

Ten at night passed, then it was almost eleven.

"Xiaoyue, is it OK if I come over?"

"OK, I'll come down to meet you." His voice was calm.

Han Ma was no longer in a state of suspense.

They converged in the middle of the courtyard.

"Kiss me, Xiaoyue."

"Wait until we're inside to kiss."

"But I have a hard time reaching orgasm."

"I thought so. We'll manage though."

They kissed in the living room. The depth and strength excited a response through Han Ma's whole body. She felt those parts of her body calling out. She didn't know how much time passed before she sobered up.

"I hadn't known you would be so good," she said.

Xiaoyue went into the bedroom holding Han Ma. She sat up, languidly letting him take off her clothes.

They stroked and kissed each other. When they were both familiar with each other's bodies, Han Ma stopped moving and lay on the bed waiting.

"Xiaoyue, what are you looking for?"

"I'm looking—I don't want you to get pregnant right now. You're at a crucial moment, you still need at least a year before things come together."

"You're so crafty! I love this crafty lover."

After he came back to bed he stimulated her again. She didn't know how much time had passed when she thought: yes, I've almost turned into water . . . At this moment he entered her. Oh . . . oh, what pleasure!

But there was more—they tried another position.

Han Ma finally started to convulse inside. She stayed in Xiaoyue's arms for a long, long time.

"Did you come, too?" she asked.

Xiaoyue nodded, gently kissing her eyes.

"You're very skillful."

"It's because I take care of my body daily. I want to spend the whole day inside of you."

They talked for a while about his new essay. Han Ma called the essay "a clarion call."

"Xiaoyue, you're excited again."

He caressed her and said:

"We can go to the sofa and try another way, with me behind—you'll enjoy this more."

Han Ma felt lust rise again as he sucked on her.

On the sofa, she leaned against his body and let him enter from behind.

Xiaoyue began to stroke her below. She felt the stimulation so powerfully that she was about to reach the peak of pleasure. So she moved his hand away and started to move herself. When she heard him about to moan, she stopped and let him touch that place. When she was almost there she started to move again. This time, they reached climax at almost the same time.

"You're very strong, Xiaoyue."

"You're pretty good, too. Now we can do this every day."

"How do you know my body so well?"

"From thinking about it. Since I couldn't have it, I've been imagining it."

"Soon we'll be practicing for a porno," Han Ma laughed.

"That's good, too."

They were both finally tired and went to sleep in each other's arms.

Midway through the night Xiaoyue woke up once to make sure that the evening's events hadn't been a dream and only then went back to sleep at ease. Han Ma, though, didn't wake. She'd set down all of her heavy burdens; her whole body felt released and cozy.

In the morning once Han Ma opened her eyes she said to Xiaoyue:

"I want to keep my apartment."

"OK," he immediately replied. "I only have one study here. I've already been watching for a suite of rooms."

"You *are* crafty. How can I escape your clutches?"

Xiaoyue smiled. He tried to suck Han Ma's breasts again.

"Don't, don't, we'll ruin our health . . . ," Han Ma said.

"One last time. Let's enjoy it all, then take a break for a few days."

So he started to move again, and Han Ma transformed into water again.

This time he entered her for an especially long time, during which they also spoke a few words with each other. Then Han Ma started to moan loudly, "Xiaoyue, Xiaoyue . . . oh!"

"I know you have high standards for your sex life," he said.

"I want to have you always inside me. But we need to get out of bed and go to work."

"You've aroused my entire body."

"It's all empty," Han Ma teased.

Han Ma went back home but couldn't quiet herself down for a long, long time.

"I was so rigid and stubborn before!" she told herself. "You could say that living with Xiaoyue has only advantages, and no disadvantages. Who else understands me like he does?"

When she sat down to write, the plot became even more unexpected. "Sex is so good," she whispered.

Her novella was finally drawing to an end; the ending was an extreme boundary. She thought: this is flying over a chasm. She would save the final leap for tomorrow, as if she were reluctant to finish enjoying it all at once. After Han Ma finished writing, she went over to the window and saw Xiaoyue out running. "He's really full of energy." She decided that today and tomorrow she wouldn't seek him out again. She would let him have a good rest.

Han Ma didn't go out and instead immersed herself in reading the whole day. Reading fiction, and also reading Xiaoyue's essay. She seemed to see a range of mountains rising up to dance, the world returned to an era of remote antiquity, species of animals she couldn't identify that ran out from the belly of the mountains, howling into the sky.

She was going to tell her father about the good news and not leave him in a state of suspension.

"Dad, I'm together with that man now. He's named Xiaoyue, and he lives just across from me. The places where we work are only one street apart. He has a job at that large bookstore. We'll get married soon. Dad? Are you crying? Are you worried about me? Don't worry, he's very dependable."

"I'm so glad, Hanhan! I don't know why, but I think he'll be dependable, too. You are amazing, so of course he'll catch you and never let you go. The heaviest burden on my mind is lifted. You can start to enjoy your happiness. Is he capable?"

"Very capable. We're going to buy a large, four-bedroom home. The most important thing is that he's also obsessed with literature. We can communicate very easily because we're both enchanted by literature. And he puts me first in everything—he's always been like this."

"You don't know how happy it makes me to hear you say this."

Finished with her call, Han Ma continued to read.

She read all the way until nine that evening and took several long paragraphs of notes.

She also went down for a run in the flower garden, debating to herself what Xiaoyue might be doing then.

When Han Ma finished her run, she read for a while again, took a shower, and then went to sleep. Lying in bed she thought back on the body in the bathroom mirror, the body which seemed to be filling out and no longer as skinny as yesterday. Good, she would conclude her old maid's life. She also wondered if she and Xiaoyue both had *too* much vitality, because they had repressed their healthy bodies for too long. If they went on this way, sleeping together night after night, it would influence their health. "Sleep apart, do it once every few days." After thinking this, Han Ma started to laugh.

The next morning they met each other downstairs again. She thought: he is so pleasurable, body and soul.

They rode the bus together, talking about their reading experiences, gazing into each other's eyes, their hearts brimming with happiness.

Then, for many days in a row, Xiaoyue didn't invite Han Ma to his place. He would give her a brief call every evening, not bringing up having her come over. Han Ma was astonished.

By Saturday afternoon, she finally couldn't stand it.

"Xiaoyue, don't you want me tonight?" she asked into the phone.

"Of course I want you. I was just going to call."

"Then why haven't you asked me to come over for so many days?"

"I was worried it would have an impact on your living habits. You work too hard, Han Ma."

Han Ma hurriedly showered. She even sprayed on a high-quality perfume that Xiao Sang had given her.

Once she came in the door Xiaoyue embraced and kissed her. Her whole body was stirred with desire. But this time, he didn't want her right away and instead had her sit down to discuss something.

"Han Ma, from looking at how things are trending, I think that in a year you will be able to make a living writing. I think that you should resign from work a little early. For example, next month. We need to conserve our strength. What do you think?"

"What you're saying makes sense. Even though I like my job, I'm also sort of tired from going to work day after day. If I don't go to work, I will have even more time for systematic reading. But this way I'll be taking advantage of you again. Things are hard for you, too."

"I don't work as hard as you do. Besides, if your fiction sells well in the future, maybe we'll be wealthy. Don't toss me aside when you're rich—my sexual technique is really first-class."

When Han Ma heard him say this she immediately took off her clothes and got in bed.

"Oh, today I'm going to devour you," Xiaoyue said.

Xiaoyue didn't enter her at first and instead brought her to climax through patient stroking and sucking. Afterward she wanted to stroke and suck on him, making him come in the same way. They were both pleased with their success. So they agreed to get right down to business again that night.

After putting on their clothes, they went back to eat at Chicken Guts Lane.

"I want to go to bed with you every day, but I have to restrain myself," Han Ma said.

"I do, too. Sometimes I want you so much that I have to take a cold shower."

"This kind of physical attraction corresponds to what you said at the book club about the relationship between readers and writing."

"The difference is that writing only conveys messages through script, while people can speak," Xiaoyue said. "One is immediate, one is indirect. We're so fortunate that every day we'll experience both kinds."

Xiaoyue led Han Ma into a xiaolongbao restaurant. Inside all kinds of soup dumplings were on offer. They ordered seafood soup dumplings and pork soup dumplings and both ate until they were full. Xiaoyue pressed close to Han Ma's ear and said: "In the evening we'll do battle."

After they returned to the apartment complex, Xiaoyue poured two glasses of champagne, and they sat down together to drink.

"I will forever remember the scene the first time I saw you at the reading group. If you ask what about you moved me the most, I believe it's your elegant air of freedom."

"Did you think of fucking me then?" Han Ma asked him provocatively.

Xiaoyue didn't answer Han Ma's question, instead reaching out to loosen her clothing. She immediately felt herself melting under the movement of his hands. He undressed her naked, then carried her into bed.

Lovers' Caprice

Xiaoyue: Every night I wake up trying to prove to myself whether what has happened is real. Inexhaustible anxiety and desperation are at an end, as I combine with her in one body. Yet I confront new calls to battle. Ah, her flesh, the freedom of flesh that I have madly longed for on so many nights! Never illusory, flesh filled with kinetic energy! What my union with her brings me is not tranquility, but instead a greater desire to struggle.

Han Ma: Youth resurrected, life arises again. In reality this body can be struck down, might temporarily be numbed, but that is only a matter of regrouping—it cannot be vanquished. My life, destined continuously to arise, even be reborn. I love him, because he is me, I am him, and we mutually realize each other. We love each other in the dreary winter; we are the youth of the Earth. While many tens of thousands of years have passed, the laws of the Earth remain unchanged from the beginning to the end. In the rumbling sound of the depths of the Earth's core we experience her will, and we turn her will into reality.

Xiaoyue: Ever since that evening, at first glance, when I was profoundly moved by her, my life changed completely and from then on only orbited one center. She is what is inside of me, a very concrete thing, that disturbs me, that compels me to act. With one look, she can raise billows, even enormous tidal waves, in the dark places inside me. To me she is a concentration, a fountainhead, that gives me certainty and faith in the activities of this human world. She caused me to become a complete person.

Han Ma: Oh, the awakening of this love! The desire to create becomes ever more pressing—my entire body is set in motion! He is perfection, and I myself in the midst of creation am perfect. What transformative magic! He leads up ahead, I come to understand later, because there is always inertia. He is actually inspiration, the incarnation of that one inside of me. That spring evening I learned about the mechanism of this inspiration with his enlightenment. Now I finally know that he has always been putting his ideal mechanism into practice. In fact, he and I both belong to those whose intentions remain unchanged, so we will ultimately always recognize the other.

Xiaoyue: I never imagined I would someday reach this state. It is the gift of the Earth, that everyone who strives will have their reward. Literature is the core of this state. This exceptional gift contains an obligation, so the people who receive it are also absorbed by a sense of urgency. Now every day I am in the process of breaking out: this is the freedom I choose. In our love there is a risk—I hope my performance won't be lacking. From childhood on I was inclined to train myself—perhaps that was my earliest self-awareness—and I congratulate myself on continuing this instinct.

Han Ma: The strange thing is that when I am writing I am not flustered, but rather can persistently "draw bamboo by seeing bamboo in my mind." I think this is a natural endowment Heaven and Earth have granted me. Yet if I will express this inheritance, letting it become gradually more formidable, that is to be devoted to life, to steel what is inside me through all types of frustration and difficulty. He and Fei and Xiao Sang were the earliest ones to point out to me that I was gifted. Perhaps this is the way the world is: when such talents appear, all around them there will be many mirrors to reveal them and enable their expression and expansion. Now he has become my mirror. He uses his body to inspire my body, facilitating my creative acts. Oh, this world, our human world!

Xiaoyue: My love for her, her love for me, always orbits this nucleus of literature. We also transform worldly love into literary sprints and risky feats. The reason I have faith in this kind of love comes from knowing its foundations—an ancient instinct is hard to lose if someone truly possesses it. Provided she and I take action, the wellspring of love won't dry. We have no use for thinking about what lasts as long as Heaven and Earth; that kind of imagining is senseless and irrelevant. Provided we persevere in the immediate action, which is also daily life, it is persevering at beauty. From the start she knew this point profoundly. It is the crux within the crux, an astonishing natural gift—so her writing will be successful and move forward unstoppably.

Han Ma: How could I not love him? Without loving him, I could not realize myself. Weren't those avoidances, the indifference, and the estrangement before also the performance of love? He sees more clearly than I do, as Xiao Sang sees more clearly than I do, because the one involved is enchanted and must draw support from the prompting of the mirrors. I finally awakened into this thick atmosphere of universal love . . . These glorious mirrors. I live in a magnificent world, where everything has really happened and is not mirage. This interaction of bodies achieved in amazingly harmonious ways demolishes timeworn ideas and goes deeper, in synchrony with my writing.

Xiaoyue: When I speak: she is there. This means that I myself am there. Amid love we cannot lose the way; all you seek will be achieved. Because love is the mother of freedom. Sometimes freedom reveals its cruel side, but that cruelty is a disguise, is a promise to love, because love itself can arrive through cruel, dangerous situations. She and I are both training in this—we don't have fixed models to adhere to, only unending desire to rely on, and the enlightenment of our mutual mirrors as encouragement. She and I are both fond of risk by nature, but in love's perpetual radiance we cannot lose our footing, even if what this illumination reveals are dangers. Once I think of this I am inspired and eager for the attempt!

Han Ma: He says that we exist at the center of history, which is what I sense constantly when I write. Otherwise, why erupt? Why do the sentences form spontaneously? Why do the descriptions that seem to have no meaning have the most profound essence? My writing cannot deviate; he knows this and feels exhilarated. My lover, he understood the mystery of my body. Together we solved an enigma—such stimulating work! Every day now we are instructing ourselves through mutual comparison, on the zigzag path leading through to eternity, while up ahead that alluring goal continuously changes shape . . .

"Han Ma, what are you thinking about?"
"I was thinking about you, Xiaoyue, of course."
"I was thinking about you, too. The book club will perfect the literary

appreciation structure in Meng. This is your and my undertaking. We will implement this structure throughout the world of letters."

"I always believed that you were a 'new power.' But my understanding of you used to be vague, and that led to complications between us."

"Let me touch you here."

"When I respond to your mouth on me, I sense so vividly how you are everything I need."

"When you and I join forces, in addition to the shared efforts of our friends, it will create history. Will you go down on me now? Come, I want so much to always be inside you."

The two of them drowsily went to sleep just before daybreak. Xiaoyue saw a hawk in the overcast sky, the same hawk Fei had seen. He said in his dream: "The globe turns, and there are countless joys still in the future."

It was almost noon on Sunday when they woke up together.

"Let me kiss you here again," Xiaoyue said, "this is the source of creation."

"Quick, stop, or else I'll kiss you again there."

"All right. Ah, never enough of love . . ."

Xiaoyue unwillingly got dressed as Han Ma laughed to herself.

Xiaoyue was in his office at midday when Jing came in again.

"Xiaoyue, sir, your whole face is glowing. Will you be getting married soon?" Jing asked.

"Mm-hmm, yes."

"Here at the bookstore, our guide Han Ma is already a goddess to us young people."

"I've monopolized your goddess. Do all of you hate me?"

"No. We feel lucky—to be so close to her. The young men all love her, and there are two young women who have been studying the way she carries herself."

"I'm truly honored. In reality, I nearly lost—no, I never really lost her."

"Her love for our guide Xiaoyue is written in her eyes."

"Thank you, Jing."

Xiaoyue reflected that the bookstore's reading group was also literature's core army of the future, and Han Ma's fiction belonged to these young people. He stood at the window, looking at the far end of the street, toward the mountain range that went in and out of visibility and where the ranks were assembling. Oh, these youths! Han Ma was a kind of hunger and thirst. Xiaoyue hadn't had a specific goal before, so he hadn't felt real hunger and thirst. While now he yearned with every moment. At the same time, he felt deeply that the way he'd regulated his life had done him a service. Otherwise how could he face Han Ma's immense seduction? These were nets, not to ensnare people, but to mold them.

Uncle Yi and Xiao Ma's wedding day finally arrived. The day before Xiao Ma went back to her family's home. She was going to proceed with her mother and both sisters from their home to Uncle Yi's home wearing the wedding dress.

That evening the four members of Xiao Ma's family held a long, nostalgic conversation in the living room. Her sisters recalled amusing incidents from when she was young, to which their mother added embellishment. Talking on and on, the family was immersed in memories of love. Xiao Ma thought: she and her sisters hadn't failed, because they had a benevolent mother. Afterward she must be better to her mother, more patient with her, and allow her to be happy in her later years. Uncle Yi was perceptive, so he knew that the two of them could only be truly happy if her mother was also happy. Such a strange feeling—that from now on the two households would become one family. There wouldn't be any problems with Uncle Yi. Didn't her sisters already love their brother-in-law? Who wouldn't love Uncle Yi? Now Xiao Ma would be given to him in marriage and bring memories from their family to his. This kind of migration would be lovely . . .

"Should I move right after the wedding?" Xiao Ma's mom asked.

"Of course you should. Then, when I resign from work, I'll go shopping with you every day."

"Uncle Yi will need your company, too," her mom said.

"Then we three will do the shopping together."

"Hmm, once I'm there, I will learn from you in all things. You have wisdom."

"At the book group we hear all about our big sister's story," Yanzhi said. "Such a beautiful tale. Xiao Hong and I feel its radiance reflected on us. Later on, when we look for partners, we will also place love first.

Of course, our fiancés will be kindhearted and cultured, too. Xiao Hong and I aren't looking now. We'll be ascetic at first, until we're closer to your level, and then see."

"As your mother I no longer need to worry about you two, because there is an example for you to follow."

"You are both pretty and, as you become more cultured, men will line up to pursue you," Xiao Ma said.

Before they went to sleep, Xiao Ma went into their mother's room and quietly said to her:

"Mom, I have something to tell you."

"What, Xiao Ma?"

"I've already been with Uncle Yi a few times, so that we can have a baby sooner."

"Then, are you . . . ?"

"I can't tell yet, maybe soon. Uncle Yi's healthy, and I am, too, so I really look forward to getting pregnant. Xiao Sang's baby is already a few months along."

"Don't be anxious, approach this calmly, and you definitely will. Is Uncle Yi as anxious as you?"

"His heart aches for me. He said if it weren't for my persistence, he wouldn't insist on us having a child. He just wants the best for me."

"You should have a child. You're right, a family without children is always lacking something."

Xiao Ma's mom also told her daughter some ways to take care of her health. They shared personal confidences for a long while, then went to sleep.

On Uncle Yi's side, he'd already reserved the restaurant and was now at home waiting for the guests to arrive. The guests included Xiao Sang and Heishi, and Han Ma and Xiaoyue. Uncle Yi hadn't met Han Ma and Xiaoyue before, but he knew all about them and had read their writing, so he was excited to meet these future literary stars, both overflowing with talent, at the time of his wedding. He knew that the four guests would arrive early, so they could exchange views on literary topics. Xiao Ma's family would only be there when it was time for lunch. Although Uncle Yi didn't have much sense of social formalities, he was moved once he thought of how his bride would arrive wearing a wedding dress. He was almost sixty years old, yet this was his first marriage. He was thinking about this when Xiao Sang and Heishi arrived. They had brought the bride and groom a small home printer, the newest product.

"Uncle Yi looks at least ten years younger in a suit!" Xiao Sang said cheerfully.

She glanced downstairs, where the other two had already entered the courtyard. She said to Heishi:

"I'd bet that they're already together."

Heishi also took a look and said:

"No mistake—just like us that night."

"What secrets are you two whispering about?" Uncle Yi asked.

Xiao Sang pointed downstairs and told him: "Joy added to this joyful event, another pair of lovers confirming their relationship."

"Wonderful! The strength of our camp is rapidly expanding," Uncle Yi said, smiling.

Soon Han Ma and Xiaoyue entered.

"Uncle Yi, hello!" they said in unison.

Uncle Yi shook their hands tight and excitedly said:

"A very handsome couple!"

Xiaoyue brought out their gift and introduced the ancient tea trees of Xishuangbanna to Uncle Yi.

"Wonderful!" Uncle Yi said, touched. "You are both so considerate. This pair of tea caddies is so elegant."

Then the five of them went into the living room and started to discuss their literary plans.

Xiaoyue was delighted to hear from Uncle Yi that he had had many years of friendly contact with several literary magazines and could consider proposing to these journals that they start running dedicated columns, and then encourage all of their literary colleagues to participate by contributing essays.

He told Uncle Yi that he had two outstanding writers in mind already, in addition to all those present, and also Fei, who was a major force. This group, with Uncle Yi taking the lead, would explode the literary world. Xiaoyue also brought up that he had established some connections in the capital and knew which literary figures from the older generation supported literary innovation, which literary magazine societies were awaiting Han Ma's work, and so on.

"Han Ma's fiction gives those of us who work in literature the greatest hope," Uncle Yi said. "It is a literary event the likes of which haven't occurred for many years. I've always felt that nothing could be more natural than for a literary event like this to come from among our nation's women. I read Han Ma's short story collection carefully, and I thought: writing like this is unprecedented, no matter whether judged in terms of intensity and depth, or in its uniqueness and essential universality. I have been profoundly moved. To meet the author herself today, and even more to work together afterward, is incredibly fortunate for me."

Han Ma blushed to hear Uncle Yi's praise for her work, a warmth welling in her chest.

"Women are always the most avant-garde," he continued. "They will be this era's trailblazers. Xiao Sang, for example, proceeds ahead of me. She enlightened me over many years of reading so that I continuously benefited. I am glad to have seen these two becoming literature's core army."

Next everyone started to discuss concrete steps to take action. It seemed like each one of them was already making an effort, so that all of them could offer one or two essays that they had already written or were in the process of writing. These essays were about Han Ma's stories and their innovations. Han Ma hadn't imagined that Uncle Yi himself would have written one, and she was beside herself with excitement, so she hastily got up and went to the window. She thought that this scene was like a dream.

The discussion grew animated, with each of them strategizing, each sensing that time was pressing and feeling the necessity of using their expertise right away. Han Ma gazed at the tree in the courtyard. Now she heard Heishi speaking, discussing back and forth with Xiao Sang. Meanwhile, Uncle Yi and Xiaoyue were planning out specific arrangements. Under the stimulus of the buzzing sound of voices in the room, *weng weng weng, weng weng weng,* her mind gradually went blank. She wanted to cry, and also wanted to shout . . . afterward she didn't shout or cry, just went back to her seat.

"Han Ma, are you unwell? Your hands are as cold as ice," Xiao Sang asked, taking her hands.

"I'm always like this when I'm overexcited. I'm very happy. I haven't accomplished much work at all yet—I have to try harder. I was thinking that I still need to expand my knowledge, enlarge my perspective, for my writing to truly open up in scope," Han Ma said.

"Just now Heishi and I saw you two entering the courtyard, and a weight was lifted from our minds. Xiaoyue understands theory and is also practical. Your union heartens us literary types very much."

"Xiao Sang, you are my dearest sister. You always show concern for me and take every possibility into consideration, and your analysis is always so sensible."

"Because you, Han Ma, are my hope and everyone's hope. We often worry too much, but Heishi believed all along that things would work out for you two, just as 'water finds its course.'"

"I am thankful to Heishi. He's someone I worship."

At this moment Han Ma saw that Xiaoyue was helping heat water to brew tea for everyone and without thinking cast grateful eyes toward him.

Without realizing it they had talked for more than three hours. Uncle Yi told everyone that Xiao Ma's family had set out and would reach the home within ten minutes.

"Xiao Ma is my close friend and also a future literary talent," Xiao Sang told Xiaoyue by way of introduction. "I've had an insider's view of her relationship with Uncle Yi. And Uncle Yi is the person who secretly brought me and Heishi together. You see, doesn't this world form out of chaos?"

"The patterns of the world's deep layers are becoming manifest," Xiaoyue said.

Still talking, everyone went downstairs to the courtyard, where they discovered that many of the neighbors from the building had come outside, where they spontaneously stood in a row. They all wanted to see the graceful bride with their own eyes.

They saw the taxi arriving outside the entrance to the courtyard. First there was Xiao Ma wearing the wedding dress and her two sisters, then Xiao Ma's mother exited the taxi. Uncle Yi led Xiao Ma by the hand into the courtyard, with her sisters carrying the train behind her. Xiaoyue promptly brought out his high-quality camera to take photos of the bride and groom. Heishi was also busily taking pictures. They both felt the occasion was precious and must be commemorated.

The neighbors started to applaud once they entered the courtyard. They exclaimed: "The bride is so beautiful!"

Afterward the party went upstairs.

"Uncle Yi, your home is very comfortable!" Xiao Ma's mother said cheerfully.

"For Xiao Ma's mom, your apartment must be excellent, too. Xiao Ma and I have already gotten it ready."

The two older people quickly fell into conversation with each other. Xiao Ma looked on from off to the side, blossoming with joy.

Then everyone stood to get ready to go to the restaurant. Xiao Ma told her mom that she wanted to take the wedding dress off, to be more comfortable, since they'd finished taking pictures.

"But you haven't drunk the wedding toast yet. Take the wedding dress off a little later," Xiao Ma's mother entreated her.

The location was nearby, so the party soon entered the event room that the restaurant had arranged.

Once they were seated, the bride and groom drank the wedding toast. Xiaoyue and Heishi helped take numerous photos of the bride and groom drinking, planning to choose the best to enlarge and give to Xiao Ma's mother. She was delighted and smiling widely. Uncle Yi went over to toast her.

"Thank you for giving your daughter to me. I will always treasure her," he said.

Xiao Ma's mother was sobbing so that she couldn't speak, then after a long time she finally squeezed out:

"Have a baby soon."

Because there was a pregnant woman present, and because Xiao Ma was anxious to be pregnant herself, no one urged everyone to drink, and the women just had soft drinks. Xiao Sang knew Xiao Ma's mother well, so she and Heishi sat with her, chatting about domestic matters. Xiao Ma's sisters sat one on each side of Uncle Yi. They were trying to be obsequious to their brother-in-law, so that they could ask him for advice in the future. He patiently answered the young women's questions, finding them cheering. Han Ma and Xiaoyue sat beside the bride. Xiao Ma said that she had read Han Ma's stories with Uncle Yi's guidance and revered her. She was going to use Han Ma's fiction for her teaching material and would study it over and over.

The wedding ended in an affectionate, joyous atmosphere.

Returning to their home, Xiao Ma said to Uncle Yi:

"Wherever you are, there is harmony and peace. It seems like a wedding isn't anything to be afraid of either."

Xiao Ma carefully took off her wedding dress and put on nightclothes. Then she packed away the dress with care, saying she would save it as a memento. She let Uncle Yi carry her to bed.

"I haven't been with you for days. I want you so much."

Uncle Yi was aroused when she said this.

They made delirious love. Xiao Ma wouldn't agree to get out of bed all the way until dusk.

Afterward Uncle Yi said he would make mung bean noodles and vegetables for her. Xiao Ma had to get up with him.

Following their meal Uncle Yi also showed her the functions of the printer that Xiao Sang and Heishi had given them.

"Our research will be much more convenient from now on with this printer," he said.

"I've matured thanks to Xiao Sang's guidance," Xiao Ma said, touched. "From now on I will request that favor of you, Uncle Yi. Tomorrow I will start to use the new study you helped get ready for me."

On the bus back to the apartment complex Han Ma fell asleep leaning on Xiaoyue's shoulder. She woke up along the way, though. There weren't any other passengers on the bus. She moved closer to his ear and said: "Today's our fifth day apart, could we do it when we get home?" He reminded her that their original plan was to indulge once a week. Still, since today was a special day, and there'd been drinking, they could break the rule.

"Wait until next week when you've resigned from your job, then we can live in a regular pattern. Once every few days is OK. I'm eager for twice a day, but then there'd be no quality guarantee?"

"You're starting to sound like a lecher," Han Ma laughed.

"I just love thinking about this subject. It's only a recent habit," Xiaoyue said.

"Mainly because of me, yes?

"I'm touched, Xiaoyue. Being with you I'm always touched," she added.

Xiaoyue told her that he had more of a sense of urgency now after spending the morning at Uncle Yi's home. He was roused to study and also do some organizing work, since the Pigeon Book Club would start up again soon.

"Can you face Fei now?"

"Mm-hmm, I think I should able to. I only have one remaining emotion toward him now—deep gratitude. My body has already turned toward you. This process wasn't easy, but I've managed it with your patient, persistent help. I often think that I just have some natural gifts and am able to write, to have so many people interested in me and show consideration for me—I really have no excuse to waste time. I will arrange my schedule to be full, not only writing fiction every day, but also enlarging my reading and research. This way I will repay all the people who place their hopes in me."

"My responsibility is to dedicate myself to literary research and promotion, and at the same time to arrange my life with you so that we both keep healthy in body and spirit. You already have spirit, though your body, well, it still waits to forge itself with mine."

"You really are effusive. I can't wait to get home," Han Ma said.

On walking through the door Han Ma took off her clothes and went into the bedroom. She heard Xiaoyue saying:

"I've suffered for a while. Let's do it now, never mind our schedule. I've really missed your body, it is my homeland."

This time Han Ma's climax came quickly, so they didn't change positions.

"Xiaoyue," Han Ma said with her eyes closed, "I've never asked about your parents, or your hometown. Are you a northerner or a southerner? No, don't answer. This sense of not knowing is good. You are the most beautiful enigma in my daily life, as well as the source of my inspiration. When I think of you there waiting for me, my writing is wilder, more fluid."

"I want to do it again. But you're tired. Sleep for a while first, I'll go get dinner ready."

She heard him go into the kitchen. After a while she just couldn't keep her eyes open.

Han Ma slept until dusk before waking back up. She saw Xiaoyue sitting by the bed watching her.

"Don't I look stupid when I'm sleeping?"

"The young people at the bookstore all see Han Ma as a goddess. Only I can observe the goddess fallen asleep, as 'the moonlight first reaches the pavilion by the water.'"

Han Ma asked Xiaoyue what delicious food he'd made, and he answered vegetable wontons. She jumped right up when she heard this.

"I never imagined you also knew how to wrap dumplings, and they're wrapped really well."

"Then you should eat a bit more."

"I will exceed my quota again, I always eat too much." Han Ma patted her stomach.

"It doesn't matter, in the evening you'll still have physical work to do."

"I just love this lecher, he's simply addictive."

Han Ma cleaned up the kitchen then went right back to bed. Xiaoyue had already taken his clothes off and lay there nude.

"Are we going to follow procedure?" Han Ma asked.

"Yes."

Xiao Sang and Heishi exclaimed profusely to each other on their way back home.

"You're always able to figure things out. You're much more responsive than me."

"You mean Han Ma's affair. There was a predestined affinity. From now on we won't need to worry. The Pigeon Book Club is a magical lair. Everyone who is lured in will turn into couples in the end."

"That was Borges's ideal. Things on Earth are all symmetrical."

"You should take time off next week and stay at home."

"I'm still fine, I have a strong body. Staying home after another month or so will be good. Going to work is more regular for me."

"Next Friday let's also go to the Pigeon Book Club for the last time, then you'll temporarily say goodbye to it.

"Thinking back to when Fei and Li Hai and I founded the book club, I really feel as though it was another world," Heishi added.

"The book club was an ideal in your youth, for all of you. Now it has become the greatest contribution you have made. Oh, I've really missed Fei—he's just like my own brother!" Xiao Sang said.

"I'll call to tell him about Xiaoyue's proposition. He has been preparing this whole time."

"Soon Han Ma will tell Fei about her and Xiaoyue. This knot has been untied. Endings aren't as frightful as Borges depicted. We Chinese people have the wisdom to come up with better solutions. We aren't as pessimistic as he was, or lose our feeling for beauty. Do you think so?" Xiao Sang said excitedly.

"You are becoming more and more profound. Write this kind of reflection into your commentary. It's brilliant!"

As they talked, the bus reached their stop. Xiao Sang's father stood there waiting for them.

"Dad, why are you here?"

"I switched my days off, because I couldn't stop worrying about you, Sangsang, so I came to see you. I'll go back after we have dinner."

"Dad, I'm doing very well. I just went to attend my coworker's wedding. Don't worry about me. The maternity hospital is near here—I can get there in five or six minutes."

They went back home, where Xiao Sang's mother came out of the kitchen. She told them that evening the family would eat century eggs in zhou and tofu with vegetables, because Xiao Sang and Heishi had eaten heavy food at lunch and needed lighter fare. Her mom was plumper, her skin was fair, and she was in an excellent mood. She'd joined the Crown Department Store reading group and started to read fiction again.

Xiao Sang's dad told her that he now earned so much more money monthly that he planned to start saving, then take Xiao Sang's mom on a trip around the whole country. Hearing this, Xiao Sang applauded in approval.

Her own intention was to take leave and spend two years with their child, while also hiring a nanny to help out. This way she could still have time to do literary research.

"Young Hei! Young Hei!" Xiao Sang's father called to him.

"What's wrong, Dad?" Heishi came out of his study.

"Tomorrow is your birthday, so I'll come back to celebrate. Invite your mom and her friend over to eat."

"OK. I've been so busy. Am I thirty-six years old?"

"You're six months older than me," Xiao Sang said.

When Han Ma called up Fei to tell him that she and Xiaoyue were in a confirmed relationship, Fei felt incredibly comforted. He congratulated her and added that Xiaoyue was his good friend, a good brother, so that Xiaoyue being together with Han Ma made him more relieved and happy than if it were anyone else—it was a weight off his mind. He asked Han Ma to say hello to Xiaoyue for him. Fei also said that he wanted to see them both soon at the Pigeon Book Club, and that he would bring his wife Yue, too, because she hoped to be an auditor.

"Is Fei all right?" Xiaoyue asked Han Ma.

"Yes. He says hello to you, and also said that you've made him feel relieved and happy. Fei and I talked about you before, so I know he has a very high opinion of you. He said you are a 'good friend, a good brother.' Xiaoyue, do you like Fei?"

"I am fond of everyone who you care about. Besides, he has integrity. Soon I am going to discuss specific collaborations with him. For a long time I've believed that someone who was able to make you feel that way about him must be outstanding. This is why I cannot disappoint you."

"According to what Heishi told me, the topic for the next book club gathering will be to discuss *Expedition*. I'm so excited!"

"We will begin to take action. This is showing our actual strength, so that our camp in Meng becomes the core army of new literature."

Xiaoyue told Han Ma more about his concrete plans and also mentioned some emerging literary types who had potential and could be cultivated as a new force. He said that developments had not yet reached an ideal situation, but there was plenty of hope. This was the usual fate of the kind of literature that Han Ma wrote. Wasn't destiny also human-made? So they had to take action to the full. Han Ma should keep up her strength, protect her health, and be ready to sprint ahead continuously.

"You and I will always be the best team: one takes action on paper, the other takes action in real life. Our strength combined grows greater. I have this sense that all my life I will keep sprinting ahead, exactly like you describe. An age-old instinct won't disappear so easily. Recently your love of life has deepened my inner experience. Loving you is also loving myself. You always enlighten me."

They also talked about the essential qualities of literature, both believing that the more of this essence there was, the more universality there was. This universality would never disappear, even if it weren't manifested at once. The best writing proliferated from an original source. Even though the majority of readers didn't understand it at first, there was no comparison between its life force and vogueish writing.

This had already been verified many times in the past. What was this essential nature? How best to explore it? These were questions Xiaoyue constantly pondered and always put into practice. He explained to Han Ma that in their relationship he had been keeping to a model he had started for himself in childhood, and he believed that he would not deviate now, because he'd gotten a response in Han Ma's body. Then he was sure that they were both seekers of essential literature. Putting this feeling into practice brought him ever closer to truth. Xiaoyue had also experienced how shrinking back, surrendering, and growing decadent were not permitted in this type of pursuit. People must persevere toward reality and take action resolutely, such that the essential qualities would be realized in both aspects, body and spirit. He believed that Han Ma was the best among this type of literary practitioners. He had witnessed her many ways of healing herself after she had suffered a deathly blow, among which the most crucial was never abandoning her intention to write, and instead writing every day, transforming her desire into writing. "Everything on Earth is transforming, and this is beauty," Xiaoyue said.

"Xiaoyue, you are the one inside of me. I cannot not love you."

"Han Ma, you are the one outside of me. You work miracles. Upholding you completes me."

Their conversation took place in the flower garden of their apartment complex. The setting sun gradually sank before them, dyeing everything golden-red in their eyes. Xiaoyue asked Han Ma whether she could still remember when she had just moved here, when they'd talked about what this scene would be like after thirty years. She said that of course she remembered: at that time they had been speaking to each other in parables, but every parable is always realized, because of the essential nature of its source. She hadn't been fully aware of what she'd said—she had only sought refuge where Xiaoyue was, based on an obscure instinct. Then it turned out to be the nets of life, and also the parables written by their bodies! Recalling the branching sequence of these "events," Han Ma finally knew that she was acting according to her inner will. Therefore, there was this outcome. "I'd never considered outcomes before," she said, smiling.

"It's in the style of how you behave, Han Ma. So you will always be able to grasp essential qualities the most quickly, the most accurately."

"This is accomplished with your help. You are my mirror. You are educating me through our interactions. So I am sure that I won't go wrong by following you from now on."

"From now on, slowly, we'll start to dance a duet," Xiaoyue said.

"Will you want me tonight?"

"I want you now. Let's go back."

They made love again. It was the position that Han Ma found the most exciting, finishing on the sofa. Xiaoyue always wanted her to reach a state of ecstasy.

After a few days they moved into their new home. The unit was on the sixteenth floor, where looking into the distance they could make out the mountain ridges on the outskirts of Meng. Han Ma liked her new study very much. It was large, and next to Xiaoyue's study. She thought that if they both sat in their studies at the same time, they could experience the rhythm of their pas de deux.

Afterward Han Ma's father and stepmother came to visit their new home. Her dad was particularly pleased with Xiaoyue, saying that he had a mature, manly air, a devoted spirit, and talent that was hard to find. Later Han Ma's brothers also came to visit and all felt happy for their beloved older sister.

Did Xiaoyue actually have a family? He hadn't brought them up, and Han Ma didn't inquire. She was willing for her lover to be an inspiring enigma, full of seductive possibilities.

Xiao Ma was pregnant. She and Uncle Yi were steeped in joy. His heart ached for her, and he wanted her to quit her job right away and stay home. Of course, Xiao Ma didn't rest, even at home. She tried even harder to study literature and took on the chores.

"Uncle Yi, count the days: we must have conceived our baby the first time. This shows how harmonious we are! You only entered me once, and my inside embraced you. Think about that happening—it's so beautiful."

"I've kept blaming myself for not doing so sooner. Why did I make you wait so long? I really am a fool! But heaven still took care of me and wouldn't let me lose you."

"Feel my body, see if there are any changes?"

"Mm-hmm—there are changes. Your breasts, thighs, also this place, they all seem to be a little different. They are getting ready to welcome young life."

"Suck on my breasts to make them develop more quickly."

"All right."

"Oh, I'm so turned on. Lick me more here, then touch . . . Ah, good. After this we'll have to practice self-control and wait until the baby comes to indulge. You haven't come inside me for days, let me go down on you?"

"Yes . . . Oh—oh! Xiao Ma, Xiao Ma, how am I so lucky . . ."

When Xiao Ma sat down in her study she told herself that, in addition to love, she also needed to sprint ahead and take risks, to dare to welcome all of the challenges of reading. She couldn't ever be lazy, since she'd worked hard ever since she was little with her mother's teaching. Now she would scale literature's peaks, with Uncle Yi's constant encouragement—he'd said that she had ingenuity.

Beyond her repeated exercises in reading and writing, Xiao Ma asked Uncle Yi to observe her body every day, touching those places, assessing the baby's environment for growing. It became a delight between them. She said she didn't want to move to a four-bedroom unit right away, because moving was disruptive and not as good as making do with the apartment at first, then waiting until the baby was a bit bigger to see about moving. Uncle Yi agreed with her arrangements. Xiao Ma felt that she was less hurried about things, and her mom also said she had the look of a young mother. "I will be a cultured mom," she said. Her mother added that Xiao Ma was becoming a little bit like Uncle Yi.

"Uncle Yi said he is becoming a little bit like me," Xiao Ma said.

Xiao Ma's mom laughed until she cried.

The days after the wedding really were what Xiao Ma had anticipated: both busy and happy, in the present and looking ahead. She felt that her activities fully engaged her, whether she were doing housework or research.

Xiao Ma was unwilling, regardless, to move out of the old residential building. Uncle Yi had brought this up once hypothetically and met with opposition. She said she couldn't abandon such a beautiful environment, with so many memories of love here. In her imagination this building had become a part of Uncle Yi. "I could smell you once I entered this courtyard and this building. An even better apartment couldn't compare to this smell," she said.

When Xiao Ma talked like this, Uncle Yi was very touched and no longer brought up moving out of the building. They lived in the old unit, both nostalgic and looking forward to their new life.

Fei jogged on the campus playing field. He'd been exercising for a while now. This wasn't only to welcome the little one who was coming (he knew that life meant the hard work of care), but also for his literary career. He'd known that the problems with Han Ma would be resolved sooner or later, and that the Pigeon Book Club would start up anew. He hoped that everyone's literary pursuits would be elevated to a new level when the book club resumed. Because a major event had taken place during this period, namely the publication of Han Ma's fiction, an event which seemed likely to continue. When Fei first learned about Han Ma remaining in their former home, he'd often sobbed relentlessly when he was alone. He thought of her facing these emotional difficulties alone, thought of her struggle with despair, until he couldn't rest at night. His agony was only relieved when he learned that she had endured with her head held high. Fei began to plan how to help Han Ma's unfolding prospects in the future. That was when he decided that he must start exercising again.

At last, when Han Ma called to tell him about the change in her life, the weight was lifted from his mind. The news inspired him at the same time, because her lover was Xiaoyue, someone he knew well. Even in the past Han Ma had believed that Xiaoyue's practical ability exceeded that of everyone in the book club—he was the most adept in transforming ideals into action. Now, with Xiaoyue and Han Ma joined in union, the Pigeon Book Club would surely be a "tiger growing wings" . . . which is why Han Ma called Xiaoyue a "new power." Fei felt that this friend was much more suitable for Han Ma than he'd been. But this idea was only a passing thought. Fei saw himself confronting the journey ahead with Han Ma's writing, which was also the future of new literature. He resolved to try as hard as he could to make his friends from the Pigeon Book Club devote themselves to action. He heard from Han Ma that his and Heishi's mentor Uncle Yi was also devoting himself to their literary activities, that he was mobilizing journal publishers . . . How imminent it all was! Fei had already written an appreciation of Han Ma's fiction. Every sentence came from his feelings, so he was pleased with himself. Now he looked forward every day to the Pigeon Book Club's gathering. He was eager to discuss concrete arrangements with Xiaoyue. He also knew that the reception of Han Ma's writing in the world of letters was somewhat indifferent, due to the lack of high-level interpretation and to inertia in reading habits. This was the significance of the Pigeon Book Club. The goal when he and Heishi founded the book club had been to establish an example, like a surveyor's pole at the front line of literature, to liberate people's thinking and experiences, promoting literature's new enlightenment. Now the key juncture had arrived, which could be seen in the flourishing of their colleagues.

Fei's home life was very tranquil and contented now. Yue had inherited her mother's talent for managing housework and making their home comfortable. The school where she taught showed total consideration for her, agreeing to give her two years of maternity leave after their child was born. Yue had also found a nanny from among her mother's relatives for when the time came. They could calmly await the baby's birth.

Pregnant, Yue was especially pretty, like a classical beauty. Fei felt indebted to her and always had an impulse to try to make up for the past. Yue was very touched, so she inwardly resolved to transform herself and try to draw closer to Fei's world. That was why she brought up wanting to audit at the Pigeon Book Club, insisting that she should go even though she knew Han Ma was one of the book club's central figures. She said to Fei that she had, objectively, stolen away Han Ma's husband and always felt apologetic to her, so she wanted to be friends. If she could become friends with this lofty woman, her own state would be elevated. Given Yue's persistence, Fei had to agree to her appeal. In fact, he had also hoped in the bottom of his heart that Yue would support his book club and learn from it, to broaden her aspirations.

"Fei, for the next few days you don't need to take care of things at home, I can cope on my own. Take hold of your plans for working with the book club," Yue said.

"Thank you, Yue. Everyone is preparing to make an effort for literature. The situation will develop quickly. This has been my dream for many years . . ."

"I want to make an effort, too. You know how our little baby was saved because you're a literary person. Put two literary types together, and they will make benevolent decisions and choices. From now on I want to learn from all of you. I won't spend my life in confusion or not taking responsibility. That would be bad for the baby."

Fei stroked Yue's hair, feeling gratified by the rightness of her words. He thought: Yue is certainly making progress. Wasn't he? He and she both were late bloomers . . .

Han Ma was writing in the study of her new home; Xiaoyue in the other study was reading an essay by Uncle Yi.

Han Ma soon finished her writing, but Xiaoyue hadn't finished yet. She lightly slipped behind him, gently held him, and said: "I'm distracting you again."

Xiaoyue looked at her cheerfully and said:

"Your distraction doesn't do any harm. It can only increase my inspiration."

"Really? Is there more?"

"Let me take off your clothes, and I'll answer you."

"I understand. Now we don't need to follow your stipulated once-a-week. Is this to celebrate?"

"I'm not satisfied, I want twice a day. Come on, sit on my lap. I won't go all the way, just letting me touch you feels good."

Xiaoyue started to tease her. Then he had her lie on the sofa again, saying he wanted to smell that intoxicating ancient forest.

"Here is the most mysterious place, I wish I could die inside here," he said as he kissed her. "I haven't today, let me come inside you."

He carried Han Ma into the brightly lit new bedroom and started to fondle her again and whisper "ancient forest." He asked her:

"What do you say, is it better to do this today or not? I'm a bit over quota."

He hadn't finished speaking when he raised her legs. This time he was able to last a long time and changed positions twice, making Han Ma moan.

"You're indulging again," she said seriously.

"It won't set a precedent. I promise not to touch you for three days," Xiaoyue vowed solemnly.

Then he reached out his hands again. Han Ma pried his fingers away, jumped up, and put on her clothes.

"Today I'll wrap wontons for you, with meat filling. You lie there and rest," she said.

As they ate they talked about the reaction to Han Ma's new novella in the literary world after it was published. There was more of a response this time, and two journals had published commentaries. One commentary discussed what the plot signified with reference to an analysis of the text's setting; while the other raised questions about the novella. Xiaoyue said that this type of response was within reason, based on his thorough knowledge of developments in literary circles. Han Ma's writing was taking them unawares. The majority of readers hadn't made the mental preparation to read her work, because reading this kind of fiction required long-term training.

"Your writing belongs to the highest reaches of literature written for the minority. The legacy of this type of fiction goes through historical waves sifting the sand. In past eras literature would often require a long time, and reversals time and again, before its status was eventually determined. The present day has taken a significant turn for the better with regard to the situation of minoritarian literature, because of advances in science and technology, the ease of communication, and the acceleration of publicity, all of which render the influence of this kind of literature not so limited as in the past. Also, a major factor is that modern people are no longer content with conventional explanations of one's self and of the universe. Readers yearn for innovative writing, especially a small proportion of high-level readers. Yet these readers haven't had time to develop or to take shape as a transformative force. They are scattered all over and lack connections among each other. Suppose that every big city had a platform for the exchange of ideas like the Pigeon Book Club, then your writing would have much greater influence than now. Since the Pigeon Book Club exists, your writing has even more possibilities and even greater potential," Xiaoyue said.

"Even though the writing of my works is not impacted by this factor, I am still very attentive to the response caused by my writing. As you've said, this kind of writing exists only in communication. Why do I write? It's because of being interested in readers—out of curiosity. The relationship of this type of literature to its readers will be more immediate, more intimate than any other. You are writing literary works, too. Beyond your essays, you do communication work daily, and you are in dialogue with people: these are also your literary works. You and I both have a major impetus because we believe that today's literature should embody everyday life." Han Ma added thoughtfully, "High-level readers can also be cultivated. If you offer them enough writing, readers eventually form themselves into an atmosphere of discussion, and some of these readers will distinguish themselves. Of course, this can take a long time: sometimes thirty or fifty years, sometimes more than a hundred years. I'm not at all pessimistic. The important thing is that the writing and the groups of readers exist."

Han Ma said that she would be happy if her writing still had readers after forty years and these readers progressively increased. Let nature take its course, along with efforts to help this materialize.

"And so Xiao Sang says we are a match made in heaven," she said.

"The setting sun, white hair, two literary elders," Xiaoyue said. "The Red Roses Apartments are the origin of a covert historical incident."

Xiaoyue told Han Ma that he'd already drafted an outline of separate activities for their friends who were about to gather at the book club. This group of people, with Uncle Yi in the lead, would continually introduce new topics into the world of letters, continually raising up their voices. The center of this literary activity would be Han Ma's fiction. He said that beyond four essays he had in hand, he knew that Li Hai and Yang had each written one. There were also Qiaozi and Yan, who were opening up discussions of literature and recording the substance of their conversations. "We need to discuss literature even more," Xiaoyue said.

"According to traditional literary conventions," Han Ma said, "authors are dissuaded from talking about their own writing. But I feel my writing breaks this convention. I must belong to that kind of modern author who can divide themselves—I am usually able to evaluate my own writing with a clear head. So I want to write some observational pieces about literary creation, too."

"That's wonderful. Your writing is an exception, and you shouldn't adhere to tradition. Once authors separate themselves from their fiction, they can become commentators on it. I believe this is also the trend of future literature. The self needs to divide itself to have any hope of growth."

Their discussion went on, becoming more and more profound, with more and more of a sense that they were becoming the center of the world. "Whoever has the most primeval force will form the center.

Even though this center won't be recognized immediately by the people of the world. History is always like this," Xiaoyue said.

"In days to come, I should continue to erupt," Han Ma said thoughtfully.

"Erupt, because the more you erupt, the more you can educate the rest of us, elevate us, and make us achieve something. My job includes protecting the source of creation and letting its vitality flow in an unbroken stream. That old theory positing mere pain as the source of creation isn't sufficient any more."

Han Ma snorted with laughter and gave Xiaoyue a noisy kiss.

"Heishi, how are you still not asleep? I've been sleeping this whole time," Xiao Sang went into the study to urge him.

Heishi put down his pen and said:

"I was just adding to my essay, and once I started writing I couldn't stop. Uncle Yi's essay is even more to the point, 'older ginger is more flavorful.' Han Ma's writing is really good—you can go deeper into it without any limitations. Let's book a taxi for Friday. I can't stand waiting."

"Me, too. Finally the day we've hoped for. Let the baby also receive an early education."

"Let me see: is the baby behaving inside you?"

Heishi lay in the dark arranging his thoughts. In Han Ma's *Expedition*, what was the significance of "expedition"? He seemed to see countless shadows making their way out of the Earth's mountain forests and caves, nameless things coming into focus, assembling, fluctuating, revealing themselves. Eventually they covered the whole ground, because they propagated with every passing second. "I need to make an expedition, too. Since time immemorial this activity has never ceased, and now evolution and differentiation are creating a new world. How has the author grasped this essence starting from her debut work?" Heishi said to himself. "The stars move as time passes; someone with an exceptional gift has heard the call coming from the cosmos . . ." He remembered that Xiao Sang acted as Han Ma's mirror to enlighten her and exclaimed at Xiao Sang's perceptiveness. "This is also connected to her and Han Ma being the awakened women of this era. Truly, as Uncle Yi said, women are ahead of men in each and every way." He thought: "expedition" is a tenacious growth continually breaking through and constructing Nature. Such astounding writing shouldn't come to a halt.

People should question their embodied selves at every moment: yes, or no? If you take action, yes, you have everything; if you stop, no, you have nothing. It's not only needing to think, but also needing to make something. Now Han Ma has made a wholly new creation, which we interact with under the provocation of what she has created, and we individually make our own objects. This is the task of readers. Nature allows for every possibility; the key is merely in making things, and what we make are natural things.

The more Heishi thought the more excited he became. He lay still, afraid of disturbing Xiao Sang. He felt his thoughts cohere the more they tunneled into deep places. His and Xiao Sang's exploration had already borne some fruit when the book club had met in early spring. Now a new turning point, Han Ma's writing, had appeared, and they could always go even deeper in this direction. For example, there were the questions: Has the age of classical tragedy passed? What type of new literature will supersede it? There should be some comparative essays and large numbers of reviews on this topic. Heishi decided to write another essay, a comparison of Goethe's *Faust* and Han Ma's *Expedition* . . . His thoughts went into the details of books, to the point of enchantment . . . Oh, if he kept studying it would soon be dawn. Now it was time to sleep, and to see what tomorrow brought.

Getting out of bed in the morning, Xiao Sang asked him:

"Heishi, you're yawning. Were you up all night thinking?"

"It's OK, I feel fine. I'm the toughest of anyone in my office."

"Take the afternoon off," she said.

"Just as well I don't have any assignments this afternoon and can take a nap at work."

Xiao Sang sank into thought on the bus. She was endlessly excited when she remembered that they would go to the Pigeon Book Club on Friday. Over the past few months the book club had calmed down after passing through the waves of turmoil that Fei and Han Ma had raised. All of the complex entanglements had resolved well. The entire incident was a literary miracle, or one could even say: a beautiful transformation. Nature is so wise! Literary people are also such a kindhearted clan! Xiao Sang was eager to meet with Fei, because she knew best of anyone everything that had happened. She felt that Heishi's old friend was just like Heishi in that his temperament contained lofty things. No wonder their friendship had lasted over a decade as if it were a single day. As the saying goes, "an army is maintained constantly for a single use," and now was the time for the Pigeon Book Club to show its sword. Xiao Sang believed that her colleagues would give an excellent performance. She'd already talked with them by phone, discovering that each of them was full of passion, leaping at the chance to try . . . As for her own essays, she would commit herself to using a precise, exquisite style to delineate the primeval scene of Han Ma's writing. Precision came first, because if Xiao Sang were not able to be exact, the essential qualities would slip away from the analysis. Han Ma had developed so quickly, with simply amazing speed, since she started writing fiction! Once she picked up her pen she was ultra-experienced. This was probably what Uncle Yi had spoken of as "lava erupting." Xiao Sang wished for her own writing to erupt—erupt in the work of communication.

Han Ma sat in her study swiftly dashing off words. She had been writing this for three days now. The daily volume she produced was more than twice her rate when she had been writing those several previous stories, but the time she spent on it wasn't too different. She calculated: only ten minutes more. Was this a new novella? It didn't seem to be. This seemed like a full-length structure. What content would she write for this full-length novel? It was unknown to her. Han Ma remembered the superb method that Xiaoyue had told her about: "Just let it be unknown." Even though she still felt a bit apprehensive, the writing itself gave her confidence: the text was so humorous and nimble! On the seventh day she obscurely realized what kind of novel she was writing.

Han Ma gave the opening section she had written, which was more than ten thousand words, to Xiaoyue to read. He looked vacantly at her after he'd finished.

"Xiaoyue, is it well-written?"

He nodded, then said:

"The very first to do this—it's unbelievable."

"I've been planning recently to write some interpretive essays and appreciations of classical works. Because now that I have experienced creation myself, I have suddenly solved the profound mysteries of what I read previously," Han Ma said.

"I have the same sense. I think you are the highest level of reader, and at the same time you are a practitioner, gathering the best of both into one body. No one can keep up with you. You must write."

"Then could you tell what this is that I've been writing for these past several days?"

"Your domain is situated at a certain frontier, with all vicissitudes—the sour and sweet, bitter and spicy—and there is too much beauty to behold. It's the arrival of a great eruption."

"I hadn't imagined that I could write so quickly."

"Lava is pouring out. It's magic that makes you laugh until you suffocate."

"Because since I left my job you have been giving me meals that encourage my writing."

"Sit on my lap, and I will hold you and see whether you're heavier."

"All right . . ."

Xiaoyue's fingers immediately reached that place. Han Ma started to tremble.

"Mm-hmm, you're a little curvier. It really makes me carried away. Let me have a closer look, then I'll arrange a light diet for weight loss."

He carried her into the bedroom.

"But I want to kiss you first," Han Ma said.

"Shh, not this time. It's been three days. In the evening you can kiss me again."

They both achieved release.

"Why do so many writers like getting into trouble?" Han Ma asked.

"Maybe it's a weakening of the literary mechanism in their bodies. Famous authors have the prerogative to regard themselves, subconsciously, as having a monopoly on literature, like an emperor, but that actually violates literature's essence. Some authors' lives separate from their writing, so they cannot have deep feeling for their lovers like you do. They only have one lover, the one inside of the text, and their lovers in real life are seen as second-class. For this reason, many authors' writing becomes word games and loses its wellspring. Love shouldn't be a matter of thought; instead it should be the unity of body and thought. Authors without this transformative ability have short writing lives."

"I've been thinking about these questions as well. I don't dare to say that from now on I will be single-minded about you; no one can guarantee this to each other. But I truly, deeply love you, and see you as myself.

My inspiration comes from life, from daily necessities, love and sex, and you are the greater part of my life. I feel so grateful once I think that, when I'm not writing, even beyond literature, I have your body to keep mine company. We hold similar standpoints when it comes to our ideas, and I like your body, which can satisfy me and give me the inspiration that is interconnected with literature. Now every day I can transform life into literature."

"Your texts are filled with a sensual wisdom and total intellectual force. Authors who unify the two are very rare. I think natural gifts are a main factor, and another main factor must be the intense love of and interest in daily life. For example, we live in an urban setting, we merge with our surrounding environment, and this kind of beauty is embodied in your writing. In this piece of writing I saw that even though there was severe criticism, it was also filled with love and humor, while never showing indifference or weariness. You have the profoundest realization of literature's essential communication, so your literature achieves the greatest universality."

"I think that because I am the daughter of a commonplace family I just naturally regard literature as commonplace happiness, anger, grief, and joy—the full range of emotions. I can also tell from this novel that my impulse for seeking out new risks comes from the commoner's perspective. There aren't any 'castles in the air.' I don't have strange ideas about 'getting into trouble.' I only want to love, in the ordinary way, and live, in the ordinary way."

"This characteristic that you've mentioned is something I've perceived since the first time I saw you. We've talked together about this kind of viewpoint. I've said you are the concrete embodiment of an ideal I've held for many years. The daughter of the people is also the daughter of the Earth. The strange ideas in your literature possess more of what is essential; your life force will also be more lasting. Motivated by your writing, I will eventually systematize my thoughts and experiences," Xiaoyue said.

"Living with you, I will write even more, even better. Sometimes I try to remember: how did I originally come up with the idea of moving to where you lived? But I don't have a definitive answer. It seems like the mechanism that you talk about started up inside of me, leading to my taking action within obscurity. In fact, from then on I started to read your body—our bodies were attracting each other from the start."

"There is often life-and-death combat in reading."

Saying this, Xiaoyue's hands wandered again. He felt that place in Han Ma opening up to him.

Outside the window it already was dusk. A large flock of pigeons flew past, and someone's children chased each other and shouted in the courtyard below.

"I'll make Yangzhou fried rice. You lay here and daydream," Han Ma said.

She got up and went to the kitchen.

After Xiaoyue lay down a few seconds, he abruptly jumped up and stepped quickly into the study to dash off some writing. He didn't know how much time passed before he stopped writing. He felt more uninhibited than ever before. Then he heard Han Ma gently asking him:

"Can we eat?"

After they finished eating and cleared up, Xiaoyue poured them each a glass of wine.

He raised his wine glass, toasting her for starting this volcanic eruption that was even greater, even more violent.

She also toasted him for achieving new inspiration and starting a brand-new series of essays.

The curtain of night had fallen outside by the time they went to bed.

Xiaoyue wanted to be first to kiss and caress Han Ma, delighting her. Next Han Ma stroked and kissed Xiaoyue, until he reached the peak.

In an excess of contentment, Han Ma murmured with her eyes closed:

"Are you a southerner or a northerner?"

She didn't get an answer, but she felt he'd already answered her. He was the boy who ran out from the depths of darkness toward her, his whole body spreading a smell she both knew and found unfamiliar . . . They'd then happened to meet at a certain turning point in life, when he brought her almost numbed body a passion like rebirth. Han Ma thought: this identical rhythm of inside and outside lovers is fantastic. Authors who didn't have genuine lovers in real life were lacking something; their one-sided forms of expression were in the end unable to last. This is what Xiaoyue had said.

The next day the two of them went back to that Guangdong restaurant they had gone to the first day when Han Ma moved into the apartment complex. Once they sat down the owner came over.

"Are you married now? Haha, I could tell right away that you had the look of husband and wife! My foresight is never wrong. That's great, pair off and marry!"

Han Ma thought: Xiaoyue had come here before to eat with his girlfriend . . .

While they ate Xiaoyue told Han Ma that he'd already asked the bookstore about changing to half-day shifts. The bookstore had immediately agreed, while also dispensing with most of his logistical work, allowing Xiaoyue to take charge of overall strategy.

"They can't do without your exceptional talents," Han Ma said happily.

"In the first place you will have royalty income soon, and in the second place I need to put most of my energy into literature, ensuring the book club's strength in publicity and communications."

"I am touched again by what you are doing."

"I will have even more time to spend with you soon. I don't want to be separated from you for a moment—I could never, ever tire of seeing you."

"Later, when I'm old, will you tire of me?"

"How could you grow old? Impossible. I've explored into the ancient forest, and I know it can't grow old. There are burbling streams and little birds singing in all seasons."

"You're dreaming of sex again, Xiaoyue. You're always dreaming and never awake, so you fell for me."

"Are you tired, Han Ma? I'm full of energy and want to exceed our quota again."

Han Ma smiled, without answering.

After they'd finished eating and were back home, Xiaoyue bit her ear and said:

"Let's do it again on the sofa with me behind you."

They did it again. They were more adept than the last time, more stimulated, and both soon fell into a frenzy.

In Han Ma's dreams she returned once again to her childhood. This kind of dream was like a series that had run for many years.

This time, in the empty classroom, the little girl Han Ma was doing her homework when a boy opened the door behind her and came into the room.

The boy's bright eyes and teeth looked like a young Xiaoyue.

"You?" He looked at her surprised.

"Me?" Han Ma said.

Dreaming, she thought: so it's Xiaoyue. Many children rushed into the classroom from the door at the front, and the two of them were scattered apart. She tried to find him, but he wasn't anywhere.

She heard someone in the dream say: "You'll only be able to find him in twenty years. It will be hard to meet such a good-looking boy, of course."

Upon waking, Han Ma cried tears of happiness. She asked Xiaoyue:

"Have you had this same dream?"

"I have. But I came to my awakening later, because my dream hasn't formed a series of dreams like yours. You've permeated my dreams ever since the first time I saw you. Often these are sex dreams, but sometimes they aren't."

"In this series of dreams, I often take off flying. I hover, though, not truly leaving the ground—instead it's like I'm tethered to the ground by invisible ropes. I use brute force to break away, then catapult back, break away again, and bounce back again. The furthest that I can reach is the height of a forty-story building. Maybe I'm performing for that boy to watch.

"That's why I often have to ask, 'Who are you?' You've refreshed my childhood dream," she added.

"Maybe we came into the world at the same place, then lost each other afterward. I must have met you before," Xiaoyue said.

Han Ma was still immersed in the writing of her new work, with her state of mind more carefree than she could say. Her efficiency was elevated, and she saw passageways everywhere within the work, so that every time she sprinted ahead, she could express herself to saturation. Whenever she sat down to write, the characters in this work started to chatter or babble away, and she became a hasty record-keeper. This astonished her: how could I have so many strange and curious things inside me? And strange to a fantastical degree. After writing them out, Han Ma would feel at ease again: so it wasn't strange at all—it was the most ubiquitous thing! She knew that readers would also need to be at this height, like her, to perceive her writing's essential universality, which destined the work to be difficult to accept. Han Ma knew though that she couldn't compromise, she only could "write like this," not "write like that."

"My readership will be small," she said.

"This is characteristic of your type of writing. I'm so proud of you. Your works are at the apex of this kind of writing."

"In any case I don't want to get rich. I have the patience to wait for readers to develop. No matter if there are only a few readers, as long as communication can take place, I will be pleasantly surprised and steadfastly continue writing for those two or three people," Han Ma declared with a smile.

"Chattering, babbling, the more the better. It comes from the people's ground level of life force. They are gathering at the deepest places, assembling, waiting to erupt," Xiaoyue said. "Think about it: this is an opportunity that only comes once in many years."

"Xiaoyue, I especially like your mouth."

"Because of the work it does?"

"Not just that, but because it can also express things. You always express yourself so precisely, and you have never said empty words."

"Then reward me—let me use my mouth there."

"Not now, we have to wait until tonight. I need to finish this interpretive essay."

"Then I will endure until evening. Oh, the agony."

Han Ma started to read ancient and classical literature and philosophy, feeling her roundabout way through those dark gullies. At first it was difficult, because there was no light to illuminate them nor any points of reference. The only thing she could do was to read one after another of the original works, allowing herself to give off light in their atmosphere. "I must illuminate them myself and not stubbornly await them giving off light," she told herself. She read a passage, then closed her eyes to meditate for a spell. In this way, after she'd experimented for a period of time, there came a day when suddenly a pattern appeared in her mind. That pattern came uninvited and became the basis upon which she solved the work's enigma. This "event" had happened recently and delighted Han Ma with surprise. From that day forward, her method was proven through repeated tests. Then, last week, she had discussed this with Xiaoyue, who finally told her that this special ability was called "intellectual praxis view" and "rational praxis view." "They are the most valuable ability. Western philosophy has not been able to define them so far." Han Ma trusted Xiaoyue, because his words could always be verified within her own literary practice. Xiaoyue encouraged her to read even more of these original works, telling her that she didn't need to study existing theory. In the future she might formulate a new set of theories relying solely on herself—theories more perfect than existing ones. "Who said women can't construct theory? Those who say this are either fools or have ulterior motives," he said. "Our century belongs to women. Uncle Yi and I both believe so." His words made warmth spread through Han Ma's heart.

Han Ma thought that classical works, in comparison to modern ones, were different only insofar as at that time literary practice wasn't yet based on conscious self-awareness. The author's consciousness often lagged behind a certain functional expressiveness. For example, the poet Dante. Even without being conscious of that kind of function, he was, however, still expressive. Though a work like *The Divine Comedy* wasn't ingenious enough and was in places awkward, it still had a life force that couldn't be vanquished. That function was the "most valuable ability" Xiaoyue had talked about. Han Ma's own writing could raise consciousness through seeking out roots and tracing streams to their sources. Hence while reading the classics she eventually understood that her writing was not accidentally, suddenly having unusual ideas. She in fact existed at a literary turning point; she herself was the turning point. Further, she sensed that she could write better, more freely than the authors from the past, because many taboos had already been broken through literary innovations. In this way Han Ma, with Xiaoyue's help, kept interpreting classical works.

The Divine Comedy enchanted Han Ma so much. She sat unmoving until late at night, still pondering and deciphering. Xiaoyue was a little worried because she'd been sitting for so long.

"Han Ma, go to sleep, you can do more tomorrow. You can work every day now."

"All right, you go to sleep. I'm still waiting."

Xiaoyue waited a while longer, then looked at his watch and saw that it was already two in the morning. He went in, knelt on the floor, reached a hand to her secret place and started to touch her. Han Ma tittered, abandoned her resistance, and let him carry her away.

"Xiaoyue, Xiaoyue, no one understands me like you do."

"We'll get right down to it today. Dante has stolen away my time."

In a dream Han Ma saw her dream-self writing: "If Dante had been as free as I am today, if he'd had a loving companion in real life or had tangible love carved into his bones, if he'd had a sex life like Xiaoyue and I do . . . But without all of these, the poet cannot but make things that follow a rigid model . . . Though in the end the characters he created have strength, and such staying power. In each and every scene there is a monument, faintly glimmering in reflection of the eternal radiance from above. Today, it's probably only a few individuals who practice literature, like Xiaoyue and me, who can return to the primeval scene of creation."

The next morning, when Xiaoyue was at work, Han Ma went a step further to express these sentences from her dream and wrote them out. She thought about how going deeper into *The Divine Comedy* was also going deeper into her own heart. The heart of all of literary art was one heart, but this heart couldn't be entered at will. One needed extraordinary willpower, and must have the support of abundant practical experience. Otherwise, reading would only stay at the surface, just like the first time she'd engaged with this magnificent work of literature. Because, at that time, she hadn't yet experienced literary practice, hadn't started up her inner mechanism. She recalled that what she had liked most then were the copperplate prints in *The Divine Comedy*. Her interest in the illustrations was greater than her interest in literature. The text had slipped past her eyes, without stirring up waves in her heart.

In Anna Karenina, *the character Anna strictly follows the laws of the body's development, so she is the everlasting treasure of the entire book. In comparison, the figure of Konstantin Dmitrievich Levin is much inferior, and there are heavy traces of 'concept first' . . . Authors from the past for the most part vacillate between the two forms of expression, conceptual and embodied; there are only a small proportion of examples that unite them,* Han Ma wrote. *The most outstanding parts of their writing often are where the body overcomes conceptual logic, so that its own logic stands forth, no longer simply obeying the commands of concepts. Therefore Tolstoy wrote Anna's death then wept—perhaps this ending went beyond what his mind had expected.*

Han Ma also remembered Dostoyevsky's *The Brothers Karamazov*, a novel that had shaken her when she was young but today seemed to have numerous shortcomings, especially those rigid divisions into religious concepts, which naturally had grown out-of-date long ago. Therefore the key was: Do people actually have a body? If so, how does the body operate in literary art? How should today's literary experts express themselves differently than in the past?

Han Ma believed that her profound exploration, which was gradually taking shape, was conducted alongside Xiaoyue. Their complementary experiences made it so that this penetration into things could go on continuously. The most valuable aspect, because most difficult, was how Xiaoyue could verify his theory through practice in real life. This was probably something that other people were very seldom able to accomplish at present. That was to say Xiaoyue was always anticipating that he and Han Ma would live experimentally, a new mold of literary life . . . He was a genius in practice. From the start of their relationship Han Ma had realized this, but never with as clear and coherent a vision as now. She saw her life unfolding before her eyes in a model that was different than before, at the same time as her exploration of fiction progressed. What the model demonstrated was Xiaoyue's creation. As Han Ma thought this over, boundless happiness streamed into her heart. Xiao Sang, Fei, Xiaoyue—they were three road signs on the path of her literary life, each one having a decisive function in enlightening her, all being her mirrors. Now Xiaoyue had become her greatest love. Hereafter she would redouble her care for the deep love that he gave her, and control herself from being too obstinate . . .

"Xiaoyue, are you back?"

Han Ma recalled all kinds of feelings from her childhood. When she was young she'd been supersensitive and curious about her body, or you could say she had never stopped exploring it or putting it to use. Fortunately, from the first day she started to write, she had discovered the kind of function she had. After that, this expressive function became freer and freer, along with the deepening of her writing and the help of those mirrors around her. She thought: direct communication still takes place in between person and person . . . She was thinking this when Xiaoyue came in.

"Han Ma, will you let me read your new work aloud?"

"That would be great, thank you."

Han Ma sat nervously, while Xiaoyue stood.

Oh, she was too moved. He blended all of his learning into the declamation, even its deep layers of subtle emotion reproduced by his tone of voice, fluctuating and pausing! He read, and read, and an hour passed while Han Ma felt herself caught up in his reading.

"Let's read up to here for today," he said.

"I feel like this is you writing."

"You're right. To read Han Ma's writing, you must dance with her."

"Just like a couple dancing at a skating rink."

"Only I haven't reached that state yet. The inner workings of the writing are too profound, but I am trying."

"If you hadn't read it out loud, I wouldn't know what's so fascinating about this new work."

"Communication passes on a kind of magic. Exactly like what we did last night."

"You're the most proficient in this magic, so I've seen you from the start as a 'new power.'

"I was excited almost to madness just now. This is a different kind of writing," Han Ma added.

Xiaoyue embraced her and walked to the window, pointing toward the distant mountain range:

"Look, there's something assembling over there."

"What could it be?"

"It must be the age itself. Downy, yet also lively."

"I often wonder: how could my special kind of writing be apart from you, Xiaoyue? And how could it be that you would arrive in my world? The activities of the body are likely very intricate: Nature from start to finish manifesting all kinds of constitutive patterns and letting beauty be revealed at its pleasure. For example, you—since my childhood, you have accompanied me in my dreams. Your face appears in that series of dreams."

"My job now is to make beauty into a functional activity for each reader," Xiaoyue said.

"You're an old hand at this, so you won't fail. The Pigeon Book Club will become a powerful force across the country. We are in the minority, but we cannot be blotted out."

"I often think that the body is the earliest force to appear, yet the latest to be noticed. The plan of Nature for the body to catch up and overtake from behind has its purpose. Perhaps it is best to wait until the material has evolved to be more abundant, to be more active, and only then to effect rebellion and division. In literature, this evolution is increasingly too beautiful to bear. Han Ma, I'd like you to go walking with me at the lakeside park in the suburbs today."

Their taxi stopped at a small sales stand outside the park. Xiaoyue bought two bottles of water.

There was no wind, and a hint of warmth everywhere. Han Ma immediately understood what he intended.

They walked along the path, Xiaoyue addressing the large lake in his mind: "I've come today to thank you. You've helped me fly across a chasm."

Han Ma said: "Such a beautiful lake, keeping all of the secrets at its bottom."

They talked about past events from the Pigeon Book Club, the renewed gathering that was coming up, and so on. Without realizing it they walked a lap around the lake. Xiaoyue said: "Let's jog a lap." So they ran a lap slowly. As they were leaving through the main entrance a voice behind them said:

"Beauty has finally become reality. Young man, I said tempering yourself would bring benefits."

Xiaoyue didn't turn around. Han Ma said: "You were at work like a secret agent."

They rode back to the apartment complex in a taxi.

Han Ma looked Xiaoyue in the eyes and said: "I just went through the process of your thoughts."

"We went through it together," Xiaoyue said.

Every day toward evening Xiao Ma and Uncle Yi went for a walk by the river. They would slowly follow the green belt along the water, walking a large circuit before returning home. They both found this highly enjoyable. "It's so peaceful, a life that is fulfilling and abundant," Xiao Ma said. She'd lived for thirty years without ever before being so content with herself. She and Uncle Yi had become acquainted when they were a bit older, but it was still all for the good, not too late, because the time hereafter was completely theirs—they didn't need to go to work, both of them were in good health, and they were committed to the same cause.

Xiao Ma asked Uncle Yi why he hadn't agreed to their spending nights together right away, and made her wait.

"It was probably from a sense of inferiority. I thought: Xiao Ma is pretty, intelligent, and vivacious, so she must have many other suitors. There might be a period of curiosity about an old man like me. After this enthusiasm passed, you might eventually notice how I'm such an old and boring person. I didn't want to marry and then get divorced, so I decided to wait and see," he answered.

Xiao Ma giggled and asked:

"And later?"

"Later—don't you know everything? You conquered the pettiness of my nature, boldly revealing your fascinating body to me. Then I knew how big a mistake I had made. I thought I would end up a corpse soon, but then you revived me. Coming back to life like this was very beneficial: not only the advantages to my body and spirit, but also in how my cause is growing even more successfully. And soon we'll have our own child. I didn't dare to imagine this before. You created all of this, Xiao Ma. I think I should be the one to follow you in the future."

"Talking about yourself this way is unfair. In my eyes, you were a fascinating, fatherlike lover from the very start. I pledged not to marry anyone but you—Xiao Sang knew all about this. So I was very careful, afraid of offending you, afraid that if you got angry then you wouldn't marry me. After all, there wasn't physical affection, so I wasn't sure of you. But the delay didn't stop me—I became even more determined. With every day that passed I tore off a page from my calendar and was happy. Then we finally went to bed together. I feel like I enjoy you too much. None of the boyfriends I had before can compare—not at all. What I wanted was that atmosphere, and only you can satisfy me. There is spiritual attraction, in addition to physical attraction. I didn't have a clear purpose in life before. I didn't know what I was good at other than my job at the store. I was awakened by Xiao Sang's enlightenment. She brought me to you here, and your very presence roused me! I thought of you at night until I couldn't sleep . . ."

They went back and forth, sharing their hearts with each other, watching the sun slowly set, sensing the tranquility and happiness of everything gradually darkening around them.

When they'd returned home, Xiao Ma wanted Uncle Yi to observe her body carefully again to see whether there were any new changes. She let him suckle her breasts, saying it was good preparation for the baby.

"Your body is fuller and fuller," he told her.

"Let me suck on you now—you've held back for so many days."

Then Xiao Ma made Uncle Yi enjoy paradise.

Uncle Yi lay there telling himself: "These young women are creating a new world . . . They aren't the abstract woman of Goethe's *Faust,* nor expressing themselves through ideas—they are taking real action instead. How shocking! How glorious! I cannot sit here and wait when I still have energy to spare. I must do solid work every day, to join in their creation."

Part Three

HEISHI AND QIAOZI QIAOZI AND LI HAI

Heishi was all of a sudden entering his thirties. Even though he had a successful career, and he'd already earned an advanced electrical engineer's license, there was still a blank space when it came to his feelings. For a while he had dated a woman from his company, but they'd broken up before very long. Heishi thought that he must not have much emotional intelligence and wasn't the type of man who attracted women. He had read numerous literary works under the influence of his good friend Fei and with Uncle Yi's guidance, which made him feel the deficiency in his own nature. One day, five years earlier, Fei'd had the flash of inspiration to propose that they start the Pigeon Book Club. Their book club had only three members then, including a young man named Li Hai in addition to Fei and Heishi. The three of them would read the same book and gathered once a month to talk about their reflections together. They always chose novels that were obscure and profound but also appealed to them. Since Fei and Heishi were essentially students of Uncle Yi, who was recognized as the literary authority of Meng, their reading level was quite high already. Fei's friend Li Hai, though, was self-taught and grew adept that way. From the beginning they chose the street of used bookstores as the book club's location, although the specific place rotated among the tearooms behind the bookshops. They were all bachelors, good men who didn't smoke or drink. Reading books was their greatest joy, and so their meetings continued. The gatherings thus became a psychological support.

Heishi lived in his company's housing. He rarely cooked and always ate out, which his high salary allowed.

* * *

One day, when Heishi was in line at a Guangdong restaurant near his company, unexpectedly everything brightened before his eyes. Queuing in front of him was a very attractive young woman, probably no more than twenty years old. After she finished ordering, she found a place to sit down. Heishi ordered some food and sat down beside her as if nothing had happened. Later the meals were brought over to them.

"I seem to have met you before. Do you work at the company over there?" she asked him.

"Mm-hmm, yes." Heishi nodded nervously. "Do you work near here?"

"Yes. I'm a storeroom employee at the supermarket next door," she answered cheerfully.

After chatting a bit while they ate, Heishi suddenly asked her:

"Miss Qiaozi, would you go out with me to the café that's nearby?"

Heishi heard that his voice was trembling.

"I'd be delighted, Mr. Heishi," Qiaozi said.

The two of them took seats in the café, which was playing classical music: Wagner.

"I don't like Wagner at all," Heishi said. "In some ways he reminds me of myself."

"You don't like some aspect of your own nature—is that it?" Qiaozi asked.

"Yes. I hope that I can change."

"Do you feel lonely in your spare time?"

"A little. I always spend the time reading."

"I'm also lonely. We should see each other often."

"That's exactly what I was just thinking." Waves of warmth surged through Heishi's heart.

After they said goodbye, Heishi kept remembering Qiaozi's large, bright, shining eyes. He wondered if this would be a turning point in his life. Had he, someone who'd always believed he wasn't popular with women, actually made such a lovely young woman pay attention to him? She seemed enthusiastic and had natural poise. She had what he lacked.

By the next day Heishi couldn't wait any longer. He went to the supermarket's storeroom.

Qiaozi had her back to him and was handing someone sample products. She wore a uniform, and her slight, exquisite figure looked pliant. She turned around and saw him.

"Heishi?" she said, astonished.

"Can you come out tonight?" Heishi lowered his voice.

"I can. But I can't stay out too late," she said directly.

"Seven-thirty, at the Messenger Bird Café. How's that?"

"All right."

Qiaozi didn't make him wait long before appearing. As she walked in, her whole body exuded a light fragrance.

They ended up chatting about many things together. Qiaozi was curious, while Heishi was happy to answer her every question. They talked about this and that, joyfully.

"Do you know why I'm so happy, Heishi?" she asked. "This is the first time I've been asked out, and by such a mature gentleman as yourself. I just graduated from college recently."

"I'm feeling like this is a pleasant surprise, too. In my eyes you are as enchanting as cape jasmine."

Heishi's heart pounded with bewilderment after he said this.

He looked at his watch. It was nine-thirty, the time specified by Qiaozi for them to part.

"I don't want you to go. Let's come back next Friday," Heishi held her hand and said.

"All right. Friday, at the same time," Qiaozi said.

Heishi hadn't imagined that things could go so well. He couldn't rest that night, repeating to himself in the darkness: "Should I change the way I see myself? What exactly does Qiaozi like about me? Is it just because I seem mature, and she's curious about older men?" He felt that the young woman was special, especially her open mindset, instead of putting up defenses like the women in his company. It seemed like she would open the doors of her heart to embrace the entire world. Heishi thought that this might have something to do with Qiaozi having just stepped into society and not having experienced frustration in relationships yet. What he liked about her was exactly this mentality, which was infectious and made him feel as though he had returned to his student days.

Friday arrived. Heishi went to Messenger Bird Café earlier in the day and reserved a private booth. He asked the owner not to have music playing. He was thinking of not having to listen to Wagner.

He ate a quick snack once he got off work and went back to his company housing. He tidied himself up, looking in the mirror (which he seldom did normally) and feeling that his appearance could do. Looking at his watch, he saw that it was almost time and promptly left.

On reaching the teahouse he was in for a surprise: Qiaozi was there first, peacefully waiting in the private booth.

He apologized repeatedly.

"It's all right, Heishi. I thought that I should get here early, since you invited me."

"You're so pretty, Qiaozi," he said in admiration.

"Do you mean my earrings? I spent two months' salary on them," she said cheerfully.

"Yes. But not just the earrings, I've rarely seen such a pretty young woman as you."

Their coffee arrived. They started to talk about this and that again. Heishi enjoyed the scattered conversation, since he'd been so lonely and in little contact with women. Now this opportunity fallen from heaven excited him terrifically.

"Heishi, you're such a good catch, and you're so well-educated. You must have had several girlfriends before?"

Qiaozi's abrupt inquiry caught him unprepared, and all at once he became nervous.

"No, I actually haven't . . . I'm a little introverted by nature, and probably women don't like that."

"So that's it. But I don't think you're boring at all.

"Maybe you're just especially honest," she added. "My mom tells me I should marry an honest man. She's ill, so she and I depend on each other."

Heishi thought to himself that Qiaozi wasn't as naive as she appeared. She had options about whom she made friends with. With this thought, he felt even more tenderness for her.

That evening when they parted, Heishi held her hand again.

"Heishi, you may kiss me," she said.

Heishi excitedly planted a kiss on Qiaozi's cheek.

He couldn't sleep when he got back to the dormitory. The girl's smiling face, her pleasant voice, and her youthful vitality surrounded him. He told himself: "I'm a decade older than her. I have the responsibility to protect her feelings and never do anything to hurt her." He felt that what he liked most about Qiaozi was her plain and unaffected nature, which was not withdrawn like his own, such that she could complement his nature.

This kind of dating at coffee shops continued for the entire spring. When the temperature turned hot, Heishi sensed his longing for Qiaozi's body more intensely.

"Would you be willing to come to my place tomorrow afternoon?" he asked her as they parted, his voice shaking.

After he said this he kissed her mouth, then kissed her a bit deeper.

Qiaozi didn't move away.

"Heishi, let me think this over for three days before answering you. I also need to talk with my mother when I get home."

Heishi reflected that Qiaozi really was in earnest. She wasn't at all bashful, nor rash in her behavior. Wasn't this exactly the kind of woman he had been yearning for so long?

Heishi spent three restless days with his mood shifting between extremes. He couldn't eat well or sleep soundly. The tossing and turning hollowed out his physique. Finally he'd waited until it was time for them to meet.

"My mom said that I can continue going out with you. She reminded me to take care of myself," Qiaozi said.

"I will surely take care of you, Qiaozi. This is the first time I've been in love in thirty years. How couldn't I treasure you?"

Qiaozi looked at Heishi and nodded. Her trust made passion swell in his chest.

Leaving the coffee shop, they very naturally held hands as they walked toward Heishi's dormitory. Qiaozi congratulated herself: "I have a boyfriend! He's so mature, and he loves me so much! And I like the way he looks: a tall frame, his introspective expression . . ."

They opened themselves up to each other in his rooms.

It was three in the afternoon as the sun of early summer in Meng paused on the curtains, witnessing the fervent sex of new love. For Heishi, it was a sudden arrival of incomparable happiness. Beyond satisfying his excitement, he felt a mixture of penetrating, tender love and sympathy toward young Qiaozi. He vowed to be good to her forever.

Qiaozi enjoyed the sex, too. This was her first experience of love, and she believed that his performance should get full marks. She thought that finding another man more considerate of her than Heishi wouldn't be so easy.

"Heishi, what do you love about me? Just what I look like?" she asked.

"Of course not only that. You and I are similar in many ways by nature. I'm also attracted to that kind of simple composure in your approach to life, and the way you pursue whatever interests you. I've become much more optimistic since I met you. Your gentle feelings about the world influence me."

"I'm reassured by your explanation. After all, highly cultured people understand things best. Our emotions have a foundation, isn't that so?" Qiaozi said.

"Of course. Our personalities complement each other. You strengthen my belief in life."

Heishi's attitude toward life did become brighter since being in a relationship with Qiaozi. Every Friday he would look forward to her arrival at his dormitory. He sat at the window, watching her lovely, petite body hurrying along in the sunlight, unexpected tears pooling in his eyes. Heishi was still an ardent reader and attended the Pigeon Book Club every month for their three-person gatherings. He knew that Qiaozi didn't like reading nearly so much as all kinds of minor matters in daily life. He believed this to be normal—she was much younger than him, so she hadn't realized the importance of reading yet.

Fall arrived after the brief, passionate summer flew by. Heishi thought he should discuss marriage with Qiaozi. He'd already met her mother, who had been ill for years, and she approved of him.

"I want to have the wedding ceremony at the Nanjing Grand Hotel and invite all of my coworkers from the supermarket," Qiaozi said.

Heishi looked at his young lover, noticing that she had gotten a little taller in the past four months. She was so young, still growing! His heart welled with a sense of responsibility.

"Invite them all," he said. "Let everyone see how beautiful the bride is in her wedding dress."

He added, "If it weren't for you, I would still be the loneliest shadow of man in Meng."

"Heishi, maybe someday I will ask to join the Pigeon Book Club. But now isn't the time. I want to enjoy everyday life, not use my brain to think about things. Can you understand?"

"Yes, I can understand. You don't need to read poetry right now, because you yourself are a little poem, the most beautiful, simple poem."

Qiaozi started to talk exuberantly about a certain coworker who'd gotten married at the Nanjing Grand Hotel, about all the details that had made a deep impression on her. Heishi was happy to listen. They settled on getting married in the winter, at the beginning of the coming year.

"Oh, I can't wait for that day to arrive!" she sighed.

"But first we still need to buy a home. We can't always live in the company dormitory," Heishi said, kissing her. "Where would you like to live?"

"In the Meng commercial district, of course, where life is the most convenient. And I must be near my mother. The environment is good around where she lives, and there are a few residential areas to choose from. Later on, I can have my mom move into our building."

Buying an apartment interested Qiaozi more than anything. They discussed back and forth, both immersed in happy anticipation. Qiaozi also told Heishi that she didn't want to have a baby right away when they got married, that she'd rather have fun for a couple of years and then see. What she wanted most was to travel—she hadn't even been to the capital yet. Heishi said that he must take her to the capital for a good time and conveniently also to visit his father.

"Didn't your father leave you when you were young?" Qiaozi asked.

"Yes." Heishi didn't like to talk about this.

"How can parents leave their children? I can't imagine what that would be like. My parents were in a car accident, so my father passed . . . oh, oh."

"Now I'm here, and your days of hardship are over. I won't let you and your mother suffer any more."

Qiaozi snuggled in Heishi's arms, kissing him. Heishi was touched to the point of tears.

One day the two of them went to a movie theater to watch a comedy. After they took their seats, and before the film started, Qiaozi suddenly stood up, saying she'd seen a friend in a row up ahead and was going to say hello.

Heishi watched Qiaozi and the young man talking in the aisle. She kept gesturing with her hands and seemed animated. The young man was about the same height as he was, but younger. Heishi thought:

maybe Qiaozi has more to talk about with someone her own age? Did she hold back when she was with him?

She only returned to Heishi's side when the movie started.

After the movie ended, Qiaozi told Heishi that the young man, who was named Boming, was a department manager at her store. They frequently played ping-pong together.

"He's so funny," Qiaozi said, then started to laugh, maybe remembering something.

Heishi felt his heart tighten with a feeling of apprehension. He thought that he might have underestimated Qiaozi, that the human heart was difficult to predict. Then he calmed down again quickly. He decided to have faith in Qiaozi, because if he started not to believe her now, how could he believe her afterward? Still, he was unhappy with her for not introducing him to Boming, though this might have been just a careless oversight. At her age she didn't consider everything.

"Are you jealous?" Qiaozi asked, then her sharp, clear laughter rang out. "Boming was just transferred here. He has the brains for management, and we have a good working relationship. But I don't love him, when I already have you. How could I also love someone else?"

"Maybe he'll fall in love with you," Heishi warned her. "He's younger than me and also better-looking."

"Oh, Heishi, you really are jealous! Don't worry, I won't fall in love with him. I only want to marry you—it can't be anyone else."

Heishi felt little uneasy after he and Qiaozi parted, for the first time since they'd been together.

Soon they began to search for a home all over the city. Qiaozi took tremendous interest in apartments and could analyze all sorts of pros and cons, which Heishi had to admire. The two of them looked at numerous units, but for the moment there were none that completely satisfied her.

Over that period of time, Qiaozi went to Heishi's place every day after getting off work, ate a quick meal with him, then she would be full of drive to go look at apartments. Slowly, Heishi discovered that she was too choosy: The living room had to be large, the child's room also had to be large, the bedroom had to face south. The kitchen had to be modernized, the bathroom had to be well-ventilated and have good light.

It couldn't be on one of the lower floors. It must have two large balconies. Apartments without elevators wouldn't do. If the property management wasn't modernized that wouldn't do either, and so on. Without realizing it they had been apartment searching for more than two months, viewing more than thirty units in all, and Qiaozi still hadn't made up her mind. Heishi was a little exhausted, and his previous enthusiasm for looking at apartments gradually disappeared. He felt that it wasn't worthwhile to spend all of both their time outside of work on this. Wasn't an apartment just a functional residence? Desiring a perfect, beautiful home was unrealistic.

When he cautiously told Qiaozi his opinions, though, she got angry with him for the first time ever.

That day they parted unhappily.

Heishi couldn't sleep that night for the first time since they'd started dating. A question bothered him: should he compromise with Qiaozi? It was only a trivial issue which he could concede, but if he conceded to her, they might quarrel between themselves over countless things like this in the coming days when they formed a family. Heishi realized that it wasn't a minor issue, but instead a difference in life philosophy. Over these months together Heishi essentially hadn't demonstrated his life philosophy to Qiaozi, or else it hadn't produced any effect on her. He had made out this matter of marriage to be too simple. He'd let the way her body fascinated him go to his head, and for a while he hadn't considered their different aims in other areas. Naturally, the major blame was with himself. He was so much older than Qiaozi. He should have considered these issues from the beginning, but he had dazedly just been getting along. He was already thirty, too old to be so naive in handling his affairs.

Heishi sank into distress. With his mood downcast, he also didn't phone Qiaozi for days in a row.

After getting off work on Friday, Heishi dejectedly went back toward his dormitory. He raised his face and saw Qiaozi standing at the entrance to his unit. Her eyes were filled with veiled bitterness.

"Heishi . . ." she called out to him and then started to cry.

Heishi hurried to let her inside and wiped her tears away.

"I love you . . . ," Heishi said, as if in a trance.

"I love you, too, Heishi. But what did I do wrong? Oh, what?"

"It was my fault, Qiaozi," he said, quieting down.

He had her sit on the sofa and sat himself opposite.

"Qiaozi, have you thought about what kind of life we're going to lead after we get married?" he asked.

"No, I haven't. Won't it be the same as everyone else's?" She looked at him in confusion, her eyes reddening.

"But 'everyone' is also different—individual people have individual pursuits."

"I know you mean that I don't read books and only want to relax and have fun, that in my eyes there are only material things and not spiritual life. But what's wrong with that? I love you, I want to marry you, and I want to find a perfect little nest. I've spent so much time and energy on this, but that's a way of showing my love for you. Why can't you tolerate me wasting a little time? This isn't how things will usually be." Qiaozi started to cry again.

Heishi couldn't respond to that and felt extremely perplexed. He fell silent, again as if he were in a trance.

"If I have fun first, then read books later on, won't that be all right, Heishi?"

Qiaozi embraced him, kissed him hard on the lips, caressed him.

So the two of them went to bed together.

After Qiaozi left, Heishi laughed bitterly. He knew she would persist in her attitude toward life. But did he really need to transform her? It wasn't some major issue of principles. She was young and enthusiastic, and she loved him. Why should he change her? Before this he hadn't even liked himself very much, then he had not at all easily welcomed love, and now he couldn't accept the young woman he loved. Wasn't he the one who wasn't normal?

Yet Heishi didn't intend to keep going to look at apartments with Qiaozi. There were so many books he wanted to read. His interests lay with the Pigeon Book Club. If he kept wasting time he would fall behind Fei and Li Hai. He decided to let go of buying a home.

Heishi and Qiaozi continued to meet. She took it to heart, while no longer bothering him about buying an apartment, with the feeling that he didn't love her enough, even though she didn't want to give up on him. Heishi was intelligent, cultured, good-looking. She believed he was the best partner for her to marry. And he was so considerate of her in bed. She thought they would put off the issue and at a certain point try to buy a home again. For the present Heishi wouldn't break up with her as long as she satisfied him physically. As for afterward, she could 'sing the tune of wherever you are,' as the saying goes.

Naturally Heishi had some different ideas. He was very fond of Qiaozi's youthful, energetic body and often touched by her enthusiasm. But he was increasingly uncertain about how their future married life would be.

The winter came, and they postponed the date they had originally planned to be married. Qiaozi wasn't happy in her heart, but didn't show displeasure on her face. She did say that the two of them should get engaged, because otherwise she would lose face with people. The so-called engagement meant his going to buy an expensive engagement ring to give her. Heishi immediately agreed.

Then a scene took place similar to their search for an apartment together. Heishi accompanied Qiaozi time and again as she lingered at jewelry shops. She chatted with the shopkeepers to see if their stores might have even better, more fashionable new products in soon. It was probably after they had gone on a dozen or more trips to jewelry shops that Heishi couldn't stand it any more. He told her that he wouldn't keep going with her; instead, he would let her make the purchase, and he would pay.

"You don't love me at all," Qiaozi said dejectedly.

"I do love you, but our life philosophies and our habits are different. I can't make a total compromise."

"Is philosophy really such a serious matter for us? Look at everyone else—don't they need to take care of everyday things after they get married? Living well is only practical." Qiaozi made an effort to set out her reasons.

"I can't be a good husband if we both insist on having our own way and don't make any compromises. We should both think things over for a while."

These two statements struck Qiaozi like thunderbolts. Her mind momentarily went numb, so that she couldn't speak. After a long while, she finally, slowly answered:

"Heishi, I never thought that you could be so cruel. Have you been thinking about breaking up for a while?"

Heishi was startled by Qiaozi's reaction to what he'd said. He moved over to embrace her and added:

"It's not like that. I love you, and I haven't ever thought of breaking up with you. But I can't find a solution for us both. Qiaozi, help me to think: what can solve the conflict between us?"

Qiaozi didn't answer and began to cry again, but she soon willed herself to stop the tears.

"I love you, too, Heishi. I am willing to change for you. What about you?"

"I can also make compromises."

The two of them started to kiss, caress each other, and then went to bed.

"I love you so much," Heishi said. "Without you, the light of my life would become gloom."

"I want to read those books you read, too, but I don't have a good foundation. I've never taken literature seriously."

"Then I will teach you, starting from a few simple beginnings."

Heishi chose the books *The Story of the Stone, The Little Prince, Little Johannes,* and *Asya,* along with others, for Qiaozi. He also specially marked with a red pen the parts of *The Story of the Stone* about the emotional entanglements among Baoyu, Daiyu, and Baochai for her to read, because he was worried she would lose patience with the intricate and meticulous descriptions of the setting. Qiaozi had encountered these books before in school, but back then she'd swallowed them whole, using them to while away the time when she was bored. Entering these books anew with Heishi's interpretations, Qiaozi really did comprehend them better.

After this they only rarely went to the movie theater or dance floors. The better part of their time they sat in Heishi's dormitory reading. When they'd sat for a long time, Qiaozi would naturally find it dull and feel discontent. She was still more used to her carefree pleasures. At such times she would drag Heishi outside to the shops to look at luxury items. She would feel total pride if by chance they came across her coworkers or classmates while they were shopping. Heishi knew Qiaozi's tiny vanities, but he believed this wasn't a major hindrance to their relationship. Qiaozi's transformation showed him the depth of her feeling for him. Apart from being moved, though, he also felt a little uncertain: was there willingness from her soul? He thought: let time put everything to the test. He was already thirty in any case. Putting off the wedding day didn't make a difference.

They began to concede to each other in this way: after work they ate together, went back to the dormitory together to read, and sometimes went window-shopping together. Heishi sensed that Qiaozi wasn't as vivacious as before and would sometimes behave inattentively. He felt like he had taken away a certain vitality from her life. However, he also thought that this was probably only a transitional phase. Wait until she adapted to a peaceful kind of life, and her energy would be restored. Qiaozi preferred popular aesthetics in life, and he wasn't at all opposed, because he liked them, too. Yet he hoped she would become a little more introspective, broad-minded, and also a little more elevated. This would require even better books and practical knowledge. Popular aesthetics could easily disappear, vanishing one day and leaving life hollow; also, these things cannot give people genuine support when they meet with difficulty and frustrations. Qiaozi hadn't considered such truths. The greatest challenge in her life had been her father's passing, but she had a mother who loved her and doted on her. So her life had been simple, even smooth. She hadn't perceived life's inner workings. She usually decided what interested her based on "fun" or "not fun." Heishi even felt conflicted about whether he should drag this simple girl into a serious life, to make her mature by "artificial" means. He couldn't decide either whether their age difference was a good or a bad thing. Seemingly everything was waiting on time to give the answer.

"I have faith in our relationship," Qiaozi said to Heishi, "because of our harmonious sex life. The older women at the supermarket tell me that a harmonious sex life is the pillar of marriage."

Qiaozi cried when she read the children's fable *The Little Prince*. She said that the things that happened in the book were just like what had happened between her and Heishi. "How can people who love each other ever be parted? I wouldn't be able to keep on living if I were separated from you."

Afterward she read *Little Johannes*, although she said she didn't understand it very well, since it seemed profound and heavy. Though it was a story about children, it was meant for readers who were older.

She praised *The Story of the Stone* effusively, rereading many times those parts Heishi had underlined in red pen that portrayed love. Only she said this kind of love was too far removed from reality. In real life she would seek out ordinary love—for example, her love of Heishi. Qiaozi added that she wasn't talented like Daiyu—that instead she wanted to be a virtuous woman and good mother, and live her life happily.

Heishi was glad to listen to Qiaozi's evaluations of literary works, thinking she was ingenious and also had plenty of feeling. She was only twenty and still growing. He needed to wait patiently for her to mature.

A dear friend of Qiaozi's was getting married, and the wedding was set for Saturday. Qiaozi wanted Heishi to accompany her to the wedding ceremony, but this Saturday was the day of the Pigeon Book Club, for which Heishi had already spent a lot of time preparing: he was planning to read aloud to the gathering some reflections he had written down. What's more the timing of their three-person gatherings was never changed.

When Heishi told Qiaozi about the book club's rules for meeting, her look darkened. She felt like she would lose face if Heishi didn't go with her to the wedding. Other people would think her boyfriend didn't think she was important. It left her brokenhearted.

"Make another compromise, Heishi!" she begged him, "just this once."

"I would go with you if it were something for work. But this is the Pigeon Book Club, and for me it's a matter of life and death. It is the highest ideal established by the three of us friends when we were young."

Heishi felt like he had no way of making Qiaozi comprehend what the "highest ideal" was. His heart filled with agitation.

"If you don't go, Boming from the store will take advantage of the loophole to fill in for you," Qiaozi suddenly said.

Heishi was stunned. He had never thought a new problem would arise with her.

After a long while, he finally said:

"If someone wants to fill in for me, then just let him. I can't always be watching over you. This is also a trial for you."

"All right, I will go by myself. I don't know whether I can stand the trial," she answered, holding back tears.

When Qiaozi left him she cried for a spell underneath a large willow tree.

Heishi spent the next several days anxiously, but he still went to attend the Pigeon Book Club and shared his ideas and impressions there.

Qiaozi came over on Sunday morning. She appeared to have already forgotten the unhappy situation from a few days ago. She started to tell Heishi about the lavish wedding at the Nanjing Grand Hotel, with all kinds of details about the ceremony. Heishi listened and was filled with suspicion, not knowing whether someone had taken his place in his absence. Qiaozi didn't bring up the subject. He knew she was punishing him, so he began to feel dejected. Whose fault was it actually? Heishi couldn't answer.

His thoughts stretched far, far away, until he remembered his parents' marriage. Maybe someone like him shouldn't get married?

"Heishi, let me touch you," Qiaozi said.

He couldn't get excited. This had never happened before. She said he must be tired.

"Probably. Let me sleep for a little while."

He closed his eyes and immediately went to sleep.

Qiaozi busied herself around the apartment. She washed the clothes Heishi had taken off and all the bedsheets, gave the tables and chairs and the floors a wiping, then changed the water in the flower vases.

"Thank you, Qiaozi," he said once he opened his eyes.

He thought: after all, she was the person in the world most concerned about him. He should have faith in her.

Qiaozi immediately turned around and kissed him, after which she asked in a quiet voice:

"Can you now?"

"We can try."

Qiaozi gently used her mouth to bring Heishi to climax, which he found very moving.

"That day what I said was on purpose to sound you out. Don't be angry with me," she said.

"I wasn't angry with you. I love you."

"And I love you, I love only you," Qiaozi vowed.

Qiaozi surely hadn't betrayed Heishi. Yet if he considered things that way, her colleague Boming was going on the offensive. Heishi was mired in contradiction: should they, or shouldn't they, get married right away? He thought that Qiaozi would eventually turn to Boming if they didn't marry soon. After all, they were the same age and saw each other almost every day. Heishi didn't think of himself as having any great charm that could bind Qiaozi's heart. He also wondered: even if they got married right away, would their marriage hold together? Maybe there would come a day, someday, when Qiaozi would feel profoundly how their being together was inhibiting, monotonous, and dull, and so harmful to her natural instincts . . .

Heishi was in agony over this conflict. He tried desperately to read literature, to study literature, thinking in this way to forget his pain. Yet how could he forget? Their first time was inscribed on his heart: Qiaozi's eager, beautiful body, her deep feeling for him, and her trust . . . She'd made him into a man, but he couldn't carry this heavy responsibility. He felt like he couldn't breathe.

How could they spend their lives together if they were unable to be of one mind? Even though she'd decided to draw closer to his way of life, she was so young and the inertia of her past life was powerful. Under the circumstances, Heishi felt that he could not contend with that power. The difference between them was that he was unwilling to be an ordinary person, while Qiaozi was comfortable living in an ordinary environment. This dispute was unforeseen when they initially got together. Back then, he had envisioned Qiaozi based on his heart's desire and not according to her actual being. Heishi's unwillingness to be ordinary had formed early on into a tendency in his nature. His family's troubles prompted him to be reflective, and he was also fortunate to have his mother's former boyfriend Uncle Yi to look after him, both crucial factors that caused him to grow into what he was like today. But Qiaozi hadn't had an environment like this, and there hadn't been anything that compelled her to reflect on things. She was only a commonplace young woman, whose habits in life were the products of her environment . . . The more deeply Heishi thought, the more pessimistic his appraisal of the future became. By nature he couldn't be ordinary, and at this late date it wouldn't change, because he took this to be where the value of his life lay. Being ordinary would destroy everything he had built up until now. Maybe he could compromise with other people being ordinary, but between husband and wife it would be hard for this compromise to work.

Qiaozi continued to read books following Heishi's guidance. It piqued her interest, and she enjoyed some of its pleasantness. But on the whole her major interest was still the popular aesthetics of everyday life. She felt in the bottom of her heart that her lover was almost arrogant, and not following human nature. Qiaozi was afraid of losing him, though, so she didn't dare to reveal this kind of feeling too much. She thought that maybe, in the future, after getting married and having children, their conflicts would eventually be smoothed over. She also thought about her coworker Boming, this young man who was similarly intelligent and also fairly advanced in specialized knowledge, and really he had so much experience of the world, such a good understanding of what people wanted. And then Boming loved her in the same way and was willing to do everything to please her. Maybe he didn't have Heishi's aesthetic standards (after all, these were profound), but Qiaozi was more herself around Boming, more able to express her natural instincts. There was the wedding, for example, where Qiaozi had Boming attend as her boyfriend because of Heishi's refusal. Boming had gone all out, even though they'd arranged in advance that it would only be playacting. His behavior had been so appropriate, while his voluble charm won the good graces of the other guests. At the time Qiaozi had wondered secretly what it would have been like if it had been Heishi. She thought things might have been fairly awkward, because Heishi wasn't very sociable and had no interest in social protocol. Even though the playacting succeeded, Qiaozi felt from the depths of her soul that she owed Heishi something. Was this betrayal, to a certain degree? This troubled her state of mind, so the next day she went right away to find Heishi and made goodwill gestures. She loved him, while also being attracted to Boming and willing to have a suitor like him at her side. She felt that the sole way out now was marriage. Once she and Heishi married, Boming would maintain boundaries around her, and they could have a lasting friendship. But was Heishi even thinking about getting married? Earlier on he'd been impatient to confirm their relationship, but now it seemingly wasn't so urgent. Oh, the hearts of men are unfathomable. How could she, as a woman, hurry him along? Thinking about this aspect of things, Qiaozi also felt a little resentment toward Heishi. She blamed him that his love for her wasn't strong enough, that he regarded his ideals as higher than anything. She believed that life was the most vital matter in the end. People take their turn upon Earth once, so shouldn't it be to live happily? Was it really necessary to be so inflexible on account of some phony ideal? Qiaozi couldn't think through these issues; she wanted as much as possible to avoid thinking about them. She had to wait for Heishi to make a decision.

"Heishi, why did your parents divorce?" Qiaozi asked him.

"It must have been because of difficulties with communication. The two of them were very different by nature. My mom is outgoing and dynamic, while my dad is more introverted. My literary research today is to help understand these kinds of mysteries in life."

Qiaozi thought: wasn't this a little like the differences in her own temperament and his? A foreboding shadow covered her heart. She found divorce a frightening topic.

"Then you must have suffered a lot when you were little?" she asked.

"Hmm, there were some challenges."

"Heishi, will you teach me how to understand such complicated issues?"

"All right, but it takes a long time. We'll also have to see whether your love for me gives you patience. I'm a dull person in most people's eyes."

"I can't leave you. I'll die if we break up like your parents. I'll die."

This was the first time Qiaozi had considered such serious problems in life, probably due to the subtle influence of the books Heishi was having her read.

"Our generation should have other ways of handling things," Heishi said, distracted.

As they talked, Qiaozi snuggled into Heishi's chest, holding him tight—she was afraid.

The weight of her reliance on him increased his concern. The power to decide was on his side, but he couldn't take that perhaps cruel step. He loved this girl—she was the only one he'd loved in his thirty years. Qiaozi was also worried, but not nearly as heavily as Heishi. If she left him, her state of mind would immediately change. For her, the temptations of life were really too much. She wished to distance herself from this melancholy and heaviness. Every night before going to sleep she told herself: "I won't think about those things." She also knew that Heishi wouldn't bring up breaking up without a reason.

Their original wedding day had passed with their relationship maintaining its status quo.

One day Qiaozi's mother asked her:

"What do you have planned for your wedding day? Have you started getting ready?"

"Not yet. Heishi and I aren't in agreement when it comes to our ideas about life. He calls me a 'material girl,' and wants me to be more spiritual. I'm trying hard, but I'm not sure that I can be what he requires. I'm this way by nature."

"So that's what it is. I always spoiled you, and you've never had to suffer, so you still think like a child. Heishi's right about what he said." Qiaozi's mother sank into thought.

"But I enjoy having a carefree life. I don't want to be too serious, or too restrained. He's not like me at all."

"Can he handle suffering?"

"Probably. He practices self-restraint and has never wasted time on entertainment in his life. He's crazy about studying."

Qiaozi didn't tell her mother everything about her sense of being wronged and her dissatisfaction with Heishi, because she felt like sharing those problems would make her lose face. Her mother knew what her daughter was like, but she had also formed a very good impression of Heishi. She hoped he would guide Qiaozi and help her eventually mature.

"Then just keep waiting. You're still very young. If you truly love him, he'll be sure to consider marriage."

"Sometimes I get upset, I feel like there's too much of a distance between us . . ."

"There are always differences between one person and another. You should learn from Heishi. He's the best kind of man to marry."

Qiaozi had a dream that night where she saw herself and Heishi getting lost in the mountains. She shouted loudly, but no one answered her. Then she started to cry, and she wept for a long time. When she woke her pillow was damp.

The next morning her mother asked her who she'd been calling for in the night. Qiaozi said she didn't know. She told her that someone had been trying to tear her away from Heishi's grasp, and she couldn't make up her mind whether to go away with that man.

"Qiaozi, do you have a foot in two boats?" her mother asked her severely.

"No. Heishi is the one I love."

"That reassures me, as your mother."

A few days later Boming started to send Qiaozi flowers. Qiaozi would not agree to accept them. He just said:

"You and he haven't gotten engaged yet, so you're friends. I am friends with you, too, and I love you in the same way. I want to compete with him. Can't I?"

"We are going to get married. I've considered Heishi my fiancé for a long time. We . . . we are always together," she said, bolstering her courage.

"This might be your one-sided point of view. I think you should set yourself free, open yourself up to more choices, and that way you'll find out who suits you best."

Afterward Qiaozi placed the flowers he had sent in the storeroom. He sent them daily, and they piled up more and more. The women who worked at the supermarket all said that Boming was a better fit for Qiaozi, adding that Heishi was too old, so serious, and unable to join in with this group of young people. If Qiaozi married Heishi, they would lose her, their playmate.

Qiaozi hadn't told Heishi about Boming sending her flowers. She knew he wouldn't come investigate or care about the details—he was too arrogant. This chilled her heart, thinking she didn't carry enough weight in Heishi's heart. Maybe it really was like Boming said: that seeing Heishi as her fiancé was one-sided? Heishi hadn't brought up marriage again, ever since the last time when they hadn't succeeded in buying an engagement ring. It seemed possible that he no longer considered her his fiancée. He might still have broken his promise, even if she had gone by herself to buy a ring. Boming's words distressed her, but in spite of everything his ardent pursuit of her aroused her interest a little. Qiaozi imagined what the scene would be like if she and Boming got married. Without question, they had many, many things in common. He could satisfy so many of her desires. Every part of her that was inhibited by being together with Heishi could be let go as much as she liked with Boming. He was in agreement with her when it came to the aesthetics of life. Still, even though Qiaozi knew many of Boming's advantages, she also realized one thing by intuition, which was that he might not be serious and single-minded like Heishi or give her a complete sense of security. He interacted with too many people every day, and women doted on him. She didn't dare believe she could keep up her attraction for such a handsome guy.

This instinctive judgment was precisely why Qiaozi was on the one hand attracted to Boming and on the other resisted his seduction. She was more willing to be close friends with him, and not to be his wife. Every time Boming came to bring her flowers, Qiaozi said to herself: "Giving me even more is still wasted effort." But it satisfied her vanity and made up for her sense of frustration with Heishi.

"Heishi, my mom asked me about our plans."

"You mean our wedding plans. Whenever you learn to put up with me, then it will be time to get married."

"You're hard-hearted."

"It's not like that at all. It's just that I'm looking farther ahead. I don't want to quarrel all the time after we get married."

"A lot of married couples fight all the time, and when they finish quarreling they make up. Isn't that getting along well enough?"

"It's not the same for me. I need a peaceful family life. I need us to genuinely understand one another. The example of my parents taught me this when I was young. Besides, after getting married we'll also have children. I'm afraid it will be bad for them if we can't communicate."

Heishi's words left Qiaozi silent. She thought a great deal afterward. She considered over and over the difference between them, trying to find a way to resolve it. Yet she knew that this wasn't within her power. Heishi must have weighed this over before, leading to his delay. What would the future be like? Would her efforts now have any effect—could she meet Heishi's expectations? Even if she could, would she feel resentful, like it contorted her natural instincts? Was the life Heishi had talked about truly what she wanted? What was "a peaceful family life"? Maybe in her view it would be deathly dull, and mean the rejection of any popular pleasures? Qiaozi couldn't see into the future or be sure what kind of fate was waiting for her after marriage, which scared her a little. She also really liked Heishi, though, especially in bed. He always satisfied her. Her mother had liked Heishi at first glance, and ordinarily her mother had an accurate sense of people.

Qiaozi, who had always gotten by without being anxious, kept thinking back and forth, and to her surprise she was startled awake several times at night, sobbing quietly. Her mother found the change in her unusual and asked Qiaozi whether she and Heishi weren't getting along.

"It's not that. But he's so arrogant, and he rejects everything I'm interested in. I don't know whether I'll get in a fight with him someday. I'm a little scared now about getting married."

"Then just keep waiting, Qiaozi. You shouldn't give up on him first."

"Hmm."

Qiaozi wanted to take a vacation. Heishi decided to take off work, too, so that he could fulfill the long-cherished dream of accompanying her on a trip to the capital for fun.

Their vacation was set for ten days. Qiaozi inwardly decided that her main goal was shopping, because the capital had the most plentiful products with the greatest variety. She brought along her savings, and Heishi also gave her a large sum of money, saying it was from when she hadn't bought the engagement ring.

Qiaozi's emotions rose and fell as they sat on the plane. She thought of the twists and turns of their romance, thought of all the ways he was good to her . . . In a daze she felt as though there hadn't been any significant conflict between them, as though the shared goal of their union wasn't very far off, so long as she didn't look too hard at things.

They'd booked a relatively high-end hotel. Qiaozi stood in front of the large window in their room watching the sparkling neon lights along the bustling street, enjoyment rising from the bottom of her heart.

"Heishi, I won't give up on you first," she said, telling him how she felt.

"I won't give up on you first either," Heishi said.

The next day they went to visit Heishi's father's family. His dad felt gratified to meet Heishi's girlfriend, because Heishi was already thirty and the question of his getting married had been a worry. Heishi's father and stepmother gave their daughter-in-law to-be an expensive pearl necklace as a welcome gift. Qiaozi made a good impression on them, and they praised her for being naturally plain and poised. They urged Heishi to hurry up and get married.

When Qiaozi and Heishi returned to the hotel, she sighed and said to him:

"Your dad is so handsome. He was a good match for your mom. Why did they break up? Was it just because they couldn't think of ways to settle their conflicts? It must have been very hard on you when you were little."

"Oh, on the surface they were a good match, but this is how it turned out. It is the most profound question between people, which also led to why I research literature."

"I can't figure out these things. Maybe I also need to study literature, and then I'll be able to know."

Qiaozi felt that she understood Heishi better now. Heishi was especially happy to hear what she'd said. He thought that such an intelligent young woman would come to understand him.

The two of them strolled the large stores of the capital for a day. Qiaozi bought a few items of clothing and shoes that she'd wanted for a long time, along with a fashionable watch.

"Heishi, I want to buy so many more things. Starting tomorrow you don't need to keep me company."

Qiaozi told Heishi this in the evening. She said he could go back to his father's to spend more time with him.

But Heishi didn't go back to see his father. Instead he sat in the hotel room reading and taking notes.

The pleasure of shopping filled Qiaozi's body and mind, even though it was a bit of a shame not having Heishi's company. The capital was enormous, and products from all over the country were gathered there—there was so much to choose from! She went upstairs and downstairs, to this store and that store, like a swallow flying back and forth. Sometimes she was so excited by buying something she'd wanted for a long time that she couldn't sleep at night.

"Heishi, I think there's hope for the differences between us to be settled," she said.

"We should be able to resolve them," Heishi said, then added, "It isn't life or death conflict between us."

The two of them were both cheerful, both looking ahead to their future. Qiaozi said that after they returned home she would make an effort to read, striving to cultivate herself in order to communicate better with him. She added that she couldn't help but want to cry once she thought of the traumas Heishi had suffered in his early years. Heishi said he would definitely help her, with all of his strength. Qiaozi had lost her father when she was little, and that was enough suffering. He was like an older brother, and in a certain sense could replace her father.

They hadn't shared their hearts with each other like this for a long time. They both wanted to make their way into the other's heart. They talked to each other until the middle of the night and then dropped off to sleep.

On waking in the morning Qiaozi thought: the trip to the capital would be the turning point in her relationship with Heishi. Any conflict can be resolved, so long as people have love inside them. How could she not love him? Without Heishi to love, life would grow dismal.

She continued her energetic shopping, knowing that she would undertake her studies after going back, so that she wouldn't have as much time to enjoy things.

Qiaozi no longer showed the items she'd bought to Heishi one by one when she brought them back to the hotel. She knew he didn't take much interest in such trivialities. She was only quietly excited, so that her good mood affected Heishi, who loved her even more tenderly. In their enthusiasm they returned to the spring of their first love.

"That time at the restaurant, you were in line behind me, and you just saw me all at once?" Qiaozi asked.

"Of course I saw you all at once. You were like the pearl in the legend that glows at night. I was completely shaken."

"And I felt you were exactly the type of man I wanted, so I took the initiative to speak with you. I wouldn't have struck up a conversation if it had been another stranger."

"What I like most about you is your straightforward, defenseless love for and interest in the world. So I fell in love with you at first sight, and loved you to the extreme."

"Wasn't I silly then, and so spoiled by my mom?"

"Your mom is also very straightforward in her ways."

"I know my mom wants me to marry you."

Qiaozi gave her mother a call to say that their trip had been a success. She was full of confidence, believing that she and Heishi would decide about their relationship right away. She also said that she knew what she should do from now on. Qiaozi's mother was glad to hear this and said that a weight had been lifted from her mind. She once again emphasized her hope that Qiaozi would learn from Heishi. "Heishi can teach you the things I wasn't able to teach you before," she said.

Something happened the fifth day Qiaozi and Heishi were staying in the capital. That afternoon Heishi was in the hotel reading and taking notes when the phone unexpectedly rang. He picked up the receiver and was surprised to hear Fei's voice.

"Li Hai was in a bike accident. He shattered his tibia, and he's in surgery right now. I'm at the People's Hospital. The situation is a bit serious." Fei's voice had changed, like he had a cold.

"I'll come back to Meng right away. I'll take the plane this evening."

Heishi called and booked an eight o'clock flight.

Qiaozi came back at five o'clock.

"Li Hai from the Pigeon Book Club was hit by a car. The situation isn't good, so I need to go back right away."

Qiaozi sat down on the sofa and didn't speak.

After a long time she finally asked:

"Doesn't Li Hai have any family?"

"He doesn't have family—he's on his own. I've arranged to rotate taking care of him with Fei. Qiaozi, I know this will be hard for you, but I believe that someday you will understand the friendship between us."

Heishi packed his things as he talked. Then he called a taxi to the airport.

"The Pigeon Book Club again," Qiaozi said to herself and started to wipe away tears.

She thought: why couldn't they hire a nurse aide to take care of Li Hai? Did Heishi have to hurry back personally? Oh, it seemed like in his mind's eye she still wasn't as important as his male friends. She immediately associated this with the previous time about going to the wedding. That time had also been because of the Pigeon Book Club. Qiaozi felt deeply how Heishi was so obsessed with this part of his life that other things regardless would all give way to it. Even the lover he referred to as loving "to the extreme" counted for nothing in comparison. Qiaozi looked around the hotel room without Heishi in it with oblivious eyes, feeling that her fate was bitter. Just a moment ago she had been ecstatic at having bought the long-cherished diamond ring.

She didn't want to eat dinner and instead sat before the window staring off into space for a long time. She felt like the glittering neon lights were full of artifice, and she was defenseless, alone and helpless like this.

Later Qiaozi picked up the phone, canceled her original flight, and booked a return trip for the next morning.

Qiaozi shut herself in when she got home. Her mother made congee for her and brought it to her room. Her face was red and she was running a fever. Her mom wanted her to go to the hospital, but Qiaozi wouldn't agree, saying that she'd drink some water and be fine. She slept until the following morning, talking feverish nonsense the whole time. After she woke up, her mom had her drink a bowl of traditional medicine. Later her temperature went down. She continued to sleep.

Heishi came over in the afternoon. Qiaozi's mom led him quietly to her own room, where they spoke in hushed voices.

Heishi told Qiaozi's mother plainly about how his best friend had been in an accident, so that he'd rushed back early.

"It was too heavy of a blow for her. She doesn't understand . . . For us this trip was like a honeymoon," he said.

"Qiaozi's been spoiled since she was little," her mother said. "Her dad passed away young. Oh, I didn't do my full duty. Heishi, keep coming here regularly, and she will eventually come around."

"Thank you. I will definitely come over."

Once Heishi left Qiaozi got up.

"Mom, I'm just about better."

She ate congee and drank some milk.

Her mother told her that Heishi had just been there and that he would be coming back. Qiaozi hmphed.

"Qiaozi, don't be obstinate," her mother said anxiously.

"Don't meddle in my business."

She went back to her room and shut the door.

Heishi came back over twice, but Qiaozi ignored him. Her mother sighed with sorrow.

Qiaozi went back to work after the vacation was over.

Heishi knew that nursing was critical for Li Hai's leg injury. He and Fei rotated shifts. Since Heishi was in better health, he took the night shift, while Fei took the day shift. They also hired a nurse aide to guarantee that nothing was missed.

Despite toiling like this at night, he would still go to Qiaozi's home every couple of days.

Qiaozi seemed resolved to break up during this interval. Every time Heishi went over he was only able to speak with her mother, since she refused to come out or acknowledge him. Her mother watched her daughter's willful behavior helplessly. Heishi eventually sensed that Qiaozi wasn't being stubborn, but instead was bitterly determined. He thought back over the two times, before and after, that he had hurt her, and about the bad impression that he had made and couldn't reverse, and felt that Qiaozi's behavior was understandable. A chasm had formed between them, leaving only a vague hope of trying to reunite again.

Half a month later, when Li Hai's leg was improving, Heishi stopped visiting Qiaozi's home.

He sank into deep suffering and hollowness. Frequently he would have aural hallucinations, as if he heard Qiaozi coming up the stairs, and he would rush over to open the door. But it wasn't her—it was some stranger.

In these days his sole consolation was reading literature.

The awful pain of losing Qiaozi was like a broken arm. Heishi knew he would have to tough it out, that no one could help him. He could only let time eventually numb the pain. The strange thing was that this kind of pain didn't affect his comprehension of literature. He felt that he was even more perceptive and had more strength to go deeper into his reading. For this he was grateful and rejoiced.

Later on, he went one day to see Uncle Yi.

They sat in the small room at the back of the coffee shop.

"You're thinner. Is your romance still a success?" Uncle Yi asked him.

"We've broken up."

"So that's what it is. Is there no room for recovery?"

"No. She's too young, and there's been a misunderstanding. She can't see the whole picture, so her resentment of me makes sense."

"It sounds like you did the right thing. You've passed through the most difficult crisis, so now you'll slowly adjust. Literary types can never give up all hope. We always have things that we can do, don't we?"

"Yes, Uncle Yi. I will apply myself as soon as possible. How can everything in life be smooth sailing? I think I could overcome the pain, if only I could convince myself of not being at fault."

"Do you still exercise every day?"

"I'll start again tomorrow."

"Good."

Uncle Yi told Heishi that he had found two books for him to take and read. These books were a level deeper than the last novel, but he believed they were just right for Heishi.

"You are always moving forward," Uncle Yi encouraged him. "Take hold of the time."

Heishi thought, "He is my father, and that man in the capital is only my uncle. I'm lucky."

Next they talked more about the topic of trends in contemporary world literature. They had both perceived a certain new tendency in literary works that had been long in coming. Uncle Yi had already written a few essays about this emerging trend, and he hoped Heishi would write one, too. Listening to him, Heishi grew excited, saying that he would strive in this direction.

After Heishi returned from the coffee shop, the severe pain he'd been feeling lightened. He reflected that it wasn't because the soreness had become numb, but instead that his endurance for the pain was increasing. He thought about how he couldn't be dispirited with a father like Uncle Yi.

He put even more effort into his studies, gaining pleasure and strength from them.

When early spring arrived, he heard from coworkers that Qiaozi had gotten married. It was a lavish wedding at the Nanjing Grand Hotel, and the groom was Boming. The newlyweds traveled to the capital after the ceremony.

Later on Li Hai's leg finally healed, though he still needed to lean on a walking stick.

The Pigeon Book Club increased by two new members. One was a composed young man named Yan, and the other an optimistic young woman named Yang. Yan and Yang had at first sought out Fei by reputation, then, following several long hours of conversation with him, also exchanged literary views with Li Hai and Heishi. Afterward the three men agreed unanimously to accept Yan and Yang as new members. They were both enchanted with books and showed selectivity in their reading along with a high degree of literary appreciation. When the five-member book club met for the first time, Fei made the prediction that if the Pigeon Book Club could expand to twenty members, it would become a considerable force. Heishi and Li Hai were especially happy and full of confidence about the future.

Heishi burned with eagerness when it came to the topic that Uncle Yi had set for him the last time they'd met. He found the two contemporary novels to function as models to start his research. Although the technique of these novels was different from each other, they showed the same tendency, which was to open up a new domain, a wholly different construction that revealed something strange and previously unknown. The more seriously Heishi read, the more he could sense the greatness of the authors' ambition and their boundless, vast vision. It seemed like entering a forest, returning to time immemorial, and from there, barehanded, expanding the world anew. A secret fervor enveloped Heishi throughout this kind of reading. Often, he didn't know why he was moved when he'd first started reading, until after he had reread the text over and over five or six times, when its inner workings would sometimes reveal themselves, towering in the distance, and then, as he searched for clues, would be led forth gradually by a force inside him. The pattern brought forth was both unknown and somewhat familiar, and, with the extension of Heishi's reading experience, would gradually become more familiar. Yet this didn't mean that from now on when he encountered this type of fiction again he could just recognize it at a glance. Instead, in reading this type of novel there was always a trial of stamina and tenacity, where the reader and the text would seesaw back and forth, this being the only way not to be knocked out of the arena of reading by the text. With Uncle Yi's enlightenment, Heishi was coming to understand this high-level reading technique. Uncle Yi always chose this category of writing for him, a kind that would steel his perceptions and reveal before his eyes new forms of ideal blueprints for humanity, one after another. There weren't many such authors in the world, contemporary or classical, so when Uncle Yi selected an author, Heishi would often read the majority or even all of their works.

Heishi experienced deeply in these gloomy days how reading gave him the strength to withstand suffering while also giving him faith in life. He knew Uncle Yi had sustained several heavy blows in love, and even now Uncle Yi was single, but he was still full of interest in life and curious to explore things, and never fell into pessimistic, low spirits. Heishi was so young in comparison, and had only just suffered his first blow—this shouldn't be so terrible. He resolved to take Uncle Yi as his example and always to study the literature he loved so ardently.

With the passing of time, his love for Qiaozi was gradually buried in the bottom of his heart. He felt himself becoming sensitive and enthusiastic again; he reflected that Uncle Yi was also sensitive and enthusiastic. "This is the function of literature," he said to himself, "a function which can show its effect suddenly when things are most difficult for you, giving you fundamental support."

Love had been buried, so now Heishi could regard the relationship soberly. He still believed their relationship had been wonderful, and the best growth experience for both of them. He was also grateful to Qiaozi, who had given him this experience. It was her influence on him that had made his heart gentler than before, more full of warmth toward the world. Beyond this, he felt himself better suited than before for his literary studies. This thought made Heishi think of Uncle Yi again—wasn't Uncle Yi exactly like this?

"It seems that as literary types we're destined to be alone our whole lives," Fei said to Heishi jokingly.

"That's possible. We are a little bit different than most people. But I won't reject any opportunity to access my emotions. We shouldn't be afraid of setbacks," Heishi said.

Heishi even imagined how Uncle Yi would be able to access his emotions, even though he had reached such an advanced age. Who wouldn't love Uncle Yi? Heishi hoped that he'd eventually become someone like him, although he fell far short at the moment. It would transgress the purpose of literature if he were to no longer love this world and the people of this world because he had suffered a setback. The new development in world literature that Heishi and Uncle Yi felt in common included these factors. Heishi took what he'd learned and wrote it into an essay. Through writing, he entered more deeply into physical and spiritual interaction with the authors he had researched, and he found this exciting and intoxicating. "All of love has a worldly aspect, except for people who disregard the body," he said to himself. For example, he thought back on his sexual relationship with Qiaozi: didn't it still shake him, heart and soul? If he hadn't been completely devoted, he would be in a much worse state today. Heishi believed that literature shouldn't be a thing of pure spirit; instead it should tend more toward the human body. When he'd jokingly called Qiaozi a "material girl," it was not entirely negative. It was her persistence and enthusiasm toward the material world that had enlivened his body. He'd only thought her enthusiasm should be somewhat more elevated in its spiritual aspect and also more introspective. Their love, then, had a good foundation; it only lacked something, and as a result couldn't withstand the test of time. Emotions in real life undergo myriad ephemeral changes. It is hard for people to be sure of themselves, although literature can enrich them so that they are able to comprehend and enter into all kinds of attachments. Now, Heishi felt that he understood Qiaozi profoundly.

"I am a little more pessimistic, because I'm older than you and still don't have a lover in real life," Fei said.

"Not having one now doesn't mean not having one in the future. There will be women who like you. Surely a woman who is different than usual, who we haven't imagined."

"I want to have a spectacular love, in real life," Fei said, with a rapt expression.

"This is also a motivation for our pursuit of literature. To not leave behind any regrets in life."

Heishi believed that he hadn't left behind any regrets in his romance with Qiaozi, which was literature's effect working on him. If Qiaozi resented him, that was only because she was so young and still lacked judgment. Now that these events were in the past, in Heishi's recollection the entire process had been beautiful and healthy, even including the conflict between them. How could that be so? Because the two of them had truly been in love and spent themselves entirely. The scenes flashed through his mind of every time Qiaozi had tried to read in order to hold on to his affection, and he was touched enough to cry. He thought that if Qiaozi were to continue her attempts to read, it would prove beneficial for her future children.

One day Li Hai said to Heishi:

"I suppose the reason Qiaozi broke up with you must be because you were on a trip that was like your honeymoon, and my leg injury dragged you back to Meng."

"Even if that was one reason, it also proved that our relationship couldn't withstand a trial."

"Ah, fate is inconstant, and how could a young woman be equal to it? I have a guilty conscience. Not even real brothers would necessarily have done what you did, Heishi."

"Don't moan and groan. Things like this always happen in life. Aren't I all right now?"

"I know you've experienced a very heavy blow. You're a real man now."

"We had differences all along—it wasn't just one single problem," Heishi comforted his friend.

"But if it weren't for my accident, you might be a father now. Qiaozi loved you so much!"

"I'm only thirty-one. There will be other opportunities in the future."

"It's so unfortunate! How could she not love you, Heishi? Oh, the human heart is hard to fathom," Li Hai sighed.

"Yes, only literature is reliable. It never abandons those who love it."

Heishi had by now shaken off being sentimental. He rejoiced: literature would always have its effect at the critical moment. He must take hold of himself, even more firmly, when so much work was arranged before him waiting for him, when he had no cause to be sentimental. Look at Uncle Yi, almost sixty years old and still keeping on. Heishi rarely saw him being sentimental. Uncle Yi's state of mind was always peaceful and clear, and he was ready at any moment to help other people, though he didn't need other people's help. He had the most wonderful demeanor; no one Heishi had met could compare.

Once the calm of Heishi's life had been restored, he spent more than a year working all out. Over this time, he felt that he'd made significant progress, not only in going much deeper with literary research, but also insofar as his worldview was maturing. He hadn't found another girlfriend yet, but he had an attitude of letting nature take its course, because he knew that most women wouldn't necessarily reach his standards, even if they didn't seem so high. He and Fei were both aware of this.

Yet in the meantime something else happened. One day around noon

Heishi went to that Guangdong restaurant to eat and was surprised to see Qiaozi also in line. He tried to avoid her, but it was too late.

"Heishi!" Qiaozi called out to him, unaffectedly.

She no longer spoke to him like an older brother. This explained how things were, so it wasn't necessary for Heishi to avoid her.

"Let's sit together," she said.

"All right," Heishi responded directly.

Heishi glanced at Qiaozi a few times, discovering she was a bit thinner, and the contours of her face slightly more defined than before. She must be twenty-two now.

They sat down at the same table.

"I've been divorced for a year and a half," Qiaozi said.

"Oh. Are you doing OK?"

"I'm fine. I live with my mom."

She still had an unguarded, genuine appearance, only she was more sedate than before.

"Is your mom doing well?"

"Very well. She's even optimistic. I'm influenced by her now and have also become enchanted by books. We discuss the fiction we've read almost every day."

Heishi thought: Qiaozi wasn't bringing up about reading books with him in the past, because she doesn't want to be sentimental. This Qiaozi was no longer the Qiaozi from before. She had shed that unripe look and was more mature.

"Heishi, I've heard that the Pigeon Book Club has added new members. Could I apply to join someday, when I feel ready? I'm not saying right away. I need to make an effort for a while and then see."

"All right. I'll tell Fei and Li Hai about your request. Wait until you feel prepared, and we'll all discuss it together."

"You are still so good, Heishi. I wanted to tell you: I wasn't trying to find you to restart our relationship. In my heart I've been certain for a long time that we can only be friends—forever. I learned many things from you, so now I want to continue to study with you, and at the same time to learn from your friends. Will you help me?"

"I will help you, Qiaozi. I'm really happy to."

When the two of them parted they exchanged their new phone numbers.

"How wonderful," Heishi said to himself. "The universe is growing, and people are maturing."

As for her drawing a dividing line between them, Heishi didn't overthink this. Because here was another Qiaozi, and he didn't know this Qiaozi at all. He did feel immense gratification when he thought of all the emotion he had invested in her before bearing fruit today. And Qiaozi wanted to enter their camp, which was elating. Thinking it over carefully, Heishi also realized that this was a matter of course. She had abundant feelings, her comprehension was strong, and in fact she could become an ideal reader, an appreciator of literature. Qiaozi hadn't been able to understand him before only because of her young age and the simplicity of her experiences—she hadn't suffered any setbacks then. From the perspective of natural instincts, she had so many points of alliance with literature and with himself. So when she did encounter setbacks in life, she had turned to literature. This was the most natural thing ever for Qiaozi. Literature is like this: on its surface it seems not to have any use, but when you suffer heavy blows, or confront choices, its fundamental effect is revealed.

"Why not get back together with Qiaozi? It's right for you to reunite!" Li Hai said to Heishi.

"I wasn't thinking about that. After all we've been estranged—we haven't seen each other for two years. I don't think that we have to get back together. Being friends is better. All of my feelings are directed to who she was before. Besides, it's what she stipulated: she said we can only be friends, forever. I'm not sure of the reason or curious to figure it out."

"Just let nature take its course with you," Fei said. "After 'winding paths through tall mountains,' good people have good rewards. It also proves that literature's power exists everywhere, as a hidden influence."

"I've guessed a little about Qiaozi's thinking. It seems she's very kind-hearted. I feel like I have a duty to help her. But we can't do anything if she really doesn't want to get back together with you. We can help her more with regard to literature," Li Hai said.

"Li Hai is right," Fei nodded repeatedly. "I think she must be an excellent seedling when it comes to reading."

In this way the question was decided. Heishi's friends were both very familiar with the events from two years ago, and Li Hai had surmised the reasons for them, so they both wanted to remedy what had happened.

Heishi told Qiaozi the book club's decision.

Qiaozi thanked everyone over the phone for their acceptance of her. She also asked about which specific novel the book club was reading now, since she wanted to prepare in advance.

Heishi told her the name of the book and asked whether she could buy it. If she couldn't, then she should give him a call.

Qiaozi said that if by any chance she couldn't buy the book, she would borrow it from the library.

After Heishi put down the phone, he noted that Qiaozi was already more independent. He was happy for her—there was truly no comparing the present to the past! Literature precipitated independence.

Heishi really didn't think too much about Qiaozi's reappearance. He felt that on the inside she was no longer the same person, even though she still looked the same. There was a significant contrast, so his passion for her wasn't rekindled. He only held on to a friendly warmth and concern for her.

When Heishi told Uncle Yi about the developments with Qiaozi, he responded:

"I admire you and your book club. Heishi, I predict that the book club will become a beacon within obscure reality. Everything that has happened will continue to exist. Heishi, you have proven this law by taking action, and I feel so proud of you."

Then they went to a bar to celebrate this transition in Heishi's life.

"Although everything now is vague and chaotic," Uncle Yi raised a glass and said, "you and your friends have discovered a path. Continue to take action. Persistence will succeed."

Heishi seemed to have heard a summons from the depths of the Earth. He was so excited, his face reddened.

"I will exert myself even more," he said. "Ever since I formed ties to literature under your guidance, the world's true face has gradually appeared before me. When I think back on the past, I was always bewildered, agitated, and in pain. My personality grew gloomy. In fact that was a distortion of my nature by its outer environment. Looking over the entire process, I see that my romance with Qiaozi wasn't a detour. Our breakup facilitated her growing more mature in all different ways. This is literature helping me in secret to finish taking action. I think this is the beauty of literature. Literature makes everything that happens become sensible and fair. It lets people grow day by day, surrounded by ideals."

Uncle Yi kept nodding, indicating his admiration for Heishi's words. The image of a thin, sheepish young man appeared in his mind. He thought: time passed so quickly and brought such elation! Although he and Heishi weren't related by blood, the affection of their interactions had long ago surpassed a father-son relationship. Heishi's steps were steady. His foundation was solid, and now he had grown into a large young tree . . .

"How do you plan to behave toward Qiaozi?" Uncle Yi asked.

"By leaving aside any personal grudges, and helping her out with literature with all my strength."

"Good!"

On returning to the dormitory, Heishi dove into his literary world, a primordial chaos yet imbued with seduction. He resolved to eventually discover unknown things as they emerged one by one, allowing the contours of that path through the forest to become more distinct with each day. He felt himself becoming more energetic than ever before.

After the call from Heishi, Qiaozi was endlessly moved. She thought of how her former lover, the dear man whom she'd gravely injured, now took no account of their past animosity and was wholeheartedly trying to help her in any way to achieve her goals in life. She was so lucky. Qiaozi had gone to that restaurant on purpose; in fact, she had been there many times before believing that sooner or later she would encounter Heishi. She had decided in advance that from now on she would position their relationship as good friends and not as anything else. This orientation showed that she could never excuse how she had hurt him. In the future, unless Heishi needed her help, which she would give with all her strength, she wouldn't cross this "good friend" dividing line. After making this vow, Qiaozi calmed down and started to implement her plan.

Qiaozi's mother was actually hoping that her daughter and Heishi would reunite. After Qiaozi told her about her plan, her mother fell silent. Her daughter was grown up—she had her reasons. She felt that Qiaozi had started to contemplate life's meaning after the divorce, so she worried less about her than in the past. Also, her daughter's life now seemed to be based on Heishi's model, which was such a welcome change! Qiaozi's mother had always believed that Heishi's path was the only right way. She'd been helpless to deal with Qiaozi's willfulness, though, because her daughter wouldn't listen to her. Now, after Qiaozi had suffered her setback, her mom didn't need to warn her to turn around. Qiaozi would grow up healthily now no matter what her relationship with Heishi was like in the future. Qiaozi's mother discussed literature with her at home, heartened at her daughter's continual improvement. She would have thoughts like this: if Qiaozi hadn't met Heishi at twenty, then today they would be such a good match. Unfortunately fate always seems to be toying with people.

"Mom, I won't get married, I will keep you company and help your health improve. We'll study literature together, exercise together, and have fulfilling lives," Qiaozi said.

"You'll still get married someday. You can't go against the laws of nature."

"Then I need to wait until after Heishi has found a lover. I owe him that much. I want to see him attain happiness. He wasn't happy with me, which shows that he and I weren't right for each other."

Her mother, after reflection, understood Qiaozi's choice and was touched by her daughter's kindness. She sounded out to herself: let nature take its course; everything will be settled.

Qiaozi's mother happened to have in her long-standing collection the exact book the Pigeon Book Club was discussing.

"Wonderful, Mom, we'll discuss it first at home. That will boost my confidence," Qiaozi said.

The novel's title was *XX XX XX*. The book wasn't too thick, but Qiaozi spent over a week finishing it the first time. It baffled her, as if something were keeping her outside of the novel. She was not resigned, though.

"Heishi used to read books in the dormitory every day, but I didn't know what about the books moved him so much. He was enchanted, so even I could faintly feel some strong emotion flowing between him and the books. Mom, I think maybe this is the key: surely there is something, or a kind of state, contained within the words and in between the lines, that exists only for those in the know who have discovered it. My skills aren't there yet—I need to intensify my efforts."

Qiaozi was somewhat agitated. She exerted herself, reading and note-taking until late at night . . .

Her mom was delighted, since she had never seen her daughter studying so hard before, even when she'd gone to college. She'd treated homework then like it was a game.

When Qiaozi had read the novel for three weeks, she could speak about a few of her impressions.

"There's an enormous yearning for communication: every character tries to enter the soul of their counterpart, imitates them, hopes to speak for them; while their counterpart also studies that character's soul, doing the same thing. The substance of this exchange becomes more and more intricate and rich. It isn't a simple one-directional passing of messages, and so most readers would recoil from this kind of scene. That's because of not being in the habit of going deeper into things, and also because our communications usually remain on the surface—right? Heishi has higher standards for communication, because of the environment his parents created when he was little; he became sensitive, so when he grew up he started to research literature. Heishi's understanding of me went much deeper than my self-understanding and experience, but I was a fool then, while he kept patiently waiting for me to grow up. When I read this book, I think back on those events from the past. I only now understand that literature is about learning the communication of emotion."

Qiaozi's mother was very excited, since her daughter's words also awakened her memories. She thought: it would have been so much better if I had guided Qiaozi onto the path of literature sooner! She regretted this to the point of tears.

"Mom, don't be sad. I'm expanding my mind now, and in the future I will surely have good fortune. I'm anxious to read even more books, to keep pace with the progress of the Pigeon Book Club."

"I'm not worried. You're taking life seriously now, so I can feel at ease."

Qiaozi studied the novel intently and wrote out long notes on her reading all the time until she went to the Pigeon Book Club. Her mother was both comforted and surprised by reading her notes: Qiaozi had real potential! Her daughter was also much gentler to her, and she no longer saw her being obstinate like before.

"Qiaozi, should I come meet you?" Heishi asked over the phone.

"No need to. I'm familiar with the location."

"Are you feeling prepared?"

"I can't say well-prepared, because I'm only at an initial stage of appreciation. This is a magnificent novel."

"Excellent, Qiaozi! You are progressing at incredible speed."

"Thanks to you."

Li Hai had been making ongoing preparations because Qiaozi was going to come to the book club. He wanted to try as much as possible to help this former girlfriend of Heishi's, whom he'd never met. He'd deduced how Qiaozi had only recognized Heishi's valuable qualities after she suffered a setback and then felt intense self-reproach. Believing that she could no longer bring Heishi happiness, she'd finally set this tone for their relationship going forward. Heishi seemed not to be thinking too much about their relationship. For him, the love from more than two years ago had died, and he wasn't familiar with this Qiaozi who now appeared with a new face; he really was taking her to be a good friend. To have a dead love come back to life could happen only if there was some exceptional turning point. Li Hai wanted to find a turning point like that in the coming days.

When Li Hai thought of those nights Heishi had taken care of him at the hospital, he couldn't help but bemoan how Heishi's care that exceeded brotherly love led to the heavy blow when his girlfriend left him because of misunderstanding. In his estimation, Qiaozi still loved Heishi deeply, but she couldn't forgive herself, so she wouldn't admit to her love for him. She was coming to the book club to study in order to elevate herself, but also as a way of apologizing to Heishi, who would be happy after seeing her progress. No matter how, Li Hai would act as circumstances required and do everything he could to make Heishi's love for Qiaozi rekindle from ashes. This was, of course, Li Hai's one-sided wish—he hoped to heaven for an opportunity to let his dream come true.

Li Hai had very minute perceptions of the things and people in his life, and was also good at deduction. He'd grown intensely enchanted with literature early on and then gotten to know Fei before founding the Pigeon Book Club with him and Heishi. He was two years younger than Heishi but understood human nature as thoroughly and profoundly as he did. Li Hai thought for a long time about Qiaozi's coming to the book club and then asked Heishi for her phone number, volunteering to meet her. Heishi knew what his old friend had in mind and was touched. He thought: Qiaozi joining this family of the book club was an extremely good thing, whether for her or for the book club itself. Besides, this would enhance their literary strength within Meng. He knew not to look down on Qiaozi's ability, once she got started.

Li Hai had prepared two books he thought Qiaozi should read, intending to give them to her on the day she came to the book club. He planned to establish a close relationship with her, like an older brother. He told himself from time to time: "As long as Heishi is single, I can't be at peace. I will inscribe his marriage on my heart."

Li Hai went to the bus station after making arrangements over the phone with Qiaozi.

He waited at the bus stop holding the two books. The bus arrived, and Qiaozi walked toward him with a smile all over her face.

Looking at the young woman, Li Hai thought to himself: Qiaozi has such a cheerful nature!

"Li Hai, you can look after me. My standards aren't high enough yet," she said.

"I am here to look out for you. Not because of standards, but because you are the youngest member of the book club."

"That's reassuring. Just a moment ago on the bus I was still nervous. What are those books you're holding?"

"I chose these two books as a gift for you. It's my own selection: I think they are must-reads."

"You're really great, Li Hai."

"Heishi and I are closer than brothers. If you have any difficulty whatever you can come find me."

As the two of them walked into the small alleyway, Qiaozi thought to herself: could Heishi have asked him to come meet me? She was affected by all kinds of various feelings. Yet Li Hai impressed her as very trustworthy. As Qiaozi thought about making a new friend, her soul shone with rising confidence. She asked Li Hai what bookstores these were beside them. He told her that the majority were used bookstores where you could sometimes also buy rare collectible books. He added that he liked to collect antique bamboo paper thread-bound editions, not for research, but purely in order to appreciate them, to smell the paper. "In those distant times, people treasured books like these, which sends me into reveries," he said.

Qiaozi had the fantasy that within the short twenty-minute walk to the book club she and Li Hai had already become old friends. She felt that this friend was different than Heishi on the outside, but the two men had similar aspects to their souls. "I can treat him as Heishi at the book club," she decided.

The other four hadn't arrived yet when Qiaozi and Li Hai entered. Li Hai started to brew tea on the hot plate, so she rinsed the teacups and teapot, then placed the tea leaves inside.

"Qiaozi, you're so pretty. I haven't gotten to know young women as pretty as you before," Li Hai said.

"I think you're great, too. You have a manly quality," Qiaozi said.

After a while the other members arrived. They all greeted one another.

Li Hai noticed that Qiaozi's gaze pausing on Heishi was always fleeting, sweeping past him. "It's like she's in a dream," he thought. Heishi and Li Hai sat down beside Qiaozi.

Everyone else sat down and drank tea while they discussed the book *XX XX XX*.

"Heishi, you speak first," Fei said, looking at him.

"I've often consider the question of communication in this novel. There is communication between two people; communication between the reader and the text; and the communication of the author through the text with the reader. Besides this there is also the communication of the reader with the communication of the author with themself; the communication at this time and at that time; and so on. In the midst of all this activity: is the most important element a common platform, or is it superb technique?"

"Qiaozi, we want to hear your response to this question," Fei looked next at her.

"I think it must be an emotional platform that is more important," Qiaozi said, her face flushing. "If two people who don't know each other are compared with a couple in love, the two strangers will definitely have more difficulty communicating, no matter what training they've received or whether they have superb technique." After Qiaozi finished she felt everyone encouraging her with their eyes, so she supplemented what she'd said: "Technique is a factor that has its effect then and there; the platform is built up over long periods of life experience. There's a saying that expresses how something 'can only be known, not conveyed in words.' I think the book emphasizes what is happening behind its descriptions, so it attracts me as a reader. Even though I don't completely understand, I am willing to try to keep reading."

"It seems Qiaozi has countless possibilities before her, even though she's young," Fei said.

"Although literary expression must emphasize technique," Yan said next. "The novel often uses the ambiguity of language to depict two kinds of mutually conflicting but also symbiotic things. Superb technique can often break the barriers of time and space, fusing the expression of entirely different emotions, allowing one's understanding to burst into even deeper levels and broader domains. When we are reading we should also train ourselves in the skills of being circumspect, generous, and able to break through. Not merely the skill of surface logic."

Qiaozi looked at Yan, full of admiration for the novelty of this speech. She all at once sensed the unusual atmosphere of the book club. She said quietly in Li Hai's ear: "You speak."

"Yan is right," Li Hai said. "When we communicate we must go deeper, even deeper, even beyond transforming ourselves into the other person or thing, so that after we enter into them we also come back out and transform them into ourselves. Think about how difficult this is. I recently started to practice listening, hoping to find clues by differentiating all kinds of tones and scales. The key, perhaps, is doing away with the fixed models, patiently catching hold, heightening our emotions, and opening up our own way through. If someone is immersed for a long time in a certain emotion, they can form patterns from their thoughts. The type of novels we are reading all have these kinds of patterns."

Qiaozi had studied shorthand and recorded Li Hai and Yan's words in a small notebook, delighting them so that they praised her loudly as the soul of the book club.

Next Fei also wanted Yang to make a statement.

"I especially admire Li Hai's method," she said. "I'm trying to operate with a similar method. I often go on work trips all over the place, and every time I reach somewhere I have a profound level of communication with my surrounding environment. I've trained my sense of smell, hoping to be able to smell cooking smoke or the fragrance of flowers and fruits in the mountains from a hundred kilometers away. No matter where I am, there are two kinds of smells—the cooking of farm households or rice straw in the sunlight—that can always place me within colorful patterns. At the beginning of this year, I climbed up a desolate hillside in order to gather these two smells together. As the scorching sun stood in the sky, a few golden pheasants moved around in the shrubs at the bottom of the slope. I sat down on a rock, concentrating my emotions, and those two familiar smells immediately floated over to me. They hovered around where I was all afternoon. Naturally, there are also patterns inside of the smells. I like to go on work trips to gorgeous regions where there are all kinds of thick smells."

At this moment Fei's face overflowed into a smile as he said that each member's speech had been extremely beautiful, all delving into the literary work. Speaking for himself, his impressions of the novel were that he enjoyed it, but it also left him agitated. He liked the beauty of its rich layers and observing their unfolding without turning his eyes away; at the same time, he worried about his own abilities: could he be missing something? Could he be reaching limits where he could go no deeper? When someone's words manifested two meanings, was there a third or even fourth kind of latent meaning? Could that latent meaning be the most beautiful, the most essential?

Once Fei finished speaking, everyone started to laugh, saying that reading literary works was seeking out hardship for oneself. Why read? Because the misery was also sweet.

Qiaozi laughed in an uninhibited way because she liked the atmosphere of the book club so much. She felt a pronounced interest in each person there, including Heishi—since they hadn't been in contact for a long time now.

Heishi was happy to see Qiaozi so carefree. Initially he'd been worried that she would feel reserved. These days he really needed to see her with new eyes.

Li Hai felt a certain optimism about Qiaozi and Heishi's relationship. He thought that if Qiaozi continued to be in touch with Heishi through the book club, their memories of the past would eventually revive. They were walking the same path, one where no obstacles existed. Li Hai thought the initiative lay with Qiaozi. Her temperament was lively and bright, and her thinking had taken a turn, so Heishi would be moved by her. Li Hai observed scrupulously, combing through all kinds of possibilities in his mind, in the hope that he could urge Qiaozi someday to change her mind. He knew that he was the only one who was trying to make this happen, since he could tell that Heishi wasn't interested for now. By nature Heishi was the kind of person who always looks ahead; he was resolute and able to endure suffering. After disappointment in love, he, like Qiaozi, had become a different person—a more strongly rational man. If Qiaozi didn't launch an emotional offensive at him, Heishi would only see Qiaozi as a good friend, a dear one. But how to make Qiaozi go on the offensive—this would be fairly difficult. Li Hai decided to take action step by step. First of all, he would make Qiaozi trust him completely.

It seemed natural enough that when it was time to go home Li Hai again accompanied Qiaozi. Heishi was suddenly nowhere to be seen and had probably left a little early.

"Qiaozi, what were your impressions of this evening's gathering?"

"It was marvelous! I don't even know how to praise how wonderful it was. You three are remarkable. I am so lucky to witness and participate in the most beautiful thing in the world. I'm impatient for the next meeting."

"Yes, we are striding together into a new era."

Qiaozi's mother was still awake when she returned home. Qiaozi excitedly described to her the book club's mystical and enthusiastic atmosphere, along with how her companions had enlightened her, how she had gained confidence from their affirmation . . . "It's hard to tell you everything all at once. For the first time in my life I experienced the fascination of literature," she said in sum. She also mentioned Heishi's speech, saying that his was exceptionally profound and also had a broad scope.

"On my way home Li Hai saw me to the bus."

"Oh, did Heishi tell him to look after you?" her mother asked.

"I don't know. I think it's more likely that Li Hai wants to act as go-between for me and Heishi. He's attentive, and I like him, but he won't be successful at playing matchmaker."

"Anyway, the members of the book club are all the best people. You should learn from them. I'm completely at ease."

Qiaozi lay on her bed for a long time, thoughts coming rapidly, unable to fall asleep. Scene after scene from the Pigeon Book Club replayed in her mind. Though she couldn't yet understand everything the members said, she was already affected by the significance of that entire atmosphere. Now she felt the pressing need to make an effort at advanced studies in literature, striving in the future to become a true literary person like Heishi or Li Hai. She felt deeply how literature could bring people immense happiness, could make everyone become kind at heart . . . She saw the light ahead, and her entire body and mind were being drawn to the light. That beautiful state was the world of Heishi and his companions. It was now changing the object of Qiaozi's seeking.

Heishi had slipped away from the book club a little early. He thought back over the other members' statements at the gathering, thinking that this truly was beautiful revelry. Being able to interpret an obscure, profound novel to this extent, to communicate to each other the feeling of the interpretation—it was truly a miraculous scene. The animated mood of the book club infected him. Especially with Qiaozi joining the group, which added to his elation. He'd comprehended so deeply every sentence that she said, knowing that these words came from her life experience and reflections. She was so young, while maturing so fast, as must be characteristic of a transformative era.

Heishi also knew Li Hai's intentions for him and Qiaozi and was touched. Yet his intuition told him that love is a mysterious emotion for which there are often no rules to follow. He had met Qiaozi at a certain moment in his life, they had loved each other, and then broken up; they both felt that they had been carved into each other's bones and inscribed on each other's hearts, because they had spent themselves to the full. This didn't mean that their dead love could come back to life. Two years had passed since then, during which all kinds of factors would have changed. People also change, even if things remain the same. He and Qiaozi had transformed in the meantime. He didn't know whether this was the starting point for why she had concluded that their relationship would be as friends. As for himself, he didn't know whether he would choose this transformed Qiaozi again after more than two years. On the whole, he felt toward her an affection that brought him joy. This emotion was similar to Uncle Yi's present feelings for Heishi's mother. Heishi thought: it's the goodness of literature. Literature had brought him and Qiaozi together again, when there was no need to worry about being hurt, only boundless gratitude.

Heishi didn't know if he would meet other women afterward, or what his choices about a partner would be like if he did. He only knew that their relationship had gone through intricate shifts before settling into a new form now that Qiaozi had taken the initiative to draw a boundary line. He was willing to obey her will and felt they would both be comfortable with this relationship.

He returned to his dormitory. He had kept the same unit from when he and Qiaozi had been in love, where so many passionate scenes had taken place. Yet Heishi wasn't a bit sentimental. He was impatient to finish his literary essay, feeling that this was a matter of life and death. His pulse beat in unison with the pulse of the times; he deeply felt the heavy responsibility on his shoulders.

After writing his essay and going to bed, Heishi thought once again of how mysterious and subtle love was. He reflected on how it was the same as literary inspiration—something that could be experienced, but not there for the asking. Maybe in Li Hai's view, the obstacles were already removed, and Qiaozi was as pretty as before, so reuniting them shouldn't be a big problem. But Heishi recalled his recent meeting with Qiaozi, and how it hadn't produced that feeling of electric shock; there had been only gladness and warmth. Qiaozi was right: he would see her as his younger sister in the future.

Heishi didn't intend to seek out women. "Obey the natural course," he thought. He was busy and afraid of wasting time. He was buried in his interests, making progress every day.

Qiaozi had a dream. She came to a large, empty room. Outside, it was apparently late at night, and only a small part of the room was illuminated by a lamp. The place lit by lamplight had a table and a chair. Someone had told her before she arrived that she needed to wait here for someone. She sat down, watching the door nervously.

In a while the sound of talking came from the hallway, the voices of two familiar men.

Li Hai entered first with Heishi close behind him. Qiaozi's heart jumped for joy.

The two men sat down beside Qiaozi, both energetically discussing something. Suddenly Li Hai stopped and turned toward her, lowering his voice to say:

"Heishi will be staying in the guestroom next door tonight."

Qiaozi, feeling that the intention of his words was obvious, answered:

"I like Heishi more than anyone else, but I don't want to impose myself on him. My greatest wish is to watch from the side as he attains true happiness."

Heishi didn't hear, because she spoke nearly in a whisper. He was looking at something through the window.

"Why are you giving up, since you love him, and it's not impossible that he could love you?" Li Hai asked her.

"Because, because I cannot let him be hurt again. That would be the death of me."

"So you have no faith in yourself," Li Hai sighed.

Qiaozi tried to explain herself, but her words were confused, and the more anxious she grew, the more jumbled they became.

She raised her head to discover Heishi was no longer there. She sighed with relief, at the same time feeling disappointed. She looked again, and Li Hai was no longer there. The familiar male voices came from the hallway again, voices that for her were filled with seduction. Her mind went blank.

Qiaozi woke up in the middle of the night and told herself: "Fortunately it was a dream. I cannot take that step, a thousand million times over." From Heishi's behavior on that evening, she could tell that his feelings had long ago quieted down. Li Hai was well-intentioned, but he didn't understand the subtle change in Heishi's emotions like she did. Qiaozi resolved only to meet with Heishi in dreams from now on.

She felt that she didn't lack faith in herself—one might say that her self-confidence was increasing like never before. At the same time, though, she was no longer the same Qiaozi. This new Qiaozi would think everything over repeatedly before taking action, and she had her own integrity, in the way that characters in fiction have a mechanism that restricts them.

Still, recalling her dream carefully, she'd enjoyed it: hearing his voice, seeing his profile, being in the same room as him . . . These things in the dream had made Qiaozi flush. Going deeper into analysis, she also felt that these were the embers of past emotions, and what the dream pointed toward wasn't today's Heishi. Just let her have dreams, then. It didn't matter, now that this sentimental kind of dream could no longer affect her: she would still do what she should during the daytime. Let the gentle, dying flames be buried in the deepest, deepest layer. Qiaozi wanted to be like Heishi, to be someone whose personality had layers.

"Qiaozi, I think you have really grown up," her mother said.

"I don't have time to blame myself—I need to hurry. It only took going to the book club once to feel this way. My friends all charge ahead, so I must redouble my efforts or be left behind."

"Was Heishi calm?"

"He could always hold back his excitement before, and now he is more calm than ever. I long for someone to fall in love with him soon. I think that there are not many opportunities, because he is so lofty and steadfast. Ah."

Her mother listened and started to smile, saying that Qiaozi seemed increasingly able to take other people into consideration.

On Li Hai's day off he came over to Qiaozi's house, making a very good impression on her mother, who said that he had a moral character like Heishi's and was a young man who could put people at ease.

Li Hai discussed with Qiaozi the literary works that both of them had read. She felt that his reading perspective was astounding and original.

"Heavens, are you listening to books?" she said.

"You could say so. When I was little I lived with my maternal grandmother in the mountains, and sometimes, when my grandma had to go out, I would be by myself at home. I imitated all kinds of birdcalls, then later several species of birds would respond to me. I could distinguish each bird's call. My communication with them lasted over a year."

"Then what did you hear at the book club?" Qiaozi asked curiously.

"I heard the voice of your heart. Once you opened your mouth, I heard your longing. But that longing is inhibited, in a way that makes you touching."

"Don't you think this kind of inhibition is necessary?"

"Under certain circumstances. In my view it's hard to say now; it will take waiting for a time. If a bird suddenly didn't communicate with me, I wouldn't get discouraged. I opened up the doors of my heart and made birdcalls over and over. Later on it would respond to me again. We can train our ears to perceive from indistinct chirping the early stages of longing's hesitation and uncertainty, then continue to make signals according to these indications, and in this way achieve communication."

"What you are referring to is the 'meaning beyond words,' something that exists in fiction and in life."

"Feeling out the laws of deep layers of emotion often depends on the sense of hearing. Patience is also very important. With the exceptionally complex emotion of love, we can simply say that there are no rules to be followed. Yet people can train their sense of hearing."

"You're right, there are no rules. My way of judging is to mobilize my whole body's experience, which might be similar to what you call a sense of hearing. Then I reach a conclusion: to have is to have, not to have is not to have. After I reach this conclusion I feel a transient peace of mind," Qiaozi said thoughtfully.

"Yet this conclusion is not one that can be reached with a single try. To approach those things in the dark depths requires patience along with trying to create the conditions that let them emerge."

"Oh, Li Hai, I like your method very much. I can make attempts over and over in books and in life. I never trained myself before, so I was a fool."

After Li Hai left, Qiaozi's mother said to her:

"What a great young man, so steady and attentive, and able to see into people's hearts and matters of the world. With his help, you could grow wings and soar."

"He is trying to bring me and Heishi back together. I won't let him move me, but I've become terribly interested in his experiences. The world of literary people is enriching. What must Li Hai's environment have been like when he was little?"

Qiaozi slipped into thought. She began to imagine the mysteries that were in books and in life. She felt that the mysteries could be solved if only she kept studying. She also sensed how Li Hai was stirring up her impulse for this kind of riddle-solving at an important juncture.

After a time, Qiaozi felt a potential change in her emotional world quietly taking place. She no longer tired herself out with sorrow. Her attention was also no longer directed toward remembering the past; instead it was greatly widened. Some new thoughts, new feelings continuously poured into her. She sensed that her world was dividing, continuously producing unique things that often surprised her with pleasure.

"Li Hai, that state you experienced when you were little seems truly miraculous. I hope that someday I can go with you to your hometown in the mountains for a few days to observe it with you," Qiaozi said, looking at him.

"Haha, there may be opportunities. I haven't been back for a long time. But wherever I go, I always carry my little wooden hut with me, and those great mountains, and those ancient trees. These must be what compose my patterns."

"What is your job?"

"I'm a city planner."

"Oh, what a beautiful profession."

"It's a profession that also trains my hearing. In the early morning, or at night, I like to stand on the main streets of the city and listen closely to the sounds made by the landscapes we have designed. Such times are really enjoyable."

"I want to learn from you how to listen, too. There are many things that on the surface appear to be one way but are another way inside, with another appearance that the eye cannot see. But no matter what it appears to be, traces will always show, and we can use our sense organs or skin to capture them, can't we? This is the skill I want to learn from you. You've pointed out a new universe to me. I've been pondering so often that world from when you were young. After thinking about it for a long time, patterns appear in my mind—but they are vague, in comparison to yours."

Qiaozi asked Li Hai whether he studied literary theory, too. Li Hai answered that he had, because theory was also constituted by the senses of hearing and of touch. Between them there were numerous communications and many passageways of exchange.

Then she exclaimed: the world was so wondrous. She added that people have no reason for sorrow when their understanding reaches this level. Even wounds could become gifts.

"My mind turns brighter after every time I talk with him," she thought.

Li Hai saw Qiaozi's eyes sparkling with radiance, and thought to himself that he could help her, even if he weren't able to bring her and Heishi back together. To help her was to help Heishi. As for himself, talking with Qiaozi made him cheerful and enlightened him every time. Because, while he enlightened her, he gained new inspiration. "It's good to be able to improve together," he thought.

These days, when Li Hai visited Qiaozi, her mother became very excited. She thought that Li Hai was the most sincere type of young man, and she liked him in just the way she had liked Heishi. She had always been fond of literature, but before this she had taken literature to be an individual accomplishment and never imagined using it to transform life. For this reason, she had not done all she could to bring Qiaozi into the world of literature. Once she'd realized, it was already too late. In the present situation, though, it didn't count as too late. Qiaozi had in the end followed a certain summons from within her soul and turned toward literature. This was a credit to how Heishi had enlightened Qiaozi before and to how Li Hai was helping her now. She felt that she hadn't done enough as a mother.

Mother and daughter started to talk about this type of thing expectantly.

"You are still so lucky, Qiaozi."

"Yes."

Qiaozi thought that all of her problems would be resolved if only she waited patiently. She believed that Li Hai was giving her confidence and wisdom in this turning toward literature of a high quality. The oblivious anxiety from before had left her. Her agitation at the moment was benign, and it could be dispelled by her forging ahead.

Time went very quickly, and another two years passed. Heishi achieved significant success in the literary field. The shared topics he and Uncle Yi were researching had already been drafted in initial outline and contour, while their bold conception was in the process of careful verification, step by step.

An incident took place when Heishi and Uncle Yi were discussing literature at the coffee shop.

The door of the coffee shop stood open, but there were no customers in the central room. From where Heishi and Uncle Yi were sitting, they could see a large part of that room, but other customers couldn't see them. Heishi noticed the figure of a familiar-looking woman coming through the door with a companion. He immediately remembered her name.

"It's Xiao Sang," he said.

Uncle Yi looked over at the women coming in from outside and added: "It is Xiao Sang. She and her friend are here to relax."

"She was my classmate. How do you know her?"

"She lives above me and is one of my young friends. She has an ardent love of literature and high standards. We've known each other over a decade." Uncle Yi spoke up to here and then looked as though he were thinking about something.

"So that's how. I can remember that during college she was always carrying a novel around campus."

"Would you like to be friends with her? She's the most accomplished young woman. Her desire to improve herself is more or less the same as yours, and she's highly talented. Xiao Sang has enlightened me."

Heishi stared at the silhouette of the women outside, then brought his eyes back to Uncle Yi.

"Is there anything else to say, since you believe this about her and me? When we were at college, Xiao Sang was good-natured, gentle, and had a lot of friends. I admired her, but didn't dare to form a deeper connection. I felt a little inferior back then."

"You and Xiao Sang will definitely have a lot to talk about. Also, going by my observations, she hasn't found a boyfriend yet. Shall I just introduce her?"

"No, don't, Uncle Yi! It would be awkward to be introduced like this. Let me wait for an opportunity."

"You're too cautious about women. Women like Xiao Sang are rare—don't miss this chance."

Heishi thought: Uncle Yi is brimming with enthusiasm, so Xiao Sang must be no ordinary woman.

Then the lights in the central room went dark. Heishi couldn't see Xiao Sang or her friend.

"You should address this part of your personal life. Your mother must be anxious. Always waiting for nothing. Besides, it's a shame for young people not to have romance."

"OK, Uncle Yi, I will go after her."

"Good. I always thought you might make things up with Qiaozi, so I hadn't introduced Xiao Sang."

"Qiaozi and I weren't fated to be in the end. She's become very loveable and mature, so she must have many suitors now. It makes me happy to think about this."

"Does Xiao Sang have family in Meng?" Heishi also asked.

"No. It makes me worry about her. She isn't anxious herself; in the same way as you, she considers literature to be the matter of first importance, so she's taking her time. But after all, she's already reached this age . . ."

Heishi took note of how Uncle Yi's agitation overflowed into his words and gestures, just as though he were speaking about his own daughter.

"Uncle Yi, don't worry. I have such a good impression of her. I'll give it a try."

Uncle Yi looked very glad to hear Heishi say this.

Afterward the two men stood up and left through the side door of the coffee shop.

Heishi didn't pursue Xiao Sang immediately, but only after some time had passed.

Not long after this conversation with Uncle Yi, Heishi attended the Pigeon Book Club gathering.

As Qiaozi and Li Hai discussed this meeting afterward, Li Hai said:

"Heishi looked distracted. I think a deep inner layer of his emotions has been activated. I heard some movements at this meeting. We'll have to wait to know definitely what has brought this out in him."

Qiaozi listened to Li Hai's verdict and grew excited, saying:

"Your intuitions are always reliable. I've been wishing for Heishi to access his feelings, and for him to solve the greatest issue of his life. He deserves happiness more than anyone."

"Mm-hmm, I've wanted this just as much as you have."

"Li Hai, how long have we known each other?" Qiaozi asked him.

"More than two years."

"The time has flown by. I feel that in these two years I've changed into a different person. Heishi will have also transformed. If one were to say that I still feel love for him, that is all in memories and has nothing to do with today's Heishi, right? Love cannot emerge now, when our backdrops and our foundations have shifted so much. Love, as described in books, is the delicate result of specific times and certain conditions."

This conversation took place in the living room of Qiaozi's home. While she was speaking she had walked over to where Li Hai was sitting and sat down close to him. She noticed that he was a little tense, but she didn't move away.

"You're becoming more extreme," Li Hai said, joking. "Now you can also hear numerous voices."

"Yes. For example, the voice inside of you. I heard it first, before you did."

"That's normal. Oh, Heishi, Heishi . . . ," Li Hai sighed.

"We may have a chance to help him."

"We should. Everything is confused now."

"Isn't that the rule of this kind of thing? To take by surprise?" Qiaozi said, smiling.

"You are more extreme than I am now. I'm willing to admit defeat." Li Hai had a bewildered expression.

"It won't bring catastrophe; it can only bring people what they want."

Qiaozi took tight hold of Li Hai's large hand as she spoke, feeling its warmth.

"Oh, Qiaozi, Qiaozi . . . ," Li Hai sighed again.

"Let's treat everything that happens optimistically. Will you take me to your hometown?"

Li Hai looked into Qiaozi's eyes and nodded, with a reddening face. She jumped up cheerfully and poured him more tea. She called to her mother in one of the inner rooms.

"Mom, Li Hai and I are planning a trip to his hometown. Inspiration is everywhere there, and people seem to have returned to a primeval world."

"Good, good! Hurry and go soon," Qiaozi's mother said.

As Qiaozi was seeing Li Hai out, she asked him:

"I haven't kidnapped you, have I?"

"No, not at all. Your sense of hearing is much sharper than mine now, so you can make quick decisions when things come up. I should listen to you now. You are my guiding light."

"This city that you and your colleagues designed is filled with birdsong. I stand on the main streets at night and hear the birds. I grow excited and think: this is Li Hai's city. Don't you feel happy?"

"The same happiness as yours."

Qiaozi went back inside, where her mother said to her:

"Very good."

"You've noticed?"

"I figured it out a long time ago. You are more charming than ever."

Li Hai returned to his home in a state of confusion. Actually, for a long time now, a vague, alarming feeling had arisen in the deepest part of his heart. Before this he'd always suppressed the emotion through willpower. As his association with Qiaozi had deepened, he'd felt that the young woman was unconsciously coming to occupy the center of his life—a situation that wasn't part of Li Hai's plan. Qiaozi simply disregarded his plan. She was daring and independent, and she could make the relationship between them feel very natural. Recently, even though he had a vague sense that something was changing in their friendship, he'd been unwilling to think about it much.

Yet today, when Li Hai had told Qiaozi about Heishi's possible attachment to someone, she had unexpectedly, implicitly, expressed her feelings for him. Faced with her genuineness, he couldn't pretend to be naive. It was she who'd illuminated the emotions inside of him: he had fallen uncontrollably in love with her. Hadn't he seen her many times in his dreams? Wasn't he anxiously searching for her in those dreams? Li Hai's intention had been through helping her to help Heishi. But the possibility of a solution for Heishi was ushered in now . . . The affairs of this world are strangely prone to error. "Without meaning to plant a tree you find shade grown there," as the saying went. Was this cause for lament or rejoicing?

That evening, when Li Hai was taking notes on his reading, his telephone rang. It was Heishi.

"I'm planning in the near future to bring a book friend to the Pigeon Book Club. She's also been a student of Uncle Yi for many years, and her standards are higher than mine. She's a former college classmate. Her name is Xiao Sang."

"Terrific! Don't worry, I will undertake this myself!"

"What will you undertake yourself? The first line isn't even written yet. It's just an old classmate I haven't seen in more than a decade, who I intend to pursue."

"Go ahead, go ahead and bring her to the book club—everything will be successful. I have a premonition that this Ms. Xiao Sang is no ordinary woman. Of course, our Heishi is hardly inferior, haha . . . Anything that happens in the book club will have a good outcome."

"Thank you, Li Hai. Nothing is definite yet."

"Isn't that so for all emotional matters? You need to have confidence."

Putting down the phone, Li Hai walked excitedly back and forth across his room.

Later he called Qiaozi to tell her.

"Oh, Li Hai, today is the happiest day for me ever! I only wish Xiao Sang had come sooner!"

"I never imagined that our efforts would bring about this result!" Li Hai said.

"This is terrific! Don't you think so, too?"

"Yes, of course. I am the one benefiting the most."

Li Hai took a cold shower, trying to clear his head. He'd felt almost frenzied all day today.

He lay in the dark thinking about Heishi's wonderful future. It really did seem that good people had good rewards. There was all possibility of success, since she was coming to participate in the book club. Heishi was so charming—especially at the book club. It wasn't ordinary fascination. Qiaozi still couldn't forget her past romance with him, even after years of separation. No matter how, Xiao Sang would be moved by Heishi. Li Hai had been able to hear that Heishi was moved by true feelings this time.

After thinking over Heishi's situation, Li Hai thought of Qiaozi: her eyes that could speak, her smiling expression, her hands, her pleasant scent, her reserved declaration—he was overcome with infatuation. He wanted to take Qiaozi to his hometown right away. But no, he needed for Heishi's relationship to be settled first. Only then would he have peace of mind.

Qiaozi couldn't help but give Li Hai another call two days before the book club was going to gather, arranging to meet him at a teahouse near her home. There were many things to share between them.

She arrived at the teahouse early, never thinking that Li Hai would also hurry in at the same time.

"Qiaozi, I was impatient to see you. I'm so excited."

"I am, too," Qiaozi said in a quiet voice.

They sat close together in the booth. Li Hai kept hold of Qiaozi's hand, which made her feel both incredibly comfortable and moved.

"We haven't taken this step on purpose, but affection has its own rules outside of the mind's control," Li Hai said. "May I kiss you?"

Qiaozi nodded.

The two of them kissed deeply, drunkenly. Then Li Hai kissed her neck.

Qiaozi gasped:

"Li Hai, Li Hai, you are a flame. We've waited too long . . . I can give my mom a call, I'll tell her this evening I'll be going to your place."

Qiaozi called her mother. They paid the bill, without drinking their tea, and called a taxi to rush straight to Li Hai's apartment. On the way Qiaozi seemed to be drawn into a dream by Li Hai. He held her tight.

She spent an incomparable night of pleasure at his home. She hadn't expected that the passions she'd excited in him would be this vigorous, lasting, and yet so gentle. Qiaozi thought she would be addicted to sex with Li Hai from now on . . . She opened herself up the entire night, letting her lover explore every part of her body many times. While she also explored his. She told herself: "That page with Heishi has finally turned." She heard her lover say:

"Heishi is my brother—you will marry his brother."

"I love you so much, Li Hai, as if we were fated in a past life. My mother will be so happy."

"I haven't seen my mother since I was little. Your mother will be my mother. I love her. The three of us will live together."

Qiaozi wanted to cry, but when she opened her mouth the crying didn't come; she also wanted to laugh, and did so.

"I will treat you like you treat me," she said.

Qiaozi returned home after getting off work. She found her mom in an especially good mood.

"Mom, your health has been a little poorer these past few years. I'm planning for the three of us to live together."

"Doesn't Li Hai have an opinion about this?"

"He was the one who brought it up. He loves you."

"I also love him as a son-in-law. From the first day he came here I imagined you marrying him."

"Mom, you're so good."

Bringing Xiao Sang to the Pigeon Book Club was a turning point in Heishi's years of bachelorhood. Without knowing why, he had a lingering delusion as if he and Xiao Sang had been in frequent contact all along instead of having been separated for more than a decade. Once they met again, he felt that they were connected. Was this because of Uncle Yi? Heishi didn't know. But at the same time, he deeply felt that Xiao Sang's affectionate attachment to Uncle Yi was as profound as his own, perhaps even more so . . . Think about it: so many years of morning and nighttime companionship, with shared aspirations . . . Possibly she was single only because she'd been in love with Uncle Yi this whole time. Later on, when Heishi drummed up the courage to bring Xiao Sang to the book club, where brilliant exchanges took place, the hesitation in his mind was not dispelled. He warned himself to be more cautious than anything, not to upset things—like "a bull in a china shop." After thinking about it, he oriented his relationship with Xiao Sang as old classmates plus good friends. "Show restraint, observe carefully," he said to himself. Even though Uncle Yi had introduced Xiao Sang to him out of goodwill and in anticipation that they would soon grow intimate, Heishi still thought that he shouldn't get all worked up. He was not sure about Xiao Sang, knowing from personal experience how fascinating Uncle Yi was. So Heishi intentionally disappeared from view after Xiao Sang attended the book club for the first time. He thought: let this affair develop slowly. Besides, he was busy with his research.

However, Uncle Yi reproved him. He urged Heishi to take the matter in hand, saying, "A woman like this is extremely rare." It seemed Uncle Yi's aesthetic was the same as his. But supposing, what if—. Why would she turn to the ordinary Heishi when she saw such a fascinating man as Uncle Yi daily? Heishi didn't usually think of himself as ordinary, but in comparison to Uncle Yi, he would seem ordinary. He was trying to ascend to Uncle Yi's level . . .

Now that he was so interested in Xiao Sang, should he enter into her emotional world, or confess his fondness toward her? Heishi thought he'd reached a forbidden zone. Out of deep love for Uncle Yi, and also out of ignorance when faced with this kind of relationship, he felt that he must not be impatient and needed to take all kinds of circumstances into account. He thought about some of the details of that day when he and Xiao Sang went to the book club, though without coming up with any clues. Seemingly, Xiao Sang also took an interest in him, but her interest was confined to her innate warmth toward a friend and her eagerness for literature. One could even say that Heishi's emotions were activated, but he hadn't been able to communicate this to Xiao Sang because he was too inhibited. Or one could say that Xiao Sang had a cautious side, too, and would rather conceal her secret feelings than reveal them. Heishi thought back and forth like this. He didn't take any substantive actions, even though Uncle Yi prompted him from time to time. Also, Heishi felt very comfortable with Xiao Sang as a friend. He could always draw enlightenment and life force from her. Her greatest quality was her ability to resist mediocrity, which made Heishi revere her. Over the years of bachelorhood he had invested his entire physical and spiritual strength in literature, but his personal life had become dreary, which he now knew to be a mistake. While there was a woman in a similar situation to his who could handle her daily life gently and peacefully, loving life with a passion—this was a major shock to Heishi. What was studying literature for? Wasn't it the pursuit of an even more reasonable everyday life? Xiao Sang had certain qualities that Heishi lacked, so he was curious about her and yearned for her to reveal her true self and to communicate with her. Heishi's friends from the book club, Qiaozi and Li Hai, for example, had seen Xiao Sang at once for her attainments and hoped fervently for the two of them to become partners.

Heishi sensed all kinds of external factors pushing him and Xiao Sang together, but their own souls hadn't yet opened up to each other. After all, they were both adults with emotional histories, so there were more aspects for them to consider. For Heishi, the major resistance came from his soul—he feared that his own behavior might wreck the finest affection in the world. This inward apprehension ran all through his relationship with Xiao Sang.

Later he went back to the book club with her, they had certain communications, and he became more powerfully attracted to her, while the friendship between them also developed deeper layers. Yet Heishi warned himself that he couldn't step over the dividing line between them on his own before there was transparency in the most fundamental question. His felt experience was that in his exchanges with Xiao Sang, everything that she said to him about Uncle Yi could be construed ambiguously. But it would be too crude to make her clarify things. He could only wait, until a certain turning point came. Heishi did not believe that he was charming enough for this woman whom he admired to open up to him. So just wait, then: this kind of waiting wasn't entirely passive, and was often rich and meaningful, although sometimes mingled with dejection. Isn't life always like this?

Heishi liked Xiao Sang, no matter what the future would hold. Even if she were a lifelong friend, she would continuously bring him life force. He'd never had a female friend like this, which showed the monotony and lack of fervor in his personal life. Besides, this lacking passion had indirectly affected his research work. Heishi thought: this was probably why Uncle Yi had instigated him to contact Xiao Sang. He was unwilling for the tree of Heishi's life to wither in loneliness and hoped for it to grow healthily upward. Uncle Yi's considerations were always so complete and full of affection.

From Heishi's contact with Xiao Sang, he could tell that she was often willing to interact with him, which made him incredibly happy. Yet after the gladness passed, he would usually then analyze and judge, deciding that Xiao Sang was by natural instinct good at understanding what people wanted, that she was enthusiastically generous, and that he shouldn't let selfish one-sided wishful thinking overinterpret her goodwill and fondness for him. At the present stage of things, delay was the sole attitude Heishi could adopt, as was also determined by the long-term formation of his personality. So long as it weren't passive delay, he was still cautiously devoting himself to life. He remembered his speech at the book club that raised the question of the "nets of life" and took note that Xiao Sang had the same feeling as him about this. Which was to say, they might be adopting similar methods to address the problem of their emotions. Only sometimes Heishi questioned his method. What if Xiao Sang's feelings weren't what he envisioned? Was his delay hurting her? Women are more emotional than men, more physical, and the delay pained him on her account, with a sense of remorse that sometimes even made him restless. Xiao Sang was so wonderful, she should gain happiness as soon as possible. Besides, now that he'd seen the nets of life, he shouldn't worry about difficulty and instead must explore the nets boldly, seeking out the most reasonable way to resolve things. This was the problem that Uncle Yi and also life itself had presented to him and that he should not elude, but face directly. Without knowing how, and to his surprise, this new problem posed in his life was identical to his current research topic. It was no coincidence, of course; instead, this once again proved in practice that what he and Uncle Yi were researching was the major question of the times, which could only be resolved via the innovations of literature. Heishi grew excited when he thought of this. He became determined to overcome his inertia and invest himself in his feelings in his own way, until someday when "the water recedes to show the stones beneath." This was how he must act, no matter if the result were good or bad. Of course, investing himself this way didn't mean ignoring everything else, but rather was proceeding with caution. He could repeatedly express his feelings to Xiao Sang at the boundary of "true friends," deepening her impression of him, and waiting for the day when she would take the initiative to open up the doors of her heart. Naturally, he didn't have much confidence about whether his approach would be effective. After all, Xiao Sang was a type of woman he had never interacted with before, so he had no experience to go by. On her side there were so many possibilities . . . Always that sentence: that he should exert himself, not grow rigid in his emotions, and keep a sensitive attitude toward life.

Now Qiaozi went to Li Hai's home on her days off to be with him. At these times she would entrust the neighbors to look after her mother, out of concern in case the elderly woman needed anything. Qiaozi often thought about Li Hai the whole day: not only going to bed with him, but also reading books with him and doing housework together. She felt the sudden expansion of her future. That first evening, after Li Hai awakened her sexual impulses with vigorous passion, she had suddenly, vividly known that this was the person she had been waiting for so long. Then Qiaozi mustered all of her desire and inspiration to respond to him. Their rhythm was intense and also in sync. Whether it were a tiny movement, or saying one word, they achieved full communication together. To herself Qiaozi called this second love "the love of literature"—Li Hai was her literature. She wanted to be immersed in his love for her and in her love for him. When they had just begun, Qiaozi only had to think of Li Hai's deeply emotional caresses and kisses for her whole body to tremble, and his sincere devotion made her breath quicken. She thought that his affection was like fire. When they had sex, he could always guess the most comfortable, most enjoyable positions for her, the rules of her climax, and how to excite her arousal with his movements. While she instinctively aroused him in turn, exploring this mysterious territory together with him.

"I've had many dreams about sex, always with you, but I was never satisfied in the dreams. Only real life can bring fulfillment," Li Hai exclaimed. "Your body is my treasure trove."

"I want to be with you every day. Only shared is each day perfect," Qiaozi said.

"Don't worry, Qiaozi, I am making preparations."

The two of them hadn't forgotten about Heishi and Xiao Sang.

"Heishi considers everything so carefully that it's been a prolonged process. I don't know what he's worrying about."

When Qiaozi complained this way, Li Hai just said that he felt optimistic.

"I've listened closely at the book club. The mechanism of the depths of their emotions has already been activated. But they've only known each other for a short time, so it's easy to have all kinds of concerns, because of not being familiar with each other. The key is in accessing emotions. Drawing back becomes impossible, once this has happened for both of them. No matter what difficulties lie ahead, in the end two will become one," Li Hai said thoughtfully.

"I want them to become one right away. Xiao Sang is the kind of woman I admire the most."

"You are the woman I admire most. So we ought to move in together as soon as possible. This kind of separation is agony, sometimes I can't rest at night . . ."

"It's just waiting until you've bought an apartment. We don't need to fix it up. A coat of paint, and my mother and I will move in right away. To avoid you losing sleep night after night, ruining your health," Qiaozi said as she kissed him.

"When the time comes I can touch you every day. Men actually fear being alone more, so Heishi shouldn't keep on delaying. It's not good for him or for Xiao Sang."

"Every day he doesn't declare his feelings for her, my heart is in my throat," Qiaozi said.

When she returned home she told her mother that Li Hai was going to buy an apartment soon, so they should get ready to move.

"Li Hai acts quickly. More and more, he can't stand to be apart from you."

"Yes, he can't sleep at night. Such a pity. So I don't want him to renovate the apartment—we'll move in immediately."

"You're right. I'm familiar with the location: life will be more convenient for us than here. Li Hai has considered every angle. He really is a good son."

Every evening after Qiaozi finished studying she would call Li Hai to kiss him and stroke those parts of his body through the phone. Li Hai always felt like crying after these calls; he didn't know how he had become so soft. He'd been in relationships twice before, but never with this frailty. It seemed as though in his whole life only Qiaozi, finally, was the best match for him. Maybe she was one of the birds he had communicated with when he was a child. Didn't her name mean "sparrow"?

Li Hai was an orphan, so his longing for family life was stronger than Qiaozi's. His greatest wish was to go to sleep holding her each night. Now, watching that day come closer, his mood brightened. His coworkers all called him "lucky in love" and said that she was very pretty. He knew that Qiaozi's mother would need their care in the future and was willing to shoulder this load, because he was the man of the family. All of a sudden more than thirty years as an orphan would end, and he would be someone with a family. How could Li Hai not be happy? And Qiaozi's feelings were strong; she loved him intensely. In the future he would bring up children with her . . . "Qiaozi, sparrow, you've finally flown into my life," he said gently, once and again remembering the sex that intoxicated him heart and soul.

Li Hai hadn't told Heishi yet about him and Qiaozi being together. He wanted to wait until after Heishi had declared his feelings for Xiao Sang to tell him. When the time came, everyone could be happy together. Whenever the book club met, Li Hai would listen with rapt attention to the voices in Heishi and Xiao Sang's hearts, judging how their feelings were progressing. Qiaozi would ask him about this as soon as the gathering dispersed. The two of them were more anxious than anyone else. Heishi and Xiao Sang remained entirely unaware and kept doing tai chi, neither fast nor slow. Then one day, after the book club ended, everyone joined together to encourage them to accelerate their relationship. That time only Xiao Sang didn't know, while Heishi was profoundly grateful to his friends for their kind intentions.

Qiaozi thought of herself as having become a different person. She still remembered about falling out with Heishi over buying a desirable apartment. While now, when she was planning to buy a home again, she let Li Hai make the decisions on his own. She simply didn't interfere, because she believed he was capable of this. Her sole concern was about Li Hai staying healthy. She was afraid he was wearing himself out and worried that the insomnia would damage his health. That was why Qiaozi had brought up buying the apartment and moving as soon as possible, which had touched Li Hai so much.

"Literature has taught me how to think through problems," she told him proudly. "Now we are just like one person at all times."

Qiaozi still enjoyed beautiful things in daily life and maintained an interest in them, but she no longer exhausted herself over them like in the past. Her popular aesthetics were continually being elevated.

At the most recent gathering of the Pigeon Book Club, Xiao Sang had been absent because of her trip to the capital to visit her family.

This time they were discussing the book *XXXXX5*. Fei guided everyone to talk about the obscurity and dominance of its deep layers of emotion, as well as the many patterns of such emotions appearing in contemporary times. Each member gave an interpretation of a pattern related to the novel's plot according to their own experience, each with a differing method, but all with points in common. This exchange left everyone very excited. They believed this kind of communication to be different than one person closing the door to read alone, in that it provoked and enlightened new possibilities. Fei said that this showed how literary communication was imperative and important at present. The reason contemporary literature could only exist and develop through such exchanges was that literature was increasingly revealing its essence. As a reader, reading that opened up an individual path became important, as did conveying personal feelings to others; through these communications, literature's target universality could be more quickly realized, and the potential value of literary works would also become evident. A new kind of literature required readers to participate in creation, because the writing depended on the readers' imaginative ideas to show its value. Precisely because new literature makes such high demands of readers, its rate of acceptance among today's readers is limited, and this is where all of them could make efforts toward improvement. Because human nature is shared and passageways for the spread of literature always exist. The difficulty of this kind of literature is similar to the difficulty of philosophy; it requires people to develop and study another function that is unlike the applications of classical philosophy. Yet everyone has discovered through practice that enigmas cannot *not* be solved: on the contrary, only solving enigmas is true reading. At this point Fei abruptly changed the topic, bringing up Xiao Sang's enquiring mind; her perseverance at interpreting the primeval scene of fiction; her consciousness of a love for life melding with the exploration of fiction; as well as her free exercise of an effective and innate gift in this regard. Fei had just stopped talking when everyone else expressed the same feelings and the book club began to confer. For a time, only the two syllables *Xiao Sang* could be heard constantly throughout the room amid the buzzing sound of conversation, *weng weng*. Heishi didn't contribute to the discussion and instead sat there with a flushed face and heart pounding, waves rising and falling in his chest. He saw that even Fei and Han Ma were whispering something in private . . . Without knowing why, Heishi felt as if everyone were blaming him a little for something. This made him doubt his previous judgments. But on the whole, the atmosphere made him feel warm—especially Li Hai and Qiaozi, who both shot expectant glances toward him (Heishi had noticed that the two of them were becoming more intimate), which almost alarmed him, with bewilderment that was also full of gratitude.

Heishi sat in his room writing a letter to Xiao Sang. The book club had shocked him so much. He thought: his friends must have reasons for their opinions, which were quite possibly more complete than his individual knowledge. He began to remember the back-and-forth over the several months of his relationship with Xiao Sang, a throughline forming from all kinds of fragments. There had always been between them a kind of mutual desire and a reluctance to be apart. Although their attachment was continuously interrupted and interfered with by external considerations, it never vanished entirely and instead quietly started to flourish as time went on. They appreciated each other and constantly had the other in mind, as reflected in each contact between them (regardless of whether successful). If Xiao Sang merely saw Heishi as a true friend, she wouldn't mind so much his efforts to keep a distance between them, given her rich emotional life and individuality. Her behavior obviously had another factor to it. At such times her anger, resentment, and impatience pointed to a different explanation; unfortunately Heishi had been too slow to react. This kind of repeated misunderstanding slowed and prolonged the development of their relationship, which may even have hurt Xiao Sang. Heishi sensed that he was standing at a critical boundary: he might lose his chance, unless he declared himself. She had offered him the opportunity of writing her letters. Wasn't that her way of asking him to open the doors of his heart? Without his opening up, what other way did she have to know his true feelings? Then Heishi wrote his implicit but passionate letter. In the letter, Heishi explained himself with the hope that Xiao Sang would take his hint, and open herself up to let him know the real state of her feelings.

Heishi walked out onto the street and, after placing this reserved love letter in the mailbox, started to wait uneasily, with rising fervor. A memory appeared in his mind of the scene at the coffee shop when Xiao Sang had angrily kissed his forehead, along with the image of her leaving, irate. It showed so obviously, but he had not been able to comprehend the deeper meaning! He had debated too much while neglecting his intuitions, so her anger was natural—then he had hurt her by not realizing his error. He had been so stupid. Heishi felt that Xiao Sang's greatest fascination lay in how good she was at understanding what people wished for, even when it came to someone as clumsy as him; she never gave up on him with impatience, but instead maintained an unchanging, incisive sympathy and gentleness toward him. In Heishi's thirty-plus years of life, only Uncle Yi had given him similar affection.

While Xiao Sang was away in the capital, Heishi immersed himself in reminiscences of the past as well as in feelings of regret. He wanted to fly to be with Xiao Sang and declare his feelings for her, and at the same time to speak of his slowness, his mistakes. Yet he knew that for now he could only wait patiently . . .

For the first time in years Heishi was enveloped in a deep sense of loneliness. Because of Xiao Sang's departure; because emotional outlets are unpredictable; because he didn't have much faith in himself.

By the third day Heishi couldn't help writing Xiao Sang another letter. This letter was also a veiled declaration of love, and told her about his family, including his admiration and affection for his mother . . . Heishi tried through the frequency of his letters to indicate what was written on his heart.

For the next several days, he could manage to forget about Xiao Sang temporarily when he buried himself in his research. But if he put down the work at hand, he became unable to sit or stand still. He even felt despondent at times.

Heishi distractedly gave Uncle Yi a call, and they decided to meet up.

"Is it things with Xiao Sang?" Uncle Yi asked him as soon as they saw each other. "Have you gotten a letter from her?"

"Not yet. Maybe she's too busy."

"Wait patiently. Xiao Sang will get back to you. Based on my understanding of her, you really don't need to worry. Wait until she's back, and then your relationship will likely be decided."

Heishi looked at Uncle Yi gratefully, but had no peace of mind.

Xiao Sang had been away for an entire week. Would he receive a letter from her tomorrow? She was the sort of person who would usually reply quickly after receiving his letters. Yet some things are hard to predict, and besides, she was no longer in Meng, so Heishi didn't feel sure of himself. Although Uncle Yi knew Xiao Sang, the world was so large, and anything might have happened to her. Ah, this had to be resigned to fate. She had come up with the idea to write letters, but she didn't seem eager to write back to him. Why not? Had something happened? Or did she think that it wasn't necessary to write frequent letters, like lovers?

That night Heishi had a dream. He came to a soccer field, not the one from his college but a soccer field in a different province. There were people kicking a soccer ball around, and other people coming and going around the field. Heishi unconsciously searched them with his eyes. They were mostly young, the men in T-shirts, the women wearing dresses and skirts. He was trying to find a young woman who was wearing a blue-gray skirt with a white shirt tucked into it and wide-framed glasses. He scanned the reddish-brown skirts here, greenish-black skirts there, and there were violet skirts, skirts the color of rice straw, and so on, but no blue-gray skirts. Agitated, Heishi walked back and forth along the playing field. Later, as evening drew on, he had to go eat at the dining hall.

The dining hall was also full of young people, and everywhere the sound of voices and laughter. Heishi started to scan the dresses and skirts. Suddenly everything brightened before his eyes: he saw a blue skirt and a white blouse tucked into the skirt. But going over to look, the skirt turned out to be black and she wasn't wearing wide-framed glasses.

"Excuse me?" She looked at him uncertainly.

"Oh, I'm sorry. I thought you were someone else."

Heishi still felt ashamed when he woke up. He thought: why hadn't he declared his feelings to Xiao Sang that time by the river? What other solution was there? Hadn't he imagined every possibility? If he had boldly told her how he felt, whether it turned out all right or not, wouldn't things have at least developed naturally? It was he who had made things so complicated—so he had to reap what he'd sown. Xiao Sang must be out of patience, so she had fixed their relationship at the level of true friends.

The next day Heishi still waited for nothing. The mailbox was empty.

In the afternoon he requested off from work. Not able to stand it any more, he went to the bar.

Heishi had two solitary drinks in a row and felt the alcohol going to his head, so he didn't dare keep drinking. He sat there in a daze. He remembered something like this happening frequently to him when he was a child: being absorbed by extreme loneliness, a feeling that made everything in the world turn murky. By contrast over the years his life had become fulfilling and strenuous, as he and his friends studied literature together under Uncle Yi's guidance. The feeling of loneliness had been left far behind him.

He ordered a glass of lemonade and drank it in a haze.

Someone tapped him on the shoulder. He turned around and saw Uncle Yi and Xiao Ma! They both seemed jubilant.

Heishi's state of mind was much calmer when he returned to his dormitory. He thought: going by appearances, Uncle Yi and Xiao Ma were together now. He knew Xiao Ma was a dear friend of Xiao Sang and that they talked with each other about everything. Now that she and Uncle Yi were in love, Xiao Sang would be sure to know. Uncle Yi's romance with Xiao Ma showed that his surmises about Xiao Sang were only clutching at wind or catching at shadows. With the knot of his greatest suspicion untangled, his task now was to wait for her to write back. It was understandable that she would not write to him for a while. Wasn't she going to stay in the capital for two whole months? She would belatedly, but definitely, write him a letter in return. Uncle Yi's judgment couldn't be wrong. If Xiao Sang sent him a letter, he would write her another letter declaring himself openly. His delays had already hurt her; he must make it up to her at once. Heishi even thought about rushing to the capital to propose to Xiao Sang.

Once his mood took a turn for the better, he delved back into literature again. He connected the thought process he had been going through to his subject of research. He thought: even though his responses had been insensitive, his actions in a fundamental way still tallied with integrity. It was a temperamental flaw that had let things delay too long, which had harmed the person he loved. Fortunately there weren't signs of failure yet.

For another overstimulated and sleepless night, Heishi tossed and turned, coming up with plan after plan to make things up to Xiao Sang. Finally he decided to go to the capital soon.

The next day, as he returned to his dormitory from the office midway through the morning, he saw a letter in the mailbox.

The beautiful handwriting unfurled Xiao Sang's scent. Heishi had tears in his eyes. He kissed the paper many times.

In the evening he called Uncle Yi to tell him.

"Xiao Sang will be back tomorrow. There are some problems with her family, so she's coming back early with her father. Tomorrow I'm going to meet her and her father."

"That's terrific, Heishi! Now I'm not as worried about you."

Heishi thought of Xiao Sang the entire night. He decided that no matter what the issues were with her family, they had to decide their relationship right away and couldn't delay a moment longer. Besides, if she'd encountered any difficulty, her problems would be his once their relationship was settled. Tiding over the crisis together would be better than her bearing it on her own.

Waking up in the morning and taking a cold shower, Heishi felt invigorated.

The lover in his dreams was suddenly coming toward him in reality. Is there greater happiness than this?

After the book club adjourned, Li Hai and Qiaozi returned to their new home together.

"Oh, this evening I'm so happy I could faint . . . ," Qiaozi sighed.

"I am, too. Heishi and Xiao Sang are an enviable and perfect match. Only, Qiaozi, we're also a perfect pair—don't you think?" Li Hai asked.

"Of course. When I think of how good you are to me in bed, I'm so excited I can hardly breathe. Not just in bed, of course—we are in rhythm together whatever we do. There is no end to this joy. I like your optimistic nature, and now I'm optimistic, too, and so is my mom. Later on our family will enjoy the sound of laughter all day."

"Qiaozi, when did you start to discover that I'd fallen in love with you?"

"Two months ago. There was something disorderly inside of you, whispering, and I could hear it all. I didn't tell you what I heard, because I wanted to wait for you to declare your love, but you never did. You always tried to hold back, and what was inside you started making a noise, a booming sound. I thought to myself: all right, he's not willing to declare his feelings, so let me tell him what is in his own heart. I took your hand and told you. When I did, you admitted it at once. Everything has gone so well, hasn't it? Haha, Li Hai struck the target without aiming for it, and captured Qiaozi's heart!"

"Qiaozi, from now on I'll go to sleep holding you every night. I've been afraid of being alone ever since we've been together. I have a hard time sleeping on my own."

"Of course you will hold me—I am your backbone. I can't be lost, not even in your dreams."

"Also, I want be inside you, every other day."

"Come on, come on, I want you now."

The two of them went into the bedroom quietly, because Qiaozi's mother had already gone to sleep.

They showered and got in bed.

"Heishi and Xiao Sang are doing the same things as we are," Qiaozi said.

"Qiaozi, do you want me to start kissing you on the left or right side?"

"The left side, the left side is tired of waiting."

Qiaozi was also caressing Li Hai. She had him enter her quickly, sensing her climax nearing.

After the first round, they started to talk.

"We turned out to be helping ourselves from the day we began to help Heishi," Li Hai said.

"Yes, because this is the way of literature. I think you are as worthy of love as Heishi. My mom has also taken a liking to you."

"I vowed: until the day Heishi marries, my conscience won't be at peace."

"You see, at long last he will be married. Good people have good rewards. You, as well.

"I wasn't a good person to start, but I've been learning to be good," Qiaozi added.

They started to talk again about going to visit Li Hai's hometown. Qiaozi said they should take this trip as their honeymoon. They planned many of the details, including to have volunteers from the community stay at their home to take care of her mother for a few days.

"Qiaozi, you are my bird. Let's fly together into the native mountains. I will search for that place. It has been entangled with my dreams for so many years. You have already fulfilled my dreams, but I still want to go there with you to see for real."

As Li Hai was speaking he wanted to enter Qiaozi again. He began to explore those parts of her body, repeatedly, and only entered her when she was at the height of excitement.

Before going to sleep they decided to purchase the train tickets and long-distance bus tickets.

The morning Qiaozi and Li Hai set out, it was raining and thunder rumbled outside.

Each of them carried a backpack. They said farewell to Qiaozi's mom and took a taxi to the train station.

After they'd entered the sleeper car, they discovered that the only passenger in the carriage besides themselves was an old man. His berth was near the front of the car, while they were in the center. He was advanced in years and seemed to not have any luggage.

"Hello, sir," Qiaozi greeted him enthusiastically.

He'd been sitting at his bunk thinking about something and was startled by her voice.

"Are you two going to Silver Mountain?" he asked.

"Yes. Are you going to Silver Mountain, too?" Qiaozi asked him.

The elderly man nodded. Then he spread out his quilt and lay down.

When the train started off, Qiaozi and Li Hai excitedly looked through the windows into the deluge. Luckily the lights were on in the sleeper car, otherwise it would have been pitch-black. Qiaozi held Li Hai close, with a feeling that they were taking a risk.

"I wonder whether it's raining at Silver Mountain, too," Qiaozi said.

"It may be," Li Hai answered in a low voice, kissing her face at the same time.

"We are so happy. Why is the old man about to cry?"

"He could be a traveler returning home who's moved to the point of tears."

When the midday food cart came by, they each ate a box lunch along with some fruit that they'd brought along. They noticed that the elderly man kept sleeping, with no sign of wanting to get up.

"It looks like there are very, very few people going to Silver Mountain. Now I'm even more curious."

"We'll be on the train for a day and a night. This bunk is too narrow—I can't go to sleep holding you, Qiaozi," Li Hai groaned.

"It will be all right when we get to the hotel," Qiaozi consoled him.

She felt that Li Hai wasn't as cheerful as her and seemed to be anxious about something. What was it?

"Li Hai, let's read," she said.

When she brought out her book, *XX XX XX*, his eyes brightened. He took out his copy of the same book.

"Let's read chapter 8 together," she said.

Chapter 8 portrayed what happened in Stone Village. The terrain of the village was rocky, with just a small amount of soil, so that farm crops and vegetables didn't grow well. To earn a living, the young and healthy all went looking for work outside of the village. While Li Hai and Qiaozi read, something happened, which was that the rain stopped, although the exterior of the train was still a stretch of darkness. Qiaozi looked at her watch: it was two in the afternoon. Why was it dark at two in the afternoon? Even so, the atmosphere suited reading the description of Stone Village. With the monotonous sound of the wheels, she felt the train moving toward that kind of overcast countryside.

"Li Hai, what can you hear?" Qiaozi asked.

"I can hear the old man mumbling in his dreams. He is also part of this book's setting," Li Hai answered.

"I imagined Silver Mountain as where there's birdsong and the smell of flowers. Now I think what I envisioned was wrong," she said.

"Maybe. I'm not sure. It's been so many years."

They continued to read their books lying down.

When dinner was brought in, Qiaozi had just reached a peculiar point in the plot, where the roots of carrots that had been planted pierced through the stones underneath them. So many carrots being pulled up, turning up pieces of rock—it made her scalp tingle. Li Hai heaved a long sigh. He'd probably also reached this place in the book.

Qiaozi discovered that the old man was still asleep and hadn't gotten up to eat at all. She couldn't help but be worried about him.

She went over to his berth and asked how he was.

He opened his clouded eyes and said:

"I want to return home on an empty stomach. I don't need to eat anything. There's everything at home . . ."

Then he turned over and went back to sleep.

"He says he wants to go home on an empty stomach, that there's everything at home," Qiaozi told Li Hai.

Li Hai's eyes darted around as if he were recalling things from ages ago. Then he said:

"Qiaozi, are you sure you want to go to Silver Mountain? If we get off at the next station and turn back, we'll be in time."

"Li Hai, Li Hai, what's wrong? Didn't we discuss this? We're going to your hometown."

Qiaozi looked at him in surprise, sensing that they were approaching some unimaginable transition. She was not willing to shrink back—going to Li Hai's hometown to see those birds was her long-cherished wish.

"My hometown's overcast," Li Hai said, as if in a trance.

Qiaozi thought: she had to go there to see. She kissed Li Hai's earlobe, trying to shake him out of it.

"I'm here with you, Li Hai, and I'm not scared."

"If you're not afraid then I won't worry. Reading about what's described in the book, it's all about what's there at Silver Mountain. There are birds, but also frightening things. I'm not afraid, of course, since I come from there."

"I want to know what it was like when you were young. This way I can love you better in the future," Qiaozi said.

She had just finished speaking when the train came to a violent halt. The old man got off the train—Qiaozi only saw his receding figure. She asked Li Hai what was happening.

"He's returning to his hometown through another passageway . . ."

Now only the two of them were left in the train car. Qiaozi was nervous that the few lights would go out. Li Hai said it wouldn't matter, because he would hold her tight if the lights went out. They would be arriving in the morning. Every morning was bright in his hometown. "Let me hold you now." He pulled Qiaozi over to his berth.

The train started moving again. It was dark outside the windows. Qiaozi heard Li Hai say in her ear:

"The nights there are long, and the days are only one-third as long as in the city and go by in a flash. Everything has to speed up to be finished in the short, short daytime, because the nights belong to reverie . . ."

"What are you thinking about?" Qiaozi asked quietly, as if startled by her own voice.

"I don't know too much from back then—I can only remember being very scared. I couldn't see anyone once night came. I couldn't see my grandma either, because she'd gone into the mountains to search for dry branches for fuel by the little bit of moonlight. Though it was dark, outside there was noise, and in the racket I could hear the indistinct sound of birdcalls. I started to imitate the birdcalls out of fear. The more I imitated the birds, the clearer the calls became, and I could better tell the difference between the traits of each bird. This kind of imitation made me less afraid. Afterward there was communication." While Li Hai gently narrated, Qiaozi kept kissing his neck, her heart tightening because she ached for him back then.

"Now you have me, Li Hai," she said.

"Eventually, I started to mobilize the birds. The surroundings of our small house weren't as gloomy, because of the birdcalls everywhere—the sounds the birds made had the upper hand. Later my grandma heard them, too. 'Li Hai, are you playing a game?' she asked me. She said I was a good boy and rewarded me with a roasted sweet potato. Back then the inhabitants of Silver Mountain wore out their strength to barely make a living, so death's shadow always shrouded us. I went out digging with a tiny hoe on my back, planting yams and potatoes. My grandma would warn me to be careful and whatever else not to get sick. She told me that if I got sick I would sink into the dark and never wake up again. Even the birds wouldn't be able to wake me with their cries."

"Now you have me, Li Hai," Qiaozi said again, while kissing him.

"On those long, long nights, with the chill wind blowing, anyone whose willpower was even a little weak would collapse. Those who remained were tough mountain folk. For instance, that old man you saw must be tenacious. Back then I used to think it must not be everyone who can hear the calls of the birds. How did those who didn't hear them last the long, slow nights? That just confirmed that there are other games. In our family, my grandma also knew the language of the birds, so I inherited her gift: grandmother and grandson depending on this gift to endure misery. My grandma encouraged me to play this game, so my skill improved, and more birds assembled."

As Li Hai said this the lights suddenly went out. It was the train's lights-off time, but neither of them was inclined to sleep. Qiaozi thought: no wonder Li Hai could understand Heishi and her so well. Every person in the book club was like the saying "one day of cold doesn't freeze three feet deep." From now on she must try to learn from all of them.

Looking out the window, there was a point of light in the distance in the darkness.

"That's a bonfire," Li Hai said. "Bonfires were another way of withstanding the darkness inside and outside of us back then. If someone couldn't endure the long nights, he or she could shoulder a bundle of firewood to an open space and light a bonfire. That small heap of flames would give them confidence."

Qiaozi saw the light leap up a few times, then it was extinguished. Li Hai said that someone must have recovered the calm in their soul.

"Before my grandmother passed away, she entrusted me to a distant relative. She urged me not to forget how to imitate the birds and to train and practice frequently. She said this would be an important way to make a living. Her words came true afterward. The book club gave me a place to train and practice . . ."

"Oh, Li Hai . . . ," Qiaozi said.

"Now I have you, Qiaozi. You flew from Silver Mountain into my heart. What an abundant life."

They held one another even closer.

Later they dozed for a while. Even later both of them suddenly awoke.

The sky was already full light, and their destination lay ahead. The train made a piercing whistle and slowly came to a stop. Qiaozi saw the three words *Silver Mountain Station* on the station sign.

They got off the train and then went to catch the long-distance bus.

Qiaozi discovered right away that their surroundings were bleak, with few signs of cultivation. She couldn't remember ever having been to a place like this. Underfoot was a road made of broken-up cement, seldom driven over from the look of it. They followed a map and found the bus station. That station turned out to be only a thatched hut with a very old bus parked on an empty patch of ground. The bus door was half-open, so Qiaozi and Li Hai boarded. They put down their backpacks, took their seats, and waited for the driver. There were thirty or so seats on the bus, and it was half an hour before departure, but its passengers had somehow not arrived. Qiaozi leaned her head on Li Hai's shoulder. She felt excited, but also a little tired. He held her hand.

When they'd waited for half an hour, the driver still hadn't arrived and there weren't any other passengers who'd come on board. Qiaozi started to feel a little doubtful, but Li Hai comforted her by saying that the driver had to come back—his thermos was in the driver's cab. He picked up the thermos to show Qiaozi that the tea inside was steaming. After they'd waited for another half an hour, a middle-aged driver unhurriedly appeared. They didn't know where he had come from, since there were no buildings anywhere around.

"Hello, you two passengers! Take your seats, and I'll drive."

The bus started violently, and Qiaozi's forehead knocked against the back of the seat, leaving a mark. Li Hai's heart ached, and he hurriedly found red flower oil to rub on it for her.

"Ah, ah, it's just like that here at Silver Mountain. Things are a bit crude."

"It's OK, it doesn't hurt at all," Qiaozi said.

After this she'd learned her lesson and held on to the armrest. Li Hai told her that the ride to the Silver Mountain Hotel would take half an hour.

Along the road was a desolate landscape with very few signs of habitation. Qiaozi only saw a few brick-and-tile houses crawling along the ground that didn't look so much like homes where people lived as dilapidated houses people had abandoned. In a while they saw the large mountain, which did appear gloomy, despite its many trees. Qiaozi discovered that Li Hai was secretly observing her expression. She could tell how tense he was, so she said, as if she didn't mind:

"Li Hai, your hometown has a unique character."

"What do you think that is?" Li Hai asked, surprised.

"Let me think. I feel like it must be—untouched by changes in the outside world."

"You're wonderful, worthy to be known as the bird who flew away from my hometown," Li Hai said.

"Let's continue to explore."

They reached the Silver Mountain Hotel, a shabby two-story wooden building situated at the foot of the mountain.

Once the bus stopped, a skinny young man ran out of the hotel, rapidly took their backpacks, and strode back inside carrying a bag over each arm. He told the two of them to follow him. Their room was on the second floor.

The hotel room was large, but utterly simple. Thick cotton blankets were spread on the bed along with a thick blue-patterned quilt. The young man put down their luggage, gave them the key, and left.

There was a desk in the room, a side table, and a few high-backed chairs, none of them polished, so that the aroma of timber issued from the bare wood. Qiaozi sniffed the printed quilt and told Li Hai that it smelled like sunshine! Their mood became spirited.

They immediately washed their faces, brushed their teeth, and took a shower. Then they each drank a glass of water.

"Qiaozi, I'm very tired. Let me go to sleep holding you first. After that we'll go get some food."

"You said that the days here are short. If we sleep during the day, won't we only be able to do things at night?"

"Yes, that's right. My grandma was usually active at night, too," Li Hai said.

They got into the cotton quilt that had the smell of the sun. Li Hai held Qiaozi and went right to sleep. She tried at first to get her bearings for where they were, but after a few minutes couldn't ward off sleep either.

The sky was dark by the time Qiaozi and Li Hai woke.

When they went downstairs to eat, the skinny young man came over again and led them to a small room arranged with a dining table. He introduced himself:

"My name is Fei. I manage the hotel on my own. Just wait here—the meal will be ready soon."

"That's a delightful name!" Qiaozi said cheerfully. "It must be difficult managing the hotel?"

"Mm-hmm. I've gotten used to it though."

"If you go up the mountain from here," Fei added, "just keep walking straight, and don't take any turnings. Because it's dark out and once you take a turn you'll lose the way. When you reach your destination, you can sit down there to take a rest, then come back down the mountain. You'll need to bring enough drinking water. Silver Mountain welcomes back every traveler."

He finished saying this and said goodbye to them.

An old woman brought their food to the table. It was potatoes stewed with beef and a kind of fish they didn't recognize. They both had an appetite and ate a lot.

"This Fei speaks words within words," Qiaozi said. "What destination is he referring to? He also knew that we were returning travelers. He must be aware of things."

"Everyone on Silver Mountain probably is, too," Li Hai said. "Can people from one's own family not be aware of things?"

They departed, each carrying a flashlight, and Li Hai with some food and bottled water on his back.

They circled around to the back of the building, identified a narrow mountain road, then started to climb. Li Hai walked ahead, and Qiaozi followed him closely. He would walk for a while and then pause, explaining that they shouldn't use up their energy all at once and ought to take the climb slowly. Qiaozi felt grateful to him, since she was climbing such a tall mountain for the first time.

Although there was a light coming from somewhere that illuminated the mountain, both sides of the path were in darkness. Qiaozi climbed for a time and then heard the sound of animals, apparently large animals, slinking through the woods. She comforted herself, "Don't be afraid. Li Hai is here, he's a native of this place. They must know by smell."

They walked and paused, climbing for more than an hour. Qiaozi didn't know how high they had climbed, because she couldn't see anything clearly. Even shining the flashlight only illuminated a small part of their surroundings. She'd also noticed that this didn't bother Li Hai, who seemed much calmer than when they'd been on the train. "After all, this is his hometown," Qiaozi said to herself.

All of a sudden something large blocked the path up ahead. She nervously held her breath, thinking maybe it was a bear. Li Hai didn't stop walking, and they slowly neared the shadow.

"You've come," the shadow spoke.

"Yes. How's the rainfall this year?" Li Hai asked him.

"All right. There are a few more people living on the mountain, so food's a bit scarce. You're not here to stay?"

"We're only here to have a look around."

"Then I won't worry."

The shadow vanished back into the forest. Qiaozi heard the man trampling dried leaves as he went.

"Li Hai, did you and your grandmother choose to live in the mountains?"

"Yes. There was also an element of being forced to—she brought me here because it was easier to survive."

Hearing Li Hai speak like this, Qiaozi felt that the mountain under her feet was now kind.

They were still walking and pausing. Qiaozi thought how she was willing to follow Li Hai and climb like this all the way until the earth and sky were no more. There started to be more animals in the woods, the sounds they made indistinct and hard to identify. Qiaozi looked at her watch and saw that they had walked for more than three hours. She asked Li Hai whether they would be at the summit soon, and he said he didn't know. Then he asked her whether she liked Silver Mountain. Qiaozi answered "Yes," three times in a row.

"Why?" Li Hai asked.

"Because it's beautiful, and there are so many sounds here."

"Your impressions are the same as mine. You must also remember things from before you flew away from here."

"You're right. I feel like I want to embrace it," Qiaozi said excitedly. "I want to be able to tell the birds' songs apart."

They sat down to listen. Li Hai told Qiaozi that there was a tiger in the area around them. It had paused, motionless, at the entrance to the cave where its den was. Someone who lived on the mountain had walked past the tiger and greeted it.

"Have the birds come out?" Qiaozi asked.

"Yes, but I can't tell their calls apart yet. We are about halfway up the mountain. Our destination will be much higher up than this. Are you tired, Qiaozi?"

"Not at all. Let's go on."

Qiaozi eventually heard every step she took making a kind of echo underfoot. It seemed like someone saying, "Hmm, hmm, hmm . . . ," appreciatively and also as encouragement.

She looked at her watch again, and to her surprise they had been climbing for five hours. They must have climbed to a high location.

"I think it's a little like our destination here," Li Hai said.

He pointed and made Qiaozi listen closely in that direction.

Qiaozi listened for a long time and finally heard. At first it was indistinct, then little by little came closer, in wave upon wave. It was many types of birds: some nearby, some farther away.

They sat down on a large rock. While Qiaozi was drinking water from her bottle, she suddenly heard Li Hai making a birdcall. It seemed like there was no response. He made the sound again, sprightly and graceful, but still no response. Then he altered the tone and rhythm, altogether making the calls of three species of birds. Qiaozi didn't hear any response. She listened more carefully.

"They're listening," Li Hai said. "None of the birds are making a sound."

"I'm listening, too, Li Hai. This is a good place. The affinity between you and me must have started long ago. I've always felt that we knew each other before."

Li Hai kept making birdcalls for a while, until he was completely satisfied and only then stood and went down the mountain with Qiaozi.

It was midnight by the time they'd returned to the hotel. Fei was still downstairs waiting for them.

He hurriedly brought them into the dining room to eat.

They had just sat down when the old woman brought out food.

"How was the harvest?" Fei asked.

"Today was reporting to the birds," Li Hai said. "Everything went well. I'm very enthusiastic."

"Here at the bottom of the mountain I heard a ceremony among the birds . . . ," Fei said.

"That was a ritual to welcome me and Qiaozi. We didn't hear it ourselves, but bystanders could hear."

Qiaozi heard Li Hai's words and thought: so communication has already happened. Why hadn't she perceived it? Apparently she wasn't skilled enough yet. Yet even if she didn't hear at the scene, Li Hai would transmit the messages to her, which was enough to make her excited.

They took showers and went to bed, both too tired to keep their eyes open.

The next day when they woke up the sky was not yet completely dark.

"Are you willing to go up the mountain again today?" Li Hai asked Qiaozi.

"Of course. I'm anxious to practice my listening."

"Mountain climbing is tiring—I'm worried you'll get exhausted."

"I won't, when Silver Mountain is protecting me like a grandfather. I heard his voice."

They ate, finished their preparations, and departed.

After they'd climbed the mountain for a while, a middle-aged man appeared out of the forest not far in front of them.

"Fellow villager, hello!" Li Hai greeted him in a loud voice.

The man's beard was disheveled, but his eyes were shining.

"Hello. Have you come here for fun? I'm the beekeeper of Silver Mountain."

“We’re locals—we’ve come to meet with old friends,” Li Hai said. “We were already here once yesterday.”

“Then your reunion has been a success?”

“Yes.”

“But today you should choose a different path up the mountain than yesterday. Your old friends won’t appear if you take the same road.”

“But there is only one road up the mountain,” Li Hai said.

“There are branching paths everywhere. Didn’t you bring flashlights?”

The beekeeper finished saying this and turned toward the forest, disappearing into the woods. They heard the noise his footfalls made on the dry leaves.

Li Hai recalled the words of the hotel manager, thinking to himself that maybe what Fei had said was a kind of encouragement. Maybe he was seeing whether Li Hai had the courage to “lose the way”?

“Qiaozi, dear, could you stay here and wait for me? If I lose the way and don’t come back, go down the mountain and ask someone to come search for me,” Li Hai said.

But Qiaozi would not agree. She grabbed hold of Li Hai, saying, “If we’re going to die, then we’ll die together.

“We won’t die. Grandfather Silver Mountain will protect us. Just a moment ago he was underfoot answering me,” she added.

Li Hai had to give up the idea and enter the forest together with Qiaozi.

The sky was entirely dark now, and their flashlights weren’t any use because there wasn’t a path to follow. Everywhere was trees, and underneath the trees were bushes and wild grass. They had to move forward slowly, squeezing their bodies through the wisteria and shrubs. There were thorns all over the bushes. Qiaozi felt at her cheeks and forehead, which were sticky, scratched and bleeding. Li Hai was opening a path up ahead and likely had even more scratches on him. Walking a ways, he asked her:

“Are you afraid, Qiaozi?”

“No, I’m not afraid,” she said.

They also heard the animals coming and going beside them. These animals seemed calm, neither running away nor attacking them. Qiaozi said, “They know who we are.”

After they’d walked a long, long stretch, the forest thinned, and there were fewer bushes under the trees.

"Li Hai, look quick—there's someone's home!" Qiaozi cried out in surprise.

In front of them there actually was a tiny house with lights on inside.

"Oh, I think it's like the house where I lived with my grandma . . ."

They saw a path, so they followed it toward the wooden house.

A woman was hoeing in the vegetable plot, though they didn't know how she could see it in that darkness.

"Don't shine the flashlight on me," she said. "Where are you going? There's no road above here."

"We want to go to the mountain summit," Li Hai said.

"This is the mountain summit. Go inside and rest."

As they entered the house, Li Hai pressed close to Qiaozi's ear and said that this *was* his former home. They had just sat down when he added that he heard the birds greeting him. She heard them, too, and was endlessly excited.

Li Hai pointed to some scratch marks on the table legs and told Qiaozi that these scratches were how he'd kept track of the birds who communicated with him when he was little. The deepest notch represented the bird he had conversations with most often. Now he took Qiaozi to be that bird. Qiaozi listened and then, moved, she knelt down to kiss the mark. "Li Hai, Li Hai . . . ," she whispered as she kissed.

Li Hai started to sing. The woman came inside and quietly said to Qiaozi:

"He sings so well. As soon as the two of you arrived I just knew you were from here. Listen, the birds are coming—they are thanking your husband for remembering them."

But Qiaozi could only dimly hear the various sounds the birds made. She knew they were numerous. It was a pity that she still couldn't tell them apart. But this didn't matter—Li Hai would explain to her later.

Li Hai was weeping, so Qiaozi wiped his tears with her handkerchief.

He sang for a long time, as if each species of bird were communicating with him.

"Can you hear them all?" Qiaozi said in the woman's ear.

"I can hear them because I've lived here for a long time, and they've become familiar."

Later the birds finally, gradually flew into the distance. Li Hai paused, looking around the room like he was in a dream. He stood, went into the other even smaller room, picked up a wooden spinning top from the windowsill, and called Qiaozi over to look at it.

"This is a top I used to play with when I was at home by myself," he said cheerfully. "My grandma cleared and smoothed a small patch of empty ground outside. I would sit there and spin the top. I wanted to bring it with me the day I left, but suddenly it went missing. It wanted to stay here."

He handed the top to Qiaozi, who gently kissed it then carefully placed it back on the windowsill.

"It spins when there's no one here. I've spied it a few times," the woman said.

"You're also from here, aren't you?" the woman asked Qiaozi.

"I am a descendant. My ancestors moved to the cities much earlier," Qiaozi said.

"I understand. So the birds are fond of you both."

Qiaozi felt a warmth in her heart. Then Li Hai found another one of his old things in the room.

It was a copper coin with four attractive bird feathers inserted into its holes, a birdie that Li Hai's grandmother had helped him make.

"It was also missing when I left," he said.

Qiaozi gently kissed the feathers on the birdie. She smelled the birds, the scent overcoming her.

"Oh, oh . . . ," she cried out in surprise.

She placed the birdie in the cabinet cupboard.

It was late when they said farewell to the woman, promising that they would come to visit her again tomorrow.

"If you do come back tomorrow, you cannot take that same path again. You need to find another way to arrive here," the woman said, smiling.

"All right, good, we'll be able to find it. Thank you," Li Hai said.

The path down the mountain was straight, however, and they easily reached the hotel.

Fei was waiting downstairs again for them to eat.

When they finished the meal and returned to their room, Qiaozi looked in the mirror in the bathroom and called out:

"How strange!"

The cuts made on her face by the thorny vines were invisible. Then she looked carefully at Li Hai. The wounds on his face and hands were also gone. Their skin was smooth.

Afterward they adventured out again twice and found the small wooden house both times. There were some alarms and dangers, but the outcomes were good. Through Li Hai's retelling Qiaozi understood the birds had cherished his memory over the many years. He said that these birds were descendants of the birds before, but they were aware of Li Hai's relationship to them.

Li Hai and Qiaozi returned home.

"Mom, we're back!"

They shouted in unison as they came inside.

"It's wonderful that you're back. Last night I saw you in my dream."

Their mother spoke cheerfully.

The first night home, Li Hai entered Qiaozi. Then they dreamed some beautiful dreams together.

CAN XUE, pseudonym of Deng Xiaohua, has written numerous works of fiction, literary criticism, and philosophy. *The Enchanting Lives of Others* received the Malaysia Hua Zong 花踪 World Chinese Literature Award in 2022, and she was recognized with the America Award for Literature in 2024. Her fiction has also received the Best Translated Book Award, in addition to international recognitions and translation into many languages. Despite deprivations in childhood and having to leave school early, she read widely in Chinese and international literature, and started writing stories in the 1980s while working as a tailor. As an experimental writer, she sees writing as the most natural activity and never plans her works beforehand or revises them afterward. Can Xue advocates in her writing for a contradictory worldview of the mutual essence of Chinese and Western cultures. She was born in Changsha, then moved to Beijing, and now lives in Xishuangbanna.

ANNELISE FINEGAN is academic director and clinical associate professor of translation at New York University. She holds a Ph.D. in comparative literature from Washington University in St. Louis. Her translations of novels, short stories, and plays from Chinese include Can Xue's *The Last Lover* and *Love in the New Millennium*.